T

TWICE A SPY

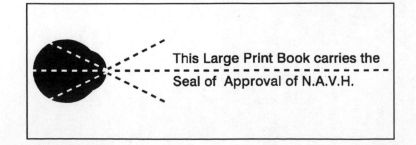

This Large Print Book carries the
Seal of Approval of N.A.V.H.

TWICE A SPY

KEITH THOMSON

THORNDIKE PRESS
A part of Gale, Cengage Learning

GALE
CENGAGE Learning™

Detroit • New York • San Francisco • New Haven, Conn • Waterville, Maine • London

GALE
CENGAGE Learning

Copyright © 2011 by TriStar Pictures, Inc.
Thorndike Press, a part of Gale, Cengage Learning.

ALL RIGHTS RESERVED
This book is a work of fiction. Names, characters, businesses,
organizations, places, and incidents either are the product of the
author's imagination or are used fictitiously. Any resemblance to actual
persons, living or dead, events, or locales is entirely coincidental.
Thorndike Press® Large Print Basic.
The text of this Large Print edition is unabridged.
Other aspects of the book may vary from the original edition.
Set in 16 pt. Plantin.

LIBRARY OF CONGRESS CATALOGING-IN-PUBLICATION DATA

Thomson, Keith, 1965–
    Twice a spy / by Keith Thomson.
        p. cm. — (Thorndike Press large print basic)
    ISBN-13: 978-1-4104-3775-4 (hardcover)
    ISBN-10: 1-4104-3775-2 (hardcover)
    1. Fathers and sons—Fiction. 2. Large type books. I. Title.
    PS3620.H745T95 2011b
    813'.6—dc22   2011009859

Published in 2011 by arrangement with Doubleday, an imprint of
Knopf Doubleday Publishing Group, a division of Random House, Inc.

Printed in the United States of America
1 2 3 4 5 6 7 15 14 13 12 11

For Richard and Winyss

All that is necessary for the triumph of evil is for good men to do nothing.

— Edmund Burke

■ ■ ■

PART ONE:
GHOSTS IN THE
SNOW

■ ■ ■

1

"Do you see a ghost?" Alice asked.

"You'd know if I did because I'd mention it." Charlie fixated on someone or something behind her, rather than meet her eyes as he usually did. "Or faint."

"*Ghost* is trade lingo for someone you take for a surveillant, but, really, he's just an ordinary Joe. When you have to look over your shoulder as much as we have the past couple of weeks, it's only natural that everybody starts seeming suspicious. You imagine you've seen one of them before. It's hard to find *anybody* who doesn't look like he works for Interpol."

"Interpol would be an upgrade." Charlie laughed a stream of vapor into the thin Alpine air. "After the past couple of weeks, it's hard to find anybody who doesn't look like a veteran hit man."

Charlie Clark owned no Hawaiian shirts. He didn't chomp on a cigar. In no way did he match anyone's conception of a horse-player: He was a youthful thirty with a pleasant demeanor and strong features in spite of Alice's efforts to alter them — a brown wig hid his sandy blond hair, fake sideburns and a silicone nose bridge blunted the sharp contours of his face, and oversized sunglasses veiled his intelligent blue eyes. But — tragically, Alice thought — until being thrust on the lam two weeks ago, Charlie had spent 364 days a year at racetracks. And that number would have been 365 if tracks didn't close on Christmas Day. He lived for the thrill not merely of winning but of being right. As he'd often said: "Where else besides the track can you get that?"

So why, Alice wondered, had his attention veered from the race?

Especially this race, a "white turf" mile with thoroughbreds blazing around a course dug from sparkling snow atop the frozen Lac de Morat in Avenches, Switzerland, framed by hills that looked like they had been dispensed by a soft-serve ice cream machine, sprinkled with chalets, and surrounded by blindingly white peaks. Probably it was on an afternoon just like this in 1868 that the British adventurer Edward Whymper said of Switzerland, "However magnificent the imagination may be, it always remains inferior to reality."

And Edward Whymper didn't have a horse poised to take the lead.

Flying past four of the nine entries, Charlie's choice, Poser Le Lapin, spotted a gap between the remaining two.

Knowing almost nothing about the horses besides their names, Charlie had taken a glance at the auburn filly during the post parade and muttered that her turndowns — iron plates bent toward the ground at a forty-five-degree angle on the open end of the horseshoes — would provide better traction than the other entrants' shoes today.

Alice followed his sight line now, up from the snowy track apron where they stood and into the packed grandstand. Ten thousand heads pivoted at once as the horses thundered around the oval.

It was odd that Charlie wasn't watching the race. More than odd. Like an eight-year-old walking past a candy store without a glance.

The horses charged into the final turn. Alice saw only a cloud of kicked-up snowflakes and ice. As the cloud neared the grandstand, the jockeys came into view, their face masks bobbing above the haze. A moment later, the entire pack of thoroughbreds was visible. Cheers from the crowd drowned out the announcer's rat-a-tat call.

Poser Le Lapin crossed the wire with a lead of four lengths.

Alice looked to Charlie expecting elation. He remained focused on the grandstand behind him, via the strips of mirrored film she'd glued inside each of his lenses — an old spook trick.

"Your horse won, John!" she said, using his alias.

He shrugged. "Every once in a while, I'm right."

"Don't tell me the thrill is gone."

"At the moment, I'm hoping to be wrong."

A chill crept up her spine. "Who is it?"

"Guy in a red ski hat, top of the grandstand, just under the Mercedes banner, drinking champagne."

She shifted her stance, as if to watch the trophy presentation like everyone else. Really she looked into the "rearview mirrors" inside her own sunglasses.

The red ski hat was like a beacon.

"I see him. What, you think it's weird that he's drinking champagne?"

"Well, yeah, because it's, like, two degrees out."

Alice usually put great stock in Charlie's observational skill. During their escape from

Manhattan, in residential Morningside Heights, he'd pegged two men out of a crowd of hundreds as government agents when they slowed at a curb for a sign changing to DON'T WALK; real New Yorkers sped up. But after two harrowing weeks of being hunted by spies and misguided lawmen who shot first and asked questions later, anyone would see ghosts, even an operator with as much experience as she had.

"Sweetheart, half the people here are drinking champagne."

"Yeah, I know — the Swiss Miss commercials sure got Switzerland wrong. The thing is the red hat."

"Is there something unusual about it?"

"No. But he was wearing a green hat at lunch."

2

The man in the blood-red knitted ski cap looked as if he were in his late twenties. Gaunt and pallid, he was Central Casting's idea of a doctoral candidate. Which hardly ruled him out as an assassin. Since he had been dragged into this mess two weeks ago, the killers Charlie had eluded had been disguised as a jocular middle-aged insurance salesman, a pair of wet-behind-the-ears lawyers, and a fresh fruit vendor on the Lower East Side.

"You're sure you saw him at the café?" Alice asked.

"When I doubled back to our table to leave the tip, I noticed him in the corner, flagging the waitress all of a sudden. What's that spook saying about coincidences?"

"There are none?"

"Exactly."

"*I* never say that. The summer I was eleven, I got a Siamese cat. I named him

Rockford. A few weeks later, I started a new school, and there was another girl who had a Siamese cat named Rockford. Coincidence or what?"

"I always wondered about that saying."

"In any case, why don't we go toast your win?"

One of their exit strategies commenced with a walk to the nearest concession stand. "I would love a drink, actually," Charlie said.

Leaving the track apron, they stepped into a long corridor between the rear of the grandstand and Lac de Morat's southern bank. While his nerves verged on exploding, she retained her character's bounce. In fact, if he hadn't been in the same room this morning when she was getting dressed, he might not recognize her now. She remained a stunning woman despite a drab wig and a prosthetic nose that called to mind a plastic surgeon's "before" photo. Ordinarily she moved like a ballerina. Now the thick parka, along with the marble she'd placed in her right boot, spoiled her stride. And her sunglasses, relatives of the ski goggle family, concealed her best feature, bright green eyes that blazed with whimsy or, at times, inner demons.

No one else was in the corridor. But

would anyone fall in behind them?

Charlie's heart pounded so forcefully that he could barely hear the crunching of his boots through the snow.

Sensing his unease, Alice took his hand. Or maybe there was more to it than that. Twelve days ago, caring only that he and his father were innocent, she decided to help them flee the United States in direct defiance of her superiors at the National Security Agency. "Girlfriend" was just her cover then. Their first night in Europe, however, it became reality. Since then, their hands had gravitated into each other's even without a threat of surveillance.

She steadied him now.

He recalled the fundamental guiding principle of countersurveillance, which she'd taught him: See your pursuers, but don't let them know you see them.

The spooked-up sunglasses — part mirror, and, to the uninitiated, part kaleidoscope — made it difficult to find a specific person behind him, or for that matter a specific section of grandstand. He fought the urge to peer over his shoulder. As little as a backward glance would be enough for the man in the red hat to smell blood.

"See anything?" Charlie muttered.

"Not yet." Alice laughed as if he'd just

told a joke.

They came to a white cabana tent with a peaked top. Inside, a rosy and suitably effervescent middle-aged couple popped corks and filled plastic flutes with the same champagne whose logo adorned banners all around the racecourse. Falling into place at the end of the small line enabled Charlie and Alice to, quite naturally, turn and take in their environs: Thirty or forty white-turf fans wandered among the betting windows, Port-o-Lets, and a dozen other concessions tents.

No man in the red hat.

And the corridor behind the grandstand remained vacant.

Charlie felt only the smallest measure of relief. Their tail might have passed them to another watcher. Or put cameras on them. Or fired microscopic transponders into their coats. Or God knew what.

"Sorry about this," Charlie said.

"About what?" Alice seemed carefree. Part of which was her act. The rest was a childhood so harrowing and a career full of so many horrors that she rarely experienced fear now. If ever.

"Talking you into coming here."

"Knock it off. It's breathtaking."

"To a track, I mean. It was idiotic."

19

"Hermits are conspicuous. We have to get out some of the time."

"Just not to racetracks. Of course they'd be watching racetracks."

"Switzerland has an awful lot of race-tracks, not to mention all the little grocery stores that double as offtrack betting parlors. And there's no reason to think that anyone even knows we're in Europe. Also this isn't exactly a racetrack. It's a course on a frozen lake — who knew such a thing existed?"

"*They* know. They always do."

"They" were the so-called Cavalry, the Central Intelligence Agency black ops unit pursuing Charlie and his father, Drummond Clark. Two weeks ago, after the various assassins all failed their assignments, the Cavalry framed the Clarks for the murder of U.S. national security adviser Burton Hattemer, enabling the group to request the assistance of Interpol and a multitude of other agencies. With no way to prove their innocence, the Clarks knew they wouldn't stand a chance in court. Not that it mattered. The Cavalry would avoid the hassle of due process and "neutralize" them before a gavel was raised.

Readying a twenty-franc note for two flutes of champagne, Alice advanced in line. "Look, if they're really that good, they're going to get us no matter what, so better here than a yodeling hall."

She could always be counted on for levity. It was one of the things Charlie loved about her. One of about a hundred. And he barely knew her.

He was wondering how to share the sentiment when a young blonde emerged from the corridor behind the grandstand, a Golden Age starlet throwback in a full-length mink. Breathing hard, perhaps from having raced to catch up to them. Or maybe it was the basset hound, in matching mink doggie jacket, wrenching her forward by his expensive-looking leather leash.

Clasping Charlie's shoulder, Alice pointed to the dog. "Is he the most adorable thing you've ever seen or what?"

Charlie realized that pretending not to notice the dog would look odd. Acting natural was part of Countersurveillance 101. The best he could muster was "I've always wanted a schnauzer."

"Why a schnauzer?" Alice asked.

All he knew about the breed was that it was a kind of dog.

The starlet looked at them, her interest apparently piqued.

"I just like the sound of *schnauzer*," Charlie said.

The woman continued past as a slovenly bald man stumbled out of a Port-o-Let, directly into her path. She smiled at him.

Women like her don't smile at guys like that, Charlie thought. Especially with Port-o-Lets in the picture.

Alice noticed it too. She yawned. "Well, what do you say we head back to Geneva?"

Charlie knew this really meant leave for Gstaad, sixty miles from Geneva.

Fast.

3

As he and Alice entered the parking lot — a plowed meadow across the street from the Lac de Morat — she maintained a vivacious conversation, raving first about the white-turf races and then about a new refrigerator she had her eye on.

They approached the silver-gray BMW 330 sedan she'd rented under a Norwegian alias. The 330 was one of the ten most popular models in Switzerland and number one in Gstaad, where they were renting a chalet, or, more accurately, where the fictitious CFO of her fictitious Belgian consulting firm was renting a chalet.

They intentionally bypassed their 330 in favor of another silver-gray BMW.

"Oh, wait, that's not us," Alice said.

Doubling back provided the opportunity to glimpse reactions from the twenty or so other drivers returning to the parking lot. Charlie spotted a man fumbling with his keyless remote. Probably a result of the champagne in his other hand. Or the champagnes that had preceded it. Everyone else proceeded directly to their cars.

Gstaad was a forty-five-minute drive from Avenches, or could have been if not for Alice's choice of SDR — surveillance detection route. At the first green light they came to, she sent the BMW skidding into a looping right turn. At its apex, with Charlie clutching his armrest so that centrifugal force wouldn't dump him onto Alice, and when she ought to have tamped the brake, she crushed the accelerator, rocketing them onto a side street. She had the right combination of creativity and controlled recklessness to win a NASCAR race, he thought.

"I think we left my stomach back at the light," he said.

Her eyes darted between the mirrors. "We'll probably be able to go back and get it. I'm pretty sure we don't have a tail."

He exhaled, before she added, "But we need to be *absolutely* sure."

She took a last-second left at the next intersection, cutting across a lane of oncoming traffic and entering a shopping mall. One car swerved. A van braked sharply, the driver screaming and shaking his fist. The car directly behind the man braked and skidded, narrowly missing rear-ending his van.

Alice concerned herself just with the vehicles that had been behind the BMW. All simply continued along.

"That sure would have surprised a tail," Charlie said. "Or convinced him that you took Driving Training at the Farm."

She laughed. "Or in Rome."

Exiting the mall, she began taking left turns at random. The odds that anyone other than a surveillant would stay behind them for three such turns were beyond as-tronomical.

"You do get to see more of the sights this way," she said blithely.

"People don't consider the benefits of be-ing a fugitive."

Another quick turn and Charlie's side mirror showed only the town of Avenches shooting aft. The chalets became specks, then disappeared altogether behind a moun-tain of fir trees laden with snow.

As Alice drove up the rugged Bernese Oberland, Charlie scanned the sky. The Cavalry sometimes deployed unmanned aerial vehicles — UAVs, remotely piloted, miniature aircraft equipped with cameras sharp enough for their operators to view a driver's face from ten thousand feet up. Some UAVs carried laser-guided missiles capable of turning the road into a crater and the BMW into shiny gravel.

Alice smiled. "Given their small size and high altitudes, the odds of spotting a drone aren't too good."

Charlie sat back, admitting, "The odds are probably better that I'll discover a new planet." A moment later, he resumed scanning. "It's harder to just do nothing."

On their descent from the mountains, wispy, low-lying clouds dissipated, revealing a valley dotted with toylike chalets, Alpine ski slopes, and cows whose bells blended into a single mesmerizing chord. The slopes converged at Gstaad's central village, a congregation of rustic Helvetian buildings, many with bright red geranium-filled window boxes. Factor in the fairy-tale turrets and horse-drawn sleighs and Gstaad was less believable than the Disneyland version of an old-world Swiss hamlet. After just a week, Charlie dreamed that he and Alice would stay for the rest of their lives.

As she nosed the car into a parking spot behind the train station on Hauptstrasse, the sun dipped behind a pair of soaring peaks, bronzing the entire valley.

They proceeded on foot through an empty

alley to the Promenade, Gstaad's main street, where the only vehicles permitted were horse-drawn. The alley was another in Alice's bag of countersurveillance tricks. Pick out the surveillants *before* leading them to the chalet.

Among the boutiques, galleries, and cafés on the Promenade was Les Frères Trois-gros, a tavern whose grilled bratwurst was good enough to persuade Charlie to stay in Gstaad even without Alice. The tavern's large front windowpane reflected no one behind them in the alley.

"We good?" Charlie asked.

"We are or they are." Alice pushed open the door, surrounding them with the aromas of roasting meat and ale. She led the way inside with circumspection in place of her usual buoyancy. If she saw or sensed anything wrong, she wasn't saying, not in a barroom with a hundred eyes upon them, all aglow in candlelight — Les Frères Troisgros had no electric lights. A collection of big smoke-darkened stones held in place by ancient beams, it had changed little from the seventeenth century.

Charlie fought the compulsion to stare at the jolly and ruddy faces. He worried he'd come here once too often.

He and Alice received their takeout orders

without being shot at or otherwise imperiled. But on the way out, in the smoky mirror behind the bar, he caught a glimpse of a ruddy middle-aged man wearing a black beret. The man was staring at them as he snapped open a cell phone.

"Ghost, I think," said Alice, taking Charlie's hand in hers.

"Because of the beret?"

"Yeah."

"Over-the-top for a pro, right?"

"One would hope."

The question became: Who was he calling?

Not someone who followed them to the car. At least as far as Charlie or Alice could tell.

Letting Alice ride shotgun — in point of fact, 9mm pistol — Charlie drove away from the village, managing the winding mountain road up to a secluded cream-colored chalet. In the dwindling sunlight, the structure blended in with the towering pines.

With a stern gaze at a field blanketed with a fresh snowfall, Alice said, "Hit teams love snow. With a few thermal-insulated, arctic-terrain ghillie suits and rifle wraps, you can turn a clearing like this into an excellent ambush site."

"Great."

"A euro says we're home free, though." She cracked a smile.

"I love you" almost slipped from his lips for perhaps the twentieth time that day, but all he said was, "You're on. And good luck."

Just tell her, he urged himself. Why the hell not?

As soon as they parked.

He pulled onto the mountainside ledge they called the parking deck. From here it was a two-minute walk through woods up to the chalet. While she climbed out of the car, he ratcheted the parking brake and turned off the engine. He heard and felt stuttering thuds from above the trees. A white medevac helicopter, common enough in winter resort areas.

The helicopter slowed to a hover directly overhead, plunging the clearing around the BMW into darkness.

Charlie felt an all-too-familiar icy terror.

"Blast," Alice said. "I owe you a euro."

4

Snow and twigs and pine needles swirled in the rotors' wash. In the general ruckus, it was useless for Charlie to shout to Alice.

Not that there was anything she needed to be told. Letting the takeout containers fall to the snow, she shot a hand toward the Sig Sauer tucked into the rear waistband of her jeans.

Doors on both sides of the helicopter's cabin slid open. The waning sun showed four men in silhouette, bracing themselves on taut ropes anchored within the helicopter. Gaining a foothold on the craft's skids, the men let their rope ends drop to the ground, giving the helicopter the appearance of a giant mosquito. In unison, the men jumped, arcing outward and rappelling down, ropes screaming through the carabiners on their harnesses. They wore thick white jumpsuits with red crosses, as a team of paramedics might, along with ski masks.

All were built like they'd spent plenty of time in the weight room.

They converged on Alice so quickly that she barely had a chance to raise her gun. On his way down, the first man dealt her a swift, steel-toed boot to the cheekbone, costing her her hold on the Sig. The next two, still attached to their ropes, tackled her, driving her into deep snow on the passenger side of the BMW.

Charlie flung himself onto the car's hood, intent on recovering Alice's gun.

She wriggled free, regained her feet, and spun two hundred degrees, gaining force and leverage and delivering a kick to the nearest jaw. The man sagged, dangling from his rope.

For better or for worse, Alice Rutherford's nature was to fight. She would have taken on ten such men. She had her hands full with two now, one corralling her from behind, the other spraying her in the face with a tiny aerosol can. She went limp, falling into the first man's arms.

As Charlie slid off the passenger side of the BMW's hood, he caught sight of a pistol capped by a silencer, pointed at him by the fourth man, who shouted something. The chop of the rotors made it impossible to hear what. Charlie guessed, "Freeze!"

And what choice did he have?

Alice and the first three men — including the one she'd KO'd — rose into the air, as if levitating. Arms extended from the helicopter's cabin, hauling them in. The door snapped shut and the ship appeared to fall upward into the sky.

Like that, she was gone, with only a faint whir as evidence that the helicopter had been present. And then it was just the breeze whispering through the bare branches.

When Charlie looked down, the remaining man was unclicking his harness. "Back up, against the car," he said, waving his gun. His accent was unmistakably American. "Put your hands where I can see 'em."

Charlie took two steps and hit the bumper.

"Now shrug off your jacket, one sleeve at a time, then toss it toward me." The gunman's rasp had a touch of cowboy. He looked the part too, with the build and bearing of a broncobuster. And when he pulled up his mask — revealing a combative leer, a pointed chin, and long blond locks — anyone would have been reminded of Jesse James.

Charlie shook at his parka until it fell to the ground. Having submitted to the same inspection before, he wasn't surprised when

32

Jesse James advanced, patted him down — everywhere — and took his car keys.

"I'm guessing this isn't a carjacking," Charlie said.

"It's a rendition."

"A rendition of what?"

"In layman's terms, a kidnapping."

"You've kidnapped Wendy? Why?" Charlie feigned the shock of an ignorant vacationer, less of a stretch than he would have liked.

"It'd be a tragedy if we've kidnapped someone named Wendy," said the cowboy. "See, we're after Alice Ann Rutherford."

"Alice Ann Rutherford?" Charlie repeated as if bewildered.

"If it helps, she was born in New Britain, Connecticut, on October 17, 1980, she's currently absent without leave from the National Security Agency, and she lives with you."

An icy gust slashed through Charlie's sweater, stinging his chest. He resisted the urge to wrap his arms around himself, afraid the movement might spur the kidnapper to precipitous use of his trigger. "Okay, okay. So what do you want?"

"An ADM. You know what that is, right?"

Charlie knew atomic demolition munitions only too well. They were portable Soviet-made bombs with a ten-kiloton yield.

Under the auspices of the CIA, his father had founded the Cavalry with the objective of putting malfunctioning ADMs into the hands of terrorists who believed they were purchasing working weapons of mass destruction. The ultra-classified operation had succeeded for the better part of three decades. When Drummond fell prey to Alzheimer's, his own men decided it best to sacrifice him in order to maintain the secret and safeguard the identities of their operatives. Charlie had learned the secret just two weeks ago, while trying to figure out why assassins were preventing him from putting his father in a nursing home. Before that, he'd known the old man only by his cover as a stern and straitlaced appliance salesman.

"You can't exactly get ADMs on eBay," Charlie said.

Jesse James grinned. "So why don't you ask your dad?"

Charlie eyed his shoe tops. "There's a problem with that."

"Isn't your father Drummond Clark, Central Intelligence Agency operations officer, born in New York, New York, on July 14, 1945?"

"He was. He passed away twelve days ago."

5

If Charlie's father — who in fact was still alive — held to form this evening, he had heard the helicopter and momentarily would appear, as if out of thin air, with a gun to Jesse James's head. Alzheimer's had acted like a wrecking ball on Drummond Clark's memory retrieval mechanism and had ravaged his ability to process the present. As with most people suffering from the disease, he still experienced random episodes of lucidity, however. And danger tended to jolt him into clarity. So Charlie's plan was simply to buy time.

"Why don't we sit in the car, where it's not freezing?" Jesse James pointed at the passenger seat with his gun, making the question rhetorical.

As soon as they were inside, he turned on the ignition, sending hot air from the vents and a delicate piano concerto from the speakers. The BMW was certainly more pleasant than the bitter outdoors, but it would complicate Drummond's assault. If he were to appear out of thin air now, Jesse James could just drive away. And the car's tinted glass might veil Charlie's execution.

"I'm sure you'd like Interpol to believe your father's dead, but I don't," the cowboy said, fishing a satellite phone from inside his jumpsuit. "Not unless you can convince me that this is his twin brother."

He punched a few keys. The phone's display filled with a shaky, greenish-gray video of the chalet taken through one of the leaded glass windows. Drummond sat at the dining table, reading a newspaper.

"I can have the mosquito drone zoom in on the newspaper's date if you have any doubt this is live feed, but it might take me a while," Jesse James said.

Charlie felt a measure of relief. "So you actually do just want an ADM?"

"Yeah. Remember the to-do with the helicopter and Alice?"

Charlie could share the secret that the ADMs were duds, but Jesse James might not believe it. And even if he did, the consequences would be grave. If Cavalry customers got wind of the fact that their vaunted arsenals couldn't blow up a balloon, the identities of countless American operatives and their foreign agents would be compromised. In any event, it was doubtful that Jesse James's principals would just let Alice walk away.

"What makes you think my father can get an ADM?" Charlie asked.

"A few months ago he delivered one to Nick Fielding, an illegal arms dealer, in Martinique. A couple of weeks ago, my employers met with Fielding there. They negotiated the purchase of the ADM, pending an inspection at its hiding place, but the trip to the hiding place never happened because Fielding got himself killed in New York City the same night. Fortunately, your dad knows where the thing's hidden. My employers need it, along with a working detonation code, no later than the thirteenth of January, which is four days from today."

Jesse James, whoever he was, had excellent intelligence, except for the fact that Nick Fielding had been a Cavalry man who trafficked *fake* ADMs. "All things considered, I'd happily make the trade," Charlie said. "My father probably did know where the bomb is hidden."

The cowboy's eyes narrowed. *"Did?"*

"Once, yeah. That's the rub. You need to understand that when he finishes brushing his teeth at night, he has to hunt for the

37

toothpaste cap, even though it's always right beside the soap dish."

Jesse James scoffed. "I do shit like that too."

"But he has Alzheimer's."

"Alzheimer's?"

"Midstage. We're here because there's a clinic with an experimental treatment —"

The cowboy's groan cut Charlie off. "The word I got was you'd trot out some spiel like this. Let's save ourselves some time, okay? Just last week, on at least three separate occasions, your daddy shut out the New York Yankees of death squads. The reason I'm talking to *you* is word had it that if I went to talk to *him,* it'd probably be the last conversation I ever had."

"He has his moments."

"Well, if you want Miss Alice to keep on being alive four days from now, he better have one more of those moments." Jesse James tapped the steering wheel. "I'll leave your Beemer in the Hauptstrasse train station parking lot, keys under your seat. Meet me outside the general aviation terminal at the Zweisimmen airport at thirteen hundred tomorrow. I'll have a jet waiting to take us to the ADM. I know a professional like your father wouldn't be stupid enough to try any tricks, like telling anyone about this, but *you* might. And if you do, your sweetheart gets your name written across her face with a box cutter."

6

Although enveloped by toasty air, Charlie felt no comfort as he stepped into the chalet's spacious living room. Usually on entry he savored the blond wooden beams and old-fashioned Alpine-style furniture. Before coming to Gstaad, he'd never given a thought to upholstery — probably never even uttered the word *upholstery*. But he'd been taken by the sofa and chairs here, embroidered with white dots that matched those on the lace curtains, which in turn afforded privacy without sacrificing a view of the skyrocketing mountains. Now he felt as if an avalanche were carrying the chalet away.

Drummond still sat at the farmhouse dining table. Of average height and weight, he'd always fostered a nondescript appearance, which served him well as a professional cipher. He was a young sixty-four, though two weeks ago it had been easy to see the senior citizen version of him waiting around the corner: His white hair had begun to thin, gravity was winning the battle with his spine, and wrinkles and spots massed as if readying to invade his taut skin's otherwise healthy glow. In Gstaad, those trends had seemed to reverse somewhat. He sat ruler-straight now. He exuded vitality. His hair even seemed a healthier shade of white.

It was too soon into the course of the treatment to detect an effect on his mind, but the medication could have been responsible for his general improvement. More likely, the upturn resulted from their strenuous hikes and the invigorating Alpine air. Or possibly Drummond benefited from the comforts of the chalet: When forced to go on the lam together, the previously estranged father and son managed not only to get along, against odds no bettor in his right mind would have accepted, but they also actually learned from each other, creating a force that exceeded the sum of its parts. As a result, they had survived. Once in Gstaad, Charlie savored the nascent affection, a nice change from his father's serial sermon about wasting one's life at the track.

"Where's Alice?" Drummond asked.

Sliding one of the heavy pine chairs out from the table, Charlie sat across from him.

41

"She was kidnapped," he said. It came out matter-of-factly; if he weren't so numb, he might have shrieked it.

"*Kidnapped!* Are you certain?"

"I guess, technically, she was rendered. Or renditioned."

"What happened?"

Charlie filled him in.

"Well, that certainly is a problem." Making a steeple out of his fingers, Drummond gazed out at the dark shapes of the mountains, seemingly contemplating a solution. After a few moments, he asked, with uncharacteristic alarm, "What are we going to do about dinner?"

7

Charlie spent most of the night gazing at the empty space on the other side of the mattress. The closest he found to a diversion was watching the digits change on the clock radio.

At 5:14 Drummond banged on the door.

"You okay?" Charlie asked.

"I woke up this morning feeling as well as I have in quite some time. And I'm almost certain that Alice was kidnapped."

"Well . . . yeah." Last night Charlie had detailed the rendition five or six times in hopes of sparking Drummond's memory of the ADM. To no avail.

Drummond made a beeline for the clock radio, snapping on Alpine folk music and turning up the volume. "I mean it was a straight kidnapping, as in an operation offering the safe return of the captive in exchange for something."

That sounded pretty lucid. Charlie

strained to hear over the accordions.

Seeing Charlie look at the radio, Drummond said, "In case of eavesdroppers. And in case of eavesdroppers who might have been able to filter out the music, I raised the heat — I hope you're not uncomfortable."

Noting the hot air whining through the registers, Charlie shook his head. "Enough about me. Do you remember all the plot points: Jesse James from the helicopter? Hidden ADM?"

Drummond sat at the foot of the bed. His eyes glowed with much more than just the moonlight spraying through the gap in the drapes.

Hallelujah, thought Charlie. Lucidity.

"If he were smart, what Jesse James told you is —"

"Lies." Charlie had already concluded as much.

"No, fifty percent lies, but you wouldn't have any way of knowing which was which. I just need to catch up on a few things."

"Shoot."

"Had Alice been in touch with anyone?"

"Yes." During the night, this had become Charlie's leading theory as to the genesis of the rendition. "The other day she took, like, eighty-seven trains and buses to Zurich, went to a public library, and sent one of those supposedly untraceable Hushmails to the personal account of an NSA inspector general she trusts."

"What did she write?"

"Basically, that she wasn't dead, and that your old Cavalry pals had framed us for Hattemer's murder in order to get the finding." A presidential finding had waived Executive Orders 11905 and 12333 banning assassinations by U.S. government organizations, thereby enabling the Cavalry to off the Clarks with impunity. "She was hoping to open a dialogue, maybe get us off the Whack-on-Sight list. She asked the guy to reply using Hushmail."

Drummond looked at the ceiling, pondering the matter.

Or so Charlie hoped. Drummond's episodes of lucidity lasted forty minutes on average, but sometimes they were as brief as two minutes.

"I think the rendition is coincidence," Drummond said.

"So you believe in coincidences too?"

"There are coincidences and there are unbelievable coincidences. It's possible that someone 'made' her while she was in Zurich or en route, but given the extensive planning and practice a helicopter rendition of this nature requires, it seems more likely that the kidnappers were already well into preproduction. Also it's possible that Alice orchestrated the kidnapping herself. She could sell the ADM for a king's ransom — she doesn't know it's a fake, right?"

Charlie waved his dismissal. "I kept the secret from her not because I don't trust her, but because there was no reason to burden her with it."

"Jesse James leveraged your feelings for her," Drummond said. "How could he or whoever he's working for have known that you'd developed feelings for her?"

"Using a mosquito drone . . ." Charlie left it at that, averse to telling his sometime-puritanical father exactly what the miniature camera might have recorded.

Also Charlie was now wrestling with the fact that during his brief time in Spook City, everyone he'd met had either deceived him or tried to kill him. Even his own mother, who had faked her death when he was four — he'd believed she was dead until encountering her just two weeks ago, when she offered him and Drummond safe haven. Fifteen minutes later, she handed them over to Cavalry assassins before reversing course and getting herself killed.

And Alice herself was no innocent. When

Charlie first met her, the day before he met his mother, Alice had posed as a social worker at the Brooklyn senior center that "rescued" his father. Her true goal had been — what else? — intel. In reality, she had no home, no money, and no family aside from her mother, who was currently serving the fifteenth year of a twenty-year sentence for murdering Alice's father. Alice's "rendition" might easily have been staged.

But Charlie wasn't convinced. "No one, not even the most sociopathic spook, is as good an actor as she would have had to be," he said.

"Probably so," said Drummond. "The bond between you would have been obvious even to a drone. It was obvious to me, after all. We can also rule it highly unlikely that the rendition was a government operation."

"Why?"

"They would have neutralized us. I'm a thorn in their side and too unstable to be deployed to locate a bomb, whether or not they know it's a fake. And if they do know it's fake, they certainly don't want anyone else knowing, which is all the more reason to silence me. If they meant to send me bomb-hunting regardless, they would have opted for a path of lesser resistance than a highly chancy airborne op."

"Like what?"

"They could have simply offered us immunity."

"So we're dealing with good, old-fashioned bad guys?"

"Bad guys with a window, however small, into the NSA or CIA. Maybe they have a confederate within one of those agencies." Drummond sucked at his lower lip, a measure of self-restraint in Charlie's experience.

"They're going to kill her, whatever we do, aren't they?" This was at the top of the list of questions that had kept Charlie up all night. "You never cooperate with kidnappers as a rule, right?"

"Actually, there's good reason to believe they'll let her live if we do what they want. Ninety-nine percent of kidnappers are in it just for the payout, and to get it, they have to trade their hostage."

"Is there anyone we can go to? Her NSA friend, maybe?"

"No. Too risky for us. Too risky for Alice."

"So then what are the options?"

"Just one: Cooperate."

Charlie raced to prioritize his questions. Drummond might go days before another episode of lucidity. "Do you know where the ADM is hidden?"

Drummond shrugged. "I might. Let me look at the map." He set a Swiss road atlas on the comforter and flipped it open. As Charlie was worrying about the choice of a local road atlas, Drummond whispered into his ear. "There's a self-serve Laundromat on rue Joseph Compère in the Pointe Simon area of Fort-de-France, Martinique's main city. As usual, the device is concealed within a Perriman Pristina model washing machine. This one is among a bunch of washers and dryers locked in the storeroom in the back. The manager is a cutout, which as you may know is a player who knows as little as possible. Her name is Odelette. She'll have the key. There also may be a key to the storeroom in the gap behind the detergent dispenser and the wall. If all else fails, it's not hard to detach the ventilation grate."

If not for the possibility that they were under surveillance, Charlie would have pumped a fist. "What about the code? Like last time?"

Twelve days ago in Manhattan, to escape confinement and make it appear that the two of them had died in the process, Drummond had detonated another ADM-bearing Pristina packed with a hundred pounds of plastic explosive — standard in real uranium

49

implosion weapons in order to generate critical mass. Without critical mass, it was still enough to take out the vast underground complex serving as Cavalry headquarters. Arming the device had been a matter of entering the washing machine's serial number onto permissive action links, a trio of numeric dials like those on safes.

As long as the ADM in the Laundromat worked the same way, Charlie was looking at a relatively simple trade.

"Yes, and just like the one in New York, dialing the numbers in reverse disarms it," Drummond said, rising. He began to pace alongside the bed, as if the motion spurred his thinking. "Of course, Jesse James can't be told any of these specifics. It's the paid cutouts in a rendition who are the least predictable. They're usually the sort you'd call to murder your wife. What we need to do is to go to Martinique, find the washer, then turn it over. We'll demonstrate the validity of the ADM code at the same time Alice is released, everything synchronized, the classic hostage exchange. They're probably expecting us to go to the Caribbean and to play it out just like that. Otherwise they wouldn't have suggested that we rendezvous at an airfield."

The mentions of "we" didn't sit right with

Charlie. "I can go to Martinique myself," he said. "These days I could teach a course on fake travel documents and disguise. And once I'm there, it's a simple trade. I can handle this myself."

"I don't doubt it." Drummond's smile belied his doubt. "I wouldn't mind coming along anyway."

"I don't know, Dad. You've spent millions and risked your life more times than I can count just to get here and try the treatment. Also this is just the first time you've flickered on since we've been in Europe."

"There you go. I need you to look out for me. And to remind me to take the pills."

"You could stay at the clinic. The fee of twenty thousand euros a month includes a private room that you haven't set foot in."

"I want to go to Martinique with you because . . ." Drummond's voice trailed off. He shifted his focus to the window. Outside, a silver streak of moonlight delineated the neighboring peak from the still-dark sky. He seemed to be searching for the right words. "I want to go for your son."

Charlie felt the chill that accompanied lucidity's departure. "I don't have a son."

"You ought to. Best thing you'll ever do, trust me. That's exactly what was on my mind when I woke up this morning, feeling so well."

Moved, Charlie placed his hands on his father's shoulders and drew him close. Although Drummond offered no resistance, he angled his head away. Charlie found himself doing the same. The boisterous music from the radio underscored their woodenness. Both broke free after maybe three seconds. They lacked practical experience in displays of affection, Charlie reflected. It didn't mitigate the underlying sentiment, though. No way would he needlessly place his father in harm's way.

"It's just a matter of turning three dials, right?"

"Yes, arming the device is simple." Drummond leaned against the doorframe, perhaps subconsciously blocking Charlie from going to the airfield without him. "The hard parts will be learning who these people really are, then preventing them from deploying the bomb."

"Because once they have the ADM, a hundred pounds of plastic explosive is sure to follow?"

"Ninety-seven point eight pounds of penthrite and trinitrotoluene, to be precise. If they detonate that in the heart of Fort-de-France, they could kill ten thousand people. But I would think Jesse James's people have a bigger target in mind than Martinique. The Cavalry's worst-case scenario has always been that if customers use a device, better the collateral be a few thousand people than an entire city. But in every case, the CIA or its liaison counterparts have been able to neutralize the customers before *anything* blew up. In this case, the customers will be shrouded in cover. Peeling it away will be similar to determining, say, why a promising horse is racing at odds much higher than you'd expect. How would you go about determining that?"

Drummond liked to use the horses to simplify matters for Charlie. Occasionally he did it gratuitously, in Charlie's opinion, venting dismay that his gifted son had buried himself at the track.

Charlie hesitated, wishing Drummond had chosen a baseball analogy instead. "They call a horse like that a 'lobster on the board,' meaning the tote board. Being wary of a free lobster, I'd study the horse's past races, then nose around the track to learn about his recent workouts. Maybe he's sick or injured or —"

"Good," Drummond said without a smile. "The job here will be similar, but more perilous. It's a matter of finding tracks and then following them through the jungle, back to the tiger's lair. The counterintelligence folks call that 'walking back the cat.' "

The more Charlie contemplated the "simple trade," the more foolish he felt for having imagined he could simply waltz in and out of Spook City, a place where everyone lied for a living and thought no more of hiring an assassin than people elsewhere did of calling a plumber. A place where no horseplayer with a half-decent grasp of the odds would dare set foot. At least not by himself.

8

They called him Fat Elvis because there had been so many unsubstantiated sightings of him. And because he was overweight, or at least believed to be. He was also thought to be Algerian, and to have done a brisk illegal munitions trade in France during the past year. As far as anyone in the CIA Paris station knew, his name was Ali Abdullah. The closest any of them had come to seeing him was the soft-focus headshot on the most wanted lists.

Yet terrorists had no trouble finding him. According to numerous accounts, he'd sold a group of Moroccan agitators the mass of penthrite they used to turn a waiter and a family of five into ashes at a Parisian bistro last summer.

"He's schtupping our nanny," Jerry Hill said. They were in the small, bulletproof conference room at the U.S. Embassy in Paris that the CIA used to interview walk-ins.

"That would be great," said Bill Stanley, favoring his prematurely arthritic right hip as he lowered himself into a chair on the other side of the table. "I'm speaking from the point of view of national security, of course, not your nanny."

"Hey, if she's collateral in terminating that prick, it'd be no huge loss."

If Stanley had first heard Hill over the phone, he would have taken the voice for that of an elderly woman. In fact the walk-in was a fifty-five-year-old Californian with the hollow eyes and gaunt frame of a refugee camper. He wore a linen blazer over a tennis shirt and a pair of sweatpants. His hair, too blond for a man of fifty — or a boy of fifteen, for that matter — stood on end as if he'd just stuck one of his fingers into an electrical socket.

Ninety-eight percent of walk-ins were either nutjobs or knew nothing of value to the agency. Based on Hill's appearance, the marines stationed at the embassy's Avenue Gabriel entrance would have ordinarily bet their paychecks that he belonged in both categories. His physique was attributable to a rigorous Pilates regime, however, and his blond hair stood on end thanks to a stylist and a hair products conglomerate in which he owned a controlling interest. And the marines knew this not from any database but from *Entertainment Tonight.* Who hadn't watched either the live television broadcast or the subsequent viral YouTube footage of Hill stabbing the air with his Best Director Oscar while delivering his expletive-laden I-told-you-so speech to a list of detractors dating back to junior high?

Stanley pulled his chair closer to the table. "The marine guards said you have photo graphic evidence?"

"We've got a place down in Saint-Jean Cap Ferrat," Hill said, almost in apology. He glanced around the room, probably just realizing that other people were watching. "There's kind of a security camera out in the pool house, in Missy's bedroom."

"Ali Abdullah allowed himself to get caught on a home security camera?" Stanley thought the arms dealer would sooner be susceptible to the gift of a giant wooden horse.

"You're CIA, right?" Hill likely sought assurance that the prospect of capturing Abdullah negated the illegal electronic eavesdropping that had occasioned it.

"State Department," Stanley half lied. Officially he was a first assistant secretary. He was also one of the twelve Counterterrorism

Branch operations officers in the CIA's Paris station.

Hill smirked. He wasn't fooled. In any case, someone of his means and reach could get the lowdown on Stanley with relative ease. The old joke was true: Anyone wanting to know who at an embassy works for the CIA just has to look in the parking garage after five o'clock. The cars still there don't belong to the diplomats.

"On the nanny's desk, which she doesn't use, along with a bunch of pens and tape and stuff like that, there's a stapler — and who ever uses a stapler anymore?" the filmmaker said. "It's really there to conceal a video camera that records up to seventy-two hours of footage — not broadcast quality, but good enough for . . ." He reddened.

"Good enough for evidence?" Stanley had no interest in busting a Digital Age peeping Tom.

"Yeah." Hill perked up. "Around midnight the last few nights, he's come onto our property by the stairs up from the beach. He throws pebbles at her bedroom window, like a teenager. She lets him in, they have their token drink, then things get rated X."

"How can I see the video?" Stanley asked and just as soon realized he'd better amend the question to forestall the laughter of the

58

marines watching through the two-way mirror. He had a collegial rapport with them, born of a mutual love of football and the fact that he'd started at tailback for Stanford. Still, they'd never let him live this down. "To know if it's Abdullah, I mean."

"Are the guys watching through the mirror going to shoot me if I reach into my pocket?" Hill asked.

"It depends what's in the pocket."

"My cell. I downloaded a couple of video files from the stapler."

Stanley nodded and Hill fished the phone from his sweatpants. A few thumbstrokes later, the tiny computer was playing astonishingly clear and vibrant footage of the nanny and her scruffy middle-aged guest. In each other's embrace, they tumbled onto a four-poster bed.

Incredible luck, thought Stanley, that the owner of the staplercam in Saint-Jean Cap Ferrat happened to be American. And on top of that, an expert with cameras. Half a dozen analysts as well as a team of techs with facial recognition software would weigh in shortly, but Stanley was certain from first glance: They'd found Fat Elvis.

It was a simple matter now to speed-dial the requisite players at the Direction Cen-

trale du Renseignement Intérieur, or DCRI
— essentially the French FBI — then go
grab Abdullah. But first Stanley needed a
CIA green light. This was the most difficult
step in any operation. Coming to terms with
that had been the greatest challenge in his
career.

Seated in his spacious office in the embassy's B Section annex, which had been built
in the thirties with a nod to ancient Athens,
he generated both an intel report and an
operational proposal for his branch chief.
Once the branch chief affixed his digital
signature, the documents would be for-
warded to the station chief, a bright and
talented man, who, like many of his peers,
suffered from Umpire Syndrome — the
umpire who makes the right call goes un-
noticed whereas the umpire who blows a
call draws the crowd's attention. The CIA's
turf system burdened station chiefs with
steep penalties for failure and relatively little
reward for success, making them risk-
averse.

Stanley suspected his station chief would
elect to hand the ball off to the French. Still
there was a chance that Stanley's proposed
plan would fly. The French were notorious
fumblers, and the station chief stood to get
the blame if they screwed up the Abdullah

op. So he might come on board. If so, he would have to cable headquarters for further authorizations.

Stanley dispatched a flash precedence cable to him, then sat back and reflected on how much easier his targets had it. Weapons salesmen and terrorists didn't have to check in with their own bureaucrats in each country. In Europe, such criminals barely needed to slow down as they crossed international borders. CIA officers could follow only with a ream of permissions.

For years the system had riled Stanley. But his piss and vinegar dwindled in direct proportion to his remaining service time. He'd leaped last year at the Paris hitch, not because of the city's aesthetic appeal — he ate most of his dinners at one of the better McDonald's knockoffs — but because of the ease of the job. Not only was France an ally, but it had a free press that provided better intel than most intelligence services could. There had been more targets in Detroit, Michigan, his first posting, because of the city's large immigrant community.

Back then, driven by unadulterated love for his country, the magna cum laude Stanford grad had turned down jobs that would have paid him more as a rookie than he could ever earn in a year in the CIA unless he was named director. Having now served for twenty-seven years, he had just three to go before he could retire with full benefits. Accordingly, like management, the last thing he wanted was a flap.

His thoughts were interrupted by the fusion of electronic beeps that signified the arrival of a cable.

He input his pass code and clicked open the dispatch. It had been just seven minutes since he'd sent his request. It was doubtful that anyone would have had time to type anything more than "NO." Instead he read:

PERMISSION FOR COVERT ACTION IN CONJUCTION WITH DCRI AND DGSE: GRANTED. OBJECTIVE: CAPTURE THEN RECRUIT TARGET TO GATHER INTEL ON TARGET'S CLIENTS.

9

Pale hazel clouds around the Cessna parted, revealing the coastal city of Nice. Stanley marveled at how, even on this hoary January afternoon, the Mediterranean beat the hell out of any painting. Even he, with the aesthetic equivalent of a tin ear, could understand why the French flocked to the patches of jagged, black-rock beach here.

From the airport, he drove a rental car twenty miles west to the village of Saint-Jean Cap Ferrat, a watercolor come to life on the Côte d'Azur. The combination of natural splendor, ideal climate, and glamour had made the Cap a favorite holiday destination of the European aristocracy and, for that reason, the latest hot spot of Hollywood's elite.

Stanley first drove by Jerry Hill's house. Last summer Hill had purchased the sprawling adobe villa, which was painted a shade of yellow Stanley speculated was called canary. Its flat roof was tiled with the traditional red clay. Behind it was a swimming pool — or, possibly, a multitiered artwork in white ceramic that contained turquoise water whose far edge ran along the hundred-foot-high seawall. The property's many bushes and hedges were so smooth and symmetrical, it appeared that they were maintained with a barber's scissors and a level rather than with a hedge trimmer. The grand front lawn was as spotless as a kitchen floor; when a tiny leaf fluttered down from a lime tree, Stanley half expected a servant to come running.

The neighboring home was nearly a twin to Hill's, but painted a robin's-egg blue with a flamingo pink roof — yet, somehow, all in all, quite conservative, if not stately. It had a commanding view of vast and exquisitely manicured gardens as well as much of the Mediterranean. According to a DCRI report, Abdullah, under the name Charboneau, was renting this property for more per month than Stanley paid in rent per annum.

Stanley proceeded two miles to the staging area, a secluded elementary school whose students and faculty were on Christmas vacation. In the cafeteria, where most of the two hundred or so undersized chairs rested upside down on long tables, he conferred with his counterparts from the DCRI and the Direction Générale de la Sécurité Extérieure, the international intelligence agency, who had brought along ninety-two members of the elite special ops unit they liked to call the Secret Army of Paris.

To avoid the risk of placing the Hill family in the cross fire, Stanley decided to grab Abdullah at the Charboneau villa, despite the presence of at least five armed guards.

Shortly after sundown, a man dressed as an Électricité de France worker cut the power to Charboneau and Hill's entire road, enabling the special ops troops to advance under cover of darkness and establish a tight perimeter around Graceland — the code name du jour for Fat Elvis's digs. Additional troops sealed off potential escape routes. Any noise was masked by the waves crashing against the rocky seawall.

There was a time when Stanley would have joined the assault team. Now he watched from the safety of a comfortable leather chair inside a contractor's van parked by an empty house eight blocks away. His DCRI and DGSE counterparts occupied identical chairs on either side of him. The three men focused on the pair of large monitors relaying Graceland through

65

miniature cameras concealed on the special ops agents.

As the troops began their covert advance, a bearded young man slid out of one of Graceland's kitchen windows, apparently making a run for it. The two agents in closest proximity swapped uncertain glances, like outfielders circling underneath the same fly ball. A third agent reached a hand from behind a topiary bush, tripping the fugitive.

Stanley wondered whether Abdullah was using the bearded man as a diversion.

A moment later, Graceland's grand, round-topped front door creaked inward. The frosted-glass transom and sidelights offered no clue as to who or what was within the cavernous foyer. As if drawn by a giant magnet, the Frenchmen's rifles swung in unison toward the opening.

Hands over his head in surrender, Abdullah stepped out. He wore only an open terry cloth robe and sweatpants. The hairy belly that drooped over his silk boxer shorts was a larger version of his bloated, scruffy face. Squinting out at the forest of rifle barrels, he said, in thick North African–accented French, "What the fuck, we forget to pay the electric bill?"

10

Stanley drove his rental car thirty minutes along Nice's winding coastal road to Haut-de-Cagnes, a tiny hilltop city practically unchanged since the Middle Ages. Because of the maze of narrow and precipitously sloped streets, it would have been impossible for another car to follow him. It was challenge enough to make the tight turns without first having to back up his tiny Renault two or three times. If he'd rented a midsize Renault, he would have had to park well shy of the safe house and proceed on foot.

He centered his thoughts on the evening's objective: Convince Abdullah to play ball. The strategy was simple. Stanley would say, "I just want a yes or a no, Ali. Yes, and you can be a hero, plus keep your millions. No, and you'll be neck-deep in shit for your remaining years — or days."

Stanley parked near an alleyway that he

might have missed without the GPS, even in daylight. At its far end sat a stone restaurant, shuttered now. The place looked at least five hundred years old. Above it was a warren of small apartments.

Getting to the third-floor safe house required climbing such a narrow spiral stairway that Stanley wondered if the portly Abdullah would have to be brought up some other way. In which case, Stanley would be envious. Half a flight and his hip was on fire.

He braved the remainder of the stairs, reaching the apartment at 1900 hours. For the first time since 0700, he realized he was hungry. It had been years since the events of a day made him forget to eat.

He liked that.

Safe houses were generally stocked with little more than instant coffee, mixed nuts, and potato chips, stale often as not. Salivating at the prospect of chips regardless, he headed directly into the sagging flat's kitchen. Although not much larger than a closet, it had two sinks — one a ceramic bathroom model, the other a steel basin suitable for washing dishes. The room also had a corner shower stall so cramped that a person could wash only half of himself at a time.

Before he could open the cupboard, Stanley heard a pair of staccato knocks at the front door.

"*Qui est là?*" he asked with a mix of wariness and grumble befitting the late hour.

"*Thierry?*" came a man's voice.

"*Qu'est-ce que tu veux?*"

"*On est là avec ton copain.*"

"*Ah, bon.*" Stanley opened the door, admitting two DCRI men who prodded in their captive, his hands bound at the wrists behind his back.

Abdullah looked younger than the forty-five years he was believed to be, due perhaps to his plumpness and the sort of golden tan indigenous to yachting. Walking appeared to strain him, probably due to "accidental" run-ins with elbows and fists belonging to members of the Secret Army of Paris — kidney shots, because they didn't leave a mark. Or maybe it was just the pain of his defeat. The Frenchmen dumped him onto the sofa and hurried back downstairs.

The plastic cuffs prevented the arms dealer from sitting up. Regarding them, he said in English, "Please take them off?"

Deciding to save this as a carrot, Stanley lowered himself into a creaky armchair directly across from the sofa and said tersely, "*Ali, je veux simplement un 'oui' ou un 'non' —"*

"Do us both a favor and skip the high school French," Abdullah said. The fire had returned to his eyes. And the rapid English was spoken with a distinctly Midwestern accent.

Stanley hid his astonishment. "I guess your high school taught you to speak English pretty well."

"Didn't have to, 'cause it was in Cleveland. Knowing that, does the name Charboneau have any significance to you now, apart from my use of it as an alias?"

"Is that the name of your high school?"

"No, Marshfield. I went to Marshfield High. While I was there, Joltin' Joe Charboneau went from being a bare-knuckle boxer down at the local railyard to starting right fielder for the Cleveland Indians. Sonofabitch not only could knock the cover off the ball; he could open a bottle of beer with his eye socket and drink it through his nose, and he did his own dental work with a pair of pliers. We would have fucking loved it if they renamed the school after him."

"I remember him, American League Rookie of the Year in 1979, right?" Stanley said. By it he meant, "What in the name of God is going on here?"

"1980, actually. Listen, there's a little mat-

70

ter I need your help with." Abdullah hauled himself up, bringing his eyes even with Stanley's. "I just got wind of the fact that an old colleague of ours, Drummond Clark, is about to sell a low-yield nuke to a Muslim separatist group."

11

"What time is the meet-up?" Drummond asked for the third time since they had found the BMW in the Hauptstrasse parking lot.

"One." Charlie pulled the car into a space among the smattering of vehicles in the Zweisimmen airfield's small lot. "Two minutes from now."

"Thirteen hundred, you mean?"

"Yes."

"I want you to get in the practice of using military time." Alzheimer's sufferers often labored to maintain the perception that they were on top of their game. Drummond in this fuzzy state was a 5 on Charlie's lucidity scale of 1 to 10 — 1 being a zombie, 10 being laser-sharp, or his old self.

In Alice fashion, Charlie reversed in favor of another spot — one more attempt at detecting surveillance.

Nobody, at least as far as he could tell.

The sleepy Zweisimmen airfield consisted of a few planes and a tiny air traffic control tower atop a proportionate general aviation building constructed of logs and painted mustard yellow; it looked more like a ski lodge.

Drummond's eyes darted about. In the throes of dementia, Alzheimer's sufferers retained the ability to bake a cake or drive a car, even create a Web site. After four decades of clandestine operations, Drummond's faculty for circumventing danger was hardwired.

"Everything okay?" Charlie asked.

"I'm fine, thank you."

Unfortunately, taking advantage of Drummond's intuition was often like straining to hear a radio with patchy reception. "I mean, are we safe here?"

"What about our escape route?" Drummond asked.

"You said that if we were going to be in a situation where we required one, it would either be at the chalet, during our walk down to the Hauptstrasse, or when I turned the car on and it started to explode."

"Oh, right." Drummond acted as if he remembered. "And just so we're on the same page: Objective?"

"Find out if Alice is okay."

"Yes, good. And then — and only then — do we get on the plane to Mexico."

Seeing no point in correcting him, Charlie turned off the engine and popped his safety belt. Drummond made no move to exit the car.

"Everything okay?" Charlie asked again.

"What time is the meet-up?"

The parking lot swirled with bitter gusts of sleet and the waxy fumes of aircraft hydraulic fluid. As the Clarks made their way to the general aviation building, Drummond reminisced — apropos of nothing, Charlie hoped — about a stealth fighter plane that had crashed in the Nevada desert during a 1979 test flight.

Jesse James bounded from the cabin of a small jet and intercepted them. Elevated to perhaps six-four by cowboy boots, he cut an imposing figure, his blue jeans and even his ski jacket conforming to muscles that were rocks. He walked with a rolling gait, arms swinging and beefy hands half open, as if poised to toss aside anyone who got in his way.

"Mr. McDonough, great to see you again," he said to Charlie, and before Charlie could respond, he reached out to Drummond. "I'm J. T. Bream. And pleased to meet you."

Drummond shook Bream's hand. "Likewise," he said with too much affection. "What's your role in this?"

"Just a glorified courier."

"Well, very nice to meet you, sir."

Bream pivoted so that his back was to the terminal, his smile fading. "Now, I need you boys to follow me over to the jet and act like you're looking the thing over. We want Jacques and Pierre inside to believe that you're a couple of suits deciding on whether or not to hire me to give you a lift to Zurich."

Charlie looked to Drummond for reassurance.

He caught his father bounding toward the jet with the zeal of a child about to take his first flight.

"So you weren't kidding about him, were you?" Bream said to Charlie.

"Wish I had been. Please don't tell me he needs to fly the plane."

"I've got that. Please tell me he knows where the thing is hidden."

"We can talk about that when we have proof Alice is okay."

"Relax, Chuck. We want the same thing here. I don't see a dime until my people get their device." Bream unpocketed his satellite phone and clicked a button at the base

75

of its oversized display panel. A video of a small room popped up. It had pale blue walls but otherwise was so featureless that it could be in a motel on the Jersey Turnpike or a budget flat in Bangkok. Alice sat on the only piece of furniture in sight, a plain sofa that possibly doubled as her bed. She was reading a magazine.

Charlie felt a swirl of joy tempered by fear that this was old video.

"Can I talk to her?" he asked.

"You are," Bream said.

As if alerted to a new entry to the room, Alice turned, then rose and hurried toward the camera, beaming, apparently, at an image of Charlie.

A potent mix of joy and guilt left him speechless. He managed, "Are you okay?"

"Wonderful," she said, "with a bow on top" — one of her codes signifying that the "wonderful" had in no way been coerced.

Charlie tried to sort through his jumble of thoughts, not least of which was their predicament. "I forget what my there's-no-gun-to-my-head code is," he said. "But there's no gun being held to anybody's head on this end. Where are you?"

"For some reason they won't tell me —"

Bream pressed a button on his phone. The display went black. "Okay, obviously, she's

76

fine. For now. So where to?"

Charlie needed to be cautious. "Martinique."

"I already knew that. Can we be any more specific?"

"Dad said the city of Fort-de-France. The way it usually works is, once he gets to a place, things become familiar to him. Don't worry, we'll find the thing."

Wariness slitted Bream's eyes. "Wonderful."

12

Now that the satphone call was over, Alice expected that her captors would again secure her wrists and ankles and duct tape shut her mouth. The tape came off only when they fed her pieces of nutrition bar or let her sip water through a long rubber tube — a precautionary measure, she thought, which they were wise to use.

Her mastery of Shaolin kung fu included the ability to sling objects with extraordinary speed and accuracy. She could toss a playing card at forty miles per hour, creating force sufficient to stab an adversary and even, if she struck certain minute pressure points, put him into a coma. If she could get her hands on the satphone, she could throw it at the man she thought of as Frank — he had the Frankenstein monster's broad shoulders and lumbering gait. His face was hidden by a novelty-store black cotton mask with reflective bulbs over the eyes. He'd yet to say anything within her earshot.

She knew less about her other captor. She called him Walt for his gleaming blowback-operated semiautomatic Walther PPK. By waving the pistol one way or another, he indicated *Get up from the sofa* or *Sit back down on the sofa and let Frank tie you up again.*

Once she took out the two of them, she would take her chances with the helicopter pilot, who in all likelihood was spending his break time in an adjacent room. Since being chloroformed in Gstaad, she could remember only this room, which might well be a cell in an upscale gulag. A better guess was an apartment in Geneva, rented under an alias. Or an isolated Swiss country house, in which case the duct tape over her mouth was a small bit of deception: She could scream her lungs out here and no one would hear. The blacked-out windows, unrelenting Muzak from unseen speakers, and an electric air freshener that sprayed a sickly sweet vanilla scent were all intended to keep her from picking up clues.

Still, she had some hints. Her old NSA-sponsored black ops unit had developed something of a niche in renditions. For discretion's sake, the number of captors was usually kept to three, all mercenaries with allegiance only to their numbered offshore bank accounts. They were fed a cover story regarding the operation. The duct tape over their captive's mouth was meant to keep the *captors* from hearing the truth.

Alice hungrily eyed the satphone. "I don't suppose there's any way you'll let me check my e-mail?" she said to Frank.

He shook his head.

So he understood English.

"How about just letting me know the score of the Patriots game?" she tried.

If he were to check the Web, she might snare the phone and launch it toward Walt.

Frank stayed mum.

Walt made one of his usual series of gestures: *Sit back down on the sofa. Let Frank tie you up again. Let him reapply the duct tape.* He punctuated each with a shake of the Walther as if to add, *Or you know what.*

She complied.

For now.

■ ■ ■ ■

PART TWO:
TRADE SCHOOL

■ ■ ■ ■

1

What the hell have you stepped in? Stanley asked himself again and again during the nightlong flight from Nice to Washington. The cable he'd received, minutes after spiriting Ali Abdullah over the border to Italy, said little more than REPORT TO HQS ASAP.

The sun had yet to appear over McLean, Virginia, when Stanley swung his rental car off a still-quiet George Washington Memorial Parkway onto the heavily tree-lined Route 123. In the darkness he nearly mistook the agency's driveway for the look-alike service road. A sign that was *not* obscured by a low-hanging bough might have helped. The location of the Central Intelligence Agency wasn't secret after all; tour bus guides pointed the place out. In many ways, he thought, this was a metaphor for the system. A second cup of coffee and he might stand a chance of puzzling out how exactly.

But for now, exhaustion made it feel as if poured cement were hardening in his eye sockets.

When he had stepped into the headquarters building as a rookie, he was dazzled by the grand, white marble lobby with its famous eagle seal spanning the floor. He was stirred by the stars, carved into the marble wall on the right, anonymously commemorating the men and women who'd given their lives in the service of the agency. As he proceeded from the security portals to the elevators, there was a bit of march in his gait.

This morning, the same lobby conjured an aging bus terminal, over-polished to compensate for wear. He shuffled to the elevators; the ten-minute trek from the parking lot against a gelid southeaster had left the hip feeling full of icicles.

Stepping out of the Europe division's hallmark Union Jack–blue elevator doors on the fourth floor, he was met by Caldwell "Chip" Eskridge. The Europe division chief engulfed Stanley's right hand with both of his own. "Welcome home, tiger."

"Good to see you," Stanley lied.

Fifty-one years old, the sinewy Eskridge tipped the scale at a pound or two more than he had as the Yale crew team's heavyweight stroke. With his crisp woolen suit, power suspenders, and slicked-back hair, he was the portrait of a bank chairman. His dynamic presentations on the Hill were videotaped and shown within the agency for instructional purposes. Although he had a battalion of deputies and administrative assistants, he did things like this, coming to greet guests of lesser rank. In conversation, he never failed to look people in the eyes, appearing to hang on their every word. If any one quality had accounted for his rise through the ranks, though, it was his ability to avoid flaps, or, better, to defuse them.

For exactly that reason, acid had been bubbling in Stanley's stomach for the past ten hours. He feared that Eskridge, acting to preempt the Cap Ferrat Flap of 2010, would dispatch him to the CIA's Anchorage bureau for the remainder of his career. Or fire him, a worse punishment since it would deny him his retirement benefits.

"How about we go to the conference room?" Eskridge asked.

As if Stanley could disagree.

Before he could reply at all, Eskridge had shifted into high gear. Trying to ignore the stabbing in his hip, Stanley hurried after him. The long corridor was like that of any white-shoe office suite and wouldn't rate comment except by someone desperate to break the silence.

"Everything looks the same," Stanley said.

Eskridge waved him to a conference room.

As Stanley hobbled through the door, applause washed over him.

He took in ten men and women standing around the conference table, all longtime colleagues of his. Eighty-something-year-old Archie Snow, Eskridge's predecessor as Europe division chief, stepped forward, handing Stanley a framed document and an envelope.

"Congrats, kid," Snow said.

The frame contained a certificate of distinction awarded to William Christopher Stanley Jr., "In recognition of outstanding performance of duty in the service of the United States of America." Which was as much specificity as Stanley had ever seen on a CIA award. The envelope contained a cashier's check for $2,500.

Stanley would have been elated if not for his certainty that the meeting was about something else. Convincing him that crucial business mandated an all-night flight just so his old cronies could throw him a surprise party definitely wasn't company style.

Each of the cronies congratulated him, meanwhile demolishing a tray of breakfast pastries. Then they filed out, leaving just Eskridge, who said, "As you've likely surmised, the award presentation was cover."

Stanley's stomach acid erupted. "I guess I won't be buying that new stationary bike."

Eskridge smiled. "Actually, the award itself is real. The certificate will have to be vaulted here, of course, but the check ought to clear, so buy away."

"To perpetuate the cover?"

"You made the right call in France. A commendable job, really. Also I needed an excuse to get you *here*." He waved at the ceiling, where tiles were suspended from a sheet of Plexiglas that continued down the wall, disappearing behind mahogany wall paneling and continuing under the floor, forming a Plexiglas room within the room, capable of locking in sound waves. "Wondering why, by any chance?"

"It crossed my mind."

"There's going to be a senior operations officer opening in London next year. It's yours if you want it."

The only post superior to Paris was London, where, in deference to the British intelligence agencies MI5 and MI6, the CIA's mantra was "Stand bloody down!" Over the past few months Stanley had lobbied for a two-year Blighty hitch to wind up his service. Now he braced for the price.

"There's a temp job I'm hoping you'll accept first," Eskridge said.

The agency wasn't the military; Stanley could turn down a dangerous assignment. The consequence of doing so, however, could be three years in Antarctica. Which beat death. So he was left to determine how risky the "temp job" was.

Eskridge sat down heavily at the far side of the conference table. "This is the part where you promise not to breathe a word of what I'm about to tell you, so help you Godhra."

Godhra, a small city in northwestern India, was home to a secret CIA prison. Time there would be worse than any of the scenarios Stanley had considered, death included.

2

Two hours into the seven-hour flight, the Gulfstream roared — presumably — above a glossy navy-blue Atlantic. Exceptional insulation made it a toss-up as to which was louder, Charlie thought, the jet engines or Drummond's light snoring from across the aisle. Their seats, like the three others, were not mere seats, but overstuffed leather recliners. Compared with this, commercial airline first class was the F train.

Charlie read a sports magazine. Or, more accurately, he held a sports magazine. He kept wondering what would become of Alice should he fail to deliver the ADM.

For the first time since takeoff, Bream glanced back from the cockpit, taking in the sleeping Drummond. "Sorry there's no in-flight movie," the pilot said to Charlie. "Heckuva bar, though." He aimed a thumb at the rear of the cabin.

He seemed bored, or at least inclined to

chat, which dovetailed nicely with Charlie's hope of learning whatever he could about him.

"This is a sweet ride," Charlie said.

"It's just a rent-a-plane, of course." Bream flashed a smile. "You know how it is, when you're flying highly wanted fugitives across international borders to go fetch a nuclear bomb. It's usually a good idea to rent, under an alias."

"Oh." In fact, Charlie would have bet the chalet that the Gulfstream was a rental. But he hoped that by playing the naïf, he might lower Bream's guard. "So how does one get into flying highly wanted fugitives across international borders to fetch nuclear bombs?"

Bream laughed. "Thinking of a career move?"

"Should I?"

Nudging a lever beneath the instrument panel, Bream pivoted to face Charlie. "I can only tell you one man's experience."

"Okay." Charlie glanced at Drummond. Still in dreamland.

"When I was in my twenties, I signed on with the Skunk Works," Bream said. "Know it?"

"Vaguely." Once upon a time, like many American boys with an aptitude for numbers and a hankering for glory, Charlie had dreamed of working at the Skunk Works, Lockheed's legendary advanced aircraft division in Palmdale, California. The closest he ever got was Arcadia, California, an hour away, to watch the Santa Anita Derby.

"I was a test pilot on an experimental stealth fighter," Bream said.

"Wow." Charlie's wariness gave way to intrigue.

"I figured I'd put in five years or so there. Then, just north of thirty, I'd be able to transition to cushy corporate jets — play that right, you can make near as much as a ballplayer and get yourself a mansion and all that. The problem was, our client was an Air Force bureaucrat in real bad need of a punch in the face. And one day I gave it to him. He saw to it that I wasn't just shit-canned but kept from flying so much as a paper plane again for a U.S.-based outfit. Then he had me thrown to the cops."

Charlie almost sympathized. "Did you have to do time?"

Bream chuckled. "Only if you count my marriages."

Lately when Charlie met men close to his age and learned that they had already been divorced several times — there was no shortage of them in horseplayer circles —

he felt he'd frittered away his youth, never even marrying once. But he didn't feel that way with Bream.

Charlie suspected he had been listening to a cover story. And why would Bream tell him the truth? Charlie cursed his naïveté in thinking that, like some sort of seasoned covert operations officer, he might "elicit" here.

"I appreciate the in-flight entertainment," he said, rising and wandering back to the bar, which held far greater appeal than it had a minute ago.

"My pleasure," Bream said, turning back to the controls.

On a crystal decanter, Charlie caught a reflection of the pilot biting back a grin. It revealed an extra helping of ego, Charlie thought.

Now he had something to work with.

3

"Ever heard of Perriman Appliances?" Esk-ridge asked.

"Rings a bell." Stanley had lived in Madrid for more than a year before he noticed that his kitchenette had no oven.

"It's basically junk that runs on electrical current. I made the mistake of buying one of their 'affordable' refrigerators *and* one of their dishwashers, back in the days when I, too, thought you could have a family in our trade."

So Eskridge had read deep into Stanley's file — or one of the division chief's adjutants had and distilled it for him. Stanley traced the disintegration of his brief marriage to the day he left for the Farm.

"You know what they say about the third generation losing the money?" Eskridge asked, rhetorically. "In the mid-eighties, one of the agency's geographical analysis sub-committees bought Perriman Appliances from the Perriman grandkids for practically nothing."

"For the usual reasons that a geographical analysis subcommittee needs a second-rate appliance manufacturer?"

"Third-rate would be kind." Eskridge glanced around, as if wary that, even here, someone might be watching or listening. "Geographical Analysis Subcommittee is how the Cavalry is listed on the books. I take it you're familiar with the Cavalry."

"Just the water cooler intel." Stanley had a nagging feeling that there was an important cable he'd neglected. Rumint — the intelligence community's brand of rumor — had it that the Cavalry was a special ops unit that recruited the gutsiest of the best and the brightest and pulled off covert operations that no one else would dare. It was hard to know, though, what was apocryphal and what was true.

"At the moment, they're an off-the-books joint project of this division, Counterproliferation, and Counterterrorism. They administer the secret side of the Perriman worldwide network, trafficking weapons. To terrorists, principally. Or any other nutjob whose check won't bounce. The Cavalry's best seller is a non-detonative version of a ten-kiloton Russian ADM from the seventies. The device looks like the inner workings of a washing machine, and its weight is only a pound or two greater. So the Perriman washer makes an excellent concealment. On top of that, the Cavalry created special insulation to veil the bomb's radiation. What the buyers don't know is that the ADM is a complete dud — even less useful than an actual Perriman washer. Once a purchase is made, the buyers are monitored by the Cavalry and taken out of play before they can use the weapon. In sum, we found that the way to beat the illegal arms dealers was to join 'em."

For the first time in twelve hours, Stanley breathed free of the worry that he'd been hoodwinked by Ali Abdullah. He'd sent Abdullah to a covert American detention facility in Genoa, purportedly to protect him from reprisal by the French but, really, to protect the arms dealer's secret identity.

"So Abdullah checked out?"

"There was no need. His real name's Austin Floyd Bellinger. I was in his wedding, in Cleveland. Your decision to keep DCRI and DGSE out of the loop was spot on. A few weeks in the detention facility will bolster Bellinger's cover. Then the special effects department will make it look like he killed some guards and escaped. Or maybe they'll just let him buy his way out. The point is, you really did earn that stationary bike. And in so doing, you've earned yourself a role in the best show on the Great Dark Way."

"What sort of role?" Stanley exhibited less detachment than he would have liked.

"Do you know anything about Nick Fielding?"

"The Ali Abdullah of the Caribbean. Is *he* Cavalry too?"

"Yes. *Was*. Died recently in an electrical fire in the New York City subway — you hear about it?"

"I don't think so." If it was something Stanley should have known, he could attribute the memory lapse to fatigue.

"Good. There was no electrical fire. What happened was, one of the Cavalry ADMs detonated in the sub-basement of the Perriman Manhattan offices, which happens to be close to a subway tunnel. As far as I know, the extent of the coverage was just a paragraph or two, buried deep in New York's *Daily News,* decrying the city's dangerously outmoded subway system."

"I thought the ADMs were duds."

"Their uranium components are essentially fake, but that sort of weapon also packs a hundred pounds of plastic explosive, supposedly to generate critical mass, and that part we can't fake, though the boys in the white coats are working on it."

"I imagine a device of that nature doesn't go off accidentally?"

"No. In an actual deployment, it would've been armed by three different Ivans, each man knowing only one-third of the code, for security's sake. In this case, one man had all the codes. Drummond Clark. Now, what do you know about him?"

"Again, only rumint, but enough that I'd bet he's a shoo-in for a Trailblazer medal."

"Stood a chance at being the first guy to win two. But he's the one who triggered the ADM that took out Fielding, along with the Cavalry's entire Manhattan office. So now he won't win anything. Originally, though, the Perriman op was his idea. He founded the Cavalry, staffed it — he plucked Bellinger out of a USO show. Thanks to Drummond Clark, lunatics who might have gotten their hands on a real nuke instead blow up the equivalent of a few sticks of dynamite."

"So why in his right mind would he blow up the Manhattan office?"

Eskridge stiffened. "He wasn't in his right mind. A few months ago he was placed on medical leave, suffering from a voracious case of early-onset Alzheimer's. More recently he developed acute paranoia, which led to an Appalachian-length trail of bodies, not least of whom was the national security adviser."

"So I take it Burton Hattemer didn't really die in a fall."

"The media weren't informed about the bullet that preceded the fall. The good news is that, as a result of it, the Cavalry obtained a presidential finding waiving Executive Order 11905, allowing them to neutralize Clark. As well as his son, Charlie, which probably isn't a bad idea regardless of the Hattemer incident. In a nutshell, the apple didn't fall far from the tree, but it bounced bloody far out of the orchard. The kid's math genius got him into Brown. He dropped out, though, and wound up an inveterate gambler. He now knows and would likely trade what is perhaps our most closely guarded secret for a good tip on the third race at Hialeah. Initially we thought that Clark and Son had done the wet work for us and detonated themselves in the 'electrical fire' along with Fielding. To say the least, this would have simplified matters. However . . ."

Eskridge hit a button on what looked to be a length of garden hose running along the end of the conference table. "This is a little something the Toy Makers have been working on," he said. Like humidifier mist, particles of light rose from a thin vent running the length of the hose. "Puts pictures on the same basic metamaterial that will soon enable us to be first to have invisibility camouflaging." He looked around the room, in an exaggerated show of paranoia. "Unless the other team has beaten us to it."

Taking on different hues, the particles formed a screen that stood at a right angle to the table and showed video of a young woman crossing a crowded city street at night.

"This is surveillance footage from a kabob place across Broadway from the Perriman offices," Eskridge said. "You're looking at former No Such Agency black ops starlet Alice Rutherford, on the night in question, going into the burning building."

Despite the dark and grainy image, the woman was stunning. Entering the drab postwar office building, she drew a gun as calmly as if it were a cell phone.

Eskridge pressed the screen. Alice's image slid to his right, the video fast-forwarding to a magnified, infrared-filter-enhanced view of her in the vestibule, blasting apart the inner glass wall.

"She was in deep cover on an intelligence

gathering op in Martinique," Eskridge said. "Fielding was her target. Like the rest of the world, the NSA bought into his bad-guy cover story. The problem with Miss Alice Rutherford was, when push came to shove, she couldn't be convinced that Fielding was actually on our side, not even by the man upstairs." He pointed to the ceiling, signifying the director, whose office was on the seventh floor. "So now we're watching her gunning down Fielding and, at least in her mind, coming to the rescue of . . ."

On the display, Alice climbed through the cavity she'd created in the glass. Eskridge tapped at the scene, fast-forwarding through about two minutes of footage of empty vestibule. Then Alice reappeared from an alley next to the office building, with a young man and an older one in tow.

"Drummond and Rotten Apple Clark?" Stanley asked.

"None other." Eskridge paused to watch the threesome disappear from the frame. "And that's the last anyone's seen of them: Alice has gone totally off the reservation."

"Any idea why?"

"She maintained that *Fielding* was off the reservation, that he and the Cavalry zapped Burt Hattemer in order to get the presidential finding against the Clarks. She also insisted that the Cavalry did this to keep a lid on their own misdoings. Under Fielding's direction, the Cavalry 'went *Lord of the Flies*,' as she put it — and to some extent, she's right. One problem with her murder theory, though, is the utter lack of any evidence. Three days ago she sent a Hushmail from points unknown to an inspector general at NSA requesting an investigation. NSA wrote her back saying basically, 'Great, tell us more,' but she never responded. It now appears as though she was just trying to smoke screen her real activity, which is putting one of Drummond's old ADMs up for sale, possibly to the United Liberation Front of the Punjab, an Islamic separatist group who are violent psychopaths when they're on their best behavior. According to our man Bellinger, their sugar daddy had his checkbook out and was waiting near Fielding's place in Martinique the day Fielding was killed. Unfortunately, everyone who knew the device's location died with Fielding. Everyone except Drummond Clark, that is. So if Bellinger is right about the new weapons deal, Alice and her companions stand to clear several hundred million clams. Which means one of those bombs could blow in the heart of New York or DC. And worse still . . ."

"The Perriman Appliances op would be blown?"

"Exactly." Eskridge stared over the screen, his laid-back manner hardening. "If you can find them, and if we can learn what they've told to whom, great. But first and foremost, we need to stop them."

The assignment was far more dangerous than Stanley had imagined. He wanted it anyway. He'd wanted an assignment like this since he first applied to the CIA.

4

Stanley sat in a temporary Europe division office with one of the unit's signature Union Jack–blue doors but otherwise as charismatic as a budget motel room minus the requisite nature print. His dream job commenced with gumshoe work about as rudimentary as it gets.

He spent much of the morning investigating PM00543MH4/7, the Science and Technology search system's designation for one of the 29,655 groups of travelers matching his criteria. This group consisted of sixty-three-year-old investor Duncan Calloway, who five nights ago had taken his Learjet 45XR from Palm Beach to Paris, along with two of his junior associates — one male, one female, both purportedly twenty-eight. Their excursion employed no small amount of subterfuge, including an 0100 departure and a layover at New York's Kennedy Airport for twenty minutes, though such a stop was unnecessary for refueling.

The subterfuge, Stanley learned, was intended to throw off a rival investment firm that had hired a Palm Beach–based private espionage outfit to track Calloway in order to determine whether he was negotiating the purchase of a French electronics conglomerate.

Stanley anticipated sitting in the temporary office for two or three more days just to wade through the computer-generated leads.

Then PM11304ZH4/9 caught his eye.

At 6:52 A.M. on December 29, thirteen days ago, a thirty-two-year-old Manhattan hedge fund manager named Roger Norton Traynor departed Newark airport for Innsbruck, Austria, aboard another Learjet 45XR, a seven-seater owned and operated by Newark-based Absolute Air Charter, LLC. Accompanying Traynor was his wife of three days, April Gail Hellinger, twenty-eight. The honeymooners checked into Innsbruck's five-star Hotel Europa late that night.

Stanley telephoned the Hotel Europa, posing as one of the groom's colleagues, needing to reach him on an urgent business matter. With even the most discreet hotels, striking the appropriate tone usually suf-

104

ficed to elicit all information save the guest's credit card number. And that, if needed, was available on Intelnet with a few clicks of a mouse.

"He was a, how you say, a *Liebling der Götter* — a lucky guy," night reception desk attendant Heinz Albrecht said of Traynor. Albrecht remembered April as a *"schöne junge Frau."*

At check-in, Albrecht recalled, Traynor paid for the entire stay in cash, which was not atypical of honeymooners, having been handed envelope after envelope of the stuff on their wedding night and eager to put it toward their hotel bill before it was lost or stolen. In the ensuing three days, Herr and Frau Traynor rarely left their mountain-view suite if at all, the *Bitte Nicht Stören* hanger fixed on their doorknob. Again, hardly unusual for honeymooners, according to Albrecht.

The rest of the staff had altogether forgotten the Traynors, although only a little over a week had passed since the couple checked out.

Stanley might have forgotten them too. But a 6:52 A.M. departure on December 29, 2009, would have allowed the Clarks and Alice Rutherford to bolt the United States shortly after blowing up much of the Cavalry and its Manhattan headquarters.

When a thorough search yielded no record of the Traynors' departure from Austria, Stanley felt his pulse quicken. Sure, they might be legitimate Americans on an extended honeymoon in Innsbruck. Or they might have left the city, taken a cozy room in a country bed-and-breakfast, and were now currently playing gin rummy by the fire. There were oddities, though. First, records showed that Absolute Air's proprietor and pilot, Richard Falzone, flew back from Austria to Newark, solo, the same day he'd deposited the Traynors. His copilot, sixty-seven-year-old Alvin Landsman of Jersey City, New Jersey, had remained in Innsbruck. Which might easily be explained. Or might not. Landsman's pilot's license had expired. Probably because a July 2008 traffic accident had left him an institutionalized quadriplegic.

The names Roger Norton Traynor and April Gail Hellinger Traynor proved equally bogus.

Stanley guessed that "Roger Traynor" had paid cash for the Hotel Europa honeymoon suite upon check-in, gone up with Alice Rutherford, and torn up the rooms so it would appear they'd enjoyed three days of romantic wildness. Then, or at least early the next morning, the couple had covertly departed the hotel. At some juncture they were joined by Drummond Clark, perhaps with a car rented under yet another alias. All three probably fled Austria after destroying their false documents, bringing Stanley's trail to a dead end.

Unless Richard Falzone knew something.

Stanley could call the charter pilot and identify himself as a CIA officer. That could spook him, which might lead him to alert Alice and the Clarks. On the other hand, if Stanley phoned and said he was anything other than law enforcement, he impeded his chances of an immediate meeting. Posing as a Homeland Security agent, for example, he stood to gain access right away and, better, leverage. An offer to cut Falzone some slack in exchange for information ought to do the trick. However, it was illegal for a CIA officer to impersonate a law enforcement official. Even pretending to be a parking cop could mean the loss of his pension.

But Stanley was permitted to pose as a Treasury official. The title encompassed coin press workers in the mint, yet carried as much clout with civilians as did Homeland Security, maybe more, as everyone who watched prime-time television knew that

Treasury also encompassed the Secret Service.

5

Stanley thought little of the three-and-a-half-hour drive through sleet and rain. The thrill of the hunt made him feel twenty years younger. He sang along with the oldies on the radio, something he hadn't done since they were released on LP.

He stopped his rental car across the street from Falzone's Teaneck, New Jersey, home, a recently constructed four-thousand-square-foot Tudor crammed into a quarter-acre suburban lot. Parked prominently in front was a candy-apple-red late-sixties Corvette that had been restored to look newer than it did the day it rolled out of the plant.

Falzone, whose greatest recorded transgression was a 1994 citation for failure to heed a stop sign, opened the castle-style front door seconds after Stanley pressed the bell. The charter pilot was a boyish fifty-three in spite of a lineman's body, dark bags under owlish eyes, and a gray mustache and goatee that matched his thick hair. He had on designer chinos and a crisp oxford shirt.

"Hey," he said, as if happy to see Stanley. "How are you?"

"Fine. Thank you."

Stanley followed Falzone through the vaulted foyer to a family room that had three walls of built-in faux-teak shelves all loaded with athletic trophies and diplomas along with framed photos of the pilot, his wife, and five children, all of whom had the misfortune of inheriting his eyes.

"Sorry my wife isn't here," he said. "She does a lot of volunteer stuff at our church." Which didn't necessarily mean she was at the church now. "Can I get you a Coke or something, single-malt Scotch maybe?"

"I'm good, thanks," Stanley said.

The pilot issued an outsized smile. Calmly — maybe too calmly, given the circumstances — he lowered himself into a leather lounge chair and gestured Stanley into a seat on the matching cream-colored sofa. "So how can I be of assistance?"

"Do you recognize this man?" Stanley handed over an eight-by-ten photograph labeled "Charles Clark." He could have flashed half a dozen images of Charlie using his BlackBerry, but blowups, printed on thick card stock, added gravity.

It was obvious Falzone recognized Charlie at first glance. Yet he made an appearance of studying the photo. "Yeah, I think so. He gave me a different name."

"That figures. He's a federally wanted fugitive."

"Holy shit." Falzone did a poor job of acting surprised.

Stanley saw no reason to go through the motions. "Mr. Falzone, how much extra did you get paid to list his associate as the copilot?"

Falzone lowered his head in an appearance of penitence. "Listen, man, please, if I'd'a had any idea —"

"Would you like immunity?"

Falzone opened his eyes altar-boy wide. "Sure, but mostly I want to do whatever I can to help."

Stanley swallowed a laugh. "Where are they?"

"Far as I know, Innsbruck, Austria." The statement was perhaps Falzone's first devoid of artifice since Stanley's arrival.

"Good. How did they come to you?"

"There's a thousand ways I get clients. I chose 'Absolute' for the company's name so I'd be at the top of the listings — that's one of the best ways, believe it or not."

111

Falzone might still give up the name of the person who referred the Clarks and Rutherford to him, Stanley thought. If the pilot didn't know, he would have said so to begin with.

Stanley sighed. "Look, I'm trying to help you out here. You pocketed a few extra bucks at Christmastime for fudging a manifest. I know, I know, everybody does it. But you're the one who stands to lose everything." With a wave, he indicated the lavish home. "Maybe even do time."

Perspiration darkened Falzone's sideburns. "If I give you a name, we're good?"

"It depends a lot on what name you give me."

"Is there a way you can work it that the person doesn't find out I told you?"

"Sounds exactly like the kind of person I'm looking for. And yes."

Falzone dug at a cuticle, saying nothing.

"I've never met him," he said finally, at a whisper. "I'd never even heard of him until he called me that night, the twenty-ninth."

"Good." Stanley meant to coax him.

"The girl, April, her company had used him in the Caribbean — Martinique, I think. He does air charter down there under the name J. T. Bream."

6

"That volcano erupted, killing all of the town's thirty thousand inhabitants but one," Drummond said, extracting Charlie from much-needed slumber.

"*Volcano?*" Charlie blinked the sleep from his eyes. He could do nothing about the whiskey-induced headache.

The interior of the jet, like the sky, was copper in the setting sun. Drummond stabbed an index finger against Charlie's window, pointing at what appeared to be a greenish cloud rising from the ocean.

"You think that's a volcano?" Charlie said.

Drummond chewed it over. Or he was focusing intently on refastening his seat belt. Charlie couldn't tell which. He figured the old man was a 4, tops.

The plane dipped, revealing the green cloud to be a round-topped mountain, coated with lush jungle. Soon Charlie distinguished individual trees, standing almost as close together as carpet fibers, their leaves shimmering in the last of the day's light.

"Mount Pelée, yes." Drummond seemed pleased to have recaptured his train of thought. "It virtually split in half on May 8, 1902. An interesting piece of information is that the lava traveled into the town of Saint-Pierre at two hundred and fifty miles per hour, thwarting all of the citizens' attempts to escape it."

Charlie reckoned that his father might be correct about the volcano. Drummond had always had an uncanny ability to retain volumes of what he — and usually he alone — considered interesting pieces of information. Upon learning that Drummond had spent his life as a spy rather than an appliance salesman, Charlie recognized that the Interesting Pieces of Information functioned like Clark Kent's plain business suit and thick eyeglasses, hiding the hero beneath. Sometimes the information offered Charlie critical glimpses of Drummond's unconscious. Other times it was drivel.

"But you said there was one survivor."

"Right," said Drummond. "Cyparis was his name, as I recall, and he was protected from the thirty-six-hundred-degree Fahrenheit ash and poisonous gas because he was underground at the time, in a stonewalled cell in the town jail, awaiting hanging. After the lava cooled, he became a star attraction in P. T. Barnum's traveling circus."

Charlie was given hope in his own predicament. "The only sure thing about luck is that it will change," he said. An old track adage.

Drummond regarded him strangely. "Where are we?"

Make that a 3 on the lucidity scale, Charlie thought. "A guess is over whatever country has Mount Pelée in it."

"Mount Pelée? That's at the northern tip of Martinique, the eastern Caribbean island that's an overseas department of France."

Charlie hadn't imagined Martinique being so expansive but, rather, a beach-rimmed dot of an island. Like Drummond, he gazed out the window. Red adobe roofs began to show through the forest. As the jet descended, the roofs grew closer together, soon outnumbering the trees. Lights from other buildings, streetlamps, and streams of vehicles created a glowing dome. Such a vast and populous metropolis would exponentially complicate their task.

"Fort-de-France," said Drummond, as if encountering a long-lost friend.

"Not the one-washer town I had in mind," Charlie said.

7

"Did you know that you're my sixth wife?" Stanley asked as their DC-8 heaved into the clouds above San Juan's Luis Muñoz Marin International Airport.

"Fancy that, you're my sixth too," Hilary Hadley said. "Husband. Plus I had a wife once for an op at the Carnaval in Rio."

In signing off on the covert action, Eskridge had suggested Stanley "honeymoon" in Martinique for the usual reasons: A "wife" would augment Stanley's tourist cover. In fact, any companion adds credibility — a mere nod of corroboration by a second party almost always causes the target's trust-governing synapse to fire. In addition, women are better able to elicit information from the Breams of the world, which is to say men.

Hadley had the sort of good looks that were accentuated by a charcoal suit, perfect for the part of a businesswoman, though

Stanley sensed a free spirit beneath the Armani. He knew that some of the most gifted actors were drawn to clandestine service for the opportunity to lose themselves in roles for months at a time.

Not everyone who could act could deceive, however.

"So what do you know about us?" he asked.

"My passport, driver's license, business cards, and all of the charge cards weighing down my insanely expensive Italian handbag say I'm Eleanor Parker Atchison, forty-seven and proud to admit it, a partner at Lerner, Marks and Hopkins, the law firm about which I'll go on ad nauseam before it occurs to me to mention that I also have been married for seven years, to you, dear, Colin Wesley Atchison, CFO of GleamCo, an industrial cleaning products conglomerate and a topic that gets your juices flowing much more readily than any aspect of *your* personal life, save golf. It is for your beloved pastime that we are currently en route to shop for a condo within a chip shot of Les Trois-Îlets' Empress Joséphine course, designed by the incomparable Robert Trent Jones. We already own an adorable hundred-and-twenty-eight-year-old farmhouse in Litchfield, Connecticut, like every Tom,

Dick, and Harriet in our Park Avenue social set, but we rarely use it because we prefer the office on Saturdays, when the phones are quiet, people don't stick their heads through our doorways, and we can get things done."

Stanley was impressed with her command of her cover. Even better was her ability to act the part: During the remaining hour of the flight, as they wove additional legend to fit their operational goals, Hadley turned into Eleanor Atchison before his eyes. He particularly liked the way her speech became clipped the moment conversation shifted to their domestic life — this was a woman with more important things on her mind. Yet when it came to the circumvention of Internal Revenue property tax codes, she was effusive, as if narrating a grand adventure.

As the DC-8 began its descent to Martinique, she argued that the quality of the material and the stitching made her handbag worth the extra nine hundred dollars. Although the argument was preposterous, her conviction left Stanley convinced.

He found himself admiring the play of the silk suit pants on her long legs, like gift wrap. Glimpsing her diamond ring and her wedding band, he felt a twinge of disappointment, before realizing that, like his own gold band, it was just cover.

8

"Not exactly an ideal airport for fugitives," Charlie said.

Night had settled over Martinique as Bream dropped the Gulfstream onto the runway. Ahead blazed a seaside airport as large as those in most American cities, or about a hundred times larger than Charlie had originally expected.

"The area for private jets is actually damn-near perfect," Bream said, taxiing away from the main airport. "Otherwise we would've just hit Dominica or Saint Lucia and gotten a boat."

They rolled perhaps a mile to the dimly lit "Executive Airport," as the general aviation area was called. It included four single-aircraft hangars, a handful of charter service offices, and a red-roofed terminal that if it were any tinier wouldn't qualify as a building. Beside the little terminal was a bar, where undulating pink lights revealed two people at the tables. On the tarmac, among the three dozen parked propeller planes, there was no sign of life.

Using a small motorized platform, Bream towed the Gulfstream into a rickety hangar that was equal parts rust and peeling silver paint. Once the jet was parked, he leaped off and lowered the hangar's garage door, the cue that it was safe for Charlie and Drummond to come out of the cabin.

As they descended the stairs, Charlie was enveloped by air seemingly composed of droplets of hot water. Despite hard strains of jet fuel and exhaust, a light breeze carried a pleasing tropical scent.

Behind him, Drummond inhaled deeply and smiled. "Lily of the Valley."

"It's nice."

"An interesting piece of information is that it's poisonous."

"Great."

"I just got a text message," said Bream, peering out the door's grease-smeared plastic porthole. "There's a coupla folks paying me a drop-by visit right now, so I'm gonna call an audible." He tilted his head to a dark corner at the back of the hangar, his eyes flashing urgency. "You'd best get to know that storage closet in case they wanna come inside here."

Charlie resisted an urge to run to the door, plant his face against the porthole, and see whoever had caused Bream's reaction. Trying to maintain the appearance of normalcy, he took the remaining steps at a leisurely pace and merely glanced at the porthole. It offered a broad view of the tarmac between the hangar and the tiny terminal. He saw no one.

Drummond stood at the base of the stairway and stared outside, something that a new arrival who was not a fugitive would do.

"They're waiting for me over in the bar," Bream said. "American couple, name of Atchison, sent by a guy I know at Air France. Supposedly just tourists wallowing in cash, looking for a flying chauffeur."

Charlie's body temperature dropped. "But they're not really just American tourists, are they?"

"Probably they really are. Probably this is just a case of bad timing. There are almost as many rich tourists on this island as there are palm trees. And I do pay the bills as a charter pilot here, so it'd attract attention if I ducked them."

Chance, Charlie realized, had presented him with his first hard fact about Bream: The pilot was based in Martinique. He

123

hadn't mentioned it, but if he was local, it might mean that he was more involved in the operation than a mercenary parachuting in for the op, or "just a glorified courier," as he'd claimed. Of course the text message — *alleged* text message — might just be a ruse to make Charlie think Bream was based in Martinique.

Either way, information about the pilot wouldn't be worth much if CIA operatives were outside now.

Bream closed the cabin door and hurried to the tail of the plane. "To be on the safe side, wait here till they're gone," he said to Charlie. "Then you two will need to get a place to lay low for the night." He flung open the luggage compartment door, revealing a pair of overnight bags. "Between the light disguises and the new travel documents you'll find in here, you shouldn't have any trouble getting through customs, what there is of it. Especially 'cause 'Capitain' du Frongipanier is on duty. The guy got the job when he bombed as a crossing guard, and in ten years he hasn't made it off the late shift."

"I don't get it," Charlie said. "Are they trying to encourage people to sneak into Martinique?"

"Anybody who wants to sneak onto this

rock can pull up at any one of a million places in a boat." Bream slid the overnight bags out of the plane, dropped one before Charlie and the other by Drummond, then inched the luggage compartment door shut to avoid noise. "From this neck of the island, which is Lamentin, it's a ten-minute cab ride up to Fort-de-France. Crash just for the night at someplace that looks like enough of a fleabag that it's not on Interpol's Fax Blast list, then tomorrow, find the goddamned bomb. And as soon as you've got it, give me a holler. Also if you run into any trouble, holler. And by holler I mean text me with the BirdBook that's in your bag."

Charlie assumed he'd misheard. "A bird book?"

Drummond said, "Encrypted communication system."

"Pop's pretty much on the money," Bream said, hurrying out. "The BirdBook y'all've got's really nothing more than a pimped-up BlackBerry — in fact, it'll pass for a Black-Berry. What you do is, type the message to me straight, though a pinch of discretion won't hurt, and the BirdBook will encrypt it."

He exited through a side door, shutting it

behind him, causing the entire hangar to quiver.

In spite of the enclosure and the darkness, Charlie had a sensation of being exposed. "What does it say that I feel less secure without Alice's kidnapper around?"

"I was just going to ask you who he was," Drummond said.

9

"Yep, the Big Apple," Stanley said, finishing off his pint of Stella lager. "Helluva town."

His game plan was to lull Bream, who'd joined them at the little airport bar, into believing that he and Hadley were urban philistines. Then blindside him with a mention of one of the fugitives. Bream's reaction could provide more insight than three hours on a polygraph.

"You know, it's funny," said Hadley, who was lit by the blinking Christmas lights atop the wire fence separating the bar from the edge of the tarmac. "Eighteen years I've been living there, and I've never learned why it's called the Big Apple. I mean, no clue whatsoever."

"I've never seen any apple trees there," Stanley added, the first thing he'd said so far that was true.

"Probably not a lot of golf courses either, I'm guessing," said Bream.

Stanley sighed. "I belong to a really nice *virtual reality* golf course. One eleven-degree morning last month, when I was playing the digital version of the twelfth hole of Empress Joséphine Golf Course, the par five that doglegs along the sea, I said to myself, 'You know, that's the place to be.' "

"We're also looking on Nevis and Saint Lucia," Hadley told Bream.

"There's no comparison." The pilot drank most of his beer in one gulp. "Folks think the Caribbean islands are all the same till they come here." His laconic speech accelerated. His lips tightened. And he ground his heel against the tile floor. All of which were indicators of dishonesty. But that didn't make him more than a jet jockey hoping to get business by pretending to agree with prospective clients.

"The issue is getting back up to Newark if I need to," Stanley said.

"For some reason, they need him all the time." Giggling, Hadley placed a warm hand on Stanley's forearm.

Bream raised his nearly empty glass. "Well, here's hoping you have lots of work crises that don't hit till you've gotten in a full eighteen on Empress Joséphine."

"How much advance notice do you require?" Hadley asked him.

Perfect setup for a boast, Stanley thought. "Ma'am, if I'm not already booked, I'm like pizza delivery: I meet you at the airport in forty-five minutes or your flight is free."

Stanley laughed. "I believe it. A friend of a friend speaks very highly of you: Drummond Clark."

Bream didn't blink. "Oh, well, I owe Mr. Clark a beverage then," he said after a pause. "How is he?"

The pause felt half a beat too long to Stanley. "Okay as far as I know."

There was no reason to let the pilot suspect they were on to him. Not yet. Better just put a little scare into him and have Langley's Caribbean Desk deploy a surveillance unit. Stanley had written a dozen cables before taking off to set this up. They now seemed worth the trouble.

10

"I'M BACK ON ISLAND. HAPPY HOUR@LE SQUASH TOMORROW?" read Bream's text.

With a double-click of the *T* key, Charlie's BirdBook translated the incoming message to "ALL'S CLEAR." Bream and the American couple were gone.

Charlie preceded Drummond out of the hangar and across the tarmac to customs, trying to appear without a care, particularly about computerized facial recognition software. He wondered, though: Wouldn't it enable the airport surveillance cameras to disregard his fake sideburns, horn-rimmed glasses, and blond wig?

Stepping into the small terminal, Charlie took a slow tour of the customs waiting area, a study in too-bright linoleum, the floor tiles a pale green not found in nature. The walls were banana-colored panels that appeared to sweat in the glare of the fluorescent tubes overhead. And best of all, there were no cameras.

Taking a seat beside Drummond, Charlie realized his khaki suit had darkened from perspiration. Although the ceiling fan's tinny rattle was audible halfway across the tarmac, he felt no movement in the air five feet beneath its bamboo blades. His mind was a feverish montage of dangerous scenarios that would play out once he and Drummond were admitted to the customs office. In more than one, their mug shots served as the customs agent's screen saver. There was just no getting around the fact that they had arrived here together. The ages listed on their documents were off by a few years, but the pairing, when keyed into the customs database, would be a bucket of blood to the sharks searching for them.

Charlie whispered, "Remember what you're going to say if the customs guy asks what brings us to Martinique?"

"I think so." Drummond smiled, as if at a customs official. "I'm John Larsen of Greenwich, Connecticut — that's Larsen with an *e* — and this young scalawag is Brad McDonough, who works for me, when the mood strikes him. I'd tell you we're here for business — we're with New England Capital Management — but even three days of Pow-

131

erPoint presentations on your fair island counts as pleasure."

Drummond waited for the imaginary official's response, a trace of worry tightening his mouth — the exact amount of anxiety an innocent man would display in this situation, thought Charlie. Incredible. Although far from lucid, Drummond could assume cover with the virtuosity of a Royal Shakespeare player.

Drummond looked to Charlie, eyes full of uncertainty. "Any good?"

The door to the customs office groaned inward, followed by "You may come in now." The voice was an authoritarian tenor, the accent French with a hint of Creole.

Willing his knees to remain steady, Charlie rose and entered the customs office, which felt like a refrigerator, more a consequence of the room's diminutive size than the throaty air conditioner crammed in the window. Charlie found the cold bracing.

The space was dominated by a vast Louis XIV knockoff desk that had to be fourth-hand and not worth the cost of hauling off. On a side table sat a computer almost as old as the desk. Its display was dark. Save a dog-eared magazine, the desktop was empty. Behind the desk sat a dark-skinned, mustachioed man of about fifty, Maurice du Frongipanier, according to the placard. His wiry features were fixed in a content expression despite a stiff pea green uniform woven from a polyester fiber that resembled plastic.

"Bonsoir, monsieur," he said to Charlie with too broad a smile for someone stuck on the late shift. "Welcome to Martinique."

"Bonsoir." Charlie approached the desk.

The official gave him a quick once-over and slid open a drawer, fishing a passport stamper and ink pad from a sea of pornographic magazines — the reason perhaps that he was eager to get Charlie on his way.

The door groaned again as Drummond shuffled in.

The ink pad clattered to the floor. Du Frongipanier's eyes bulged as if he were seeing a ghost. "Marvin Lesser, you must be crazy coming here," he exclaimed.

Charlie felt as if he'd been pushed off a cliff.

Drummond's eyebrows bunched toward his nose, as if he were straining to fathom the official's words.

Not pretense, Charlie suspected. Trying to appear unruffled, he said to the customs man, "Begging your pardon, sir, this is my colleague —"

Turning to Charlie, du Frongipanier thrust an accusatory finger. "So Lesser has a new accomplice."

He lunged for the small metal box beside the telephone, smacking a red button atop it. The result was a hollow click, but surely, somewhere close by, an alarm was ringing.

With a new upsurge of dread, Charlie said, "Sir, this is some sort of mistake."

"Yes, yours."

The far door burst open, admitting a brown-skinned young man who wore an Airport Security uniform. Easily six-six, he had massive shoulders and tree trunks for legs. If that weren't enough, he brandished a black baton nearly as big as a baseball bat.

Exhibiting no intimidation, and perhaps unaware that intimidation was in order, Drummond set down his overnight bag and wandered over for a closer look at the baton. He chuckled. "That a Louisville Slugger?"

With a shrug, the security guard glanced down at the baton.

Drummond's right hand blurred into a karate slash, striking the underside of the man's jaw with so much force that his boots left the floor. He sank to the linoleum tiles and lay motionless.

To the customs official, who looked on in horror, Drummond said, "When he comes to, please pass along my apologies." Turning to Charlie, he added, "It was necessary, right?"

"I don't know." Charlie speculated that Marvin Lesser was Drummond. Or Drummond had been Marvin Lesser at some juncture. It was enough to process that du Frongipanier would almost certainly send them to prison now.

The customs official opened another drawer and jerked out a gun in a dusty leather holster. The revulsion twisting his face left little doubt about his intentions.

He needed to unsnap the holster in order to draw the gun. Trembling hands slowed him.

"Lights!" Charlie shouted, hoping his father had noticed the wall plate behind him and would understand.

Without glancing at the wall plate, Drummond reached behind his back and swatted the switch, plunging the room into what would have been complete blackness if not for the trickle of runway light through the air conditioner grate.

Hearing Drummond drop to the floor, Charlie did the same.

A gunshot thundered in the tiny chamber as a plume of flame revealed the customs official wielding a big revolver in two shaky hands.

The bullet bored through the wall to the left of where Drummond had been standing. Exterior light shone through the hole, illuminating a cloud of sawdust.

Du Frongipanier leaned forward, placing both elbows on the desk to brace the revolver, then aimed at Charlie. From less than ten feet away a miss seemed an impossibility.

With a heavy metallic clank, the thrown baton struck the barrel of the gun, evidently snaring the official's gun hand as well. He screamed in pain as the gun dropped from his grip and banged against the floor.

While Charlie looked on, incredulous, Drummond whisked him out the far door.

11

Charlie ran after Drummond across a broad expanse of crumbling tarmac, a patchwork of shadows and spill of runway and instrument lights. In contrast to the jumbo jets screaming overhead toward the main airport, the little executive airport was dark and still, so still that it seemed possible that the unconscious guard and the customs official were the only other people present.

"Who's Marvin Lesser?" Charlie asked.

"How should I know?" Drummond said defensively.

He was not *on,* yet his evasion software continued to fire: He distanced himself from the terminal, hugging the razor-wire fence separating the airport from the parking strip.

On his heels, Charlie made out an opening in the fence about a hundred feet ahead, near the charter company offices. Just then he heard a staticky version of du Frongipanier's shout, *"Ils visent le parking!"* The sound emanated from Drummond's suit pants.

Surprised, Drummond shot a hand into his pocket, withdrew a walkie-talkie, and eyed it oddly. Its provenance was less of a mystery to Charlie: Relieving an unconscious security guard of his communication device was probably second nature to the lifelong spy.

"They're headed for the parking lot," Drummond said.

"Who?" asked Charlie.

"Us." Drummond tapped the radio. He understood French — who knew?

"Well, good, we can get a car," Charlie said. "Right?" Even at his murkiest, Drummond could, in seconds, snap open the ignition barrel on the underside of a steering column, pluck the proper two from the tangle of wires, touch them together, and bring an engine roaring to life.

Drummond pressed the walkie-talkie to an ear and relayed, "They've sent men to lock the gate leading to the parking lot, and all of the exits from the airport."

Sirens erupted with the distinctive hee-haw of European emergency vehicles.

A pair of police cars were racing from the main terminal. Parked planes popped out of the darkness, alternately red and blue, reflecting the cars' light bars.

"It sort of begs mentioning that there are planes everywhere," Charlie shouted through the chaos. Last week Drummond had demonstrated that he could fly a helicopter. "Can you get a plane started?"

"Simple as flipping a toggle switch or two. But I'm not a licensed pilot."

"Whatever. I'll spring for the fine."

"I mean, I barely know how to fly planes like these."

"*Barely* sounds pretty good right now."

"I'm . . . I'm sorry, son . . ." As if to hide his shame, he looked away, fixing his gaze on the dark alley between two hangars.

Just as well, Charlie thought. Suffering a precipitous drop in lucidity, Drummond had crashed the helicopter last week.

Drummond perked up. "Now *that* is perfect!"

He pointed to a big vehicle parked in an alley. It looked part fire engine and part tugboat, or something a mad scientist might have created in an automotive junkyard. Its rectangular cargo hold flashed olive green in the bright light cast by a third police car rolling along the far side of the fence.

"Perfect for what?" Charlie asked. "Ramming the gate?"

"I think you'd need a tank to do that."

139

Drummond hurried toward the vehicle.

Charlie trailed him, thinking this was no kind of exit plan: If they managed to start the behemoth, the police cars would catch them in seconds.

Drummond darted to the front of the vehicle, which was shaped like a ship's prow. Bold metallic letters on the grille proclaimed AMPHIBUS. Charlie guessed it was used for rescues when planes landed in the water, short of the runway.

Drummond grasped the driver's door handle and tried to get into the cabin. The door didn't budge. Charlie added his weight to the footlong handle. The creak of the hinges was masked by the sirens, fortunately.

Drummond dove upward, landing prone on the driver's seat. He flipped onto his back, reached under the control panel, and went to work on the ignition barrel.

Usually he needed to find a way to pry loose the panel. With a nothing tap, this one clunked to the floor. A mass of wires spilled onto his face. Although they all appeared black in the dark alley, he somehow knew which two were the reds — or at least he appeared confident as he touched two ends together.

The engine hiccupped.

Then fell silent.

Maybe for the best, Charlie thought.

A patrol car crept even with the mouth of the alley.

Charlie resisted an impulse to dive out of sight. Even in the shadows, his sudden movement would have the effect of a signal flare on the policemen's peripheral vision. So too would the contour of a man pressed flat against the side of a vehicle, but the Amphibus had a wild outcropping of tires, life rafts, and rescue devices. Charlie blended in.

The patrol car continued past.

A moment later Drummond tried the wires again, this time pressing the accelerator with his palm. The engine coughed, six or seven bursts, the intervals between them decreasing in duration and culminating in one pleasing grumble.

Drummond scrambled to the passenger side of a front bench larger than most couches. Charlie jumped in, taking the wheel. Despite the obvious antiquity of the vehicle and the sour stench of old seawater, the cabin was in pristine condition. Evidently the Amphibus hadn't seen much action.

Perched at the edge of the bench, Charlie needed to stretch to keep hold of both the gear shift and the steering wheel. "So do you think we should try for a diversionary tactic? Or just gun it for the water — assuming this thing guns?"

Drummond made no reply.

Charlie looked over to find his father shaking his head as if to stave off sleep. Over the past week the experimental medication had slowed Drummond down in general, a function of the p25 protein booster's beta-blocker component, which brought his metabolism to a crawl. The brief flight from the customs official seemed to have drained him.

"Any thoughts, Dad?"

With a forearm that seemed to weigh a hundred pounds, Drummond pointed ahead.

Customs official Maurice du Frongipanier strode around the corner and into the alley, eyes blazing with fury, revolver locked on Charlie.

12

The customs man took a deep breath and squeezed the trigger.

Charlie imagined that he heard the click over the clamor of sirens. A white muzzle flash lit the alley and the report drowned out all other sounds.

Like Drummond, Charlie ducked, not just beneath the window line but to the nonskid metal floor, his instincts overriding his awareness that even the monster's metal plating offered little protection against a bullet traveling near the speed of sound.

The bullet drilled through the windshield, spider-webbing much of the surrounding glass and blasting shards against Charlie's hands, which he was using to shield his head. The round continued its course through the vinyl seat just above Drummond's head, disappearing through the door to the cargo hold.

With his raw left hand, Charlie punched

the clutch, meanwhile ramming the gearshift into first and pressing the accelerator, sending the Amphibus lurching forward. He pounded the horn.

The customs official jumped, sending his subsequent shot high. It struck one of the spotlights on the vehicle's roof. Orange fragments of glass bounced down Charlie's window.

Emboldened by the sight of the official scurrying out of the way, Charlie sat up so that he was even with the wheel and stomped on the accelerator. The Amphibus chugged to seven or eight kilometers per hour.

Drummond rose too, heavy-lidded and irritable, as if he'd been rudely awoken.

"You okay?" Charlie asked.

Drummond grumbled. "Why wouldn't I be?"

"No reason."

As the truck reached the end of the alley, something thudded against the passenger side of the cargo hold.

"I was afraid of that," Drummond said, eyeing his side mirror.

Checking the mirror, Charlie saw du Frongipanier improbably clinging to one of the flotation devices dangling from the Amphibus.

"Hang on," Charlie said. "Tight."

Drummond braced himself against the control panel. Charlie crushed the brake pedal. The tires shrieked to a halt while the chassis and Charlie's stomach hurtled onward.

The customs man ought to have been flung thirty feet ahead.

But he hung on and, what's more, managed to point his revolver at the passenger window and line up Drummond's head in his sights.

Charlie shifted back into gear, costing du Frongipanier his aim. Mashing the gas pedal, Charlie hoped to gain enough speed to shed the unwanted passenger.

Rapid acceleration was not one of the Amphibus's features.

Three successive rounds pounded through the wall behind Charlie and Drummond. The air filled with particles of seat-cushion foam. More shattered windshield fell inward, scraping Charlie's face and sticking in his wig. Rolling out of the alley, he saw no choice but to duck again and hope that no planes or fuel trucks were in his path.

Shielding his eyes from the continuing influx of glass, Drummond sat up and jerked one of the levers beneath the control panel. With a rush of air, a pontoon shot away from the Amphibus — a horrified du Frongipanier aboard.

The flotation device thumped against the tarmac then reversed course, the rope tethering it to the Amphibus snapping back to the vehicle. Despite repeated bumps and asphalt burns, the customs official not only hung on but also raised his revolver.

Another glaring muzzle flash and a bullet penetrated the steel door dividing the cab and the cargo hold, ricocheting around like a mad bee.

"Any chance there's another lever you can use?" Charlie asked.

Drummond brightened. "Yes, thank you! *That* is what I was trying to remember."

He leaned forward, jerking another handle.

A red life ring disengaged with a feeble click and floated backward, like a frisbee.

It clipped du Frongipanier in the shoulder with a disheartening *pfft.* But enough force still to knock him off the pontoon. He tumbled backward along the tarmac, his revolver bouncing along with him. Right into his hand. As he slid to a stop, he fired again.

The bullet sparked the tarmac well wide of Charlie's door. The Amphibus bounced, Charlie along with it, his head striking the roof liner. "What the hell?"

"Grass," Drummond said.

Now Charlie saw it. The Amphibus was crossing the strip of lawn that paralleled the runway. A moment later the heavy vehicle clomped onto the runway itself.

Charlie looked up, bracing for impact with a descending 747.

The sky was empty, but a trio of police cars was converging on the Amphibus.

Extraordinarily composed, or perhaps just drained of panic, Charlie focused on the Caribbean, outlined by the moonlight, a mile up the runway. He tried to turn the Amphibus, wrestling gravity for control of the wheel. The tires howled. Whines and groans suggested the vehicle was about to collapse into a mass of spent automotive parts. It careened toward the water with the exception of a cylindrical tank — *a fire extinguisher?* — which burst through the rear door and bounced down the runway, leaving a comet trail of sparks.

The first police car slalomed to avoid being struck, then accelerated, closing to within a city block of the Amphibus. The two other police cars fell behind the first, forming a triangular formation, suggesting to Charlie that they intended to "T-bone" the truck, or disable it by ramming its flanks.

Although the engine roared like a blast furnace, the Amphibus seemed to have maxed at seventy kilometers per hour.

The police cars closed to within striking range.

The water was half a mile ahead.

"Now would probably be a decent time to figure out how to turn this thing into a boat," Charlie said.

Drummond stared across the cabin as if Charlie were the one with lucidity issues. "Turn this into a boat?"

13

One of the police cars was now close enough that Charlie could make out the driver's mustache — the traditional Burt Reynolds model. He also saw the gun that the man's partner braced on the passenger side window. Getting closer. The options were to get rammed, get shot, both, or to stay the course to the Caribbean at the runway's end.

"Dad, this thing is an *Amphibus,*" he said. "If we can't make it live up to its name, when we reach the water" — seconds away — "we're literally sunk."

"Oh, that. We could always retract the wheels. The power train will shift from driving the wheels to driving the jet propulsion system."

Charlie exhaled. "You've been in one of these things before."

"I don't recall. On the other hand, once, back in the early seventies —"

"How do you retract the wheels?"

"Push this." Drummond pointed at a big button on the console. Pictured on the peeling decal directly above it were a tire and an arrow that curved upward.

The police car closest to Drummond slammed into his side of the Amphibus. Charlie felt the crunch of metal in his teeth. Impact with any more force would knock the ungainly vehicle onto its side.

His eyes went to the blur outside his window. The second police car was charging straight at his door. He clenched head to toe in anticipation of the blow.

The police car suddenly slowed, braking close enough that Charlie could read the lips of the man at the wheel: *Merde!*

The runway ended, and the Amphibus took off into the sky, or so it seemed.

An instant later, it belly flopped into the Caribbean. And began sinking. Seawater rose above the windows, darkening the inside of the cabin save for a few faint white circles on the instrument panel.

Charlie groped for the button that turned the thing into a boat, found it — he hoped — and hammered down.

The wheels ground inward, and the inboard engines roared to life, bringing the water around it to a boil.

The craft popped back to the surface.

And, incredibly enough, floated.

As far as Charlie could tell, just one problem remained: "How do we make it go?"

"Just keep doing that." Drummond indicated the accelerator, which Charlie still had pressed all the way to the floor.

Indeed the Amphibus continued to function, distancing them from the runway. But at a turtle's pace.

"You sure about the 'jet propulsion' part?" Charlie asked, watching the cops spring out of their cars, all with sidearms drawn except for the last man, who had a shotgun.

"An interesting piece of information is that it took ten million man hours to develop amphibious vehicle technology," Drummond said.

The shotgun roared and a round barreled into the cargo hold, creating a fist-sized hole in the wall behind them and boring into the dashboard. The radio spat out sparks.

More bullets rained against the vehicle, with such frequency that the dings and chimes formed one continuous peal. Too many bullets to count entered the cabin, kicking up a confetti of vinyl bits from the dashboard along with a geyser of sparks, and turning any remaining glass into gravel.

The air filled with a salty mist.

Crouched as far down as possible, Charlie kept his hands on the accelerator. He tried to steel himself by remembering that he and Drummond had escaped worse.

That reduced the odds of their succeeding again, come to think of it. Better not to think, he decided.

The Amphibus reached thirty kilometers per hour, according to the speedometer, slashing through the waves.

The hail of bullets dwindled to a sprinkle, then nothing. The ruckus of gunfire and sirens receded and was soon drowned out by the inboard engines' hums. Charlie felt safe enough to emulate Drummond and climb back onto the bench.

Through what remained of his window, he glanced aft at the policemen standing at the water's edge, their heads lowered.

"Now what?" Charlie asked.

Drummond didn't reply, fully attuned to the French chatter from the walkie-talkie pressed to his ear. After a moment, he said, "They're dispatching two Coast Guard cutters."

Charlie looked to shore. The airport now appeared the size of a dollhouse. Other than the engines, he heard only the patter of waves against the hull and a faint cry of a seabird. The moonlit seascape could have been used by the Martinique Travel Bureau.

"How about we get out and let this thing keep on chugging to sea, so that when the cops get to it, there's nobody aboard?" Charlie said. "We can use one of the life rafts to get back to the island." He thought back to what Bream had said: Anybody who wants to sneak onto Martinique can pull up in a million places by boat.

"They're also sending a helicopter." Drummond indicated the walkie-talkie.

"Super. With a searchlight?"

As he sometimes did, Drummond massaged his temples, as if trying to trip the button that activated his memory. "Sorry," he said in conclusion.

"Okay, how about a more basic survival question?" In this respect, Charlie thought, Drummond's tradecraft was practically ingrained. "If you were now, hypothetically, a fugitive, what would you do?"

"Swim to shore."

"But they'd still see you."

"Not if I swam underwater."

"It's got to be a couple of miles at least."

"Well, that would be my best course of action, if I were a fugitive."

The distant cry, which Charlie had thought of as a seabird's, grew louder, into a whine. He recognized it. Helicopter rotor.

He gripped his door handle. "Well, either way, we need to get out of here now."

"This way," Drummond said, unlatching the door to the cargo hold.

"What difference does it make?" Charlie asked.

Pushing open the door, Drummond pointed into the dark hold. The glow from the console outlined walls blooming with vests, masks, fins, and cylindrical tanks like the one that had flown out the rear door and onto the runway.

"I guess you've scuba dived off an amphibious rescue vehicle before too," said Charlie, who had never even snorkeled.

Drummond pulled on a wet suit. "Maybe so."

A minute later the whine of the rotor turned into a series of raucous thumps. The moonlight delineated the approaching helicopter from the night sky. Dressed like frogmen, Charlie and Drummond sat on the edge of the open cargo doorway.

"Some handicapper I am, thinking coming here would be simple," Charlie said, effectively to himself.

With a splash, Drummond fell backward into the sea.

Charlie followed suit, sinking into water that was warm and, better, ink black.

14

In a preposterously small rented Peugeot, Stanley and Hadley raced to Les Trois-Îlets, a seaside village off the coast where the Amphibus had just been found.

Undercover as the well-heeled Atchisons, they checked into the five-star Hôtel L'Impératrice, a remnant of the 1960s' embrace of garish opulence. The lobby was dominated by a lush rain forest replete with a three-story coral cliff enshrouded by luminescent mist, the result of a booming waterfall and as many filtered spotlights as a Broadway stage. At the frothy base of the fall was an emerald lagoon, populated by fish representing every shade of neon.

Stanley thought of the hotel as the perfect venue for the espionage fantasies of his youth, in which the Ritzes of the world constituted the everyday operational locale. In reality such accommodations had been far from the norm. Even in Paris, the job took him to the sorts of hotels that offered hourly rates. His agents weren't just people willing to sell out their own countrymen; they were willing to do it for a pittance. Not quite habitués of the posh spots.

With a Serge Gainsbourg melody in his head, he walked onto the bamboo terrace that extended from the open-air lobby and overlooked the purple-black Baie de Fort-de-France.

"Hoping to spot our rabbits swimming ashore?" asked Hadley, joining him at the rail.

The inability to do anything frustrated him. "At least we're close to the action in the event there is some."

She checked her BlackBerry. "The local officials have come to the conclusion that Drummond Clark is an international money launderer and arms dealer named Marvin Lesser. Old cover, mistaken identity, or whatever, it's working better as a pretext for a manhunt than anything we could have come up with."

"So what can we do now?" Anything seemed preferable to sitting idly.

Hadley hesitated, then asked, "How about we get a bite?"

"I guess we can keep an eye on the bay."

The hotel's outdoor restaurant, Les

Étoiles, was lit for the most part by candles and tiki torches, but also, as advertised, by the stars, beneath which the Baie de Fort-de-France was a mosaic, flickering from black to white. Along with a smattering of other late diners, Stanley and Hadley were serenaded by a calypso band in tuxedos the same turquoise as the pool. They both ate Colombo, Martinique's national dish, a coconut milk curry of fish, served with spicy fried plantains, at a price probably close to the per capita income. Stanley would have happily quit after the salad course. Primed for a hunt, his body wanted no part of food.

Hadley set her BlackBerry on the table. "You ready for the latest?"

"I can make the time." He ate a forkful of fish for appearance's sake.

"Our pilot friend went straight home to his apartment in Anse Mitan, about five miles from here. He microwaved a burrito for dinner, and had" — she glanced at the BlackBerry's display — "five *red stripes:* I'm going to have to check my codebook."

"You'll do better with this." Stanley tapped the leather-bound drinks menu propped between a candleholder and the pepper mill. "Red Stripe is a beer brewed in Jamaica. If our boy's had five, he's probably not plan-ning to drive. Under any other circumstances, I'd say: 'I hope not.' "

"Currently he's surfing the Web. No calls, no new e-mails, two text messages, one sent to a local woman asking her if she'd be at Le Squash for happy hour tomorrow, one from a Dutch woman who tends bar at a nightclub in Fort-de-France inquiring about his plans later tonight."

"She looking to book a 'flight' with him?"

"It would seem so. He didn't reply."

"Maybe he's waiting to hear from two men."

With a groan, Hadley kicked Stanley's shin, as she would have if she knew him well. "Those men would know that contacting him by telephone or text would effectively be contacting us."

"Unless it's encrypted text."

"Good point." Hadley began typing a cable.

"How about this?" Stanley asked. "Do we know where on the Web he's surfing?"

"As a matter of fact, yes. EBay — auto parts."

"We're capturing it?"

"Are you in the market for auto parts too?" Hadley resumed eating.

"When I was in Algiers, an MI6 tech intercepted bad guys' messages embedded in online classified ads for used bathroom fixtures. They were using an encryption algorithm to mix the secret text into the pixels of the photos in a way that didn't distort the pictures."

She paused, fork midway to her mouth. *"Used bathroom fixtures?"*

"Would you ever look at classified ads for used bathroom fixtures, let alone buy a used bathroom fixture over the Internet?"

She smiled. He sat back and admired her. No acting required.

Throughout the rest of their meal, thoughts of covert operations receded.

15

The black water lightened to violet. Landfall. Charlie wasn't sure whether he was happier about that or the fact that he hadn't needed to use his speargun en route.

He and Drummond surfaced about fifty yards short of a secluded beach that shone silver in the moonlight. On the dark and densely wooded hills, thousands of lights glowed like embers. A gentle breeze whistled through palm fronds. Charlie thought of his surroundings in terms of obstacles to circumventing the local authorities — who were undoubtedly scouring the island — and getting to the Laundromat. Contacting Bream was out. The BirdBook had been left in the overnight bag last seen in the customs office. They had fled the airport with only what they had on them, wallets and the pill bottle Drummond always kept close at hand.

Charlie spat out his clammy mouthpiece.

"It's been over an hour since you hot-wired a vehicle. What do you say we find another one?"

Drummond held his mouthpiece close to his lips, as if ready to resubmerge. "Okay."

A hundred yards up the beach stood a mass of stacked wooden lounge chairs. "Looks like a hotel there," Charlie said. "What do you think?"

"It does."

"What do you think we should do? Head toward it? Or away?"

"I don't know."

"How about this? Say you were a fugitive looking to shed your scuba gear and steal a car in order to get to a Laundromat in Fort-de-France. Would you be wary of a big hotel, where the security might be watching out for us, or would you be psyched about a crowded place where there are probably a lot of other people with our skin color, many of them on their fourth or fifth umbrella drink by now?"

"Ah. In that case, the relative ease of obtaining clothing and a vehicle would outweigh the cons, which would largely consist of a faxed alert that the graveyard-shift guards and receptionists may not even have seen."

Unbelievable, Charlie thought.

They swam closer to the beach, then walked along the sandy sea bottom in their flippers. Gas-fed torches showed the way to landscaped gardens fronting a large resort hotel. As they drew closer still, the dark forms of guests came into view.

Drummond slowed a few yards from shore, body low in the surf, apparently casing the surroundings. When no one was in sight, he ambled onto the beach, his flippers and speargun bunched under one arm.

Charlie followed. The sand ended at a wall of bamboo stalks twenty to thirty feet high, red at their bases before morphing into a brilliant green. Drummond deposited all of his gear but his wet suit into their midst. Which made sense to Charlie. The lightweight neoprene suits had short sleeves and pant legs, not entirely out of place on guests strolling along the beach.

Without the wigs they'd worn at the airport, they looked less like the two men sought by local authorities. On the other hand, they looked more like the two men sought by the rest of the world's authorities. But Drummond's intuition seemed to be firing. So Charlie didn't hesitate to replicate his father's every move while trailing him up the beach and toward the hotel.

They crossed paths with a handsome

middle-aged couple, apparently walking off dinner, arm in arm, their wedding rings and her diamond aglow. Flush from a bottle of wine or just the warm air, they both smiled, the wife offering a warm "Good evening." Awaiting a reaction to the dripping scuba suits, Charlie could only muster a nod in greeting, but Drummond said, "How're you doing?" as if he hadn't a care in the world.

The man and woman appeared to care just as little, intoxicated with each other. As they passed, a wave sizzled up the sand, lapping their shins. "God, why didn't we change into our swimsuits?" she said. "I'm dying for a dip."

Charlie spotted a bamboo hut fifty yards ahead, between the beach and the hotel's swimming pool. Nailed to the hut's grass roof, at a slant, was a sign that read SANDY'S, hand-painted, intentionally slapdash. Probably a shop that sold suntan oils and lotions at three times the price guests would pay in town. Pointing it out to Drummond, Charlie said, "That place ought to have shirts and stuff."

"It's closed," Drummond said.

"I know, but I was thinking that someone who can hot-wire an amphibious vehicle might be able to open a hut."

The hut proved to be nearly as secure as a

vault, an industrial version of the prefabricated metal storage sheds sold at home improvement stores — the bamboo façade was hot-glued to the exterior walls, synthetic grass was stapled to the roof. Its door and window were fastened by combination locks.

"An interesting piece of information about combination locks is that many have small keyholes on the back," Drummond said.

Charlie eagerly flipped the lock over and spotted a tiny round keyhole in the upper right corner. "Excellent piece, Dad!"

"Did you know that many people use the same combination lock for years without ever noticing the keyhole, until a thief defeats it."

"How does the thief defeat it?"

Drummond gazed down the beach, as if regarding a beautiful painting. "How would I know?"

"Say you were a onetime CIA operations officer, who took a five-day course in lock-picking when you were at the Farm . . ."

16

The shock of actually finding the Clarks might have bowled Stanley over if Hadley hadn't seized his hand and steered him behind a grassy rise in the sand, out of the fugitives' sight.

"Good choice of hotel," he said under his breath.

"Next time we decide to take a 'romantic stroll along the beach,' remind me to request permission to bring a sidearm."

Stanley had an AK-47 and three handguns in his apartment in Paris, but rarely took them to work, although, like now, they often would have come in handy. As opposed to FBI agents, CIA officers didn't carry firearms — the bureaucrats usually withheld permission for fear of their operatives being exposed as CIA officers and of the resulting flaps.

Antibureaucratic vitriol sharpened Stanley's senses. He regarded the stretch of beach where the Clarks had disappeared. "We ought to go after them."

Hadley opened her purse and drew out her BlackBerry. "And take them ourselves, with no weapons?"

"Just tail them. In a minute or two, they'll have a whole new wardrobe from that beach supply shack or the shops in the lobby. Another ninety seconds and they'll have helped themselves to a car in the guest parking lot that no one will realize is gone until morning at the soonest. By the time our backup mobilizes, the rabbits will have blended into the half a million people on this four-hundred-square-mile jungle."

"They'll know we're tailing them, though."

"I can live with that. If we can stall them for as little as two minutes, we'll have half a dozen police cars and a helicopter in play."

By way of agreement, she started back to the hotel, scrolling down her phone menu. "I'll call the dry cleaners." She meant their backup unit.

Stanley looked past her, toward an odd rustling in the bamboo.

Drummond and Charlie emerged from the stalks just a few feet away, crisp new Hôtel L'Impératrice T-shirts over their wet suits. They brandished pistols of sorts with four-foot barrels and spearheads protruding from the muzzles.

Stanley was hit with a one-two punch of surprise, then fury. Why hadn't he heeded his instincts and rushed the criminals the first moment he saw them?

"Fort-de-France Dry Cleaning," came the Yankee-accented voice of the backup unit's chief over the BlackBerry.

Holding a finger to his lips, Charlie held forth a thick sheet of hotel stationery. With the point of his speargun, Drummond directed Stanley and Hadley to the big block letters on the stationery, although Charlie's intent had been obvious.

By the light of Hadley's BlackBerry, Stanley read:

FOLLOW THESE INSTRUCTIONS IMMEDIATELY OR WE WILL SHOOT YOU:

1. RAISE YOUR HANDS.
2. ONE OF YOU, SAY, ENTHUSI-
   ASTICALLY: "LET'S GO FOR A
   DIP ANYWAY!"
3. SAY NOTHING ELSE.

Raising his hands, Stanley glanced at Hadley in hope that she had a better plan. Her hands were already in the air, and though the night made it hard to tell, she was pale.

"Let's go for a dip anyway," she said with enthusiasm so convincing that Stanley wondered if she weren't in fact happy to enter the water.

As Drummond frisked him, Stanley waited for an opportunity to launch a knee into the old spy's groin. The spear pressed into his own inner thigh made him think better of it.

Drummond snatched away Stanley's phone and flung it into the sea. The satellite device splashed down and sank, followed by Hadley's.

Now that they were at liberty to speak, Charlie looked to Drummond, who just shrugged.

"It's okay, I got this," Charlie told him, before turning to Hadley. "Ma'am, gently toss your purse onto the sand in front of you."

Trembling — or probably pretending to be trembling — Hadley needed both hands to do it.

Charlie scooped up the bag and sifted through its contents. "I hope it won't inconvenience you too much, but I'm going to keep all of this stuff. After seeing your fellow civil servant Nick Fielding shoot Burt Hattemer with a keyless remote from a Lincoln Town Car, I'm not taking any chances with lipsticks and eyeliners."

According to a brief Stanley had read, the national security adviser was killed with a single .22 caliber round. Although Stanley had never seen such a device, a keyless remote could be rigged to fire a bullet; the museum at headquarters had an entire exhibit of pens, lighters, and even a roll of Tums that fired small-caliber bullets, most of the weapons dating from World War II. However, since forensics had conclusively determined that Drummond Clark had fired the .22 caliber bullet that killed Hattemer, either Charlie hadn't seen the shooting or he was simply a good liar, in which case he'd likely inherited the trait. Back in the day, another CIA brief had noted, Drummond Clark could have convinced a polygraph that it was a toaster.

Hadley's chattering teeth seized their attention.

Stanley gleaned her intent. "It's going to be okay, sweetie," he said, adding a tremor to his own voice.

Charlie tightened his grip on his speargun. "Please cut the act. You're way too teenagers-on-a-date for a married couple your age."

Ironically, the affection was authentic,

Stanley thought. At least on his part.

"I wouldn't have given you a second thought," Charlie added, "but while we were trying to get into the supply shack, my father kept looking back down the beach. You weren't there. And you weren't in the water. Which meant you'd ducked behind this grassy rise just after we passed you. Now why would you do that?"

Hadley blushed. "My husband was a bit frisky, that's all."

Charlie shook his head. "By your stage of the game, everyone knows it's just not worth getting sand in those parts. Also you were calling the dry cleaners . . . Come on!"

Continuing to play dumb was futile, Stanley thought. Better to just stall. The backup unit commander probably had people on the way.

"All right, Charlie, you've made us, except we're on the same team as you." Stanley turned to Drummond, who peered back as if through a thick fog.

"In that case," Charlie said, "before more of our 'teammates' show up, you two need to turn and head to the hut, holding hands, like you were before. And if you try anything, you will get speargunned in the leg — wait, I should qualify that: We'll *try* for the leg. My dad could probably split a jelly

171

bean from fifty yards away. But I've never shot one of these things before, so I can't make any promises."

Stanley turned toward the hut and took Hadley's hand, which was cold and clammy. Not part of the act, unfortunately.

17

A few minutes later the couple sat on the hut's linoleum floor, Charlie aiming his speargun at them while Drummond bound their wrists and ankles with kite string.

They looked like Superman and Lois Lane fifteen years after their first meeting, Charlie thought, out on a date night now while their kids were home with a sitter. According to their driver's licenses, their names were Colin and Eleanor Atchison. Odds were high that their real names were something else. And it was even money that they were now plotting to turn the tables.

For fear of drawing the attention of hotel security staff, Charlie kept the lights in the hut off. Drummond worked by the pink beam of a children's flashlight, a miniature of Mount Pelée — squeezing the green mountain activated a tiny bulb within the red peak, theoretically simulating a volcanic eruption. His technique was to thoroughly tie captives' legs together at the ankles, knees, and thighs, then practically mummify them from the waist up. Although the process was complex, Charlie had previously seen him execute it with the same dexterity that party magicians display when turning balloons into dachshunds. But now, lids heavy, head lolling, Drummond faltered.

The conditions weren't helping. With the doors and windows shut, a small grate provided the only ventilation in the hut, which was stifling and thick with the scent of suntan lotion to begin with. Perspiration streamed down Charlie's face, soaking his shirt. Like being slow-cooked in coconut oil, he thought.

The woman broke the heavy silence. "So . . . have you been in Europe?"

"I don't believe so," Drummond said before pausing to reconsider.

"Didn't you just fly in from there?"

Almost certainly, Charlie thought, the spooks had gotten hold of Bream's flight plan listing Warsaw as his point of origin, a ruse capitalizing on Poland's lax documentation requirements. A minimal amount of detective work on their part and Gstaad would be blown.

Unwilling to assist them, Charlie looked

away, which, he realized, probably served as an admission — in his experience, people like these two were human lie detectors.

"Please try to understand that we're on your side," the man said.

"Interesting," said Drummond, as he often did to avoid creating an awkward gap in conversation. He fastened the knot behind the man's neck and moved on to the woman.

"We can help you," she said.

Charlie considered that the sole aim of their conversation was diversion.

The man craned his neck to look Charlie in the eye. "We all want resolution to your case, right?"

There was a certain affability etched across his broad face, and his eyes were full of a forthrightness that didn't seem like artifice. Langley must have invented a new sort of contact lens, Charlie thought. But on the off-chance this really was one of the good guys, he said, "The problem is that your company's idea of resolution is diametrically opposed to ours."

"I'm not so sure. What's yours?"

"Life, liberty, pursuit of happiness, stuff like that."

"Those perks come with responsibilities," the man said. "In your case, answering to charges of a capital crime."

Charlie sighed. "Have you asked yourself why you don't have spears running through you already? The only times we've ever hurt anyone have been in self-defense."

"What about Hattemer?"

"I'm sure the Cavalry did a great job of littering the scene with our fingerprints and nose hairs and whatever, but anybody who thinks the Cavalry are good guys has to have been drugged by them."

The man shrugged. "What motive would they have had to kill Hattemer?"

"Not *Burt* Hattemer?" Drummond said.

Drummond had fled the scene of the killing just two weeks ago, yet his friend's murder seemed to be news to him.

"We'll talk about it later," Charlie said. They could ill afford the distraction now. He turned to the man. "Their motive was to keep him quiet."

"Interesting," the man said, with a bit too much enthusiasm.

"We'd better gag them now," Charlie said to Drummond.

"Check." Drummond pressed a rolled-up T-shirt over the man's mouth, stretched it around his ears, and knotted it behind his head. If Hattemer's murder remained on Drummond's mind, he gave no sign of it.

"I wish you could trust us," the woman said.

"Same," said Charlie.

She smiled. "In the interim, my only request is that you don't leave my arms so high behind my back. One of my fellow officers in Farafra developed blood clots in both shoulders after just one hour with his arms tied behind a tree."

Grunting acquiescence, Drummond loosened the kite string, allowing her wrists to fall even with her waist.

Charlie thought of Farafra, or at least the silver screen version, with its centuries-old sandstone spires and backdrop of date palms on sparkling Egyptian sands. What he wouldn't give to go there someday with Alice. As much as any city on earth, Farafra conjured romance and adventure and . . .

It was an extraneous detail.

"Dad!" he screamed.

Drummond looked up from refastening the woman's ankles in time to dodge the glistening barb she swung like a dagger.

Charlie didn't dare fire the speargun for fear of spearing his father. Instead he flung a family-sized bottle of sunscreen, striking her in the jaw. The container bounced harmlessly to the floor, but the diversion allowed Drummond to swat the weapon away

177

from her.

It landed in a tall wicker basket full of flip-flops. Retrieving it, Charlie nearly sliced his fingertips on the razor-sharp edge of what had passed for the woman's engagement ring. Pressure on the spring-loaded diamond must have caused the metal band to uncoil into a blade. She had probably cut through the twine around her wrists a while ago, then waited for the opportunity to strike.

As Drummond refastened her wrists and gagged her, Charlie heard footsteps outside. Kneeling, he peered out the ventilation grate to see two young men, but only from the neck down. He didn't recognize the bodies, but there was no mistaking the muscular, boxy builds — ex-military contract agents were the darlings of black ops personnel directors. Both men wore polo shirts, crisp Bermuda shorts, and, probably in a nod to pragmatism over tourist cover, cross trainers rather than sandals. They strode purposefully toward the beach. In a moment, even if they found nothing suspicious, they would rush back to the lobby and lock down the resort.

"The fun never stops," Charlie said to no one in particular.

"Finished," Drummond said, looking up from a pile of spent kite string spools.

"Good. Unless there's anything in here that they can use to draw attention to themselves or to escape — flashlight circuitry that could turn a tube of aloe vera into high explosive, anything like that?"

Drummond shrugged.

"What if you were them?" Charlie waved at their captives.

"I'd try to get my hands on *that*."

Charlie followed Drummond's eyes to the telephone by the register. Seeing no need to chance it, Charlie rendered the phone inoperable by slicing the outside wire with the woman's ring. At the same time, he thought of a way to stymie the two searchers. Unfortunately, his plan required using a phone.

18

During the crash course in espionage that had been his past two weeks, Charlie had learned that intelligence agencies of the United States and her allies maintained house-sized computers that continuously intercepted and analyzed billions of phone calls, e-mails, and text messages. In one instance, a captured conversation between two terrorists over a pair of children's walkie-talkies enabled the Mossad to corral a major weapons shipment from Cyprus.

Even on the hotel's intercom, Charlie's intended lifeline, his voiceprint would raise the digital equivalent of a red flag, simultaneously spitting his whereabouts — to within a five-foot radius — to those agencies seeking him. Paramilitary assault teams would storm Hôtel L'Impératrice in a matter of minutes.

If things went according to plan, however, in a matter of minutes Charlie and Drummond would already be driving away from the hotel. But first Charlie needed to get to an intercom. Followed by Drummond, he slipped through the bushes behind the re-locked beach supply hut. He stopped short of the paved pool deck, within reach of a fiberglass coconut mounted on a pole resembling a palm tree. Inside the coconut was a house phone.

Reaching for the handset, he glimpsed the two young men in polo shirts and Bermuda shorts, no more than thirty yards away, prowling the beach like bloodhounds. He froze. And immediately regretted it — he knew his pursuers were trained to detect unnatural motions on their peripheries. In contrast, Drummond hid behind a thick tree, never breaking stride.

Neither young man appeared to notice.

Charlie couldn't reach far enough into the fiberglass coconut to grasp the handset without exposing his position.

As he waited for the men to continue down the beach, a cool gust off the bay made the tree limbs and bushes sway noisily. A variation on opportunity knocking, he thought. He reached slowly until his fingertips knocked the handset from its cradle and into his other hand.

The men on the beach didn't turn to look.

Charlie extended the handset back toward the coconut until the rounded earpiece pressed the CONCIERGE button on the telephone's keypad. As the line rang, Charlie took the handset and withdrew, in synch with a windblown palm frond, into the shadows between the bushes and the shack.

"Concierge," came a chipper male voice.

"Hi, this is Mr. Glargin," Charlie whispered. "We're staying here at L'Impératrice and, well, my young daughters and I were just walking on the beach where I'm afraid we saw two young men engaged in — I don't really know how to put it — lewd behavior."

Within seconds, hotel security guards appeared from the main lodge and discreetly headed down to the beach. Much as Charlie would have enjoyed staying to hear the contract agents' protests, he knew that each second could make the difference between escaping or not.

19

The N5 to Fort-de-France wasn't the crudely paved, single-lane road alongside sugarcane fields that Charlie expected, but a sleek and ultramodern highway with elevated ramps that wound around, across, and, occasionally, directly through mountainsides. Fortunately, Drummond had relieved the CIA man of his car keys while tying him up, because Charlie found driving the Peugeot challenge enough, particularly keeping up with the local traffic, blazing vehicles whose proportions, unlike the Peugeot's, were suited to the snaking curves and narrow passageways between rock walls. To allow past a flaming orange Micra — an amalgam of a go-kart and a flying saucer — he swerved right, nearly shearing off Drummond's door against a cliff that doubled as a retaining wall.

Finding Fort-de-France was also a problem. Although the highway wrapped around the western border of Fort-de-France, because of the dark night, the blinding LED billboards, and the giant outcroppings of rock that blocked the view, the precise location of the city wasn't clear. Not until signs began popping up indicating that Charlie had already driven past it.

"Do you have any idea where we're going?" he asked Drummond.

No response.

Drummond was balled up in the cramped front footwell, his usual countersurveillance position. Somehow he'd managed to fall asleep.

Probably a good idea, Charlie thought. Although there was no correlation between rest and episodes of lucidity, rest generally sharpened Drummond's faculties.

Anyway, how hard could it be to find a large city?

Hoping to make his way to the opposite side of the N5 and head back toward Fort-de-France, Charlie shot onto what had to be an exit ramp. It spiraled into the empty parking lot of a dark six-story supermarket. He navigated a dozen rows of parking meters before reaching a ramp he felt sure would bring him back onto the opposite side of the highway. It dead-ended inexplicably behind an unlit warehouse.

A few moments later, after he had back-tracked and found the right way onto the N5, a gap in the retaining wall finally yielded a view of a tight grid of well-lit, three- and four-story Belle Époque buildings. It was so stunning, Charlie nearly missed the exit.

Descending the ramp, he spotted a road sign for Pointe Simon, the area to which Drummond had instructed him to go when they were still in Switzerland. During a series of left turns to check for surveillance, Charlie noted the street signs mounted on the walls of corner buildings. Dark blue plaques with white letters, exactly as in Paris. The streets themselves were packed with bustling boutiques, cafés, and bars. He cracked a window. The balmy air, wonderfully redolent of fresh pineapple, resonated with French banter and jazz.

More wonderful, no one was following them. At least not by car.

At rue Joseph Compère, the supposed location of the Laundromat, the city grew darker and quieter, the chic boutiques yielding to simple fish stores and produce markets with hand-painted signs. The urban thrum dwindled to a lone sax playing the blues, with traffic declining to one or two cars per block. Pedestrians included a handful of adventurous tourists and, mostly, locals returning home.

The odd television screen shimmered through lace curtains as well as holes in regular curtains. The dwellings themselves, almost all three-story apartment buildings, were either old and dilapidated or new constructions done on the cheap, with views not of the sparkling Baie des Flamands, a block away, but of a four-story, graffiti-covered municipal parking garage. In short, they were apartments where residents would depend on a self-serve Laundromat. The closest thing to a Laundromat Charlie saw, however, was a hairdresser.

He reached down and nudged his father awake. "Sorry, I need you to take a look."

Drummond tried to shake away his sleepiness.

"Does this look familiar?" Charlie asked.

Drummond rose the fraction of an inch necessary to peer out his window. He smiled, as if in reminiscence.

"Familiar?" Charlie asked, meaning the question to be rhetorical.

"No. Should it be?"

"If for no other reason than we flew four thousand miles to go to a Laundromat here."

"What Laundromat?"

"That's a good question."

"Thank you."

"How about this, Dad? What if you were, say, a CIA operations officer working under nonofficial cover and you had a fake ten-kiloton atomic demolition munition concealed within a washing machine and you needed to hide it in an urban residential area. Where would you put it?"

"Plain sight." Drummond's mouth tightened, as if he were annoyed that Charlie would ask such a stupid question.

"Like where?"

"Is that why you were asking about a Laundromat?"

"Right."

"For an operation of that magnitude, I might buy an existing Laundromat to use as a front, or open my own."

"Where, ideally, would you locate it?"

"Easy. A place with access for a delivery truck."

"Close to a parking garage?"

"Exactly."

Charlie sped to the end of the one-way street, turned left on Boulevard Alfassa, took another left onto rue François Arago, then doubled back to the top of rue Joseph Compère, bringing the car to a stop at the municipal garage he'd noticed earlier.

Still no Laundromats in sight. Just a quartet of three-story apartment buildings painted in repeating pastel squares and adorned with enough architectural flourishes to prevent the residents from realizing that they lived in concrete boxes. The buildings were new, evidenced by the freshness of the paint and the clean stretch of cement fronting them — without any of the stains or ruts on the sidewalks that were everywhere else on rue Joseph Compère.

Charlie indicated the apartments with a sweeping gesture. "How much do you want to bet that the Laundromat used to be there?"

Drummond reacted as if he'd just swallowed vinegar.

Charlie spun in his seat. "What's wrong?"

"Always with the betting," Drummond grumbled, taking Charlie back to the years when the two of them still got together on major holidays, always at restaurants where they could eat in less than an hour, ideally with televised bowl games to minimize the time Drummond lectured on squandering one's life on the horses.

A truck shaped like a baby's shoe — and not much larger — whizzed past, snapping Charlie back to rue Joseph Compère.

"Well, you'll be happy to know that I now

wish I'd become an engineer at the Skunk Works," he told Drummond. "If only because I'd be in Palmdale, California, instead of on this wild Laundromat chase, unsure if I'm going to live through the night."

Drummond regarded him as if through a fog.

The bluesy saxophone drifting down the block offered a fitting sound track. The music emanated from a slender two-story hole-in-the-wall. Hand-painted on one of the smoky windows, in a feathery silver cursive, was "Chez Odelette."

The hair rose on the back of Charlie's neck. "Your cutout, wasn't she named Odelette?"

"Nice girl," Drummond said.

20

Charlie drove the Peugeot into the parking garage, where the vehicle was less likely to be spotted than at the curb outside Chez Odelette's. He found a space hidden from the street by a delivery van. Keeping himself and Drummond from detection posed a greater challenge.

"We need to blend in with the other tourists around here," Charlie said, slipping on the fake-tortoiseshell reading glasses he'd taken from the counter at Sandy's beach supply shack.

Eyeing Charlie's image in the rearview mirror, Drummond said, "Since when do you wear glasses?"

"Since they make me look less like the guy on the wanted posters."

Drummond nodded. "Interesting."

Charlie had learned almost all he knew about impromptu disguise from Drummond. Foremost among the old man's dictates was that bulky clothing veiled stature. Second was that individuals attempting to avoid notice should wear different styles and colors than when they were last seen. Accordingly, from his new Sandy's tote bag, Charlie drew two cotton polo shirts, two baggy floral-print board shorts, two pairs of rubber flip-flops, and two baseball caps.

Hats draped faces in shadows and compressed hair, altering the shape of the head, but Drummond avoided them as a rule because they aroused surveillants' suspicions. In the Caribbean, however, young men wore baseball caps as often as not, and Charlie believed that the old man could pass for a young man. Drummond was in better shape than most men half his age, present company included. Charlie hoped the two of them would appear to the occupants of a passing patrol car as just another couple of young guys in a neighborhood catering to that demographic, as opposed to the young guy/senior citizen duo for whom the authorities had their eyes peeled.

Wandering from the parking lot onto the sidewalk, Drummond indeed appeared much younger. His slight hunch vanished, his shoulders squared, and his chest appeared to inflate. His stride went from sluggish to a strut.

Finding himself standing and marveling, Charlie had to jog to catch up.

Chez Odelette's front windows afforded a view of the saxophonist, a spindly native with a white beard. He stood on a pillbox platform, spotlit in a sultry blue whose wash illuminated the face of the bartender, a brown-skinned woman of about thirty with attractive, strong features.

"Is that her?" Charlie asked.

"Who?" said Drummond.

"Odelette."

"How would I know?"

Jesus, Charlie thought. "She's the only person working there, other than the sax player."

"Probably it's her."

"That's what I was thinking. What do you say we go find out?"

Hearing no reply from Drummond, Charlie turned to him. Drummond was no longer beside him. Or anywhere in sight.

How the — ?

A pair of big brown hands fastened around Charlie's collar and yanked him backward into a pitch-black alley.

21

The alley wasn't much wider than Charlie.
Halfway down it, the unseen man propelling him whistled like a parakeet. As if in
response, hinges groaned and a diagonal
shaft of white light illuminated the crumbling bricks. It came from the bottom of a
flight of stairs, where a doorway led to the
basement of an automotive shop.

The man prodded Charlie down the stairway with such strength that resisting was
pointless, at best.

A woman inside whispered: "You can
come in."

As if Charlie had a choice.

He was practically carried into a hot and
stagnant basement that smelled of motor
oil. The dim light from a pair of sputtering
fluorescent tubes revealed a grimy cinder
block room full of salvaged parts — shock
absorbers, belts, hoses, steering wheels,
hubcaps, entire bumpers — either in the

cityscape of piles or jammed into the floor-to-ceiling rusty shelves lining the walls. In a minimal clearing at the room's center, Drummond sat slumped in a wooden office chair. He nodded hello to Charlie, exhibiting no awareness that anything out of the ordinary had transpired. Across a small desk from him sat the pretty bartender. She stared at Charlie with steely hazel eyes.

"You're Ramirez, yes?" she asked him.

At check-in to a motel on the New Jersey Turnpike while on the run a couple of weeks ago, he had given the name Ramirez. Seeking to keep a lid on the story that the Clarks were in Martinique, the CIA might have fed that name to the local authorities.

"McDonough, actually." He had a passport, driver's license, and a walletful of other cards to back him up. "Brad McDonough."

The woman waved at Drummond. "That's what he said." She spoke with a blend of Parisian French, strong Creole patois, and an even stronger skepticism.

The muscular handler dropped Charlie onto the chair beside Drummond, then returned to the door, blocking the only escape route. Not that Charlie would think of escaping now that he'd gotten a glimpse of the brute, particularly after he drew a

black revolver from his ankle holster. A water pistol would have been no less redundant, thought Charlie.

The woman tilted her head at Drummond. "He told me his name is Larsen."

Charlie shrugged. "John Larsen, that's right."

The man at the door said, "If you *mecs* wanna play games, my sister may as well go and claim the ten-thousand-euros reward the cops are offering now."

"We've known Monsieur Clark since we were kids," she told Charlie.

At *Clark* Charlie froze, then struggled not to show it. He eyed Drummond, who raised his shoulders slightly.

The woman groaned in indignation. "Monsieur Clark, you can't really expect us to believe that you don't remember us."

Drummond swiveled in his chair, plucking a steering wheel from the nearest mound of auto parts as if fascinated by it. "An interesting piece of information is that most American car horns beep in the key of F," he said.

The bartender turned to her brother. "Ernet, you keep an eye on them, I'll go upstairs and call Officer DuFour." She placed her palms on the tabletop, preparing to rise.

"Wait, Odelette, please," Charlie begged.

"You think I'm Odelette?"

Charlie again looked to Drummond, who was now fiddling with a fan belt. Again he shrugged.

"I'm now going to guess you're not Odelette," Charlie told the woman.

"I'm Mathilde. Odelette was our mother."

Out of the corner of his eye, Charlie noticed the pistol pivot his way.

"*Maman* died in October," said the man, biting back emotion.

Charlie said, "I'm sorry." For their suffering and, at the moment, his own.

The woman spun toward Drummond. "*Maman* revered you, Monsieur Clark. I don't know what you're trying to pull here —"

"He has Alzheimer's," Charlie said.

"Yes, I'd heard that," said Drummond.

Mathilde's eyes narrowed with skepticism. "A man so young, comparably. That's difficult to believe." She looked to Ernet, who nodded in strong agreement.

Charlie wanted to ask him where he'd studied neurology.

"Alzheimer's at his age is rare," Charlie said. "And it's tough to prove without an autopsy. It's no wonder those old Mafia guys keep using the Alzheimer's defense in court."

"What we need you to prove to us is that these charges are false." Mathilde snapped open a Martinique Police flyer with photographs of Charlie and Drummond, followed by details of the transgressions for which they were wanted. Stabbing a finger at the picture labeled MARVIN LESSER, she said to Charlie, "You prove that our old friend Monsieur Drummond Clark is not this thief, and that the club we named as a tribute to our mother wasn't paid for with blood money."

"Let me ask you something first?" Charlie said. "He paid for the club?"

"Yes, after the Laundromat was closed."

"So there actually was a Laundromat?"

"Our mother worked there for twenty-seven years," Mathilde said. "Monsieur F knocked it down and put in tenements."

Charlie saw a shining ray of hope. *"Monsieur F?"*

"Fielding. Cheap *salopard* didn't give *Maman* a centime in severance."

"Shame what happened to him," Ernet said, not meaning it.

"By any chance, do you know what happened to the old washers and dryers that were in the Laundromat's storeroom?" Charlie asked.

Mathilde rolled her eyes. "Yet another

example of Fielding's cheapness: a man who spends three million dollars for a swimming pool at his home but does he spring for a new washing machine for his pool house? Hell no. Comes here himself and hauls a dusty old Perriman off to his island."

Mindful of the pistol pointed at him, Charlie fought the impulse to pump a fist.

"I am left to ask God, 'What is it with all these thieves?' " Mathilde said. "First our father, then our uncle, and then Monsieur F. Now the club has to pay so much for 'protection' that Ernet's forced to take off the semester from college." She gazed at Drummond, who hastily set aside a shiny, curved chrome band, apparently the trim that ran along the front edge of a car's hood. "After Monsieur Fielding let *Maman* go like that, you were extremely kind, helping her start the new business. But if it is true, if you are just another thief, we want nothing from you."

"Except the reward," Ernet said.

Mathilde pushed her chair away from the dcsk, apparently preparing to leave.

"I can explain," Charlie said. "Or try to."

Mathilde remained in her seat, eyes fastened on him.

With a tilt of his head at Drummond, Charlie said to Mathilde and Ernet. "Believe it or not, he's a spy."

Mathilde smiled without mirth. "Not."

"Jésus Christ." Ernet sighed. To Mathilde, he added, *"On appelle la police?"*

She nodded.

"I wish we could show you a CIA badge, or had some way we could demonstrate it," Charlie said. "Actually, here's one thing: He speaks French."

"That's news?" Mathilde said. "Perriman would never send the island a salesman who couldn't speak French. Monsieur Clark and my mother never spoke English — she couldn't."

Charlie tried, "He can hot-wire a car —"

Ernet spat. "So he's a car thief too?"

Mathilde looked down, her head seemingly weighted by dismay. "Embezzler and money launderer: These things I *might* believe our Monsieur Clark capable of. But Monsieur Clark, the doddering appliance salesman, a spy? I can't think of a less likely spy in the world."

As Charlie scrambled to find another way of convincing Mathilde, some sort of projectile buzzed past his head. He turned toward the door, where, with a clang, Ernet's pistol fell from his hand and clattered to the floor, along with a metal tailpipe extension. Ernet's eyes bulged with astonishment. Mathil-

199

de's too.

Drummond loaded another length of tailpipe — or makeshift arrow — onto the curved piece of chrome and rubber fan belt he'd fashioned into a bow.

"And you should see what he can do with an actual weapon," Charlie said.

22

"Hibbett can help," Ernet said after Charlie had filled in the remaining blanks.

Mathilde explained that Alston Hibbett III's trust fund enabled the young Californian to vacation permanently in the tropics and pursue his passion, tropical drinks. At some point every night, their cumulative effect sent him sliding off his accustomed bar stool at Chez Odelette. The utility room in back, with its battered couch, had become his second home. Most of the time, he didn't stir until Mathilde or Ernet unbolted the club's door the following afternoon.

Tonight, with the help of four shots of Jägermeister, on the house — Mathilde's idea — Hibbett plunged off his bar stool earlier than usual.

After laying him down on the couch, Ernet exited the utility room with the keys to Hibbett's lesser-used first home on Boulevard Alfassa, a few blocks away, where

Charlie and Drummond could stay the night.

Ernet also took Hibbett's distinctive green and gold Oakland A's cap, with which Charlie might pass in a blink for the similarly built Californian.

"It would also help if you stumble a lot," Ernet told Charlie.

Charlie staggered every now and then, as Drummond played Good Samaritan helping him home. They used Alice's technique of stair-stepping through the Pointe Simon grid. It turned the two-block walk into six blocks, but allowed Charlie to check the reflections in car and storefront windows to see if anyone was following.

Rounding the corner to Boulevard Alfassa, Charlie spotted Hibbett's building, an only-in-the-tropics Creamsicle orange, four stories trimmed in spearmint green and overlooking the Baie de Fort-de-France. Up and down the block, a light crowd bopped into and out of lively clubs. Across the street, a similar number meandered along the bayside promenade and ferry docks.

At Hibbett's well-lit entrance, Drummond stopped and gazed at the starlight at play on the wave tops. Eager to limit their exposure, Charlie hurriedly produced the keys and opened the door. "Come on, the view's even better from upstairs."

Drummond remained planted on the sidewalk, turning his focus to the sky.

Had he detected something? A surveillance drone? Charlie's stomach clenched. "What is it?"

"An interesting piece of information is that Mozart was just five years old when he wrote the music for 'Twinkle, Twinkle Little Star.' "

"Interesting really isn't the best term." With a tug at his elbow, Charlie led his father into a small foyer furnished with contemporary flair. Best of all, it was unpopulated. "I'm in 3-A, kind sir," he said with a Dean Martin slur, in case anyone was listening.

As they reached the stairs, the door to 1-C, a few feet to their left, swung inward. Out darted a heavily made up young blonde in a low-cut satin dress. Her cherry perfume devoured much of the oxygen in the lobby.

"Hey," she said, eyeing Charlie with recognition and, he hoped, mistaking him for Hibbett.

He grabbed onto Drummond as if to prop himself up, but really to hide his face. "Hey," he replied into Drummond's sleeve.

The blonde turned to say thank you to

the man in 1-C, but found herself facing a hastily shut door. The man, evidently her customer, seemed disinclined to encounter any of his fellow residents at this juncture. With a self-conscious air, the young woman fled the building.

Helping Charlie up the stairs, Drummond said, "That was lucky, wasn't it?"

"I guess," said Charlie, thinking of the old horseplayer expression: *Luck never gives; she only lends.*

Apartment 3A was a spacious loft with a collection of curvy Plexiglas furniture that, from the standpoint of functionality, might be more aptly considered art. Charlie imagined Hibbett buying the whole lot in an effort to win over a modern furniture store saleswoman.

The living room bolstered the theory. This room probably reflected the real Hibbett: just a single piece of furniture, a soft, black sofa made to look like a baseball mitt from Ty Cobb's day. It faced an enormous plasma television mounted on the wall. Littered on the hardwood floor were two laptop computers, three game systems, and too many game cartridges to count. And in the corner was an antique Coke bottle vending machine retrofitted to dispense cans of Red Bull.

"Think we're safe here?" Charlie asked Drummond.

Drummond sank into the baseball mitt. "From what?"

"The usual: getting killed. Or getting arrested, then getting killed."

Drummond luxuriated in the cool leather. "Why did we come here again?"

"We decided it would be too conspicuous to row out to Fielding's island in the middle of the night."

"Right, right." Drummond sat up with an air of determination. "So we can find the device."

"First we need a better way to get there than rowing."

"Well . . ." Drummond thought. The exertion seemed to have sapped him. His head fell back onto an Oakland Raiders throw pillow. His eyes burned with frustration. "I'm so sorry, Charles . . ."

"Did you remember to take your medicine?"

"Of course," Drummond said, indignant.

"That explains it."

Drummond was supposed to take a pill before bedtime, and he did so with the reliability of a Swiss train. Drowsiness invari-

205

ably followed.

Drummond yawned. "What was it you needed to know again?"

"How to get to Fielding's island."

"Oh, right. You know who might know?"

"No. Who?"

"Odelette's children."

"Mathilde and Ernet?"

"How many children does she have?"

"I don't know," Charlie said. Nor did his father, he realized, at least not now. "I figured it would be best not to tell them what we were up to."

"That sounds about right."

"So any idea how to get out there?"

"Where?"

"The island where Fielding lives. Or lived, I should say."

"Oh, right, right. I don't know." Drummond stretched out on the sofa.

Charlie rushed to capitalize on his father's last moments of consciousness. "What if some other organization figured out what Fielding was doing with washing machines, then tried to storm the island?"

"They'd be in trouble. Police patrol boats would open fire on them once they got within a mile. And there are armed guards there as well. Everyone is scared to go out there, by design."

"Let me guess? The chief of police got a boxful of money?"

"Rings." Drummond studied the blank plasma TV as if it were playing a thriller.

"A boxful of rings?"

"Rings a bell," Drummond said, his lids lowering. "It's a figure of speech."

"Dad, what rings a bell? Please, we have to get out there somehow."

Drummond opened his eyes. "We donated thirty-caliber machine guns to the police department. Whatever you do, do not try to go to that island."

"But —" Charlie stopped short.

Drummond was out.

Maybe for the best. Rest was his Red Bull. Charlie could try again in a few hours.

Now, careful not to make too much noise, Charlie sat on the floor and hit the space bar on one of the laptops, bringing the computer to life and flashing its display image on the plasma screen. The system was already open to the Web, a site selling coin-operated air hockey tables.

Charlie debated entering as little as FIELDING into a search engine, let alone HOW TO COVERTLY REACH NICK FIELDING'S PRIVATE ISLAND. What if the CIA had programmed its house-sized computers to set off alarms if anyone did?

Wouldn't that person's location flash at once onto the agency's computer screens or cell phones or tricked-out wristwatches?

Charlie was willing to bet against that happening. Fielding's cover as a dashing and colorful hunter of pirate gold had made him a worldwide celebrity. Teams of his divers were still combing the Caribbean in search of the sunken ship containing the legendary treasure of San Isidro. Charlie's horseplayer cronies, who regarded treasure hunting as gambling's highest form, kept track of the San Isidro expedition team with the same dedication with which other people followed athletic teams. In reality, according to Alice, the treasure of San Isidro was the maritime equivalent of an urban legend.

Thinking of her, Charlie considered for the first time that the expression "missing someone like crazy" wasn't entirely hyperbole.

Clicking to a search engine, he entered what he considered a relatively innocuous FIELDING ISLAND MARTINIQUE. The screen filled with 10 of the 871,222 results, the first being a computer-generated map of Fielding's private island, Îlet Céron, located a few miles northwest of Fort-de-France.

Charlie opted for the satellite picture of the island. He gaped at the pentagonal swimming pool, so big that it was probably visible from outer space without satellite assistance. He also made out the slate roof of the sprawling château and what appeared to be a wall around the entire island, topped by bushels of barbed wire.

His eye fell to the search engine's automatically generated advertisements, all but one from online stores selling replica gold doubloons and pirate swag. The exception was a real estate listing of a thirty-room château on Îlet Céron. The ad had been placed by the Pointe du Bout, Martinique, office of Caribbean Realty Solutions.

Charlie hoped that the company would have a solution for him.

23

Located on the ground floor of a three-story tangerine French Colonial building on Pointe du Bout's ritzy yet quaint main street, Caribbean Realty Solutions filled its broad front window with striking color photographs of the best listings. "Bait," the Realtors called these pictures. "Fish" often stopped and lingered, openmouthed. Frank DeSoto, an eleven-year veteran of the realty game, sat at the reception desk, watching two such prospective catches, men wearing expensive polo shirts and Bermuda shorts, crossing the street. Without a glance at the bait, they entered the agency.

Fabulous, DeSoto thought. They know what they want.

Filled with the exhilaration a fisherman feels at a tug on his line, DeSoto did a five-second check of his hairpiece and breath.

The men approached the desk. Striking the proper balance between deference and social equality, DeSoto asked, "What can I do for you?"

The younger of the two men, who looked moneyed enough, said, "We're interested in seeing the Céron Island property."

DeSoto's exhilaration evaporated, although he continued smiling. Chances were these men were GCs — gate-crashers, a minor-league brand of thrill-seeker whose idea of a thrill was wandering around a property they couldn't afford.

GCs were normally couples, however, and tended to dress as if they'd just stepped off a yacht. Like the authentic rich, this duo placed comfort ahead of appearance. The key was their footwear. The younger man wore the distinctive boat-shaped Bettanin & Venturi loafers, handmade in Italy. And he wore them without socks, as if he didn't care whether they fell victim to sweat, sand, or saltwater. The other man, although at least twenty years DeSoto's senior, wore a pair of Day-Glo orange Crocs, the over-priced neoprene beach clogs that were cute on little kids. Anyone over the age of eight wearing a pair of kiddie clogs didn't give a hoot what others thought. He was loaded, DeSoto suspected.

He decided to find out for sure. "I would love to share Îlet Céron with you," he said, extending his hand, rattling his eighteen-karat gold Rolex. "I am Franklin DeSoto."

The young man's grip was firm and his eyes never wavered. "Brad McDonough," he said. Then he cocked his head at the older man, who hovered by the entry. "And this is Mr. Larsen."

Larsen stepped forward, bumping his young companion without apology. He placed his hand in DeSoto's and let the Realtor do the work. "*John* Larsen," he said as though it were some sort of secret.

"Great to meet you," DeSoto said. "This happens to be the first slow day I've had since Thanksgiving." *If only.* "I could take you to the island this morning if you'd like."

McDonough looked to old Larsen, who nodded his consent, though grudgingly. Maybe he would have preferred a nap first. Or a Bloody Mary.

"The agency just has a minor security requirement," said DeSoto. "I need to have my assistant photocopy either your passports or your driver's licenses. Then I can call down to the dock and have Marcel ready the motor launch."

Licenses in hand, DeSoto proceeded to the copier in the back room, glancing at his BlackBerry en route. Just the usual boasts from colleagues. Bettina Ludington was showing the old Delacorte estate to a Goldman Sachs senior partner. DeSoto replied with an insincere wish of good luck and *btw, i'm showing ceron to a couple of whales.*

But were they really whales?

Taking a few moments longer than necessary at the photocopier, DeSoto used an array of Internet tools to search for his prospective clients' occupations, real estate holdings, and credit histories; Realtors were as adept as private investigators at getting the lowdown, and, by necessity, they were faster. If DeSoto's digging indicated that his men were in fact whales, he would immediately plunk down fifty euros to rent a Riva Aquarama, a vintage mahogany runabout known alternately as the maritime version of a Ferrari and the Stradivarius of the sea. Should he discover that they were plankton, getting rid of them would be a simple matter of requesting a fax from a bank stating that they had the financial wherewithal to close on such an expensive property. Plankton usually claimed that they had to return to their hotels to get their bank information. Invariably they were never seen again.

It turned out that Larsen was CEO of New England Capital Management, LLC, about which DeSoto could find no useful information. He hoped that it was one of those ultradiscreet hedge funds. Larsen's address was 259 Cherry Valley Lane in Greenwich, Connecticut. DeSoto knew Greenwich was a Manhattan suburb where two million got you a house in the part of town that formerly quartered the servants. Cherry Valley Lane was located in Greenwich's lushly forested "Back Country." According to a Web site that generated instant appraisals, the eight-acre property was worth $10.5 million.

McDonough lived on the other side of Greenwich's proverbial tracks in a $3.2 million converted barn. He popped up on DeSoto's computer as the proprietor of the nearby McDonough Thoroughbred Farm, whose Web site offered only the most rudimentary information. Like good restaurants and colleges, successful horse breeders had no need to advertise.

It was enough to go on, DeSoto decided.

If worse came to worst, he always had his Beretta.

24

It was a bright morning with a colorful array of spinnakers in bloom on the Baie de Fort-de-France. The Riva Aquarama runabout skipped across the waves at an exhilarating forty knots, its chrome trim sparkling. Just stepping aboard the iconic craft had made Charlie feel like a movie star.

In the next seat, adding to the illusion, DeSoto steered the boat with one hand and held a thermos of espresso in the other. Sure his tan was too orange, his teeth were too white, and his hair was too fake, but when Charlie squinted against the sun's glare off the water, the real estate agent passed for Cary Grant.

Charlie might have enjoyed the experience except for the police cutter bobbing ahead, a monstrous black thirty-caliber machine gun mounted on its foredeck. If the policemen glanced at the Riva through binoculars and recognized the fugitive Marvin Lesser

— or if the forest of instruments sprouting from the cutter's wheelhouse included a camera with facial recognition software — Charlie would wind up in a cell. Then things would get bad.

Drummond lay behind Charlie and DeSoto on the sundeck, his recently Clairol-ed black hair flapping aft; Charlie had gone "Golden Sunshine" himself. Drummond's lethargy was genuine, the side effect of his medication. Charlie thought the attendant crankiness added a bit of plausibility to his role as a man reluctant to part with twenty-eight million of his hard-earned greenbacks.

"So what do you think of the Empress Joséphine?" DeSoto asked.

Preoccupied by the policemen, Charlie struggled to find a response. "Terrific golf course, underrated empress."

DeSoto laughed as only someone hoping to sell a $28 million property could.

Charlie watched the policeman at the machine gun crane his neck to speak to the pilot. Eyes glued to the Riva, the pilot reached for the controls. Water began lathering around the cutter's stern and, sure enough, the craft launched onto a course to intercept the runabout.

Intolerant of gaps in conversation, DeSoto

said, "I always say that golf is the only game where you strive for a subpar performance."

Charlie faked a laugh. And asked himself why he and Drummond hadn't simply chartered a dive boat, taken it to within a mile of Fielding's island, then swum the rest of the way underwater. Anyone who'd seen a Saturday morning cartoon knew that was the way to go.

He reached back and nudged Drummond from his slumber. "Hey look, Mr. Larsen, a police boat with a thirty-caliber machine gun." He hoped the reminder of the gift to the police, if not the imminent danger it posed, would spur his father's mind.

Drummond looked up. "Oh," he said. Getting comfortable again, he closed his eyes.

The police cutter chugged to within a hundred yards.

DeSoto cut his engines, bringing the runabout to a skidding stop. His only concern seemed to be his appearance, which he checked in the control panel. "As opposed to a lot of the other Caribbean islands, one thing you won't have to worry about here in Martinique is crime," he said. "The police don't miss a trick."

"Glad to hear it," said Charlie. If he could grab hold of DeSoto's thermos, he might heave its steaming contents at the policeman on deck and gain control of the machine gun.

The cutter pulled to a halt, paralleling the Riva. Both the machine gunner and the pilot were young Martinicans with muscles that swelled their dark blue uniforms.

"Ça va, Monsieur DeSoto?" asked the pilot.

"Ça va, Sergent François," DeSoto said, a little New Jersey evident in his French. He dug an envelope from his breast pocket and handed it across the three-foot-wide lane to the pilot. *"Ça va?"*

"Ça va." Stuffing the envelope into his own breast pocket, the cop offered a crisp salute and returned to the controls.

DeSoto then threw the throttle and the Riva was off. "The toll," he explained to Charlie.

Charlie felt no relief. If experience was any teacher, that wasn't the last they'd see of the police cutter.

"So what's your first impression?" DeSoto asked.

"It depends on how much the toll is."

Laughing, the real estate agent pointed at the mass of land looming before them like a low-lying thunderhead. As they drew closer, it turned greener and sharpened into picturesque, sprawling meadows.

"Originally Îlet Céron was home to a rum distillery." DeSoto waved at the ruins of a long warehouse coated in moss. "That was the factory."

"Oh, good, I was worried that was the château," Charlie said.

With a belly laugh, DeSoto drove the boat around a stretch of coast, bringing them into a small cove. A long, weather-grayed pier terminated at a gorgeous beach.

To tie up, the Riva had to gain admission. DeSoto slowed alongside a guard post resembling a prison watchtower. Atop it, in a small roundhouse, a man stood, shadows obscuring his features but not his machine-gun barrel.

"Why are there guards here?" Charlie asked DeSoto under his breath.

"The seller's concerned about looters."

Certainly it was a better answer than *The security staff has been retained in hope of preventing anyone from retrieving the bomb disguised as a washing machine.* Charlie suspected that the latter was the case, however.

"Who's the seller?" he asked.

"I ought to have mentioned that before," DeSoto said. "Mr. Fielding had no marital partner or descendants. His closest living relative is an uncle in the States who's motivated to unload everything and collect the proceeds ASAP." He nodded at Drummond, now sleeping on his stomach. "From his point of view, the ideal seller."

The uncle in the States was in fact none other than Uncle Sam, Charlie speculated. Without Fielding, the CIA was probably eager to roll up its operation here. Charlie hoped that the island included no new personnel who would recognize him and Drummond. According to Alice, Fielding's staff had had no idea that he was a spy. In fact, to add to his criminal cover, the Cavalry hired heavies from the Colombian Bucaga drug cartel.

The guard stepped onto the square platform surrounding the roundhouse. He was a tall Hispanic with the build of a Greek statue. He peered down through binoculars. Thankfully Drummond's face was pressed against the cushioned sundeck.

Flashing a toothy smile, the guard waved the Riva ahead.

25

"It would seem we had one margarita too many, and three or four after that," Hadley said as soon as Kyle loosed her gag. "As for our friend who left us tied up here like this, I don't think there is any earthly explanation for her behavior."

"It happens," said Kyle, the amiable aquatics director.

Stanley hoped that Kyle was sincere, or, at least, that any curiosity the hardy Australian harbored would go no further than war stories the staff shared at happy hour. Although young — twenty-seven or twenty-eight — he had probably seen his share of oddities on the resorts circuit. Certainly he'd never opened up shop to find a couple bound and gagged. Yet he exhibited no surprise beyond the natural shock of discovery, nor any misgivings after hearing Hadley's yarn. He asked only, "You folks want a Powerade — get some electrolyte action going?"

"That would be wonderful," Hadley said. "Anything would be, except a margarita."

"A margarita might not be such a bad idea, actually." Kyle regarded Stanley. "You look like you could stand some hair of the dog, mate."

Stanley decided to leave Kyle's recommendation out of the report he would write Eskridge, who had never been in the field and would have enough trouble digesting the rest of the events at Hôtel L'Impératrice.

On return to their hotel room, Stanley took a seat at the rolltop desk. Blocking out the postcard view of the Caribbean through the balcony window, he clicked a featureless area of his computer screen four times in rapid succession, opening a fresh cable form. He filled it with a blow-by-blow account of the past fifteen hours. If adversaries were to intercept the transmission, they would view only an e-mail from Colin Atchison to his secretary asking her to call some other fictitious person and reschedule the morning's round of golf.

Then Stanley launched into putative next steps:

PERMISSION FOR OVERT ACTION.
OBJECTIVE: DEBRIEF CARTHAGE

He heard Hadley turn off the shower. He did not hear her approach. The pile carpet was so thick, she might have long-jumped into the bedroom and he would have been none the wiser if it were not for the pleasing perfume of honey and lavender. He didn't turn around, largely to avoid gawking, not until he felt her standing just inches from his back.

"Overt action?" she said. "In other words, we call up Carthage and say, 'Actually, Mr. Bream, we're professional spies from the CIA.' "

"Breaking cover is the most expedient way I can think of," said Stanley.

"Why would a couple of spooks — spooks with a track record of deceiving him — be the people best able to get the truth from him?"

"Because we'll best be able to convince him that he'll be in deep kimchi otherwise."

She took a seat on the nearest corner of the bed, crossing one glowing dancer's thigh over the other. "I know a really good way that won't leave any marks," she said with an enthusiasm that transformed her in Stanley's perception from a sensuous woman into something darker and colder.

He was troubled already by her rush to slash Drummond's jugular last night with her switchblade ring — which would have certainly come in handy *after* they were tied up. Their track record notwithstanding, the Clarks very obviously were not bent on murder. It would have been more expedient for Drummond to snuff them than to tie them up. Also Charlie's assertion that they had acted in self-defense seemed free of artifice.

Stanley wondered if Hadley had her own agenda.

26

DeSoto had been to Îlet Céron twice before, first to view the property himself, then to show it to a couple from Dubai who ended up buying a Bettina Ludington listing, an Italianate mansion with no business on a French island. Both times here, on ascending the crushed clamshell pathway from the pier he had halted abruptly when the château came into view. The structure was breathtaking.

As its limestone façade appeared now, the crotchety Larsen didn't even pause. If DeSoto didn't know better, he would have thought the old man had already seen the place.

McDonough slowed, but only to allow DeSoto to catch up.

"Wow," McDonough exclaimed.

After eleven years hustling houses, DeSoto knew *wows* the way a jeweler knows diamonds. The kid's was pure zirconium. Possibly he lacked education. New money often didn't aspire beyond a McMansion with superfluous turrets, their sensibilities shaped by Donald Trump.

Thankfully, such clients could still be educated. "Le Château d'Îlet Céron is celebrated for perfectly capturing the period of architectural transition from the rococo of the mid-eighteenth century to the more refined neoclassical style," DeSoto said. "As *Architectural Digest* put it, 'The palatial limestone façade dazzles new arrivals with its towering Corinthian pilasters and detached pillars while at the same time heeding simplicity in order to capitalize on sunlight bouncing from passing waves.' "

McDonough slowed at the marble staircase leading to the entry. "Dazzling," he agreed. Larsen took in the façade and was no more dazzled than if it were a split-level in Sheboygan.

A young chambermaid heaved open one of the monolithic copper-faced French doors. In lieu of a greeting, the old man nodded. He shot inside before she had a chance to open the other door. McDonough hurried after him.

The grand reception hall was like a skating rink made of marble. Elephantine columns supported a gilded and improbably high ceiling, the painted sun and clouds realistic enough to be mistaken for a skylight view.

"DuVal, one of the greatest living realists," DeSoto began, pointing up at the work.

But his clients were on their way into the den.

A Realtor is supposed to precede his clients, but these two were bloody racewalkers. DeSoto hurried in pursuit. Greenwich, he reminded himself, was a bedroom community of New York City. New Yorkers rushed even through cheesecake.

If the den was a den, then the White House was just a house. The giant room was still furnished, including sofas and chaises and divans dating back to Louis XIV, restored and reupholstered well beyond Versailles standards. The best part was the far wall, which opened onto a golden beach.

"Mr. Fielding had the sand imported from Venezuela's Paria Peninsula," DeSoto said.

Too late. The clients were out the far door.

He labored to keep pace, calling after them, "The lower level includes an old-fashioned billiards room as well as a tavern with an authentic mahogany Victorian bar. There's also a squash court, a gym, a marble steam room resembling an ancient Roman bathhouse, and a game room with enough arcade games to keep grandchildren occupied for a whole weekend."

Larsen and McDonough gave the lower level maybe a minute before going out to the pool deck. Mopping his forehead with his ascot, DeSoto resumed the chase.

McDonough stopped and waited for him. Although the waves and wind made such discretion superfluous, the young man said, sotto voce, "The house is lovely, but old Mrs. Larsen's going to redo everything regardless of what Mr. Larsen thinks."

"I'm sure she has wonderful taste," DeSoto said, dabbing his brow again.

"Hey, how about we give you a breather while the boss checks out the pool house?" McDonough waved at the building. "*That* will be his; Mrs. L. doesn't go into water — hairdo-related reasons."

"I look forward to recommending decorators," DeSoto said, thinking of his $1,120,000 commission.

The dutiful McDonough hurried after Larsen, who was rounding the enormous pool. Plopping onto a chaise lounge, DeSoto checked his BlackBerry. There was a text message from Bettina Ludington: "CHECK UR EMAIL!!! URGENT!!!"

The cellular reception was poor. While waiting for the e-mail message to appear, DeSoto chewed away a good part of a thumbnail.

Finally:

Frank: if ur 2 whales r these 2, u can get a 10K bonus . . .

Attached were photographs of two men wanted by the Martinique Police for multiple counts of fraud and racketeering.

27

Charlie slid open a door leading to the enormous pool house. The living room looked like a nightclub, not only because of its size, but also because of the mirrored walls, expensive erotic art, and enough low-slung, Euro-posh furniture to accommodate half the jet set. The giant bar was stocked with, it seemed, every spirit known to man, in every possible configuration of decanter. The pale morning light set the crystal and fluids aglow.

"Been here before?" Charlie asked Drummond.

"I don't remember."

"My guess would be that a lot of the people who've been here don't remember it."

"Oh." Drummond blinked at his reflection on the mirrored back wall, as if expecting something altogether different. He pressed his palms against the mirror.

A door sprung inward.

Charlie felt a charge of excitement. "Well, that's something, isn't it?"

"A door," Drummond explained.

Charlie followed him into a plush-carpeted hallway opening into two guest rooms. Like those in the main house, the rooms would have suited guests accustomed to Buckingham Palace. Not the sort of area where laundry was done.

Drummond started down the hall with an air of determination.

Charlie trailed him. "Going anywhere in particular?"

"We're trying to find the washing machine, right?"

Rounding a corner, Drummond opened another door, revealing a stairway with relatively plain carpeting. He tromped down the steps. Charlie's hope was rekindled.

At the base of the stairs, luxury gave way to dark, featureless walls and a hint of mildew. Drummond threw the light switch as if he'd known exactly where the wall panel was, illuminating a large basement of bare concrete.

At one end, a central air-conditioning unit heaved air into a labyrinth of foil-coated ducts. At the other end of the room stood a hot water tank sufficient in size to service

231

an apartment building. The center of the basement included a laundry area, with an industrial-style sink and an ironing board that folded out from a wall compartment. Both devices appeared to have never been used. Ditto the gleaming stainless steel washing machine and dryer.

Charlie recognized the models from the display window of the ultra-chic kitchen and bathroom store in the West Village that carried the French brand name. "They're gorgeous," he said. "The thing is, the washer we want is a three-hundred-buck Perriman piece of crap."

Fielding might have upgraded to a pricier nuclear bomb container, but it was unlikely: The Cavalry's Perriman Pristina models had specially modified linings to thwart radiation detectors.

Charlie snapped open the round door on the machine's face, knelt, and looked in. "This is only good for doing laundry."

As Drummond bent over to take a turn inspecting the machine, a Hispanic baritone resounded from the stairwell. "You looking for a bomb?"

Startled, Charlie spun around.

The watchtower guard took the last three steps in a leap. He was armed with a smaller machine gun than before. More than ample to shred two intruders, though.

"I was just wondering what in the world this washing machine does that makes it so expensive," Charlie said.

The guard rubbed his chin, as if trying to make sense of Charlie's words. Meanwhile Drummond unfolded himself from the washer.

"I knowed that was you, Señor Lesser," the guard exclaimed.

Fear, like molten metal, filled Charlie's intestines.

"How are you?" Drummond asked.

"Real, real good, *gracias*." The guard smiled, seemingly flattered by Señor Lesser's interest. "Except that real estate fucker called the cops on you."

"Didn't see that coming," Charlie said.

"I have an idea," the guard said, waving for them to follow him up the staircase. "Also, the washer you want's not on the island no more."

Charlie looked to Drummond for a sign of assurance.

Drummond started up the stairs.

Good enough.

At the top of the staircase the guard hurried to the kitchen and opened a screen door, taking them out the back of the pool house.

Drummond looked the guard over. "You're Henrique, right? Or Hector . . ."

"*Sí,* Hector. Hector Manzanillo." He led the way across a cricket field as lush and well tended as a golf course.

A smile creased Drummond's face. "With the brother who pitches in the Milwaukee Brewers farm system? Rico, yes?"

Charlie could almost see lucidity surging into his father: As Drummond walked, he appeared to grow taller, his stride becoming more resolute, and the old glow returning to his eyes. Had Hector Manzanillo sparked him whereas du Frongipanier or Odelette's children had not? Possibly. Sticking his head inside a washing machine might also have sparked him. Whichever, Charlie was elated. They needed an exit strategy, and when Drummond Clark was on, he was an escape artist.

"Rico blew out his shoulder last season," Hector said.

"I'm sorry to hear it," said Drummond.

"Don't be. He's doing way better now selling 'bananas' for the Bucagas."

"First-class operation," said Drummond of the drug dealers.

The trio reached a staircase whose eight flights zigzagged down a cliff face speckled with patches of grass and scrawny trees.

From this far up, the choppy sea looked like tinfoil.

Hector pointed down to the beach that wrapped around the rock wall. "Follow the shore 'round to the pier, shouldn't take you no more than a minute, then blast off in that fancy-ass speedboat you came in. I'll go the other way, gunning one of the launches from the private dock, do what I can to draw away the cops."

Drummond nodded his approval. "I owe you one, Hector."

"I still owe you way more than that, señor." The guard clambered down the stairs, unconcerned by the creaks and groans that suggested loose moorings.

Right behind him, Drummond said, "Hector, do you have any idea what Fielding did with the other washing machine?"

"The Perriman Pristina? Wish I did. Woulda saved me two broken ribs and fuck-near getting drowned."

Drummond reddened. "Who did that to you?"

"They said they was Interpol."

"That means we can rule out Interpol."

Struggling to keep pace, Charlie surmised that whoever Bream was working for had interrogated Hector. They would have exhausted every means of locating the bomb

235

before mounting their Gstaad operation.

Continuing down the stairs, Hector said, "I told those fuckers what Señor Fielding told me, which was pretty much *nada*."

"Tell me anyway," Drummond said.

"When we loaded the Pristina onto his boat, he said he was gonna run it over to some new hiding place he got on Bernadette Islet or Antoinina Islet — you know, there's tons of them little isles around here, no people on 'em, no nothing. The boss, he liked to cruise around, find new ones and draw 'em onto his map. He'd name 'em after the ladies he took there . . ." Embarrassment tinted the guard's beefy face. "On dates."

"I imagine your 'Interpol officers' searched all these islands?"

"Bernadette's just a giant-ass sandbar, maybe three kilometers north of here. High tide, thing's underwater. So you couldn't really hide nothing there. So of course they didn't find nothing."

"What about Antoinina?"

"That's the thing. There's no Antoinina on any of Señor Fielding's maps. Or on any map. Closest thing's Arianne Islet, which is far, forty clicks easy. They tore that rock apart too. Found shit."

"Could there be some meaning to

'Antoinina' that they missed?" Charlie asked Drummond.

"Damned if I know," he said.

Which was reason to hope otherwise. Drummond opposed even mild profanity.

28

Charlie had difficulty keeping up with Drummond on the slender beach, which was piled with round, sea-smoothed stones that could broadcast their whereabouts.

"While it's on my mind, I should say that I might know what Fielding meant by those islets," Drummond said.

"That could come in handy," Charlie said. He'd presumed Drummond had chosen to keep mum in the presence of Hector. Nice guy and all, but probably a hardcore criminal who would have been less concerned for their well-being once he knew the whereabouts of a weapons system that could net him enough of a fortune to buy this island several times over.

"Do you remember the false subtraction cipher?" Drummond asked.

"Yeah. You're thinking alphanumeric values of 'Bernadette' and 'Antoinina'?"

"Ought to yield the latitude and longitude

of Fielding's hiding spot. I'd need to do the math on paper. But perhaps you can do it in your head."

With each letter assigned a number based on its alphabetical order, BERNADETTE minus ANTOININA translated to:

$$25181414520205$$
$$-11420159149141$$

As the cipher's name implies, false subtraction isn't true subtraction. Charlie worked left to right, subtracting numbers on the bottom line from those directly above. $2 - 1 = 1$, $5 - 1 = 4$ — if this were true subtraction, $5 - 1$ would yield 3 because the 1 that comes next borrows from the 5 in order to subtract 4. As for the rest . . .

$$25181414520205$$
$$-11420159149141$$
$$14761365481164$$

"One-four-seven-six-one-three-six-five-four-eight-one-one-six-four," said Charlie.

"Good." Drummond nodded. "That gives us latitude and longitude, using decimal values. Latitude of 14.7, longitude 61.3. Or about fifteen nautical miles off the coast of Martinique."

Bream's people surely used potent decryption software to parse every permutation of Bernadette and Antoinina, but without the simple cipher Drummond had taught Fielding years ago, they might as well have searched for the mythical treasure of San Isidro. The single-degree latitudinal difference between the 14 and the 13 yielded by actual subtraction equaled 69 miles, a margin of error of some 15,000 square miles.

Charlie was suddenly distracted by the sound of an approaching police boat's siren — what had been a distant drone became a shriek.

Drummond broke into a jog, continuing to stay close to the seawall, depriving DeSoto or anyone else atop the cliff a glimpse of him. Over the resulting ruckus of stones and clamshells, he shouted, "Now all we have to do is get there."

Charlie joined Drummond in peering around the edge of the rock wall to see DeSoto on the pier, pacing alongside the bobbing Riva. The real estate agent's back was to them. They could easily overpower him, if it came to that.

As Charlie followed Drummond onto the pier, DeSoto spun around, the pistol in his hand ignited by the sunlight.

Instinct sent Charlie sprawling onto the hot, splintery slats.

Drummond remained on his feet. Without flinching, he stepped toward DeSoto.

"You best stop right there." DeSoto's salesman façade was history.

Drummond continued walking toward him.

"They'll be here in less than a minute." DeSoto gestured to sea. The police cutter was now visible, its siren growing louder.

"Give me the gun, please," Drummond said.

Taking a measure of the older man, in his beach garb and Crocs, De Soto scoffed. "I suppose you want my ten-thousand-euro reward too?"

Drummond advanced until only the length of the runabout separated them. "I want to avoid hurting you."

DeSoto aligned the muzzle with Drummond's chest. "Stop now," he said evenly.

Drummond took two quick steps, wound back and threw something, some sort of shimmering white disk, too fast for Charlie to track.

The object struck the real estate man in the hip, then dropped to the deck with a clink.

A clamshell.

Glancing down, DeSoto smirked. "That's all you got?"

His smirk faded when, with one more step, Drummond launched himself into the air. He effectively flew, feetfirst, at DeSoto.

The real estate agent pulled the trigger. The ear-splitting shot scattered birds from unseen perches all over the island. The bullet struck the shore, several small stones leaping upward.

Drummond's sole smacked into DeSoto's elbow, causing him to lose his grip on the gun.

Drummond landed on his side, rolled, and sprang back toward the weapon.

The real estate man rallied, snatching it off the slats. He wheeled around and pressed the nose of the gun against Drummond's neck.

Drummond balled his left hand into a fist and drilled it into DeSoto's gut. Staggering backward, the real estate agent fired again.

The bullet sent up a water spout fifty feet away.

Drummond heaved a roundhouse into DeSoto's jaw. The real estate agent sank to the pier. Grabbing the gun on its way down, Drummond regarded him with remorse.

From her hiding spot behind a bush at the top of the clamshell pathway, the young chambermaid shrieked, distracting Drummond. He didn't notice DeSoto draw a keychain from his trouser pocket and fling it at the darkest blue patch of bay.

Having anticipated this action, Charlie jumped to his feet, sprinted down the pier, and sprang off a rickety slat in what he meant to be a dive. Cold water slapped his face and chest. His momentum carried him down, to about fifteen feet below the surface, where the pressure made his head feel as if it was about to burst.

The key ring was a veritable strobe light in the colorless depths. He snatched it and launched himself upward, breaking the surface to find DeSoto flat on his back, out cold now, and Drummond ensconced at the runabout's wheel.

Hauling himself over the opposite gunwale, Charlie tossed Drummond the key.

Turning it in the ignition and adding throttle, Drummond glanced at the police cutter, now close enough that Charlie could make out the two men aboard, until, with a boom, the entire craft was obscured by whitish smoke streaming from its thirty-caliber cannon.

A shell screamed toward the Riva.

29

The shell — or small-caliber rocket — zoomed wide of the bow, sending up a twenty-foot-high spout of seawater. A second shell hammered the Riva's stern. Everything not tied or bolted in place slid or tumbled to starboard. Drummond fell from the portside captain's seat, slamming onto Charlie. It felt as if the runabout would flip over.

In apparent defiance of gravity, Drummond heaved himself against the elevated portside gunwale, righting the boat and catapulting hundreds of gallons of seawater out.

Now maybe he could contend with the islet directly in their path, a mound of sand and rocks not much larger than a porch, but enough to turn the runabout to splinters.

He clocked the wheel. The Riva sashayed past the landmass, slicing through the waves as if they were air. But the corner of her stern was a mass of splinters, and the big police cutter appeared to be gaining on them.

"I thought the Riva Aquarama was the fastest boat made," Charlie shouted.

"At the time it was made, fifty years ago, that was true." Drummond turned the wheel a degree or two, allowing the runabout to slalom past another tiny islet.

A third blast shook the air.

With an eardrum-piercing clank, the starboard half of the Riva's windshield disappeared. A column of seawater rose over the bow, lashing Charlie, the salt lodging in and burning each cut and scrape in his now-extensive collection.

His father was also struck by the water but remained steady at the helm. And, oddly, at peace. Charlie recalled one of Drummond's favorite adages: *There's nothing so enjoyable as to be shot at by one's enemy without result.*

"We need to keep them close," Drummond said through the onrushing air, more forceful with no windshield to deflect it.

Before he could ask what his father was thinking, Charlie glimpsed sparkling sand ahead, capping a diminutive islet that was long and winding, like a sea serpent. He shot a hand forward. "Do you see that?"

"By my reckoning, that's Bernadette," Drummond said.

Even within a hundred yards, it would have been easy not to notice the large sandbar, then sail smack into it.

Drummond ought to begin to steer clear of it about now, Charlie thought.

Another mammoth round walloped the Riva, cleaving the sundeck and sending slivers of mahogany flying like darts. Like Drummond, Charlie ducked. One shard whistled past him, carving a groove alongside his left cheek before knifing into the black plastic radio at the base of the control panel.

The searing pain barely registered, as Drummond continued straight for the islet, focused on it, as if he were trying to hit it.

"Dad?"

"Hold on!"

Charlie grabbed the sides of his seat and braced himself.

The Riva's prow hit Bernadette Islet with a deafening crack. If the police cutter hadn't already blasted away his side of the Riva's windshield, Charlie's face would have pancaked against glass. His joints felt like they'd been struck individually by a mallet.

Mostly intact, the entire craft took to the air.

The stern came down onto the sand first, like a giant's gavel. Every one of Charlie's cells seemed to throb. Then, with a boom, the prow landed too.

The runabout sleighed forward through wet sand and puddles, the irregularities in the surface having a bumper-car effect. Sand grated away the caramel varnish, rocks abraded the hull. The inboard engines gasped, the propellers spitting a gritty brown haze in place of a wake.

Still the craft's momentum carried it forward, fast.

Charlie hung on, white-knuckled. Drummond retained a firm grip on the wheel, his head lowered against the rush of sand and water and other bits of Bernadette Islet.

The far shore came into sight, a dune in miniature.

The Riva slid off the land, going airborne again, entering a stomach-wrenching plummet, then thumping into the Caribbean, walls of water erupting all around.

Surely the battered craft would now collapse into flotsam, Charlie thought, but the engines purred and the Riva shot forward through the waves.

Charlie was shocked just by the fact that

she remained in one piece.

"Now for the real test," Drummond said, looking at the rearview mirror until he discovered that the glass there had been broken away.

With a shrug, he throttled the runabout ahead, accelerating to an even faster speed than they'd gone before.

Charlie turned to see the police cutter within a hundred feet of Bernadette Islet. He read the horror on the machine gunner's face as the man scrambled off the foredeck and leaped toward the wheelhouse while the pilot threw his full weight into turning the steering wheel.

Bernadette was too wide. The cutter smashed into the shoreline. Charlie momentarily lost sight of the craft behind a cloud of kicked-up bits of earth. The propellers on the giant engines hacked away like saw blades before being smothered by sand. The behemoth lurched to a stop twenty feet inland. Beached.

30

Although one of the inboard engines sputtered, the Riva was in the clear, save for the sea. Water sprayed onto the deck through the bullet holes and fissures — too many to count. Parts of the craft, or parts of parts, intermittently fell off. Yet Drummond managed to maintain thirty knots.

The seascape soon became cluttered with uninhabited landmasses, none of them larger than a football field. With the sun nearing its peak, the blue of the sea matched that of the horizon so that the two appeared to be one and the Riva seemed to be floating through the heavens.

Charlie might have appreciated it if he hadn't been on the lookout for police boats. Even the colorful birds flitting about the islands gave him pause. In the Middle East, Alice's NSA unit had deployed remotely piloted attack aircraft that could pass for barn swallows. A macaw was nothing.

Drummond slowed the engines.

"Are we there yet?" Charlie asked.

"This particular GPS is only accurate to within a latitudinal minute, or 1.15 miles. So all I can tell you is we're within 1.15 miles." With a sweeping gesture, Drummond indicated the eight small islets surrounding them, distinguishable only by the placement of the trees. "It could be any of these."

Hardly simplifying matters, each islet lacked an obvious hiding place. If Fielding had buried the washer, which made sense, he wouldn't have left the ground looking like someone had dug an enormous hole. The odds of finding the washer before the police made the scene were best not to calculate.

"Other than whipping up an astrolabe, what can we do?" Charlie asked.

Drummond brightened. "Actually, all we would need to make an astrolabe is a thick piece of paper, something to cut notches along its end, a straw or reed, some string, and a small weight, like a ring."

Charlie wondered if his father was fading — a fade was well overdue. "Then what? Wait for the stars to come out so we can calculate latitude?"

"Planets work too." Drummond accelerated the runabout toward the furthest of the eight islands. "But I have a feeling that that's it."

"Washer Island?"

"I recognize the tree on the southern shore." He pointed to a huge oak atop a high ridge that sloped at almost a right angle to the sea.

"You've been here?"

"It's where I found the treasure of San Isidro — you don't forget a thing like that."

Charlie felt the cold draft that usually accompanied the opening of Drummond's chest of broken memories. "Just like you don't forget seeing your first unicorn?"

Nosing the Riva onto a shelf of golden sand, Drummond cut the engines. "You'll see." He hopped over the gunwale and secured the bowline to a giant root.

Charlie slid off the bow and waded after his father. The oak's myriad roots and tendrils fanned down the ridge like a bridal train, several disappearing into the high tide. Between the roots, where Charlie would have expected sand or soil, he saw dark apertures nearly his height. Waves tumbled into these gaps, breaking with a rich echo, indicative of an enormous subterranean cavern.

"Go on in," Drummond said.

Charlie hesitated. "How do I know this

isn't a giant squid's lair?"

With a laugh Drummond reached into the mouth of the cavern and patted the roof until, with a rip of Velcro, he extracted a moss-green nylon sack the size of a hard-cover book. He unzipped it, drew out a pair of slender black Maglites, and tossed one over his shoulder. Charlie set aside his incredulity to make the catch.

Drummond fired his Maglite's laserlike white beam through the roots, casting spidery shadows onto mossy rock walls, then sauntered into the cavern. Charlie stuck close behind, hunching every few steps to avoid a stalactite. The air was cold and clammy. Goose flesh rose on his arms, not attributable to the temperature alone: Although he saw no movement, he had a tingling sense that the place was teeming with slithery life forms.

"Dad, you know how I used to get on you for never taking me camping?"

"Yes. What about it?"

"I take it back."

The cavern floor rose out of the water to a platform of red clay. Within the far wall of the platform was a tunnel large enough to allow a man to wheel in a washing machine.

31

Charlie aimed his Maglite into the tunnel, revealing an opening fifty or sixty feet down, maybe the entry to another cavern. Shifting the beam to the right, he saw a wall coated in silt and dirt. Unlike the ceiling and floor, the wall was flat, undoubtedly man-made.

"That's the gold," Drummond said with no more enthusiasm than if he were showing Charlie the contents of his sock drawer.

"What's the gold?"

"That wall."

"What are you talking about?"

"The other wall too."

Charlie swung his beam across the tunnel. Amidst the grime, streaks of yellow metal flashed. "Walls made of gold. How would that even be possible?"

"Fielding and I used to putter around this area, using sonar to find places like this that couldn't be picked up by eyes in the sky. The idea was, if you're a prospective client and you're taken to a subterranean weapons cache on a tiny deserted island fifty miles from anywhere, you more readily believe that you're seeing an actual nuclear device."

"I'll buy that. What about the fifty-foot-long slabs of gold?"

Drummond ambled into the tunnel. "Oh, that, right. Long story."

Charlie followed him. "So you didn't just order them from Sears and Roebuck?"

"In 1797, the Venezuelans organized a conspiracy against the Spanish regime. The Spanish colonial governor in San Isidro worried that the rebels would seize the gold that the Spanish colonists had previously seized from the natives, chiefly the golden roof of the church, which was worth two million dollars."

"In 1797," Charlie repeated, brushing a stripe of the metal and pondering its current value.

"So the Spaniards found a sea captain whom they thought they could trust to take the roof panels to Spain. But they were wrong about him: He and his crew turned pirate. The loot's infamy made it impossible to traffic, though. So the pirates secured it here, intending to return when things cooled down. But they died in a cannon fight with a Spanish man-o'-war before they had the chance. And although there have been hundreds of attempts, no one found the treasure."

At the tunnel's end, half thinking he'd imagined the gold, Charlie turned, taking it in again. "Until you did?"

"Right."

"So why was Fielding hunting for it for the last couple of years?"

"He had his dive teams search in the wrong places, which allowed him to go about his real work. Eventually, he would have 'happened on' this cavern, I suppose."

Charlie bounced his beam off the floor to better see his father's face. "I don't get it. Why didn't you sell the gold off yourselves? You'd still have your secret cavern."

"For one thing, we would have had the same problem the pirates did."

"You and Fielding? Come on. You guys trafficked nuclear weapons."

Drummond shrugged. "I suppose we could have sold the treasure, if we had wanted to."

Charlie, whose upbringing had been modest bordering on Spartan, couldn't fathom his father's indifference. "You ever even consider it?"

"We were occupied with the job that brought us here in the first place."

"That gold is easily worth a hundred million —"

"We thwarted an actual nuclear incident in 2005," Drummond said with finality.

"You would at least have bolstered your Marvin Lesser cover. We could have lived in a villa on the Baie de Fort-de-France, driven Lotuses . . ."

"Living the Lesser cover would have been too time-consuming. I needed to be either in the field or at the office."

Drummond's base of operations was Perriman's musty, overheated, low-rent office in Manhattan.

"If memory serves, the washing machine is in here," he said, rounding a corner into another, darker cave, not much larger than a van.

And, other than dirt and a spiderweb the size of a volleyball net, empty.

If memory serves resounded harshly in Charlie's mind.

"Latex," Drummond said, batting aside the spiderweb. "Otherwise we'd get bugs."

He leaned into the damp, rocky wall and a door opened inward, revealing a small room. Charlie shot his Maglite beam inside, illuminating a white, top-loading Perriman Pristina, bound to a wooden pallet that rested on a dolly. The washer's housing had dings, spots of rust, and a light coating of muck. A good deal of the spongy orange insulation around the power cord appeared to have been chewed away, as if rats had mistaken it for cheese.

"Probably in all of history, this is the happiest a man has been at seeing a washing machine," Charlie said. "Unless it is just a washing machine."

Wrestling with the plastic strips binding the machine to the pallet, Drummond pried open the lid and peered in. He grunted his confirmation that the Pristina indeed contained a nuclear device.

Charlie felt a jubilation well up in him, like bubbles in champagne.

"Better check that the serial number's still there," Drummond called, interrupting Charlie's reverie of life with Alice enhanced by the proceeds from the treasure of San Isidro.

Charlie shone his light, revealing a metal band glued to the top of the control panel. He recognized the sequence of fifteen one- and two-digit numbers as the detonation code made to look like the manufacturer's serial number.

He waited for the reality of their accomplishment to sink in. Then he would leap up or shout or —

"Well, are you going to lend a hand?" asked Drummond, setting about getting the washer out.

"Okay." Charlie helped push the dolly into the tunnel. He guessed his father was averse to celebration prior to the completion of a mission.

"I was a big fan of our Pristina line even before we increased the cubic footage of the wash basket," Drummond said, batting aside a tree root. "No one's going to argue that we have the vibration control or that we're designed as well as some of the highfalutin brands, but you won't find as many wash cycle options at twice the money."

The spy had reverted to the old appliance salesman suffering from Alzheimer's. Charlie felt shortchanged; the transformation had robbed them of the shared exultation their discovery warranted. At least the timing wasn't terrible for once, he thought, until, displacing a vine, he saw a tall policeman standing near the beached runabout.

Drummond came to a halt.

Charlie had DeSoto's Beretta wedged into the back of his waistband. The policeman's gun was holstered on his right hip. His right hand was occupied with a flashlight.

Spinning toward them, the cop called out, "They're here!"

Five other officers came galloping from the parts of the tiny island that they had evidently been searching.

Returning his attention to Drummond and Charlie, the cop said, "Luckily the owner of the Riva installed LoJack."

32

Bream's condominium complex consisted of about fifty luxury duplexes, amalgams of classic colonial and modern beach houses with weather-browned clapboard walls and doors trimmed in a sandy cream. A sun-tanned blonde out of the pages of a swimsuit issue dozed, gently swaying in an oversized rope hammock by the pool. Lying on a floating chaise lounge was a second woman, possibly the blonde's younger and bronzer sister. She glanced up from her paperback and smiled as Stanley and Hadley got out of their new rental car.

Stanley gave a tight smile in response.

"Bonjour," Hadley said to the women. Nudging Stanley, she said under her breath, "Don't you want to give them a thorough once-over, make sure they're not sentinels?"

He looked down at her and saw her grin. He liked that she never missed a beat.

He hoped like hell that the switchblade

ring business was just an aberration.

She rang Bream's buzzer. A moment later the pilot appeared in the doorway, pulling an old sweatshirt over a pair of gym shorts. He might have put on the sweatshirt *before* opening the door, Stanley thought, but then he wouldn't have been able to show off his Muscle Beach abs. The pilot's eyes were rimmed red with sleeplessness, pleasing Stanley, who didn't like it when scumbags with that much free time for the gym slept well in their cushy island pads.

"Mr. and Mrs. Atchison, hey." The pilot acted pleasantly surprised. "Nice of you to drop by."

"We're here on United States government business," said Stanley, glad to be spared the song and dance of why the golf-obsessed CFO and his self-absorbed wife were on the pilot's front stoop.

Bream leaned closer, as if he hadn't heard right. *"Government business?"*

"We should go inside and talk about it," Hadley said.

The pilot shrugged. "So long as you don't mind a little mess. The maid hasn't been here, well, to be honest, ever."

Stanley stumbled, intentionally, as he followed Hadley across the threshold. He fell against Bream, who reflexively caught him by the shoulders.

"Excuse me," Stanley said, clinging to the pilot's waist to remain upright while he felt for a gun hidden in the small of the man's back.

Bream released him. "First thing on the maid's list will be that doorstep."

"Much obliged." Stanley added a pat of gratitude, feeling no holster in the vicinity of Bream's underarm, bolstering his confidence that the pilot had no weapon on him.

Still Stanley knew he needed to keep an eye out for a knife or gun produced from a hiding spot and against which his only defense would be the surveillance team in a hotel room fifty yards away. In such situations, the old joke went, the best your backup team can do is avenge you.

The condo itself wasn't as bad as advertised. Empty Red Stripe bottles, randomly flicked bottle caps and clothing abounded, but were lost in the grandeur of the space — ten-foot ceilings with gleaming ceramic tile crown molding, lustrous hardwood floors, and slabs of granite atop every counter.

Whisking a weight-lifting belt off the back of one of the dining room chairs, Bream ushered Stanley and Hadley into two of the other three seats at the table. "I can offer you water, or water with a tea bag in it," he said, indicating a stout Victorian teakettle on the burner.

"How about you just join us, Mr. Bream?" Hadley tapped the glass tabletop.

"Okay, then." Bream spun around a chair and sat so that his chest was pressed against the backrest, providing himself an extra layer of protection whether or not he consciously intended it. "So are you folks CIA or FBI or I don't need to know?"

"You were right the first time." Stanley leaned over the table to minimize the distance between them. "I take it you're aware that you've been ferrying some fairly sought after individuals."

"I heard about the dustup at the airport last night. You've gotta understand, though, I'm just a glorified courier. Those guys came to me through an American company that does lots of business here."

"We know all about them," Stanley said of Alice Rutherford's NSA unit, which had operated under the cover of a Maryland-based insurance agency and obviously hadn't placed background checks for charter pilots high on their priority list. "I want to let you in on something that the CIA has learned: John Townsend Bream is a thirty-nine-year-old resident patient at the Four

Oaks mental institution in Tunica, Mississippi. Has been for nine years."

Bream stared across the table in open-mouthed wonder. "So you're saying I'm a mental patient in Mississippi and, what, that I'm just imagining that I'm in Martinique?"

"That's possible. It's also possible that you assumed the identity of someone who wouldn't be going anywhere . . ."

Bream scowled. "Maybe the mental patient assumed *my* identity —"

"If I were you, I'd deny everything too," Stanley said.

"Don't worry, we're not here about that," Hadley added.

"Not necessarily." Stanley let a beat of silence underline the threat. "If you'll help us locate your two passengers, J. T., your only involvement in this case will be collecting the ten-thousand-euro reward for their arrest." In fact, Stanley expected Bream, or whoever he was, to wind up penniless in a federal penitentiary.

"Do you have any idea where they are?" Hadley asked.

Bream sighed wistfully. "I wish I did."

Stanley didn't believe him. "How about your best guess?"

"The only unusual part of the deal is they're planning on bringing back some supersize cargo. I'm supposed to find a bird with an extra-large cargo door. But that's okay. I once had a client who bought a statue in Athens and flew it back to Palm Be—"

Hadley cut in. "Do you have a rendezvous time or place?"

"They're gonna call me as soon as they find whatever it is they're looking for. They've got me booked for the whole week." Bream broke free of Stanley's stare, shifting his focus to the copper teakettle.

Hadley set her BlackBerry on the table and cupped her right knee, signaling to Stanley her belief that the pilot was dissembling. Stanley twisted his wedding ring, indicating his agreement.

The BlackBerry vibrated, rattling against the table. Hadley snatched it up.

"Well, how about that?" She relayed the text message. "Lesser and Ramirez have been captured at sea by the Royal St. Lucia Police Force and are on the way to a detention center."

Bream grinned. "Well, it's a good thing you came to see me, isn't it?"

33

The forty-foot Royal St. Lucia Police cutter chugged toward a remote island known as Detention III, a dismal, rocky place, apparently immune to vegetation, and so tiny that the architects had had no choice but to build up: The four-story brick prison stood at a slight incline. Painted battleship gray, it was part tenement house, part lighthouse, surrounded by two rings of twenty-foot-high electrified wire fencing and, in the event of a power outage perhaps, an outer fence topped with coils of old-school razor wire.

Drummond was handcuffed to a long bench in the police cutter's stern. If he had a plan, he had to have dreamed it up, literally, while napping during the hour or so since their capture. Escape seemed impossible to Charlie, who was handcuffed to the other end of the bench.

"Lesser" and his young accomplice "Ramirez" might be able to buy their way out, though. Charlie had gleaned that Detention III was administered by a private maritime security firm called Starfish, contracted by Saint Lucia, Dominica, Martinique, and other islands in the area.

In the rest of Charlie's scenarios, Detention III would effectively be a CIA detention center for him and Drummond. And the grave for Alice.

The washer sat on the prow, still strapped to its pallet. If the Saint Lucia policemen didn't already know what the Pristina held, they would soon, when one of them peered under the lid — which someone would do eventually, out of boredom if not simple curiosity. They would then place urgent calls to the bomb squad. Enter the Cavalry.

While tidier than the exterior had led Charlie to expect, Detention III's plain tile interior smelled like it was hosed down with seawater in lieu of proper cleaning. At the intake desk, three of the Saint Lucia cops uncuffed Charlie and Drummond and handed them over to two Starfish jailers, men who wore generic navy-blue fatigues with badges identifying them as Guard L. Miñana and Guard E. Bulcão. Both West Indians, Miñana and Bulcão spoke English with the sharp Hispanic accent familiar to

Charlie from Brooklyn.

Miñana, with his slight build, quiet demeanor, and round spectacles, could have passed for an actuary if it weren't for the worn wooden cudgel, which he gripped as if it were a cutlass. As the trio of Saint Lucia policemen prepared to depart, he slipped them a small stack of greenbacks. On the way out, one of the cops drummed the lid of the washing machine. Miñana smiled, seemingly pleased with his new purchase.

The heavyset Guard Bulcão meanwhile frog-marched Charlie to the wall next to the intake desk. "Face the wall, arms and hands apart," the guard barked, then proceeded to pat Charlie down.

Miñana gave the same treatment to Drummond, who, although awake, didn't seem that much more alert than when he was asleep.

"Now the both of you turn around real slow and take off all your clothing, drop it to the floor, then say 'Ah.' " Miñana demonstrated by sticking out his own birdlike tongue.

The guards probed Charlie and Drummond's mouths as well as every other body part where a weapon might be hidden.

Bulcão scooped their clothing and possessions from the floor, stuffing the lot of it into a large brown paper bag. "You guys can get this stuff back when the Martinique Police take you into custody in the morning," he said, sitting down at the desk and filling out the intake form on the computer, at four words per minute.

L . . . E . . . S . . . S . . . E . . . R . . .

To Charlie, anything other than C-L-A-R-K spelled hope.

The rough orange prison jumpsuit chafed Charlie's underarms and inner thighs as he mounted the three flights of stairs to the cellblock. Drummond followed close behind, trailed by Bulcão, who prodded them now and again for no apparent reason. Their footsteps in the cramped stairwell were amplified by the moisture on the moss-spotted walls, making it sound like a racquetball game was taking place.

"I heard about another innocent guy in a fix like this," Charlie said, as if trying to make small talk. "A war hero. Happened to be very wealthy too."

"From selling weapons?" Bulcão glanced sidelong at Drummond.

"I'm in appliances, actually," Drummond said in earnest. "Perriman."

"The guy I'm talking about made his fortune in the stock market," Charlie said.

"One of the jailers believed that he was innocent and let him 'pick the lock.' To show his gratitude, the guy gave the jailer five thousand dollars." Charlie and Drummond had about half that much in their wallets, last seen at intake being dumped into the brown paper bag.

Bulcão spat an invisible seed out of the side of his mouth. "I know you're not trying to bribe a law enforcement official, my friend."

Charlie widened his eyes. "Huh?"

"You guys are Public Enemies number one and number two in Martinique. If you somehow escaped, even without any help from me, and without Guard Miñana and Alejandro the maintenance guy looking the other way, we all would be let go, probably do some time too. Just speaking for me, say you gave me a million bucks. After I got out of the can — if I ever made it out — the cops would be watching for years to see how I'm paying my bills. Best job I could get probably'd be hacking pineapples, and if I spent more than a field hand's pay, the Inspector General'd throw me right back in jail. If my wife goes to some fancy store in town and gets herself a dress, back to jail. If my son gets a bicycle that isn't second-hand . . ."

In other words, Charlie thought, no.

34

Carlo Pagliarulo thought little of the Servizio per le Informazioni e la Sicurezza Militare, Italy's military intelligence agency. He got the message that SISMI felt similarly about him. In 2005, after twelve years as an operative, he was demoted to deputy operations coordinator, a glorified term for gofer, hardly the job he'd hoped for when first signing on out of college. The salary was decent, though, the benefits even better, and he felt secure in his job since terminations were rare in the intelligence community — agencies were usually reluctant to have an ex-operative out and about with a grudge, and, of course, secrets to sell. Yet within a year, due to chronic lateness to work, drunkenness, and allegations of sexual harassment, Pagliarulo was let go.

It was his big break.

Foreign intelligence services scoured associations of former soldiers and law enforcement officers in the hope of securing assets with half of Pagliarulo's skill set. Two weeks after his termination, he was making more per week than he had at SISMI just to run a pair of Geneva safe houses for MI6, a job that took no more than a couple of hours a day, leaving him plenty of time for other gigs, like the rendition in Gstaad and subsequent work as one of the captive's babysitters. And this evening alone, while shopping for groceries, he stood to pick up enough additional cash to buy a villa in San Remo.

At an under-heated but still crowded supermarket in Moudon, an unremarkable town about an hour northwest of Geneva, he resisted a fresh Parmigiano-Reggiano, instead dumping a cardboard cylinder of factory-grated Romano into his cart. The American woman was supposed to get as few clues as possible about where she was being held.

"Excuse me, do you know if the pesto's any good here?" asked a man pushing a cart half full of TV dinners.

His Italian was good, but he sounded American, and despite an Alpine parka over a French suit, he looked it. Like Gary Cooper, Pagliarulo thought.

"You want good pesto, you gotta go to

Corrençon," Pagliarulo said, which may or may not have been true, but it was their recognition code.

The man was Blaine Belmont, the U.S. embassy's legal attaché — official terminology for spook. Belmont pushed his shopping cart to the end of the line five deep at the butchers' counter, where a pair of bleary-eyed meat cutters worked in slow motion. Pulling his own cart up behind Belmont's, Pagliarulo checked for surveillance. Belmont nodded his own assessment that they were clean.

Pagliarulo wasted no time. "I'm doing grunt work for a guy who I've figured out is planning to flip an ADM to the United Liberation Front of the Punjab."

Belmont turned to face him, with no more excitement than if Pagliarulo had said it was going to snow tonight. "Yeah?"

"He's somehow getting it from another American. I've only caught a glimpse of that guy, over satphone, but I could ID him from photos. The deal is, he delivers the bomb, he gets back the package we're storing. I'm pretty sure you know her, Alice Rutherford."

Belmont shrugged.

"I could give you enough information to get the bomb and the bad guys," Pagliarulo added.

"If?"

Afraid the American would laugh at the price, Pagliarulo steeled himself. "One million."

Belmont studied a tower of sausage links behind the smudgy glass. "That's probably fair for a tip that bags a rogue WMD. Which means HQS'll have me counter six hundred and settle at seven-fifty — if they determine it's worth a dime. Seven-fifty about what you really figured on?"

Pagliarulo's confidence rose. "The price is one million dollars."

"Look, I don't give a crap, it's not my money. I'll tell you what, I'll talk to my chief of station when I get back to campus. If things go like they should, we'll have a dollar amount tomorrow morning at the latest. Then somebody will send a text message to your cell addressed to a Hans, asking Hans if he wants to down a few at the Hofbräuhaus, something like that. Delete the message, then hightail it to the *hypermarché* in Corrençon and we'll see if the pesto lives up to its reputation. Fallback, meet right here tomorrow, same time. How's that for a game plan?"

Pagliarulo's answer was forestalled by a butcher's summons to the counter. Presum-

ably to maintain his cover, Belmont bought
a chicken.

35

Sure, Alice would have preferred traipsing across an Alpine snowscape with the man she loved. But most of her life had been spent either dodging bullets or the metaphoric equivalent. Once, in fact, she'd been hit — just a flesh wound. At times, she would happily have paid for the peace and quiet now inflicted on her.

Especially because the Shaolin liked to practice meditation before a fight.

As Alice had learned in nearly a lifetime of devotion to Shaolin kung fu, channeling her inner energy allowed her to do things that her corporeal body alone could not. But it wasn't easy. Shaolin monks had to spend years mastering meditation before they were allowed to think about fighting, or as little as throwing a playing card. Prior to writing the book of Shaolin kung fu, the Buddhist monk Bodhidharma faced a wall for nine years without uttering a word.

Alice began by clearing her mind of all destructive energy. Combat, whether in self-defense or on the attack, demands pure intent, with all emotions under complete control, which is to say turned off.

After several hours, a plan came to her. It depended on a light switch plate the size of an index card that was fastened to the wall behind the sofa, two and a half feet from where she sat. If it were slung like a throwing star — the flat, star-shaped projectile that was the Shaolin weapon of choice — the light switch plate's speed might exceed fifty miles per hour, making its sharp corners as lethal as a dagger.

The plate was held to the wall behind the sofa by two ordinary slot-headed screws, one above the light switch, one below, the latter a bit loose already. It would be a simple matter to undo the screws.

Well, not exactly simple.

First, Alice needed to position herself on the sofa so that the light switch was directly behind her, concealed from her captors' view. Following each bathroom trip — they permitted her one every four hours — she inched closer. The fifth trip gained her position sufficient to execute sleight of hand, which time and again had proven the most useful component of her operations training. Sleight of hand is widely believed to work when the hand is quicker than the eye. In fact, it depends on psychology, primarily misdirection, larger actions distracting from smaller.

That her boots and socks had been confiscated presented an opportunity. When she stretched, which was only natural after so many hours on a sofa, the men's attention went to the action of her legs and her feet. Initially, the goons appeared to pay little if any attention to "itches" she simultaneously scratched on her face or behind her ears. Soon they seemed to pay none at all. Moreover, Frank spent a lot of time surfing the Web on his phone. Walt, though he never let go of his Walther PPK, spent hours picking his cuticles. And the third man in the rotation — the Teutonic-looking helicopter pilot Alice nicknamed the Baron — as in Red — sometimes nodded off for a few minutes.

After about thirty hours, the light switch plate was ready for deployment.

And when Frank came on duty in place of Walt, Alice was primed.

The Baron took over the armchair as well as the Walther while Frank disappeared into the kitchen with a bag of groceries. Alice heard him bring a pot of water to a boil, then add a bag of pasta. Warm air, laden with buckwheat and garlic, seeped into the living room.

A few minutes later, Frank brought her a Styrofoam bowl full of steaming macaroni. He'd topped it with grated Romano cheese, very likely an act of kindness. She put his gesture out of mind.

With the Baron's gun fixed on her, Frank undid the cords around her wrists, enabling her to take the bowl from the floor and use the plastic spoon in it to eat.

When she finished, she set the bowl on the carpet, and Frank kicked it away. The Baron gestured for her to extend her hands. Frank started to reapply the cords to her wrists, staying as far from her as he could, wary of a head butt or a bite. Which was exactly what Alice had been counting on. When he attempted to tie the first knot, she surreptitiously rotated her left forearm in such a way that the cord merely formed a loop. This was the key step in Houdini's famous rope-escape trick.

Finished, Frank retreated to a chair. Pretending to settle back onto the sofa, Alice worked her left hand free of the loop. It took her about thirty seconds, or about twenty-seven more than Houdini.

When Frank dug his phone from his pants, she swiped at the light switch plate with her freed left hand, dislodging the fixture from the wall. She caught it with her right.

Frank dropped the phone and drew a switchblade, snapping it open, as the Baron leaped up, aiming his gun.

Alice bent her arm ninety degrees at the elbow, drawing the makeshift weapon toward her abdomen. With a motion similar to that of a Frisbee toss, she sent the plate slicing through the air, so fast that it gave off a metallic whip-crack.

As the Baron leveled the gun at her, a corner of the plate sank into his neck as if his muscles were butter.

He plucked it free, but blood poured from his jugular. Eyes white, he collapsed over the armchair. His Walther dropped to the carpet, the powder blue fibers rapidly turning purple from the vital fluid streaming from his sleeve.

Alice needed to get to the Walther before Frank, who no doubt had a few combat tricks of his own. Plus he had a knife. She expected to sustain injuries, but never contemplated any outcome other than success. *To doubt is to be defeated before the enemy has thrown a single punch.*

She dove headlong for the Walther. Frank slipped on his phone and lost balance.

If not for the cords still restricting her legs, Alice would have fielded the gun, rolled into a kneeling position, and shot him. As it was, she landed on the carpet, her fingers within inches of the gun, as the Baron snatched the weapon off the sticky floor. With what seemed his last gasp, he tossed it over her head, to Frank.

The Baron thumped down from the chair, dead, momentarily pinning Alice to the floor and enabling Frank to get a firm grip on the gun.

"You are lucky we are not allowed to kill you," he said in a thick Italian accent.

"You have no such luck," Alice said.

But that was just adrenaline talking. She knew she would be in chains from here on in. At best.

36

Mountain peaks speared the feathery clouds above Saint Lucia. Through the window by his seat in the DC-3, Stanley could see the entire island, which was about half the size of Martinique. He watched the plane's shadow pass over verdant mountains and meadows with galaxies of vibrant tropical flowers. He'd thought all Caribbean islands looked alike, but this was Eden with typing-paper-white beaches.

Leaving Hadley to finish questioning Bream, he had initially procured a de Havilland Twin Otter seaplane to fly directly from Martinique to Detention III. He made the mistake of cabling the plan to headquarters. Saint Lucia's CIA base chief, a man named Corbitt, requested — demanded, really — that Stanley first come to Castries, the tiny capital city of Saint Lucia, to be debriefed. This was the base chief's right, to an extent. Headquarters needed Corbitt to exert his influence so that the Starfish people would hand the Clarks to the CIA rather than to their primary employer, Martinique's police department.

Stanley deliberated cabling Eskridge to request that the Europe division chief tell the Latin America division chief to order Corbitt to stand the hell down. Jesus Christ, a base chief on an island with the population of New Haven? His job was to make life *easier* for operations officers. Ultimately, Stanley decided that he could chat with Corbitt in less time than he would spend waiting for the succession of cables.

At George F. L. Charles Airport, before Stanley was halfway down the plane's stairs, someone thrust out a right hand. It was connected to a short and doughy fifty-year-old in a just-pressed suit, starched shirt, and gleaming golden 1990s power tie. "Clyde Corbitt," the man said, the words accompanied by a gust of wintergreen-minty breath.

Although Stanley had read nothing about Corbitt, not even his first name, he suspected he knew everything pertinent. Low rank, to begin with. GS-12, maybe. The "base" of which he was chief consisted of a nothing-special office. Either he was a one-man shop or he was aided only by an operations support assistant — government-speak

284

for "secretary" — almost certainly a local, whose most dramatic clandestine operation would be using the special telephone with the encryption device. And, as sure as the sky was up, this was Corbitt's first command, bestowed upon the career desk jockey either as a reward for twentysomething years of service or because Langley simply needed a body in Castries. Probably when he received the cable — C/O IN MARTINIQUE ON COVERT OP. GIVE HIM ALL ASSISTANCE HE DESIRES — Corbitt had an inkling that he was about to embark on the most exciting chapter of his tour.

Shaking the base chief's moist hand, Stanley said, "Great to meet you."

Corbitt had arranged for a driver and a stretch Town Car with tinted bulletproof windows. He helped Stanley into a cavernous backseat. The air was set to Arctic. Clad only in a polo shirt and chinos, like every other white-collar type in the islands except Corbitt, Stanley labored not to shiver. At least there was no need to worry that the ice in the minibar would melt during the trip to the American consulate, which the driver speculated would be half an hour on unusually congested roads.

Corbitt sat on the opposite leather bench,

285

his back to the Plexiglas divider separating them from the driver. "I took the liberty of scheduling us a lunch."

"Very thoughtful of you," Stanley said. "It's a shame I already ate lunch." In fact, that had been yesterday.

He just wanted to get to the damned detention facility.

As the limo rolled away from the airport, he asked, "How about saving some time and going straight to the dock?"

"Maybe just a drink then. We're meeting the CEO of Gotcha-dotcom." Corbitt's smile faded when Stanley failed to register recognition. "They're the world's largest private manufacturer of electronic surveillance devices."

"It sounds really interesting, but —"

"Trust me, bud, you do *not* want to miss this." With the air of a magician, Corbitt reached for the bar and unscrewed the top from the crystal scotch decanter. The round bottletop was sculpted with so many facets that it sparkled like a disco ball. "Would you believe this contains a camcorder that can hold sixteen hours of video and sound?"

"Only from context," Stanley said, to be polite. At least five years ago at headquarters, one of the Toy Makers showed him a collar stay containing far superior micro-camcorder technology. Probably Saint Lucia wasn't a Toy Maker priority. "The problem is time, or the lack of it. The men we're chasing —"

Putting a finger to his lips, Corbitt turned and glanced nervously at the driver. "We'll discuss it in the SCIF," he said as if any other course of action would be utterly reckless.

An hour later, Stanley was still in the sensitive compartmented information facility within the American consulate, a small suite of low-end offices on the ground floor of a white building resembling a sheet cake.

"One more time, for the record," said a flushed Corbitt, pushing the strands of hair back into place over his bald spot. "You expect me to tell Claude Beslon, the Saint Lucia chief of police, to just release the criminals into your custody, no questions asked?"

"Alleged criminals, for the record," said Stanley, even though the point of a secure conference room was that there would be no record.

"Can you even tell me whether or not these guys have actually done any of the stuff they're charged with?"

Stanley leaned forward over the confer-

ence table. "Listen, Chief Corbitt, if you
—"

"What? 'Need to know'?"

"I was going for a less trite way of phrasing it."

Corbitt jerked off his trifocals, which were misted by perspiration. "I *do* need to know. I don't want to be a prick, but, come on, bud, this is my turf."

"The chief of the Latin America division was told less."

"I've built relationships here based on trust. A flap and it all blows up. I mean, what in the world am I supposed to tell my friends here?"

"Make up whatever you think will impress them the most."

"How about a pinch of truth to fortify the deception?"

"What I can tell you is that Lesser and Ramirez pose a threat to national security with what's in their heads alone," Stanley said. It was certainly more than Corbitt needed to know, and, Stanley hoped, enough to placate him.

37

The three holding cells constituting the fourth floor were vacant, giving the stocky Starfish guard, Bulcão, his choice for Charlie and Drummond. He chose the smallest, an eight-by-ten-foot cement box fronted by a sliding wall of thick, rusty bars.

Inside the cell, two cots hung from a moldy wall by chains, one on top of the other. A metal sink sprouted from the adjacent wall. On the floor lay a filthy porcelain platform the size of a notebook, with slip-resistant shoe-shaped pads on either side and a hole in the center: the bathroom.

"Same interior designer who did Leavenworth, am I right?" Charlie asked Drummond.

Drummond put a hand to his chin and regarded the cell, as if giving the question serious consideration, until Bulcão propelled him and Charlie inside. Disappearing into the corridor, the guard heaved a breaker switch, sending the barred front wall shut with the force of a locomotive.

"Supper is at nineteen hundred," he called over the ringing echo as he disappeared down the stairwell.

Taking a seat on the lower cot, Drummond remarked, "Surprisingly comfortable." He looked underneath for the label, as though contemplating a future purchase. Finding nothing, he shrugged, then lay down.

"Don't go to sleep just yet," Charlie said.

"It's nighttime, isn't it? Speaking of which, I need my medicine."

"Actually, it's only about two in the afternoon," Charlie said, but he understood why his father would think it was nighttime. The perpetual fluorescent twilight of the cellblock offered no clue to the actual hour. Outside light didn't reach the floor, and for that matter, neither did fresh air. "Also we need you to come up with one of your exit strategies."

"You want to break out of here?" Drummond asked, more vociferously than discretion dictated. Or maybe it was just the relative silence. Only the buzz of the fluorescent tubes could muffle their conversation.

Charlie whispered, "Of course."

"Impossible."

"Why? This isn't exactly a state-of-the-art maximum-security penitentiary."

"Well, I have no idea how to do it."

"Listen, if any of your good old ex-colleagues gets wind of us being here — I should say *when* they get wind of us being here — we'll be lucky to get life imprisonment. We'll be lucky to get life anything."

Charlie paused to listen to a low-pitched whine, like that of a small plane, flying low.

Had a Cavalry hit team arrived on cue?

The noise died away.

He turned to his father. "You get the deal here, right?"

"Yes, yes, they'll neutralize us immediately. Alice will be in big trouble too. Where's our attorney?"

Charlie's hope shattered.

He gripped one of the rusty bars, expecting it to give a little.

Not a millimeter.

The rust wasn't even skin-deep. Drive a truck into these bars at full speed: The truck would be accordioned.

How about the breaker switch that opened the wall of bars?

Not just out of reach. Out of sight.

Studying the rest of the cell and coming up empty, Charlie remembered what should have been Step One.

Taking a seat beside Drummond, he asked, "What might a professional covert operations officer do to get out of a place like this — say, a guy who took the two-month Escape and Evasion course at the Farm?"

Drummond sat straighter, only an inch or two, but enough for Charlie to feel a spark of hope. "Spies are only human, and as such can't pass through solid walls."

"What about through bars?"

"There's a gap of, what, three inches between each?"

"But it's been done, right, and not just by people who went on extreme diets first?"

Drummond nodded. "You do hear those Wild West stories of horses tied to the bars and yanking them free."

"There's a start . . ."

"Taking into account the laws of physics, even with a team of especially strong draft horses, I'd say those stories are apocryphal."

"Well, we probably won't have the chance to put it to the test, given that we're three floors up from the ground and don't have a window. But, come on, jailbreaks are in the papers all the time."

"Because they're news. Are you thinking about breaking out of here?"

Charlie sighed. "It crossed my mind."

"Would you like to hear an interesting piece of information?"

"Does it have anything to do with getting out of a jail cell?"

"Yes."

"Then, yes, I'd love to hear an interesting piece of information," Charlie said, undoubtedly a lifetime first.

"In 1962 three prisoners at Alcatraz used spoons and a vacuum cleaner part to chisel away at the concrete around a fan vent leading from their cell to a utility corridor. They worked during the cellblock's music hour, so the guards wouldn't hear, and they concealed their progress with bits of false wall, good enough that the cell passed its inspections. When their escape route was finally ready, they left papier-mâché dummies in the beds, then they climbed through the fan vent — they'd removed the fan blades and the motor ahead of time. That got them into an air shaft. On the way out, they stole some raincoats, which they used to make a rubber raft to get across San Francisco Bay."

"I thought that no one ever escaped Alcatraz."

"Correct. They either drowned, or they were shot to death, I forget which."

"Whatever, you lost me at *spoons.*"

"They used the spoons to chisel away —"

Drummond was cut short by a gunshot-like crack that reverberated throughout the detention facility.

Charlie froze. "I don't think that's supper being prepared."

"Sounded like a three-fifty-seven," Drummond said. Lying down, he pulled the pillow over his head, presumably to prevent additional .357 reports from disrupting his sleep.

He was kept awake by the two men racing up the stairs, amplified by the damp concrete so as to sound like two bulls. The first to appear was Hector Manzanillo, the toothy Îlet Céron security man. The long barrel of his steel revolver shone in the wash of the overhead fluorescents. Miñana accompanied him.

Drummond rose from the bed. Recognizing Hector, he smiled.

"Hola, Señor Lesser," Hector said with warmth that seemed genuine.

Misgiving still flooded Charlie. A physiological malfunction, he hoped, a by-product of fatigue in combination with two weeks during which everyone he'd met had tried to deceive or kill him. The thing was, if Hector had known that the Riva was fitted with a LoJack, he might have bribed someone in the Saint Lucia police force so that he could sit back and wait for the elusive $100 million washing machine to be delivered to his confederate, Starfish Guard L. Miñana.

"You're not here to liberate us, are you?" Charlie said to Hector.

Hector flashed a car salesman's smile. "I am."

"If?"

"If you tell me the detonation code for the bomb hidden in the washing machine. Alejandro's wheeling it down to my brother's boss's cigarette boat right now. I can go down and test it. If it works, you're outta here."

"Detonation code?" Drummond shouted, prompting Miñana to blanch.

"There's something wrong with his head," Hector reassured the guard. "But the other one, he'll tell us."

Miñana, Hector, and Drummond all looked to Charlie, who did not know the code but could learn it with a quick glance at the Perriman Pristina's serial number. Were he to share that information, Hector would liberate them. From the cell. He wouldn't permit them to live much longer than that, though.

Charlie's only other idea was to stall until Drummond blinked on. "The code's on my cell phone," he said. "It's listed in my phone book under 'Dry Cleaners.' "

Hector looked to Miñana.

"They didn't have no phones on them," the guard said.

"Yeah, I figured it was a lie." Hector's big mouth twisted in disgust. "The college boys Lesser used to bring down from the States, they were all fucking math geniuses. Memorizing a thirty-number code for those dudes is like memorizing a name for me or you." He spun at Charlie. "I'll tell you something, man. There was some pretty slick spooks on Céron last week, packing state-of-the-motherfucking-art code-breaking software. Not one of them made sense outta that Bernadette and Antoinina thing, though. But you turned it into latitude and longitude in, like, five seconds. In your fucking head, too, am I right?" Without giving Charlie a chance to respond, he asked Miñana, "How does your piano piece go?"

The guard indicated the wall of bars fronting the cell. "He lays his fingers flat on the crossbar. Then I play them" — he raised the cudgel as if it were a hammer — "until he sings."

"Go for it, maestro," Hector said.

Miñana advanced to the crossbar. Hector pointed his revolver at Charlie, directing him to come forward.

Drummond looked on with anguish that Charlie judged, unfortunately, legitimate. And warranted.

"Stick your fingers through the bars," Miñana told Charlie.

The guard tightened his grip on the cudgel.

Charlie placed his fingertips on the cold and grimy crossbar and slid them forward, a hairbreadth at a time, scrambling meanwhile to come up with an alternative.

All he came up with was nausea.

"Wait," Drummond said — ordered, actually, in that Patton style he employed when he was at the top of his game and things got hot.

Electrified, Charlie withdrew his hands and looked to his father.

There was no fire in Drummond's eyes. "What if we work out some sort of arrangement, Hector?" he asked. As if he believed it was a truly novel idea.

"Like when the bomb gets sold, I get half of the money?"

"Something like that, yes! How about it?"

"I'd rather get all the money." Hector flicked his gun, directing Charlie to return his fingers to the crossbar to be broken.

Just then an explosion shook the entire building, slamming both Hector and Miñana against the floor.

Grabbing the bars kept Charlie upright.

Drummond plucked him away, flinging them both toward the corner of the cell near the cots. They landed on their knees. Drummond pressed a pillow over the back of Charlie's head, guided him into a crouch, then reached up, snaring the other pillow and placing it behind his own head — all of this was done in about a second and as naturally as if Drummond had been zipping his fly.

"Grenade?" Hector shouted to Miñana.

The guard gave no indication of having heard Hector, likely due to a near-deafening onslaught of machine-gun fire. Hurrying to his feet and waving for Hector to follow, he ran for the stairwell.

The barrage continued, darkening the air with dust and loosened mold. Individual bullets ricocheted, shattering glass or ringing against metal fixtures and furnishings. After about a minute, the gunfire dwindled to sporadic pops. Finally the building's familiar silence returned, followed by the sound of somebody running up the stairs

— somebody new, judging by the squeal of rubber-soled shoes.

38

The smog parted, revealing Bream standing outside Charlie and Drummond's cell. Dust whitened the pilot's hair and coated his face, except where blood dripped down. He carried an assault rifle, his pants pockets bulged with fresh mags, additional guns protruded from his waistband, and grenades dangled from his belt along with a sheathed knife almost as big as a machete.

"I had to whack an attractive lady from the CIA in the head with a teakettle to get out here, but otherwise you fellas did well in getting thrown in this clink," he said. "I had no damned idea how we were going to get you off Martinique after we took care of the bomb business."

Could this be Bream to the rescue? Charlie was at a loss.

The pilot stepped out of sight. The cell's front wall slid open with a resounding clank. Reappearing, Bream grumbled. "Course, now we gotta get off *this* island."

"Thank you, J. T.," said Drummond, exiting the cell.

"My pleasure." Bream drew one of the pistols from his waistband.

Charlie was too far away to do anything more than watch in horror: Had Bream decided that Drummond was now expendable? Drummond, for his part, barely registered the pistol.

"Either of you got a preference for the Glock 17?" Bream asked.

"I do." Drummond claimed the stout black pistol as if slipping on a glove. He racked the slide, inspected the chamber, hit a button ejecting the clip, and studied its contents. Satisfied, he rammed it home, checked the safety, and found a comfortable grip. "Nice."

"Fly me, you do get some frills," Bream said.

He offered Charlie a rugged gray pistol, a Sig Sauer. Charlie happily accepted, though in his estimation his skill as a marksman was limited to hitting a target directly in front of him. If the target was large and stationary.

He followed Bream and Drummond to the stairs, imitating the way they led with their guns, as if lighting the way.

At the lower landing, Bream sidestepped the crimson pool surrounding Miñana. "I got this guy and Ricky-Ricardo-on-Steroids on their way down from the cellblock. The other guard was dead on my arrival. Who else have y'all seen since you've been here?"

"We heard there was a maintenance man." Charlie tried to avoid looking at the dead man.

"Yeah. Overalls. Him and a ponytailed version of Ricky Ricardo and another thug were loading the washing machine onto a cig boat when I puttered up. They dropped what they were doing and started shooting at me. I had to fire blind." Bream pantomimed ducking beneath his boat's gunwale and firing without looking. "I got lucky," he concluded with false modesty.

Sticking his gun out ahead of him, he hugged the doorframe, then darted out of the stairwell.

"We're good for now," he called back.

Drummond exited with catlike movements similar to Bream's. Charlie brought up the rear, clumsily, slipping off the short step down from the landing to the intake desk, almost falling onto the bribe-proof Bulcão. The guard sat at his computer terminal as if still typing, except his neck was at an impossible angle and there was a dark cavity where his left eye had been.

"Don't forget your personal items," Bream said with a wave at the brown paper bag now labeled LESSER/RAMIREZ. "Also it might be slightly less conspicuous if you two changed out of those fire-colored jump-suits."

Charlie snatched the paper bag. Nause-ated by Bulcão's body, he raced to check the contents of the bag — everything was there — then rejoined Bream and Drum-mond.

Like them, he flattened himself against the front wall and peered out a window. The Hector look-alike and two other men lay outside, on the stretch of dirt between the building and the water. The late-afternoon sun cast long shadows of their bodies, mak-ing it all the more apparent that the men were not moving and never would again. If there were more of their gang, the barren, rocky ground offered nowhere for them to hide.

"Exactly what I was hoping to see," Bream said. "The only bad news is this rock's now too hot for us to do the bomb-for-Alice swap. We gotta go somewhere else."

"Where?" Charlie asked.

"There's an uninhabited spit of land a few clicks off Saint Lucia. An associate of mine is standing by with a scientist who'll do the nuclear physics version of kicking the ADM's tires." Bream started toward the giant speedboat bobbing at the dock, the washing machine visible in silhouette in the stern. "Here's hoping the dead guys won't mind if we take their boat."

39

Stanley peered through binoculars. Even before he could see the cigarette boat's javelin-like bow, he recognized the craft's characteristic contrail wake.

"It's them," he said, passing the binoculars to Corbitt, who was stretched out on a lounge chair on the second highest of three decks of what was listed in the House Intelligence budget as an Escape and Evasion Craft. In fact it was a svelte, seventy-foot-long pleasure yacht, or, as Corbitt put it, "a perk."

Setting down his scotch, Corbitt pointed the twin lenses at the tall building on the little detention island.

"Three o'clock," Stanley said.

Corbitt panned. "The cigarette boat?"

"Aye." There were no other boats in view for miles. There was nothing but water. "We need to get on commo and send a flash to headquarters."

"A flash cable? What for?"

"An eye in the sky."

"You're not kidding, are you?"

"Cigarette boats can go ninety miles an hour, and even faster if the folks on board don't mind burning out the engines. The DEA in Miami finds 'cigarette butts' all the time."

"But a *satellite?* What's wrong with radar?"

"Practically useless against craft that fast."

"Okay, high-speed helicopters?"

"They're fine, but to chase anyone, they'd have to get out here, by which time . . ."

Corbitt sat up, still looking through the binoculars. "I can't make out anyone on the boat," he said. "I mean, I'm sure there is someone, but —"

Frustration cooked Stanley. "It's. Them."

"A gut thing, eh?" Corbitt said, no doubt itching to recite the line emblazoned on posters in Langley's corridors since the sixties: *The Agency has hundreds of brilliant analysts so that operators won't have to rely on hunches.*

"This isn't some kind of sixth sense," Stanley said. "Just two hours ago, after learning that the targets were at Detention Three, Carthage KO'd one of our officers and gave her backup team the slip. In any case, why would a cigarette boat be at a

306

detention facility?"

Corbitt hoisted himself from the chaise and walked aft, struggling to maintain his balance, a landlubber if there ever was one. "Javier," he called up to the bridge. "Radio Detention Three and see if anyone's escaped or anything like that."

He returned to his chair and his drink while the man at the helm punched a number into the radio set.

Stanley stared down at his own ordinary cell phone, a temporary replacement for the satphone that Drummond Clark had thrown into the Baie de Fort-de-France last night. Nothing close to a signal now, damnably.

Corbitt patted him on the shoulder. "You know the playbook, bud," the base chief said. "I need confirmation. If it just turns out to be a drug dealer visiting an inmate, my division chief would come down on my ass like you wouldn't believe."

"If it is the men we're after, and you lose them, what will your division chief do?"

"It certainly wouldn't be my fault for going by the book. Do you have any idea what it costs to redirect a satellite? More per hour than flying a 747."

This was why Stanley admired the Cavalry. Their operations incurred collateral damage — put bluntly, innocents fell victim to cross fire — but at least there was action.

"Nobody's answering," Javier called down from the bridge, mystified.

Corbitt relented, cabling the chief of the Latin America division, who flashed the satellite request to headquarters.

Twenty-one minutes later, headquarters approved a redirect. Thirty-four minutes after that, the Latin America desk had a picture. Given the analysts' subsequent assessment that the cigarette boat had landed at one of fourteen small islands within a fifty-eight-minute radius of the detention center, that imagery came approximately three minutes too late.

40

It was hard to believe, but the nuclear weapon inspection site was idyllic, a sparkling white beach ringing a secluded clear blue lagoon. A canopy of palm fronds provided both shade and protection from eyes in the sky. While Drummond lay against a coconut palm, watching the gentle waves curl and whiten, Charlie stood on the beach alongside a slight, bespectacled man of about forty who had introduced himself as Dr. Gulmas Jinnah, nuclear physicist. They watched Bream and his brawny "associate" — whom he called Corky — haul the washing machine off the beached cigarette boat.

Jinnah certainly looked the part of a scientist — he was thin enough that Charlie would have believed he absentmindedly forgot to eat. In spite of the high temperature, the man wore a starched white long-sleeved dress shirt and a tie.

"So you are from where?" he asked.

"Brooklyn." Charlie hadn't anticipated that the serious man, about to inspect a nuclear weapon, would shoot the breeze.

"I so would love to go to New York City someday."

Charlie took that to mean that New York City wasn't the bomb's destination.

"How about you?" he ventured. "Where are you from?"

"Lahore. Underrated city. Definitely worth a visit if it were not for the strife in the Punjab. I hope we shall see a resolution to it soon."

According to Alice, a Muslim separatist group from the Punjab had dispatched representatives to Martinique to purchase the ADM the same day that Fielding died. Charlie now speculated that, having left Martinique empty-handed, the same group had devised the rendition plan.

Taking into account Bream's tight time-table for the delivery of the bomb, Charlie asked, "So you figure the strife will end with the 'special occasion'?"

"What special occasion?"

"Isn't there a special event in India a few days from now?"

"Vasant Panchami?"

"What's Vasant Panchami again?"

"It's a Hindu festival celebrating Saras-

310

wati, who many believe is a goddess of music and art."

"So the ADM will be part of the Vasant Panchami fireworks?"

Jinnah stared at Charlie as if he were speaking an alien tongue.

"I take it Vasant Panchami's not the day you're planning to detonate the bomb?" Charlie said.

"*Detonate* the bomb?"

"What else would you do with it?"

The Indian drew away. "I am here on behalf of the Bhabha Atomic Research Center in Trombay. Our aim is to prevent illegal arms dealers like your father from selling such weapons to parties who would not hesitate to detonate them — for instance, the terrorists in the Punjab."

Jinnah was an excellent liar, Charlie thought, or an even better cutout.

What mattered was that Jinnah was not an excellent physicist, or at least that his arsenal of electronic gauges would fail to detect that the ADM's uranium pit contained the enriched uranium version of fool's gold.

After a careful examination, the Indian deemed the weapon "the real deal," to the satisfaction of everyone but himself.

Bream placed the satellite phone call, commencing Alice's liberation, and video of her face flickered onto his satphone display, terribly out of focus. Still, Charlie drank it in.

The picture sharpened, revealing her to be standing outdoors, in a rural location, at nighttime. She was pale and, despite a parka and a thick woolen cap, shivering, exhaling streams of vapor that were illuminated by a streetlamp.

"Chuckles," she exclaimed. Another of her safety codes. "How's it going?"

"It's a laugh a minute here," he said, signifying all was well on his end. Relatively.

"And my other friend?"

Bream pushed a button near his mouthpiece, possibly initiating voice alteration. "Hang on," he said. He angled the lens at Drummond, who had fallen asleep. "Captain, you have a call."

Drummond rose wearily. He eyed the satphone's display without recognition. "How are you?"

"Very excited about the prospect of using a ladies' room without people watching me."

"Oh."

"Okay, enough chitchat." Stuffing the satphone into a pocket, Bream waved at the washing machine. "Time for you fellas to step up to the plate."

Charlie suddenly thought of all the things that might have gone wrong with the bomb's delicate inner workings after sitting in a damp cave for weeks and then bouncing around the Caribbean. "Dad, do you remember how to use this?" he asked.

"Of course," Drummond said. "I helped write the Perriman manual."

"This is the souped-up model."

"Oh, right. It isn't an ordinary washing machine, is it?"

"Right." Charlie felt the weight of his responsibility triple.

With a yawn, Drummond stepped to the water's edge, then smiled as the bubbly surf trickled through his Crocs' ventilation holes. Corky traced Drummond's movements with an Uzi. In his late twenties with long tangles of sun-bleached hair, Bream's associate could have passed for a surfer if it weren't for the especially grim Grim Reaper tattooed over much of his back, its outsized bloody sickle curling around his neck.

Charlie carefully opened the washing machine's lid. Even the fool's gold of uranium was highly volatile, and it was hot enough inside the machine to broil a chicken. Hoping to sidestep the demonstration altogether, he pointed out the steel strip on the control panel. "The code is this sequence of fifteen numbers," he said. "Five for each of the PAL knobs inside."

"Ah." Jinnah squinted. "Show us, if you please."

"Yes, if you please," Bream repeated, without any of the cordiality.

Charlie bent into the machine. He cleared a path through the jungle of wires to the permissive action links, three big numeric dials, like those on floor safes. If he were to misdial the fifteen numbers more than twice, an anti-hacker device would render the system unable to detonate. Or worthless for today's purposes.

He carefully clicked to the first number, 37. Sweat stung his eyes. Millimeters at a time, so as not to dial past a number, he input the remaining two-digit numbers on the first dial, then began on the second.

In a bit under five minutes, though it seemed like well over an hour, he finished. Now, even if he had correctly entered the code, who was to say that the sensitive detonation mechanism still functioned?

The readout panel duct taped to the inside of the lid was lifeless. Then it began to glow a pale green. Black characters formed against the backdrop . . . *20:00.* And a second later, *19:59.*

Charlie pumped a fist. "Your turn," he said to Bream.

His eyes on the readout and his face a shade whiter than before, Bream snapped open the satphone. "Okay," he said into it. "Give her her bus fare and her parting gift."

Alice's captors had agreed to hand over ten 100-euro notes and a loaded gun before releasing her in proximity to public transportation, presumably somewhere in Europe. She would then tell Charlie that she was safe.

Bream showed his satphone to Charlie. On the display, Alice stuffed a sheaf of bills into her parka, checked the mag in a pistol, then walked backward, keeping the barrel leveled at whoever held the satphone on her end.

"We're good, Chuckles," she said. "See you in St. Louis."

By St. Louis she meant Paris. Dr. Arnaud Petitpierre, the neurologist who ran the Alzheimer's clinic in Geneva, had a daughter studying art history at the Sorbonne. Without drawing undue attention, Petitpierre could minister to Drummond at a safe house with a view of the Île Saint-Louis — hence the code name.

Charlie watched Alice recede down a deserted, snow-lined country road. The odds of seeing her again seemed awfully long.

His thoughts were interrupted by Bream. "Chuckles, how about you do everyone here a favor and turn off the nuclear bomb?"

Once Charlie did, Bream let out a whoop, quickly adding, "Now let's get the hell off this rock."

Corky dollied over a black plastic case big enough to hold a man. The ZODIAC logo gave Charlie a clue to both its contents and Bream's plans. He knew Zodiac boats as the wobbly rubber rafts on *The Undersea World of Jacques Cousteau.*

Watching Jinnah help Corky lower the case to the sand, Charlie asked Bream, "Is that our ride home?"

Bream laughed. "No, that's transport to the mother ship for Doc Jinnah and Corky and their passenger." He cocked his head at the washing machine. "The Culinary Institute of America won't think to look for a rubber raft. You, me, and Pop can take the rent-a-plane Corky and the doc came in." He pointed to a clearing on the far side of the woods. The tail of a small airplane glistened in one of the few rays of light that pierced the ceiling of branches and leaves.

"To where?"

"You want to go back to Europe, right?"

"You'll take us there?"

"Would if I could. That plane is from Saint Lucia and it's not good for much more than a dime tour of the area. But if we fly it back to Castries, you won't need to go through customs — there's no need for you to even leave the tarmac. Just play rich tourists and buy your way onto a general aviation flight. Go to some little airfield in Europe."

It sounded like a fine plan to Charlie except for one large blemish: Bream's clear incentive for him and Drummond to be dead. Then again, the pilot knew that if he let them live, they wouldn't dare go to law enforcement. So, from his standpoint, giving them a lift ensured their silence as well as bullets would. Allowing them to leave safely also meant two less bodies left on his trail, and no risk of reprisal from Alice or Drummond's former colleagues.

Charlie looked to Drummond for reassurance. His father just stood watching the Zodiac assembly like a kid at the circus. From the big case, Corky had produced bright red fiberglass boards that snap-locked together, forming a plastic deck big enough to support a Clydesdale. Jinnah meanwhile unrolled a giant rubber bladder and plugged an electric pump into a portable generator.

317

In seconds the bladder took the shape of a hull and the men transformed metal pipes into a cargo hold and a base for seats and a control panel.

Turning back to Bream, Charlie asked, "Wouldn't two tourists suddenly chartering a flight to Europe set off alarm bells?"

"Yeah. That's why your pilot files a local flight plan. Once you're out of Saint Lucia, he'll call in a revised or emergency flight plan — he'll know how to play it. When you land, you may have to answer a few questions . . ."

"But at least we'll be out of Dodge," Charlie said. He was generally satisfied with the plan, in no small part because it gave him one more chance to draw Bream out. And this time, he knew just how to do it.

41

The twin-engine plane climbed into clouds.

"You have to tip your hat to those Indians," Charlie said to Drummond, across the aisle in the first of three rows. "I mean, all the intelligence and law enforcement agencies in the world couldn't find us, but somehow they did. And now they've managed to score themselves the terrorists' equivalent of the Holy Grail."

Despite the conversation, following the bumpiest takeoff since Kitty Hawk, Drummond nodded off.

As Charlie had hoped, Bream turned around in the cockpit. "The thing you've got to ask about your so-called intelligence agencies is just how bright their best and brightest really are," the pilot said. "For one thing, why are they making less money than plumbers?"

"Or even charter pilots?"

"Some charter pilots do better than others."

Charlie sensed Bream could be persuaded to talk. He had first noted the pilot's surplus of pride during their flight from Switzerland, when Bream gloated over fooling Charlie with his Skunk Works story. While clothing that made a man more difficult to identify was de rigueur in Spook City, Bream dressed to accentuate his physique. When fleeing the cellblock, he'd taken precious time to detail his "lucky" marksmanship on arrival at Detention III. And he was burning now to claim his share of credit for this operation. Charlie could practically feel the heat.

"So how do you think the Indians found us?" Charlie asked.

"You know I can't tell you that."

"So they did tell *you?*"

"Gimme a molecule of respect here, Chuckles."

Bull's-eye. "I thought you're just a glorified courier."

Bream sat back, shifting his focus to the instruments.

Charlie feigned interest in a cloud.

Bream cleared his throat. "After Fielding bit the dust, I heard from one of his goons, a guy named Alberto."

Drummond stirred. "Gutierrez?"

"Know him?" Bream asked.

"Alberto Gutierrez and Hector Manzanillo were practically joined at the hip," Drummond said.

Had the mention of the criminals sparked another episode of lucidity?

"Yeah, he was working for Fielding in Martinique," Bream said. "He offered me a piece of intel so he could raise bail and have flight money. A hundred grand. It was the best investment I ever made. The Injuns are gonna pay me so much, even you couldn't calculate the rate of return, Charlie."

"So this guy, Alberto, knew about the bomb?" Charlie asked Bream.

"The bomb wasn't exactly a secret at that point. The Culinary Institute of America had sent an interrogation unit to Îlet Céron. NSA and Defense Intelligence Agency, pretty much the same deal. But Alberto told me one thing that he hadn't told anyone else: Korean Singles Online-dot-com."

Charlie looked to his father for an explanation, but Drummond was drifting back to sleep.

With the satphone, Bream beckoned from the copilot's seat. Charlie braced himself against the bulkhead and entered the cockpit in time to see the pilot open the Internet to a Korean Singles Online page dominated by a photograph of "Suki835," a chubby teenage girl with warm eyes and a pretty smile.

Bream moused to her left earring, then zoomed in by a factor of a hundred or so, revealing eleven rows, each with ten columns of six seemingly random alphanumeric sequences. "If you figure out how to decipher this shit — which, thanks to some very expensive software and ten espressos, I managed to do — you get, *Hounds lost Rabbit and Rabbit Junior at Utica and Fillmore in Brooklyn at half-past midnight.* That mean anything to you?"

It had been two weeks, but Charlie would never forget the middle-of-the-night car chase through Brooklyn. A pair of Cavalry gunmen just missed him and Drummond. About fifty times.

"No idea," he said.

Dropping the satphone back onto the copilot's seat, Bream said, "That's how Fielding communicated with his henchmen while they were hunting for you, Rabbit Junior. Reading through the rest of Suki's private messages, I got the gist of the story. In one entry, Fielding warns that you boys might make a run to an experimental Alzheimer's clinic in Tokyo, Jerusalem, or

Geneva. And I already knew you'd gone to Europe — remember, I recommended the charter pilot who flew y'all to Innsbruck. So I thought, How many Alzheimer's clinics could there be in Geneva? I put tails on a few Swiss docs. A day later, Arnaud Petitpierre drives to Gstaad and voilà . . ."

"I'm amazed," Charlie said, which was an understatement. Not only had he just been handed proof of his and Drummond's innocence; he now saw Bream's laconic cowboy act as exactly that, an act. Clearly the pilot had managed every facet of the operation. The odds were irresistible that he would transfer the ADM personally.

The multimillion-dollar question was: Where?

"So have you got your mansion picked out?" Charlie asked.

"Haven't been mansion-hunting yet. I'll be sure and send you a postcard, though."

Charlie played wistful. "I'm sure you've at least thought of how you'll celebrate your successful delivery of the ADM."

"Not really. I play 'em one at a time, and this ballgame ain't over."

"If it were me, as soon as I got paid I'd head straight to the best restaurant in town, order a bottle of 1954 Louis Latour and a lobster the size of a tricycle."

Bream scoffed. "It'll be 2010 Budweiser, thank you, and, if you must know, a rack of ribs."

"The collateral won't affect your appetite?"

Bream reddened. "*Collateral?* You've been hanging out with too many 'governmentals.' You mean 'innocent folks turned to red mist'?"

"I suppose so."

"If I told you it keeps me up just about every night, would that make me less of a villain in your eyes?"

"Should it?"

"Yeah. It's not an easy decision to make. But our country needs the wake-up call. If the best and brightest were really on this case, it wouldn't be so easy to pull off."

That was the last thing Charlie heard.

Until the air, rushing like a freight train into the cabin, woke him.

The cabin door dangled out of the plane.

Bream was gone.

Maybe he was beneath the chute that bloomed behind the plane, framed by a violet sunset.

Charlie was back in his seat, buckled in. The sky was really beautiful, he thought.

For some reason, he wasn't worried. Plus

Drummond was still asleep. If this were any big deal, he'd be up, right?

If not, there was a long way to go before they splashed into a sea so mild that it probably wouldn't hurt. Warm probably. Beautiful too. Molten bronze in the waning light.

"Hypoxia," Drummond shouted over the gale. He rubbed sleep from his eyes.

"Is that what this is? That's not good, is it?"

"Correct."

The incoming air chilled the cabin. Charlie's thoughts began to clear. "Why not?"

"It affects people differently, but in all cases it's brought about by a reduction in oxygen." Drummond unfastened his seat belt. "Either the cabin needs to be properly pressurized or we need supplemental oxygen."

Charlie looked out a porthole. No longer any sign of Bream.

Wobbly, Drummond started into the cockpit, reaching for the W-shaped yoke in front of the empty pilot's seat. He toppled, his forehead cracking into the yoke. He fell sideways, landing on the other seat, and lay motionless.

The plane started to dive.

"Dad!"

No response.

"Come on!"

Nothing, not even as the buzz of sky rushing past built to a holler. Charlie wanted to get up and rouse Drummond, but he remained seated. His limbs wouldn't respond to his will.

Adrenaline rocketed through him.

Still, he couldn't move.

42

Bullets bit into Alice's parka, creating a cloud of ice, fabric, and goose feathers. When the cloud dissipated, it appeared as if she'd been replaced on the dimly lit bus shelter bench by a rag doll, her head hanging grotesquely in one direction while her body slumped the other way, flattening against the sidewall housing a Christmas movie poster.

Having pretended to let her go, Walt and Frank emerged from behind the snowy woods across the otherwise deserted rural road, intent on confirming the kill and reclaiming the Glock, as well as the cash.

Halfway across the street, they realized they had not shot Alice but a mannequin made of packed snow, and adorned with her parka, jeans, and hat.

"I'll let you live," she called out to them from the thick woods behind the bus shelter. "You're just going to have to put down your weapons and then slide them to me along the pavement."

Walt flipped the selector on his silenced gun to an automatic setting and sent a torrent of bullets in the direction of her voice. Brass casings shimmered in the scant light as they arched over his shoulder and tapped onto the icy asphalt.

For this reason, when Alice had called to them, she'd pressed her tongue flat against the base of her mouth and pushed the sound from her abdomen through her larynx in the direction of her palate. This manner of throwing one's voice tricks listeners into believing the voice is emanating from a greater height than it actually is.

She fired back, once.

Walt lay dead on the street long before the report had finished resounding through the bare woods.

The muzzle flash having revealed her position, Frank whirled, firing.

She dove headlong toward the bus shelter. The metal sidewall offered a measure of protection. One of Frank's bullets sparked against it, cracking the glass over the movie poster so that it appeared to be a jigsaw puzzle of Santa Claus.

Alice returned fire. Her bullet struck Frank's right wrist. His gun clattered against the ice, bouncing toward her.

"Good job, Frank," she said, springing to her feet. She stepped out from behind the bus shelter. "Now, what I really want is your coat." She had only her T-shirt and underwear to counter the well-below-freezing night. "Unbutton it, shake off one sleeve at a time, then toss it to me."

Gritting his teeth against the pain of his wound, the hulking Italian complied.

Before daring to pluck the overcoat off the road, she wedged her gun against Frank's kidney. With her free hand, she patted him down, turning up his switchblade as well as a satphone and, an unexpected bonus, Mercedes keys. She pocketed the lot, saying, "As if the bus driver was going to have change for a hundred-euro bill."

The big man gripped his injured wrist and moaned.

"That's what you get for trying to kill me."

She prodded him into the woods until they were out of sight of any passing motorists. About twenty yards in, she kicked his knees out from under him. Toppling forward, he attempted to break his fall with his bad arm. He came to rest on his side in a pile of snow, sticks, and dry leaves.

Squatting beside him, Alice pressed the muzzle of her gun against the base of his skull. "I don't want to shoot you again," she said. "And I won't if you tell me who hired you —"

He rolled to his left, at the same time launching his steel-toed boot at her face.

She ducked, slashing his ankle with the side of her hand, breaking bone.

With a scream, he leaped to his good foot and threw a roundhouse that eluded her parry, hitting her jaw like a truck.

The world flickered. She dropped against frozen ground.

He sat astride her stomach, trying to wrest the gun free of her grip, leaving her no choice but to pull the trigger.

The shot snapped his head backward. Hot blood lashed her. He thumped into the snow and lay still, the angle of his head oddly similar to that of the mannequin in the bus shelter.

Admittedly not one of the six billion most patient people in the world, CIA case officer Blaine Belmont had paced perhaps five miles in his office at the American embassy in Geneva until, finally, a cable from a deputy director of operations authorized payment of $1,000,000 to Carlo Pagliarulo. As soon as the Italian gave up the goods, the funds would be wired to him.

But now Belmont was unable to reach him. Fighting to keep the exasperation out of his voice, he instructed the techs to triangulate Pagliarulo's cell phone.

Two hours later, the CIA officer stood over the Italian's corpse about fifty feet into a wooded area on the road to La Vernaz, an hour east of Geneva.

"Not the end of the proverbial road," Belmont told his team, if only to boost his own spirits. The snow mannequin in the bus shelter and the pair of bodies were almost as good as videotape of what had taken place there. Unfortunately, Rutherford could be anywhere by now.

Within twenty minutes, things were looking up. Belmont flipped open his phone to watch two-day-old National Geospatial-Intelligence Agency KH-13 satellite overpass footage of Pagliarulo hauling an unconscious young woman from a black SUV to the small La Vernaz farmhouse that had been rented a week beforehand by a man named Hans Baehler.

The landlord, whom Belmont's people woke as they raced by car to the farmhouse, said that Baehler had paid cash and seemed like a nice person in his e-mails, which turned out to be untraceable. Belmont would have been surprised to hear anything different.

At the isolated farmhouse, the CIA team found ample traces of both Rutherford and Pagliarulo, along with the body of helicopter pilot and all-around German thug Lothar von Gentz, apparently stabbed to death with a light switch wall plate.

There were no signs of current life in the farmhouse, though. Nor would there be, in all probability, until the landlord found a new tenant.

This was the end of the proverbial road.

"Shit," Belmont said.

He spent much of the night back at his office putting all but the expletive into his report.

43

The cold air screaming into the cabin helped Charlie regain control of his muscles. His panic abated, or at least moved aside, allowing him to wonder how his father was doing and hope that, if he was okay, he would know what the hell to do now.

Drummond was crumpled on the copilot's seat, breathing, but not much more.

Charlie jumped up from his seat in the cabin, but the rush of air swept him off his feet, sucking him like a dust ball toward the aperture where the cabin door used to be.

He grabbed for the bulkhead. Gritting his teeth, he pulled himself around it and into the cockpit. As he noticed the Caribbean leaping toward him, his stomach jumped into his throat.

He glanced at the instrument panels. There were a hundred times as many dials, knobs, buttons, gauges, and other glass bubbles as there were controls in the Play-

Station aerial dogfight game that constituted his aviation experience. Save the pair of yokes, one in front of each seat. A yoke acted like a steering wheel. It also moved the nose of the plane up and down. At least on PlayStation.

He grasped the yoke in front of the vacated pilot's seat and pulled it toward him.

The nose of the plane turned up. Too much — the sensation was just like that on a roller coaster when the car transitions from plummet to climb. Gravity thrust Charlie backward. He grabbed the seat in time to avoid being thrown back into the cabin.

PlayStation didn't do this.

He reached forward and ever so gently nudged the yoke forward.

The plane fell into a nosedive.

Stomach imploding, Charlie gripped the seat so tightly that he tore the leather at a seam. He tried the yoke again.

The nose turned up, and — incredible — the plane settled. But for how long?

Out of tricks, he knelt by Drummond, shaking him. Drummond rolled the other way.

"Dad, please?"

Drummond struggled to open his eyes. "Where are we?"

"Airplane. Sky. Caribbean somewhere. You with me by any chance?"

"Check." Sitting up, Drummond glanced out the cockpit windows. He exhibited no alarm. Possibly a good sign. "Are you okay?"

"I am if you know how to fly," Charlie said.

"You mean a plane?"

Charlie battled terror to think of a way to communicate the exigency in a way that might spark his father's memory. "Bream's trying to make it look like we died in a plane crash."

"What kind of plane?" Drummond asked.

"This kind."

Struggling to sit up, Drummond took inventory of the cockpit. "Use the autopilot," he said. His speech was sluggish. He tried to reach forward, toward the instrument panel. His arm seemed leaden. He teetered.

Charlie propped him up. "Hang in there, Dad," he said.

As Drummond tried to recompose himself, Charlie searched for the autopilot. The search could take half an hour. If there even was an autopilot.

He looked back at Drummond, who appeared transfixed by the passing clouds.

"Where is the autopilot?"

"Oh, that, yes, right." Drummond seemed grateful for the reminder. "Sorry, we need to find someone to help."

"Say you were the only person on the plane?"

"I'd radio for help."

Charlie dropped into the pilot's seat, snatched up the headset, and brought the microphone to his lips. "Mayday! Mayday!"

No response.

Drummond pointed at the talk switch located on the top of the yoke.

Charlie hit it. Then tried more distress calls.

Still nothing. Not even a crackle.

He wiggled the headset jack at the base of the instrument and tapped the radio. The channel selector read 118.0 MHz.

He looked to his father. "Is there an airplane equivalent of nine-one-one?"

"I believe so."

Charlie waited.

"Any idea what it is, Dad?"

"Maybe one-two-one-point-five?"

Charlie clicked the knob to 121.5. "Mayday! Mayday! Mayday!"

Only static back.

"Mayday!"

Drummond said, "It's often out in places like — " He fell backward, out cold before

336

the back of his skull struck the headrest.

"Dad?"

44

Something beneath Drummond began buzzing. An egg timer, it sounded like.

Wedging his hand between his father's left leg and the seat cushion, Charlie plucked out Bream's satphone. Forgotten in haste. Or had the twisted fuck left it behind so he could call and deliver a parting shot?

Charlie thrust the phone to his ear. "Cockpit."

"Listen, J. T. Bream," came a voice through the earpiece, "I know where you are, and I'm going to come and kill you if —"

Charlie couldn't believe his ears. "Alice?"

"Chuckles?" She remained the pro, avoiding using a real name, and, at the same time, employing her safety code.

"Yeah," he said, adding a safety code of his own: "It's a laugh a minute here."

"Did you get away from Bream?"

"We're away from him, put it that way."

"Your dad?"

"He got knocked out when Bream bailed, but I think he'll be okay, if, to make a long story short, you can help me land a plane."

"Maybe," she said. Charlie assumed she hadn't blinked. "Do you know what kind of plane it is?"

"Propeller . . ."

"Start reading off the labels on the instruments."

"There are labels on most of them —"

"Read whatever you see." She was as cool as a call center operator, which had the effect of dissipating enough of Charlie's panic so that he could focus. "Maybe a model name?"

He found one on the yoke. "Beechcraft."

"Good. How many propellers are there?"

He checked the side windows. "One on each wing."

"Okay. How about this? When you got going, did the engines make a noise like a car starting, or did they whine?"

"A whine, I think."

"Turboprop, then. What seat are you in?"

"The one on the left."

"Pilot's seat, excellent. Directly in front of you there should be a glass-covered dial that indicates what's known as 'attitude.' "

Finally, something PlayStation had. "Yeah.

Tells you which way's up, right?"

"Exactly. Blue's the sky, brown's the dirt, and the little white bars in the middle are our wings."

"Well, if it's working, we're flying level now."

"Good. Now, just to the right you should see an instrument that looks like an old-fashioned clock."

"Uh-huh."

"Our altimeter. I know you know what that is. Should be a window across the top half with numbers. Can you read them?"

Charlie's stomach settled, somewhat. Alice knew what she was doing; she wasn't just trying to calm him down. "About fifty-two hundred feet."

"Stable?"

"I think so."

"Great. To the left is a speed indicator. Read it to me."

"One-ninety." According to the gauge, it was 190 KIAS. Knots? Knots Incorporating Air Speed? No time for Q & A.

"We have to find out how much flying time we have. On the wall to your left, there should be two gauges on a separate panel."

"Okay."

"Those are the fuel gauges."

"There's one-twenty-five on both gauges."

Not a bad total, he thought, if this was anything like a car.

Alice was silent.

A sticky foreboding spread over Charlie.

He glanced at Drummond. Still out.

Finally, Alice spoke. "What do you see outside?"

"Not much," Charlie said. "Just tranquil Caribbean, a couple of clouds."

"No land?"

"No."

"I was hoping — sometimes there are islets there that don't make the GPS maps."

"We've run into a couple. Just not lately."

"Listen, Charlie, I'm afraid there's no way you're going to make land."

"Not with two hundred and fifty gallons of fuel?"

"That's not gallons, that's *pounds*. Two hundred fifty pounds of fuel is around thirty-five gallons. We'll be stretching it to fly another fifteen minutes."

Charlie turned to ice. "Don't tell me we're going to do a water landing?"

"Fine, I won't tell you. But I'll bet that, afterward, you'll say it was no big deal."

"A bet I'd be happy to lose."

She laughed. Briefly. "Between the two yokes, lower down, you'll see some levers. Grab the pair on the left, the biggest ones.

They're the throttles. Pull them back half-way."

Easy enough, he thought. The throttles gave more than he expected, though. "Shit, the nose is dropping!"

"Hold it up."

He pulled the yoke toward him, inducing a blast of g-forces strong enough, it felt, to push him through the floor. Finally the nose evened out.

He tried to keep his voice from shaking. "Piece of cake."

Alice added a rapid series of instructions involving altitude adjustment and controls for the tail. He tried to follow, head still aching from hypoxia. Worse was the nagging certainty that he'd forgotten at least one crucial step. In spite of a few bumps, however, the plane began a smooth descent.

"Now, take the two levers for the props and push them all the way up," she said.

Setting the phone on his lap, Charlie scrambled, groping for the levers. When was his damned adrenaline going to kick in?

He snatched up the phone. "Done," he said. And hoped.

"Are you all right?"

"Yeah, except my stomach is so knotted up, I'll only be eating soup from now on."

"I know a good New England clam chowder recipe."

He forgot about his stomach. He wanted to say he loved her.

"Now, push the nose down, not a lot," she said. "Remember our attitude indicator: Push it down just under the line."

"Got it."

"What's the airspeed now?"

"One-eighty."

"Dandy. Pull the throttles back another quarter. We want to be going slow close to the water."

"Airspeed's slowing."

"Tell me when that needle gets into the white arc; should be around one-fifty. Also you need to head into the wind, which is coming from the east, according to my phone. So where's the sun?"

"Behind us."

"Perfect."

"And speed's now one-fifty."

"Altitude?"

"Thirty-one hundred."

She gave him instructions for the flaps and throttles.

Easy to follow, for a change. "Flaps, check. Throttles, check. Twenty-four hundred feet."

"Good. Where's your dad?"

"Copilot seat."

"Belted in?"

"No." Drummond's safety belt had fallen by the wayside because of Charlie's concern over how long a person was unconscious before it was considered something worse, like a coma.

"Do it up. Yourself too. When you hit the water, you're probably going to get thrown around a bit."

Reaching over and pulling the straps across Drummond, Charlie considered that a cage match with a professional wrestler equated to "thrown around a bit" by Alice's standards.

Drummond didn't stir, not even with the loud metallic pop of the seat-belt buckle.

Even Alice heard it. "Okay, Charlie, now bring the throttles back an inch or so and keep the plane coming down. Try and settle the speed at around a hundred, otherwise the airplane will stall. You know what happens then, right?"

"No. Do I want to?"

"Probably not. Just don't go less than ninety knots or raise the nose higher than ten degrees. I'm telling you, that chowder will make this worthwhile."

The plane continued to descend. Easy enough, though Charlie knew full well that actually setting the thing down would be the most difficult thing that he had ever done and ever would do. If a wingtip touched the water first, the plane could turn into a skipping stone. Set the plane down in proper sequence but at the wrong angle, and the impact forces would obliterate everything.

"Eight hundred feet now, speed one-ten," he said.

"Bring the throttles back about an inch and keep coming down."

"Speed's around a hundred."

"Keep the nose down. Altitude?"

"Three hundred." Although the sea was a placid blue green, he had the sensation of entering a dark alley.

"When you hit, get out, as soon as you can. Among other things, the plane might flip, it might fill with water, or it might get too dark for you to see. So just go for the cabin door. There should be a life raft and vests there. Can you see the raft?"

There was an orange pile of rubber next to the door. "Needs to be inflated."

"On the way out of the plane, put on the vests as soon as you can. Inflate the raft after you get out or you won't get *it* out."

"And then what?"

"Category of desirable problems."

Charlie was sorry he'd asked. "At a hundred feet now," he said.

The looming sea made him feel minuscule.

Alice maintained her calm. "Pull the throttle back just a hair, then leave it alone."

He set it, glad to have one less item to worry about. "Seventy feet."

"Both hands on the yoke."

The moment that he'd continued to hope would not come: It had come. "Forty feet."

"Slowly now, pull the yoke back. Keep the wings in the center of the circle."

He did. His stomach contracted to the size of a Ping-Pong ball. The water flew up at him. "Fuck. Twenty feet."

"Bring the nose slowly up 'til you hit the water."

The water was so close that Charlie could taste the salt. He fought an impulse to close his eyes.

A perfect shadow of the plane floated on the waves ahead, slowing, as if trying to meet him. The water was serene. He made out individual, sparkling droplets in a gauzy mist lofted by the waves, when — WHACK — the tail hit water, pulverizing his muscles, joints, and tendons. His face smashed into the yoke, forcing him to release his grip. With a whine, the left propeller dug into the water, throwing a mass of spray that battered the fuselage. The nose of the plane slammed down onto a swell, sending his body in different directions at once. Water rose over the front windows.

Finally, the plane settled afloat in a gentle drift, but not for long. Seawater rushed into the cabin.

"We should get out, don't you think?" said Drummond, unbuckling his safety belt. He appeared rested, and unperturbed by the events of the past few minutes.

Charlie popped free of his harness. "Sure, why not?"

Drummond led the way out of the cockpit, fighting the influx of water to reach the cabin door.

Tugging the life raft free of its Velcro mooring and grabbing the vests, Charlie said, "Now we just need to reach land, which was too far to fly to, using two rubber paddles."

Drummond pointed outside at the svelte yacht heading their way. "Actually, I think that boat is going to rescue us."

45

Stanley sat below deck of Corbitt's USS *Perk* in a startlingly spacious living room with taxpayer-funded, rich mahogany paneling and a copper-plated bar containing a transatlantic crossing's worth of single-malt whiskey. Every fixture or component involved either precious metal or crystal — even the Kleenex, dispensed from a crystal cube within silver latticework. There was a fireplace, too, with antique brass andirons piled with logs that required a third look before Stanley was sure they were fake. The only reminder that he was at sea rather than in an English gentlemen's club was the set of pedestals, in place of legs, to fasten the seats to the floor — a floor swathed in antique Persian carpet.

The captives sat in a pair of red leather wing chairs. Wet and bedraggled, they seemed far less menacing this time around. Drummond was struggling to stay awake.

Charlie was so frenetic in his narration of their adventure that he could barely stay seated. "Your capturing us is the best thing that possibly could have happened," he was saying. "I know that sounds crazy now, but let me tell you what we've learned."

"The best possible thing would have been if we'd gotten to you before you sold the bomb," Stanley said.

"Who was the buyer?" asked Hadley. She sat to Stanley's left on the camelback sofa, facing the fugitives — her thousand-euro heli-taxi ride from Martinique would probably be overlooked by headquarters in light of their having coralled the Clarks.

She aimed a Glock at them. After her experience with Bream, Eskridge had finally granted her permission to carry. The teakettle's purple imprint was visible on her forehead. The gun was unnecessary, though. Shortly after Charlie's Mayday calls had enabled Echelon to pinpoint his whereabouts, a second helicopter had landed on Corbitt's yacht, depositing four marines with enough weaponry to stage a coup on some of the area islands. The yacht resounded now with the dull thuds of their combat boots. The opportunity to stay on deck and "command them" — Corbitt's words — ended his protest over his exclusion from the debriefing.

"When we last saw the device, Bream's men were loading the washer into a Zodiac," Charlie said. "We have reason to believe they're planning to ship the bomb to India. So you ought to have plenty of time to intercept them."

Hadley looked to Stanley. "What do you think?"

"Nothing to lose by checking it out."

She dropped the Glock into her shoulder bag and withdrew her new BlackBerry. She began tapping out a cable to Eskridge, at the same time saying to Charlie, "The thing that puzzles me now is how you could sell a weapon of mass destruction in the first place."

"I was thinking the same thing," Stanley said. His concerns actually ran much deeper.

"It wasn't a sale," Charlie said. "It was ransom."

He was polite, Stanley reflected, not petulant, or acting in any way that pointed to dissembling. "Why didn't you go to the authorities?"

"The bad guys would have killed Alice. And the authorities would have tried to kill us. Like last night." Charlie indicated Hadley with a tilt of his head. "But things are different now. Now we have proof of everything I told you. The Cavalry's plot is all right there on the Web. A few minutes online and you'll be able to see exactly how we were set up, plus how Bream was able to learn about the existence of the bomb."

Her cable dispatched, Hadley placed the BlackBerry back into her shoulder bag. "This story sounds familiar," she said to Charlie. "Don't tell me: Bream revealed the whole plot to you as he was leaving you to die in a plummeting airplane instead of simply shooting you?"

"I wondered about that too," Charlie said. "Whoever he really is, he's got more than his share of ego. He was proud of his plan and wanted to brag about having outsmarted the best and the brightest. But he's nobody's fool. Maybe he wanted our deaths to look accidental. Why add the murder of a CIA Trailblazer to the list of reasons you have to hunt him? In any case, to verify my story, all you have to do is flip on the Internet, go to Korean Singles Online-dot-com, and throw some decryption software at Fielding's hidden text. His mistake was not living long enough to delete it."

"Well, I'd be shocked if Corbitt doesn't have this brig equipped with high-speed satellite Internet access." Hadley started to rise, presumably to go up on deck and ask the base chief.

"Hold on just a second," said Stanley, turning to Charlie. "If what you're saying is true, why wouldn't Alice Rutherford or her NSA colleagues have taken action?"

"I was too busy landing the plane to mention Korean Singles Online-dot-com to her. And once we hit the water, I lost the phone — not that she'd have been able to stay on long. Odds are the same people who wanted us have sent a hit team after her too, right?"

"Probably so," Stanley said. "We need to ensure that no one ever sees that Web content."

"But it could exonerate these men, Bill." Hadley searched his eyes for a clue to his thinking.

"It would be the death knell for the Cavalry." Stanley lifted the Glock and its silencer from her shoulder bag.

Charlie froze. "You're one of them, aren't you?"

Even Drummond sat up.

Hadley looked to Stanley, eyes wide.

"I'm sorry, Hilary." Twisting on the silencer, he aimed the gun at her.

The other night in the Haut-de-Cagnes safe house, Ali Abdullah — aka Austin Bellinger — had tried to make the case that his

Cavalry was made up of bright and gallant patriots who gave no thought to flaps and didn't waste time on the chains of cables seeking permission for action. They just went ahead and acted. Their actions often brought them into legal gray areas. Sometimes they simply broke laws. But always for the greater good.

Stanley left the safe house convinced that the Cavalry was the clandestine service he had dreamed of joining as a young man. He believed that exposure of the unit's efforts to stop the Clarks, particularly the truth about the unfortunate Hattemer episode, would force soft and cowardly bureaucrats like Eskridge to roll up the operation. Stanley wanted to help prevent that. So when he was assigned to the Clark case the next day by Eskridge — it turned out that Bellinger had planted the seed in the head of his onetime groomsman — Stanley felt that he had found his calling, at long last.

Now he found himself hesitant to extinguish the lives of Hadley and the Clarks.

Unfortunate but vital to national security, he concluded.

Frozen in astonishment on the sofa, Hadley was an easy target. With the space between her eyes centered in the Glock's sight, Stanley pulled the trigger.

46

As Stanley pressed the trigger, there was a bright orange blur on the edge of Charlie's peripheral vision.

Drummond's Croc bounced off Stanley's gun barrel.

The report was muted, probably sounding like an ordinary cough to someone on deck, assuming it was heard at all over the big yacht's engines. Hadley's head snapped sideways. A red circle appeared in her hair just above her right ear. She collapsed, falling to her left, with enough force that the massive camelback sofa toppled with her, the pedestal snapping free of its moorings. The sofa landed directly over her, shielding her from another round, or at least from Stanley's sight.

Stanley knelt, shifting his gun to the armchair in which Drummond had been sitting. Drummond was in midair now, diving headlong at Stanley.

With both hands around the handle of his gun, Stanley tracked his flight. With a click of the trigger and another muted blast, a bullet sliced a channel along the right side of Drummond's collar, cleaving the air by Charlie's left shoulder before particling a glass porthole.

Slamming into Stanley's abdomen, Drummond tried to wrap his arms around the spook's waist. Stanley twisted free, dropping his elbow onto the base of Drummond's skull.

On his hands and knees, Drummond sought the cover of the copper-faced bar. As he pulled himself around the corner, Stanley fired. The bullet clanged into the copper plating as Drummond disappeared from sight, save one Croc.

Stanley fired instead at the face of the bar, repeatedly, the bullet holes tracing Drummond's probable path behind it. Glass exploded and scotch jetted into the air, spraying Stanley and raining onto the fancy carpet.

Charlie noted that the pilot light in the fireplace was on. The handle to turn on the gas was open as well. So he flung himself at the button for the burner, pounding it as hard as he could. Gas hissed through the pipe and created an instant blaze. He redirected the pipe at the spilled liquor, which burst into flames that streamed along the carpet toward Stanley.

The spook sidestepped the fire. Still one of his pant cuffs ignited, and, in a blink, flames coated the liquor-soaked front of his khakis. In obvious pain, he tried to beat the fire out. He was nearly successful, when Drummond popped up from behind the bar and hurled a stout highball glass.

Stanley ducked and the glass disintegrated the crystal sconce on the far wall.

Drummond threw another, this time striking Stanley's gun hand, forcing him to drop the Glock.

Charlie lunged for it. Stanley kicked at Charlie's head. Charlie rolled, averting the spook's toe, but the heel caught his ear — slashing it so sharply he was surprised it remained attached. Stanley wound back again, like a field goal kicker. Charlie sat up, getting a solid grip on the gun and leveling it at the spook, freezing him.

Suddenly the door to the cabin was smashed inward. A crowd of marines in gray-green body armor, guns drawn, filled the small aperture.

Stanley waved at Charlie. "He shot Hadley." The marines appeared to believe him. "I think she's dead."

"*He* shot her," Charlie said. "Look at the way she fell over. To his left. We were sitting *across* from him. Plus we didn't have a gun at the time."

The marines exchanged looks.

Charlie realized he'd offered nothing, really, in the way of evidence.

Two marines rushed down, swept Hadley off the floor, and carried her up the stairs, leaving a trail of crimson drops.

Stanley followed.

Charlie heard the whine of the engine and the tingling of the rotor blades as the marine helicopter prepared to take off.

"Sir, we need you to surrender your weapon," said one of the two marines remaining below deck, a stone-faced bruiser who towered over Charlie.

The other locked his rifle on Drummond.

"It's *his* weapon!" Charlie said, regarding the door through which Stanley had exited. As soon as the words left his lips, he felt foolish because they didn't prove a thing.

"Slowly set it on the floor and tap it to me."

Charlie lowered the Glock an inch at a time. "Listen, we have proof that we're being framed."

He looked at Drummond, now being frisked by the other marine, probably the

357

unit's superior officer given his graying hair.

"Yes, that young man wanted to kill us!" Drummond said of Stanley, with so much indignation that it rang false.

The marines exchanged a dismissive glance.

"Let me just tell you guys one thing, while we have the chance," Charlie pleaded.

The superior said, "Sir, it would help if you would refrain from speaking now. When we return to the American consulate, you'll have a full debrief by the CIA."

Charlie set the gun down. "You've got to understand, 'debrief,' in this case, is a euphemism for 'execution.' "

The younger marine knelt and snatched the gun. "Please stand, slowly, and face the bar with your arms and legs outstretched."

Charlie complied. "Just listen, for posterity if nothing else: The proof of everything I've been saying is on Korean Singles Online-dot-com." He received a shove in the small of the back. "Go to Suki-eight-three-five's page, magnify the left earring —"

The older marine sighed, seemingly in frustration. "Sir, we'd prefer not to have to sedate you."

A short, chubby man in a suit and tie barreled down the stairs.

"Chief Corbitt," both marines said by way of greeting.

Charlie looked up at him with a glimmer of hope.

Corbitt looked past them at the lower deck and gaped at the smoldering wreckage. "Holy *merde*," he said.

47

Pointe Simon pulsated with a variety of music and chatter, a good deal of which was pickup lines, Stanley supposed. He stepped into the relative quiet and cool of the sort of bar no one bothered to name — it went by 107, its number on one of the little streets in the maze near the ferry docks. Neon distillery promotions cast red and purple on the frayed bar island and the establishment's two dozen patrons, a mix of locals and travelers on a budget. Although 107 served no food, it smelled vaguely of hamburger.

He spotted an attractive brunette sipping a drink. She wore a slinky floral-printed cocktail dress, the sort sold at the tourist bazaar at the ferry docks, revealing a lithe figure. Most anyone would guess she was a young American or Euro tourist bent on a night on the edge.

Settling onto the barstool beside hers,

Stanley asked, "What do you think the chances are that I'll meet my wife here?"

"A sure thing," she said, leaning over a salt-rimmed margarita and kissing him on the lips. Recognition code, safety code.

This was Lanier. First name or last, Stanley didn't know. Probably pseudo anyway. Rumint had it that she'd authored the Ayacucho hit, notable not because she trekked a hundred miles alone through Peruvian jungle and snuck past two hundred Shining Path Senderistas, but because she'd put the whole op together during a half-hour taxi ride from the Lima airport.

"So how was your day, honey?" she asked.

"I've had better."

She regarded the mirrored rear wall, which offered a view of the whole place. Turning back to him, she asked, "So what the fuck went down on the boat?"

"The old man kicked a Croc while I was firing and wrecked my shot. I mean, a *Croc!*"

"How about that?" She spread a cool, comforting hand over his. "Just another one for the list of You Never Damned Know."

The bartender slid Stanley a tall glass of something redolent of rum.

"What would you have done?" he asked.

"Don't know. Spilled the milk. Maybe not spilled the milk. Either way, what we have is

361

Hadley in brain surgery. Doesn't look like she'll make it, but even if she does, we'll see to it that she doesn't. So all is far from lost."

"What about the other two?"

"The night, as they say, is young."

Stanley had been trying to devise a way to get at the Clarks. "FBI's flying down an excessive number of agents to extradite them first thing in the morning. Meanwhile they'll be at the consulate guarded by an excessive number of marines."

Lanier licked salt from her margarita glass. "The good news is, father and son are bound for impromptu detention rooms, in the true sense of impromptu." All embassy and consulate holding rooms were technically improvised because neither the State Department nor the CIA had the authority to arrest or detain anyone. Nevertheless their architectural plans tended to include oversized "storage vaults" and "fallout shelters" that afforded confinement at least as secure as police holding cells. "The only reason there are bars on the windows there is to keep people from getting in."

Stanley didn't see where she was headed. "But we're people."

She flashed a smile. "People with sniper training."

48

After a three-minute drive from the Pointe Simon docks, two giant, beige Chevy Suburbans entered a quiet pocket of the city, sliding to a stop in a pitch-black cul-de-sac service alley beneath the American consulate, which occupied the lowest two levels of a nine-story contemporary glass hotel. The monolithic tower, bisected by a block of terraces lit sapphire-gray, reminded Charlie of a stainless steel refrigerator.

Two marines propelled him from the lead Suburban and toward the consulate's service entrance. Foreboding filled him, so heavy that he strained to put one foot in front of the other. What were the odds, he thought, that the Cavalry would *not* drop by here tonight?

Before he could see if his father was in the second Suburban, he was prodded down a short flight of cement stairs. Punk rock, from a club in the hotel lobby overhead, shook the clammy air. The men whisked him into a back office hallway. Fluorescent tubes caused the white tile walls to shimmer a pale blue.

Halfway down Charlie spotted another marine, whose uniform said he was Private First Class Arnold. The man's baby face clashed with his 270-pound weight-room physique. He pushed open a wooden door, revealing an empty room suitable for a copier and some office supplies. "Mr. Clark, sir, you are being placed here for the time being for your own protection," the marine said.

Two to one the exact words lawyers had fed him.

Charlie's eyes fell on perhaps the smallest toilet seat in the world. Standing on spindly foldout legs, it fed a disposable plastic bag. Beside the toilet lay a ham sandwich in a vending machine's triangular container.

Hefting his massive shoulders into an apologetic shrug, Arnold said, "I'll get you a Coke if the guys outside have got the right change." He pulled the door shut.

Charlie heard a jangle of keys, then the raspy slide of a bolt, possibly the only detainment measure other than Arnold himself. The window was covered with a cage of bars, but so were all the others along the lower two floors of the building. Probably just to keep the locals out.

Charlie supposed he could stab the windowpane using one of the plastic toilet legs, in which case fragments of glass would rain onto the sidewalk, snaring the attention of someone in the apartment buildings across the street. Maybe the residents would call the local cops, who in turn would call the consulate and then the marines would — what? Deny Charlie his Coca-Cola?

He leaned his full weight against the door. The wooden slab, although not thick, didn't budge. Who exactly were the men who broke down doors, he wondered, and how did they do it? If he were to kick at this one, he suspected, he would break his foot. And still fail to budge the door.

The ceiling was an ordinary office-style ceiling, eight soundproof tiles suspended by a tic-tac-toe board of thin metal strips. At one side the strips tripled into a vent from which cool air trickled, suggesting that there was an air duct above. Charlie thought of Drummond's tale of the prisoners who had escaped Alcatraz via the fan vent.

Standing directly beneath the vent, he could see the air shaft. It was about ten inches high and fifteen inches wide. Even if he could somehow gain access to it —

springing from the windowsill or climbing from atop the spindly legged toilet, for instance — a freak-show-caliber act of contortion would be required to enter it, let alone crawl through it. If he were to crawl atop the ceiling grid, like they always do in the movies, the whole works would almost certainly collapse.

He had no better ideas. Not even any other ideas.

But his father might. Hearing the three sets of approaching footsteps in the hallway, Charlie's hope rose.

On the other side of the door, Private First Class Arnold grunted, "Hey." He received similar salutations from two other men.

As the new arrivals continued past the detention room, Charlie heard Drummond say: "I'm going to have to take my medicine before bedtime."

49

They looked like the three-story flophouse's typical guests. Ideally, that's what they hoped the prematurely hunched woman at the reception desk would remember about the too-loud American couple who, while checking in for an estimated stay of two hours, debated which was the best of the daiquiris they'd just had at various Pointe Simon bars.

Stanley's other reason for debating tropical drinks with Lanier was to divert the attention of the woman behind the desk from Lanier's duffel bag. It was a good Louis Vuitton knockoff, decent camo. But the woman might think it odd that someone checking into a seedy hotel for a couple of hours would pack a bag, let alone such a big bag.

It contained a forty-four-inch-long Remington bolt-action M40A1, the M40 variant with the relatively lightweight McMillan

HTG fiberglass stock. Lanier would have preferred to use a Mark 14 Mod 0 rifle with a collapsible stock, but the M40 wasn't bad given that she'd had just over an hour to devise this op. M40s were common enough; she'd rented this one from a hunting and fishing supply store in nearby Lamentin for "target practice."

She initially set the bag on the floor of the lobby, so that the woman would miss it from her elevated seat in the Plexiglas-encased front desk. The bag would come into view, however, as Lanier climbed the spiral stairs to the rooms.

So after Stanley got the room key, he lingered at the reception desk and smiled his appraisal of the warbled drinking song cascading down the stairwell from one of the upper floors. The woman smiled along with him.

Then he asked, *"Avez-vous des cartes de Pointe-Simon?"*

While she rifled through a drawer behind her for a map — the staff here probably didn't get this request often — Lanier and her bag disappeared up the stairs.

The third-floor room was shaped like a wedge of cheese and smelled a bit like one. The furnishing included a pipe-frame twin bed that looked as if it had survived a flood, a dresser missing one drawer and all its handles, and a nightstand that belonged in a child's room. Bolted to the top of the dresser, evidently in an effort to thwart theft, was a clock radio that emitted a mechanical grunt each time the digits flipped. It read 6:51. According to Stanley's watch, the time was 22:13.

"All in all, not bad for forty euros a night," he said.

Lanier flashed a smile and returned to assembling her bipod near the room's key feature, the mullioned dormer window overlooking the Forêt Communale de Montgérald parkland. She had a clear shot, save for a few palm fronds, at the American consulate.

Peering into her scope, Lanier said, "You're not going to believe this, but I think I can make out Charlie Clark standing right by his window."

Charlie turned away from the window when his door opened and Arnold entered with a plastic bottle of Coke. Charlie was about to say thank-you when something or someone crashed against a door down the corridor, followed by a heavy flop of a body against tile floor.

Charlie glanced beyond Arnold. Outside of the next room down the corridor stood the young stone-faced marine from the yacht — the name silk-screened onto his uniform was, fittingly, Flint.

Regarding the closed door, Flint asked, "Mr. Clark, are you all right?"

There was no response from Drummond's room.

"Mr. Clark?" Flint again asked.

Still no answer.

Did Drummond have an escape plan? Charlie should have felt his hope surge, but he sensed something was wrong.

Sergeant King, Flint's graying superior officer, came bounding around a corner, an assault rifle in hand. He slowed, leveling the weapon at Drummond's door.

"Go ahead," he told Flint.

Kneeling to the side of the door, the younger marine inserted a key, twisted the bolt free of the lock, and tried to push the door inward. When it barely moved, Flint peered through the crack between it and the jamb. "He's just lying there, sir. Doesn't look like he's breathing."

Charlie held his breath. A cold perspiration coated him. Protocol surely dictated that Private Arnold shut the door to his room, but deferring to basic humanity, perhaps, the marine allowed Charlie to remain in the doorway.

They both watched King move closer to Drummond's room and Flint throw a shoulder at the door, grab an edge with his free hand, and drive Drummond's body back. An orange Croc rolled from the room and into the corridor, coming to rest upside down.

With King covering him, Flint ducked into the room.

"I don't feel a pulse," he called out.

"Roger that," the sergeant said. He squatted, disappearing into the room. "Let's get him to the infirmary."

The two men picked up Drummond then backed into the corridor, King holding him by the shoulders, Flint by legs that were now white to the point of translucence.

Charlie launched himself toward his father until the barrel of Arnold's gun lowered like a gate arm.

"Sorry," the marine said, backing Charlie into the small room and jerking the door shut.

Charlie was pummeled by horror and sorrow, and, at a hundred times the intensity, anger that a hero like Drummond Clark could come to such an inglorious end with

371

proof of his innocence just a few computer
keystrokes away.

50

Alice reached Geneva by midnight. To get travel documents, she had to pay a visit to Russ Augenblick, the forger, who did a lot of his business out of a nightclub on the rue de la Rôtisserie, L'Alhambar, known for jazz.

She parked the Mercedes on a sleepy residential side street three blocks away, then walked. Her route, with the usual strategic left turns, added four blocks.

Tonight L'Alhambar featured a brass quartet with a predilection for volume. Among its throng of early-twentysomethings, she spotted the slight, fair-haired forger, in a Red Sox T-shirt. He stood by the curlicue bar, part of a small crowd vying to order drinks.

"I need one too," Alice said, sidling up to him. "Big-time."

At twenty-five, Russ Augenblick could pass for a choirboy, his wispy attempts at a mustache and beard, paradoxically, high-lighting his youthfulness. He regarded Alice as if she were insane. "Dude, you're hotter than Satan."

"Oh, you like my new jacket?" Frank's gray overcoat gave her the form of a traffic cone. "Thanks."

"I mean, showing up here. This place has more cameras than a camera store. What kind of super-crazy-desperate trouble are you in?"

"The usual kind. I need your 'full suite,' *tout de suite*."

He looked down at his sneakers. "I can't. Not now. Sorry, man."

"By all means, go ahead and have your beer. My treat, in fact — if the bartender can break a hundred-euro bill . . ."

"I can't take you to the workshop while you're listed as shoot-on-sight. Not even you would take that risk."

"Yes you can, Stew."

Despite himself, he blanched. Russ Augenblick was an alias.

"I know about California," she continued. "But there's no reason to tell tales out of school, is there?"

While at the NSA, Alice had learned the truth about "Russ," but she allowed him to continue operating in case he might be of use at some point. Like now. She was prepared to tell what she knew of Stewart Fleishman's freshman year at Berkeley, where making the scene at off-campus bars was mandatory, the drinking age was twenty-one, and his Massachusetts driver's license showed his true age. The fake California license he'd bought proved useless because the bouncers ran licenses through magnetic strip scanners — a flashing red light resulted in a long and expensive night with Berkeley's finest. Fleishman chose to replicate a Delaware license because of its simplicity and relative obscurity. A quick trip to San Francisco netted him a sheet of the same PVC the Delaware Department of Motor Vehicles used, plus a magnetic strip that he programmed so the scanners informed the bouncers that this fair-haired young man was a twenty-one-year-old from Wilmington. His classmates wanted Delaware driver's licenses of their own. He went into business, and business had boomed, enough that a college degree in economics was redundant. Because it was illegal in the United States to possess, produce, or distribute falsified government documents, he set up shop in Thailand, where counterfeiting was something of a national pastime. He now sold $500,000 worth of fake U.S.

driver's licenses over the Internet per year. Passports, much easier to forge, netted him ten times as much money.

If Alice were to spend three minutes on the Homeland Security tips site now, Stewart Fleishman aka Russ Augenblick would face extradition, at the least.

"I need you to hack into the customs database," she told him. "I want you to make me a passport with the information of an American, Canadian, or Brit actually traveling in Switzerland right now." With such a passport she could waltz out of the country.

He grumbled. "Buy me a mescal shot too and I'll try. A double."

After their drinks, she followed him through the back exit and down a windy but otherwise quiet side street to his vintage VW love bus.

Demonstrating surprising courtliness, the forger trudged through slush to open the front passenger door for her. The entire van, apparently restored without regard to cost, smelled new.

With a hint of fresh male perspiration.

Alice knew without looking, but turned anyway. Four men in black jumpsuits and matching body armor sat in the back of the van, each gripping a Sig, the silenced barrels pointed at her.

By way of greeting, the man closest to her said, *"Dienst für Analyse und Prävention,"* German for "Service for Analysis and Prevention," the Swiss domestic intelligence agency, which, evidently, had a working relationship with a certain forger.

51

Despite the antiseptic scent unique to medical facilities, along with walls, cabinets, and a sparkling tile floor that matched the hospital white of a medic's lab coat, the lack of windows suggested that the infirmary originally had been a locker room or showers.

Sergeant King said, between gasps, "He's not breathing, Ginny." The medic's badge read GENEVIÈVE in big block letters.

"I don't think he's got a pulse either," said Corporal Flint, angling Drummond's feet toward the examination table.

"Set him down and we will see if we can fix that," Geneviève said.

Although barely into her twenties, she had the composure of a battle-hardened veteran. She whipped a fresh sheet from the roll of paper at the foot of the table, clamping it into place just as Drummond's head hit the headrest. Lifting his chin upward with one hand and pressing back on his forehead with the other, she tilted back his face. She opened his mouth and checked for obstructions, finding none. No breathing either.

Pinching his nostrils shut, she fit her mouth over and around his, then commenced breathing for him, inhaling and exhaling slowly into his mouth. His chest rose and fell, again signifying no obstruction. She provided two more breaths, each about a second long, then pressed two fingers to the side of his throat.

"No carotid pulse, as far as I can tell," she sighed, not so much a lament as a prognosis.

"What can we do?" asked King.

"Call for an ambulance. Say the casualty is having a cardiac arrest."

King said, "Corporal?"

Nodding, Flint ran out.

Pointing to a white blanket, Geneviève said to King, "Sergeant, if you could roll that up and use it to elevate his feet by about fifteen inches . . ."

He did, offering better blood flow to Drummond's heart, which Geneviève prepared to resuscitate by placing the heel of her right hand two or three inches above the tip of his sternum. She lay her left hand on top of her right and interlaced her fingers.

"It was probably his damned pills," King said.

"What pills?" Geneviève locked her elbows and moved herself directly above Drummond, so that she could use the weight of her body, rather than her muscles, to perform the compressions, minimizing fatigue.

"Some kind of Alzheimer meds. Could that have anything to do with this?"

She nodded. "Do you have them?"

The sergeant whisked his hands over Drummond's pockets without finding the bottle. "I'll be right back." He tore out of the infirmary.

Geneviève compressed Drummond's chest wall by about three inches, or enough to break a rib, the desired amount. Compressions any weaker were ineffective. The point of squeezing the rib cage, after all, was to pump the heart.

She had repeated the process fifteen times, at a rate of approximately one hundred compressions per minute, when Drummond decided that it was time to end the cardiac arrest act he'd initiated by swallowing eight of his ten remaining pills. The experimental drug's beta-blocker components — atenolol and metoprolol — had weakened his pulse to the point that it was undetectable, at least by harried marine guards and a medic in an under-equipped infirmary. He'd augmented the effect with a ploy as old as predators and prey, holding his breath.

He may have done the job too well, he thought, as he tried to get up from the examination table: A chill crept over his body, leaving him cold, clammy, and feeling weighted down, as if he were at the bottom of a deep sea. His extremities stung and the pressure neared skull-crushing. Everything around him blurred. The hiss of the overhead lamps, Geneviève's breathing, and the rustling of her lab coat had the effect of trains blowing past. And both vomit and diarrhea burned within him.

Had he miscalculated the dosage?

Highly likely. His faculty for making calculations lately had been like an old television set that gets reception only at certain angles. Still, getting reception at all had been fortuitous. His son was locked in a detention room. And any moment might bring the return of the Cavalry agent who had tried to kill them — what was his name?

Steve?

Stanley?

Sandy?

Like the beach.

Saint Lucia's beaches were as white as sugar.

Until he'd seen them for himself, he'd thought "sugar sand" was just the hyperbolical concoction of an advertising copywriter.

Drummond felt his thinking careening off the rails.

What matters, he told himself, is that Steve or Stanley or whoever *will return,* almost certainly with backup from the misguided Cavalry. And the marine guards here would prove no more potent than scarecrows in defense.

The world seemed to revert to its normal pace.

Drummond exhaled, with a cough, for effect.

Geneviève jumped, pleasantly surprised.

He tried to raise himself on his elbows and fell flat.

"Easy," she said.

"I accidentally swallowed some . . ." he said just above a whisper before letting his voice trail off.

She leaned closer to hear. "Yes?"

He shot up his left arm, encircling her neck, clamping the crook of his elbow at her trachea.

She tried to cry out.

With his left hand he grasped his right bicep, placing his right hand behind her head, then brought his elbows together, applying as much pressure as he could generate to both sides of her neck, restricting the blood flow to her brain.

Unconscious, she sagged against him. He slid off the examination table, keeping a grip on her so that she wouldn't fall. His knees buckled, but by force of will he remained standing.

He hoisted her onto the table. She would regain consciousness in seconds. The marines who had brought him here would return sooner.

There was simply no time for infirmity.

He took the white blanket from the foot of the examination table and cast it over her. The marines would mistake her for him, at least for a few seconds.

He crouched behind the crash cart, the portable trolley with the dimensions of a floor safe. It contained all equipment and medication required for cardiopulmonary emergencies, and he would need one of the meds momentarily. In the shorter term, the cart would hide him. He rotated it so that its drawers faced him.

Sergeant King entered at a jog. On seeing the fully covered body on the examination table, he froze. "Damn it," he said to himself.

Hidden by the portion of the blanket hanging from the examination table, Drummond slowly opened the crash cart's drawers fractions of an inch at a time, searching for succinylcholine, the swift-acting neuromuscular blocker used to facilitate endotracheal intubation. Drummond intended to use a small dose of the drug to temporarily paralyze King.

The sergeant wandered toward the table. "Ginny?" he asked at a whisper, as if worried about disturbing the corpse. "Where'd you go?"

Drummond found three pencil-sized preloaded succinylcholine syringes, each packing an eighteen-gauge needle.

Warily, King peeled the blanket from the head of the examination table. He recoiled, drawing his gun and shouting, "Flint!"

Drummond reached beneath the table and slung the needle sidearm into King's calf. The sergeant looked down in mystification — he probably felt no more pain than if he'd been stung by an insect. Drummond sprang, hitting the floor on a roll, then reached and tapped the plunger, driving succinylcholine into King's muscle.

King twisted away with such force that the needle jerked free and flew across the infirmary. It struck a cabinet on the far wall, lodging there like a dart.

Flint ran in, gun drawn. King pointed, superfluously, to Drummond, then crumpled to the floor, where he lay, unmoving.

Glad of the diversion, Drummond dove back behind the crash cart.

Flint pivoted on his heels, firing. Strips of linoleum slapped Drummond. The air clouded with sawdust that had been a chunk of the examination table.

From his knees, Drummond shoved the red cart at Flint.

The marine spun, shooting and ringing the face of it. The bullet exited through the uppermost drawer, whistling past Drummond's ear, followed by a spray of glass and a milky white substance that smelled of alcohol.

Pushing the cart ahead of himself, Drummond picked up the gun King had dropped.

Another bullet pounded into the cart.

Drummond said, "I have a clean shot at you, son. Neither of us wants me to take it. So, slowly, set your sidearm down on the floor and kick it toward me."

"Mr. Clark, sir, there is no chance whatsoever that you can get out of here, so —"

Drummond fired, aiming to Flint's right. The wall a few inches from Flint's right ear exploded into plaster dust. The man dropped to the floor.

Drummond tracked him through the gunsight. "We're making progress. Now, all you have to do is surrender your weapon."

Ashen, independent of the haze of plaster dust, the marine complied.

As Drummond reached for the weapon, something hard slammed into the back of his head. He fell against the crash cart, toppling it. As he hit the floor, he saw the metal bed rail swung like a cricket bat by Geneviève.

Meanwhile the crash cart's five metal drawers dropped open and pounded him, the sharp corner of one ripping through his shirt and slicing into his chest. All manner of medical supplies rained onto him.

He implored himself to maintain focus; he had one last play in mind.

White light devoured his consciousness.

52

Snipers aim for the "apricot," better known as the medulla oblongata, the part of the brainstem that controls the heart and lungs. To reach Charlie Clark's, Gretchen Lanier needed to fire from the barely opened window of the third-floor hotel room, across and through more than three hundred yards of parkland, and into the barred detention rooms.

If only every job were so simple, she thought. A year ago in Afghanistan, she'd recorded a kill from 2,267 yards away, or 1.29 miles, on icy and mountainous terrain.

She dropped to a kneeling position at the foot of the bed. In her year and a half of sniper school, her instructors had placed almost as much emphasis on proficiency in camouflage and concealment as on marksmanship. More often than not it involved wearing a ghillie suit in order to pass for a bush or clump of weeds. Tonight's camo involved surrounding the rifle with a well-placed pillow and the blankets bunched just so. Wrapping the comforter over the works simulated a person lying in the bed she and Stanley had rolled against the window.

She needed to accurately estimate and balance the many components in a bullet's trajectory and point of impact. Range was simplest. From this relative proximity, she would have zero difficulty placing the red laser dot smack on the base of Charlie's head. But if she made a mistake in calculating the effects of wind direction or velocity, among other factors, the round might fly several feet wide of Charlie and bore instead through the far wall of the detention room, possibly taking out the marine guard stationed on the other side.

Shooting at a downward angle also complicated matters. Gravity could wreak havoc on a shot traveling three thousand feet per second. Fortunately, the wind was almost nil, the conditions otherwise were practically ideal, and sniping technology had advanced at a head-spinning rate lately: The ballistic calculator in Lanier's telescopic sight — and this was an el cheapo telescopic sight available in a Caribbean version of a hick gun shop — all but offered a glimpse at the future in the form of an animated preview of the shot.

She leaned into the stock's cheek-piece and squinted against the cold scope to find not a view of an impromptu detention room, as she'd expected, but the profile of a young man with sandy blond hair. Charlie Clark, no doubt about it. The back of his head was centered almost exactly within the crosshairs.

She half expected him to turn around, feeling her eyes upon him.

He stood still, an ear pressed against the door, as if trying to hear through it.

She disengaged her conscience. The target became a piece of paper with concentric circles around a bull's-eye rather than a human being with loved ones who would suffer from his loss.

Rather than draw attention with the laser range finder, she used the mil dot reticle in the scope — a sort of electronic slide rule — to find the range. 194.8 meters, or, as she thought of it, nothing.

Anticipating the target's behavior was integral to a precise shot. With moving targets, the point of aim was ahead of the target, the distance depending on his speed and angular movement. A stationary target like this was the sniper's version of a three-inch putt.

Lanier zeroed the scope, then looked over her shoulder at Stanley, who sat in an executive-style simulated-leather desk chair with a gash in the back.

"How're things in the Sound Department?" she asked.

He tapped nine digits on his BlackBerry. "Just waiting on your cue now."

When she pulled the trigger, he would dial a tenth number, sending a radio signal to detonate a C-4 shaped charge not much larger than a Tic Tac. She'd stuck it to a transformer hanging within easy reach of the roof. The blast would obscure the thunderous report of the M40. The simpler solution, a suppressor, would skew her shot. When possible, she opted for loud sounds heard in the environment, exploding artillery shells in an Afghanistani combat zone, for example, or, in places like Martinique, fourth-rate transformers that blew as often as the wind.

She pressed her eye against the scope, locating Charlie where she'd last seen him.

The bullet would require .93 seconds to reach the point of impact. She would squeeze the trigger straight back with the ball of her finger to avoid jerking the gun sideways. She took a deep breath, then let the air out in small increments, the idea being to hold her lungs empty at the moment she took the shot. To further minimize barrel motion, she would fire between the beats of her heart.

As always, a calm enveloped her, removing Stanley and the room and the rest of Martinique from her consciousness — everything but herself, her weapon, and her target.

53

Drummond regained consciousness, but his vision remained cloudy. Flint knelt beside him, along with King, who seemed to have fully recovered from the succinylcholine.

"They said he was good, but who could've anticipated this?" King was saying.

The words came at Drummond as if through a bullhorn. He yielded to the need to vomit, letting it spill out of his lips and, purposefully, down his shirtfront.

The rest of the infirmary came back into focus as the marines each grabbed him by an armpit, hoisting him to his feet. Flint patted Drummond's shorts in search of a weapon. Geneviève stood by, still gripping the bed rail, at the ready.

"Cheee-rist," Flint said, turning his nose away from the vomit.

Drummond staggered. With intent.

Flint lost his grip on him.

Drummond shot his right hand into his

shirt pocket, drawing out one of the succinylcholine syringes he'd gathered from the floor. In the same motion, he swung it into Flint's shoulder, then popped the plunger.

Flint whirled around, swinging.

Drummond ducked the fist.

As Flint reared back for another try, he dropped unconscious into Drummond's arms, providing a shield against King, whose gun was aimed at Drummond.

"That's enough, Mr. Clark," he said. "Set him down."

Drummond flung the sedated corporal toward King, who instinctively reached to catch the younger man. At the same time, Drummond dove at King, jabbing a second syringe into the sergeant's bicep.

King threw a heavyweight blow to Drummond's jaw.

Again, the room began to fade to white.

Drummond flailed, catching the edge of the examination table to keep from falling.

King plucked the needle free of his arm. He retrained his gun barrel. "Hands in the sky."

With effort, Drummond raised his arms.

"Now back against the wall and —" King teetered.

Drummond snatched the Glock away from him and whirled toward Geneviève.

Mouth open, she let the bed rail fall, ringing on the floor tile.

"I don't want to hurt you, believe it or not," Drummond said.

"Why should I believe you?" She had to shout over the wail of the arriving ambulance.

"I might be able to convince you if I had a minute." He clapped the handcuff that had been intended for him onto her right wrist. "But I don't."

Charlie's thoughts were whirling like a roulette wheel, the ball popping from anguish to denial, when the detention room door swung inward. Stepping clear of it, he heard an odd pop behind him. Something buzzed past his head. A bullet hole appeared in the doorframe, venting smoke.

"Sniper." Drummond beckoned from the corridor. "Hurry."

Charlie set aside his joy at seeing his father to run from the room, just as a second bullet shattered the window, turning the door's upper hinge to shrapnel.

Drummond limped down the corridor, leading with a Glock. Charlie scrambled to follow. More glass broke and another bullet disintegrated a tile on the corridor wall.

Charlie caught up with Drummond, who

winced with each step. "You okay?" Charlie asked. Nothing short of a garroting would cause Drummond Clark to wince ordinarily.

"I'm better off than him," said Drummond, pointing ahead to the giant Private First Class Arnold, splayed across the floor, unconscious. "The issue is, he ought to have answered the doorbell by now. We have to get up there before our getaway drivers start thinking it's fishy that nobody's come."

"Our getaway drivers?" Charlie followed Drummond up the short flight of stairs to the consulate's back entrance.

"You heard the ambulance, right?" Drummond said.

"I heard a siren."

"With a little convincing, they'll be our getaway drivers." Drummond reached into his waistband and passed Charlie a second Glock.

Taking hold of the heavy gun, Charlie felt an uneasiness that had nothing to do with hijacking an ambulance. These days, that was no more intimidating than hailing a taxi. "Won't an ambulance be kind of conspicuous?"

"We're going to need them because . . ." At the landing, Drummond's heavy coating of perspiration blinked between orange and yellow in the reflection of the ambulance parked outside. Still he appeared eerily pale. "Earlier, I tried to make it seem as if I was having a heart attack," he continued, his breathing labored. "I may have overplayed the —"

His gun dropped from his hand and bounced down the stairs. He teetered then fell along the same trajectory.

54

With his father flung over his shoulder, Charlie backed out the service door and onto the sidewalk, which was lit by the ambulance idling at the curb. Two paramedics, laden with cases and duffel bags, wheeled a gurney from the opened back of the ambulance. A glance at Drummond, now an alarming shade of blue, and they began to run.

In seconds, Drummond was lying on the thin mattress. One of the medics, a small young man whose name badge read GAILLARD, asked, "Sir, can you hear me?" He shook Drummond gently, trying to rouse him.

Nothing.

Gaillard looked up at his partner and said, "Still breathing. Pulse is faint."

In seconds, the paramedics transformed their bags into a temporary hospital room. They elevated Drummond's feet and fitted him with an oxygen mask fed by a cylindrical tank. A heart monitor and a cluster of other instruments whirred to life.

"BP is seventy over forty," Gaillard read, which meant nothing to Charlie, but the paramedic's tone made it clear that this wasn't good.

Gaillard's partner, a slender, middle-aged man named Morneau, hoisted an IV pole and hung two bags of clear fluid on it. "Point four mils of atropine and a milligram of epinephrine," he said, adding, for Charlie's benefit, "To get his heart rate back up."

Gaillard launched into rapid chest compressions, counting to himself. *"Un . . . deux . . . trois . . ."* as Morneau scrutinized the readouts. "Dropping," he said, biting his lip.

Gaillard ripped open Drummond's shirt, sending buttons clicking onto the pavement. Next he snapped open a case that resembled a laptop computer. "Trying two hundred joules," he said, withdrawing a pair of defibrillator paddles. "Stand clear."

On the other side of the gurney, Charlie took a step back, at once hoping and bracing himself.

Gaillard aimed the paddles. Both paramedics' absorption was such that they seemed oblivious to the tire-screaming arrival of a sporty black Fiat, until a young brunette in a floral-print cocktail dress climbed out of the passenger seat, gun in hand. Stanley followed from the driver's seat, a sidearm drawn as well.

Charlie's jumbled emotions were slashed away by fear.

Stanley looked through him to the paramedics. "Gentlemen, I'm Special Agent Stanley and this is Special Agent Lanier, FBI." He waved an FBI badge. "These two men are wanted for capital crimes in the United States. We need to take them into our custody."

Gaillard, poised to use the paddles, looked down at Drummond. "He's in ventricular fibrillation. I need to shock him *now*."

Lanier pointed her gun at him and pulled the trigger. The muzzle flash spotlit Gaillard's shocked face. The paramedic dropped behind the gurney, apparently dead before reaching the sidewalk. The defibrillator clunked down beside him.

55

Shielded from Lanier and Stanley by the gurney, Charlie watched the surviving paramedic, Morneau, leap into the rear of his ambulance and disappear behind one of the van's double doors.

Dropping to a knee, Lanier leveled her gun at the section of door likely between her and the paramedic's heart.

The roar from the barrel, the metallic fracture, and Morneau's wail all resounded within the cul-de-sac.

Charlie looked at his father, hoping the din would rouse him. The only movement was Drummond's EKG, descending, accompanied by a lethargic blip that lasted for at least a minute.

Or so it seemed to Charlie, adrenaline surging into his veins, accelerating his mental acuity and, he sensed, slowing the pace of the rest of the world.

He reached through the undercarriage of

the gurney for the defibrillator, on the pavement at the edge of a pool of Gaillard's blood. He drew it back, trying to weave through the gurney's elaborate network of springs and crisscrossing shafts. A sharp bolt ripped a red strip into his forearm. He felt nothing.

Gripping the handles on his side of the gurney, he propelled Drummond toward the ambulance.

Lanier rotated toward them, slow as a second hand in Charlie's heightened sense of things. She tweaked her aim.

Before she could fire, Charlie pulled the trigger of his Glock twice. The first bullet plowed into the Fiat's passenger-side mirror, sending the mirror's chrome housing bouncing end over end along the asphalt. Unfazed, Lanier dropped behind the passenger door to the street.

Charlie's second bullet sailed into the crack between the windshield and the open driver's door. Blood spouted from Stanley's shoulder. Writhing, he fell from view.

Charlie adjusted the Glock and snapped the trigger again. He was conscious not only of the thwack of the firing pin, but of the explosion of the primer, and the heat pushing on the base of the bullet — hotter and harder until there was enough force to overcome the frictional bond between the bullet and its casing. With a plume of flame, the projectile leaped from the barrel and seemed to wade into the Fiat's windshield, just in front of the steering wheel. Particles of glass wafted into the air like confetti. Blood spurted from Lanier's right arm. Her gun arm.

The front of the gurney banged into the ambulance's rear bumper. Charlie vaulted in, hauling Drummond after him. Drawing him really; Charlie wasn't experiencing weight or friction as he normally did.

The ambulance wasn't a van so much as a hospital on wheels, its multitude of cabinets, compartments, and pouches crammed with supplies. Charlie set Drummond on the floor, then fired the Glock over his shoulder, exploding more of the Fiat's windshield.

Lanier's barrel, propped on the dashboard, sashayed sideways as it discharged.

Charlie threw up his left arm, shielding Drummond's head. The bullet slashed into Charlie's shoulder, picking him up. Tearing out of him, it dragged him to the floor. He crashed face-first into the grainy metal.

He tried to use his newfound command of his senses to turn off the searing pain. It didn't work. He had been hit by a bullet once before — it had just grazed him, really, yet felt like certain death. *This* was death wielding a razor-sharp scythe. Still, Charlie pulled the second ambulance door shut, grabbed for the IV bar suspended from the ceiling, and hauled himself to his feet.

Drummond lay still, two shades bluer than before. Morneau was slumped beside him, trying to adhere an enormous bandage to his own belly, over a hole that oozed blood with each beat of his racing heart.

"Here," Charlie said, making his way to the front of the van. He handed the man the defibrillator. "Can you try and use this now?"

A bullet smashed a cavity in one of the rear doors. The glass casing of a wall clock shattered, raining shards.

"Now's not such a good time," Morneau stammered. "They're still shooting at us!"

"I noticed." Charlie jumped for the driver's seat and released the parking brake. "How about this? You take care of my father, I'll take care of them."

He mashed the clutch, shifted into first gear, and flattened the gas pedal. The van lurched forward. He watched in his side mirror as the lanky paramedic lowered himself to the floor.

Another bullet pounded through the back before digging into the radio, releasing an acrid stench of burning rubber.

"We'll never get away from them in this thing," Morneau cried.

"Best we can do is try." Charlie aimed the ambulance toward the street behind the consulate. "And if it works, we won't be dead."

With a relenting sigh, the paramedic turned to Drummond. "He probably needs more atropine." He drew a syringe from a drawer, too slowly, his rigidity suggesting he was bracing for the next bullet.

"I'll tell you a story my father once told me," Charlie said. "My grandfather — well, not my grandfather, actually, but a hit man in witness protection whose cover was my grandfather — he lived in Chicago during Al Capone's heyday. You know who Al Capone is?"

"Of course." Morneau sounded concerned for Charlie's sanity. But at least he was administering the atropine to Drummond.

"Every once in a while, Grandpa Tony would hear machine-gun fire. He would peek out his window and see these mobsters racing by in a Cadillac that had been shot up like Peg-Board, and chasing after them were the cops, in a police wagon, same condition. The point is, every single time, everyone was alive. The moral of the story:

It's extremely difficult to fire from one moving vehicle at another with any degree of accuracy. They're just trying to fluster us."

Morneau pressed a button on the defibrillator and set the paddles on Drummond's chest. The charge wasn't as percussive or otherwise dramatic as on TV medical dramas — the jolt of electricity merely quivered Drummond, but a healthy pink returned to his face. He opened his eyes.

"Pulse is much better," Morneau exclaimed.

"Dad?" Charlie cried, his excitement tinged by disbelief.

"I'm fine," Drummond said, obviously as white a lie as had ever been told.

Still, the words were music to Charlie. He crushed the accelerator and, with a screeching slide that pushed the van to the brink of capsize, swung onto the street, remarkably with no more disturbance than a compartment door swinging open and a spool of gauze rolling out.

The sideview mirror showed the black Fiat rocketing after them, however.

56

The Fiat was catching up. Charlie saw Stanley at the wheel, face speckled with blood, but as determined as ever. In the passenger seat, Lanier squinted against the onrushing air, aimed a preposterously large assault rifle through the cavity in the windshield, and fired.

The bullet hammered through the back of the ambulance, struck the metal handle of the open compartment door, and ricocheted into a computer display, smashing it to pebbles. Morneau regarded the computer with heightened dread.

"It's okay," Charlie said. "The bullet didn't come close to us." He shifted into second and made for the well-lit cross street about half a mile ahead; it appeared to be bustling with pedestrians and other vehicles.

"I just thought of one problem," Morneau said. "In your Al Capone story, the vehicles were not carrying highly flammable oxygen tanks."

Charlie nodded. "That is a problem. Pass me the defibrillator?"

Although clearly puzzled, Morneau handed the device forward.

Charlie rolled down his window, causing an eruption of blood from the gunshot wound in his shoulder and pain to match. Alternating glances between the Fiat and the road ahead, he tried to aim the defibrillator at the large cavity that had formerly been the Fiat's windshield.

"The big red button puts this thing in zap mode, right?" he asked the paramedic.

"Yes, but it can't shock anyone unless both paddles are in contact with the body simultaneously, forming a circuit."

"Well, what are the odds he'll know all that?" Charlie let the defibrillator fall out of his window.

It wobbled backward through the air, its paddles flapping wildly, toward the Fiat.

Eyes wide, Stanley spun the wheel to avoid the device, sending the Fiat crunching into a parked delivery truck. The Fiat's hood crumpled, Stanley slumped in his seat, and the fender flopped onto the asphalt.

"That sounded good," said Morneau.

"Yeah . . ." Charlie hesitated at the sight

of Lanier climbing out of the sports car, leveling her assault rifle.

A monster bullet punched through the rear of the ambulance, sounding as if it had exploded on impact. The entire vehicle jumped.

"The oxygen tank!" Morneau shouted. "We need to get out!"

Flames began to sprout throughout the ambulance. Charlie hit the brakes and punched open his door. He clocked the wheel so that the driver's side would face away from Lanier, allowing the ambulance to provide cover for their egress.

Morneau hauled Drummond to his feet and dragged him toward Charlie.

Before Charlie could help, a bigger explosion spat him out the open driver's door. The ambulance itself disappeared in a blob of fire. Scalded, Charlie fell backward, landing on the asphalt, on his spine, the pain unbearable, then even worse as Drummond and Morneau slammed into him. He was pleased, though, because neither appeared seriously injured. At the same time, shock tugged him toward unconsciousness.

He would have allowed himself to glide there if not for the click of Lanier's heels.

Scrambling out from the tangle of limbs, Charlie grabbed for the Glock beside him.

The Glock that had been beside him.

Now, nowhere in sight.

Stanley rounded one end of the van, leading with a gun. The massive barrel of Lanier's rifle preceded her around the other side.

Morneau fainted, probably a consequence of the blood pouring from his reopened wound.

Seven or eight vehicles, several with flashing lights and sirens, charged toward the remains of the ambulance. Leading the charge were the same two beige Suburbans in which Charlie and Drummond had been transferred from the docks to the consulate.

As if Stanley and Lanier needed reinforcements, Charlie thought.

Turning to his father, who lay on the street beside him, he said, "I'm sorry."

Drummond's response was lost under the shrieking halt of the Suburbans. A passenger door opened and Corbitt slid out. He wore a rumpled linen business suit over a pajama shirt.

Staggering out from behind the van, Stanley said, "Chief Corbitt, your timing is excellent once again." He waved at Charlie and Drummond. "The rabbits nearly gave us the slip."

"Really?" Clasping his hands behind his

back, Corbitt started to pace. "Remember how this morning I was telling you that we now have miniaturized digital camcorders capable of recording up to sixteen hours of video?"

Stanley smiled. "Of course."

Corbitt stopped pacing, squaring himself with Stanley. "Tonight, after I reviewed today's footage from the decanter on the yacht, I decided I'd better get down here."

Charlie sensed the odds had taken a fortuitous if not incredible turn. He kept his cheer in check, however. In his experience, such a turn was unprecedented, and, with the Cavalry involved, impossible.

Stanley sighed. "Listen, Corbitt, there are factors you know nothing about, and that needs to remain the case."

"Maybe so. But until I hear otherwise from the State Department or from headquarters, you two are going into custody." Corbitt indicated the other members of his party. Six Martinique policemen, two paramedics, and three marine guards had emerged from the vehicles, all but the paramedics carrying sidearms or rifles.

"What authority do you have to take us into custody?" Stanley shouted.

"French law," Corbitt said. "On the way here, we received a report of a Martinican emergency medical technician who'd been gunned down in cold blood." Turning toward the local policemen and paramedics, the Saint Lucia base chief pointed at Stanley and Lanier. "I believe we'll find that they're the ones who did it."

57

"I owe you a pot of homemade chowder," said Alice over the phone from the American embassy in Geneva. "And whatever else you want."

In the Martinique consulate's secure conference room, Charlie should have leaped in elation and told Alice that he loved her.

But the ADM was stuck like a splinter in his thoughts.

She said she didn't recall Bream by name, only that the copilot who flew her to Newark three weeks ago had been handsome in a roguish way. "Not in the good way, like you," she added quickly.

Their catch-up otherwise was of the bullet-point variety, a function not only of his preoccupation but of a rush on her end — a battery of NSA debriefers awaited her. Hanging up, Charlie couldn't believe he'd neglected to mention that he'd found the treasure of San Isidro.

Eager to check on his father, he shot out of the secure conference room and into the hallway, hurrying down to the infirmary. Drummond had been under anesthesia for the better part of three hours, during which cardiac catheterization had enabled the surgeons to determine that the extent of the damage to his heart was minimal. As also was the case with the CIA's Hilary Hadley, Drummond had made it out of the medical equivalent of the woods.

Corbitt jogged out of an adjacent office, pulling even with Charlie. "Eager to see your dad?" the base chief asked.

"Yes. And to see if he knows where Bream took the bomb."

"It's only a matter of time until we find that son of a bitch." Reaching the elevator landing, Corbitt gazed into the gilded-frame mirror as if already seeing himself with the medal he would receive.

Charlie hit the down button. "I wish I were even half as sure."

"Look, our commo folks sent an encrypted cable — flash precedence — to the director, the chief of the Europe division, plus all the honchos in India, Pakistan, and pretty much everywhere else boats go. The U.S. Coast Guard and Homeland Security have cast the satellite and radar version of a tight net over the water between Saint Lucia and the coast of India. And as we speak, the agency's unleashing NEST teams."

"*What* teams?"

"Oh . . . uh . . . Nuclear Emergency Search . . . something?"

"Team?"

"Right. They have dedicated 707s decked out with radiation sniffers, the works. They've already taken off, on their way to swarm the Caribbean. It's only a matter of time until we get the news that they've disabled Bream's boat."

"What if the radiation is masked?" Charlie didn't want to give away the fact that the supposedly enriched part of the uranium was essentially pabulum, lest the operation's secret be cabled flash precedence pretty much everywhere boats went.

"We still have a squadron of UAVs plus a few tricks that you don't need to know about, but put it this way: Given the intel *you* provided us, we'll know about every object larger than a baseball that comes within five hundred miles of India. Either our people or our liaison counterparts will board any ship they can't swear by, and a good percentage of those that they can."

"Great, unless the bomb's not really

headed to India."

"What would make you think that?"

"Half of everything Bream said was a lie." The groans and sputters of the cables within the elevator shaft seemed to echo Charlie's thought process.

"There's no reason to think he was lying about India, and every reason to think you snagged grade-A intel," Corbitt said. "You're probably just tired."

Tired? If only. Fifteen straight hours of sleep and Charlie might be upgraded to tired. "I just feel like we're overlooking something."

A chime announced the arrival of the elevator. Brass-plated doors slid open. Corbitt led the way into a car whose Victorian décor predated electric elevators. "I'm telling you, you've got nothing to worry about. It probably just needs to set in is all. Take a long bath and crack a cold bottle of beer. You've won, bud. The stuff on that Korean Singles site has completely exonerated you — you're a hundred percent free."

The doors closed with a hydraulic hiss. Charlie, who had never experienced claustrophobia before, felt as if the mahogany panels were about to close in on him.

Clapping a hand on Charlie's good shoulder, Corbitt said, "And it gets even better.

Stanley and that Lanier woman are locked up someplace really dark, key thrown away, the works. And every U.S. agency this side of the Department of Agriculture is teaming to roll up the rest of the Cavalry — I saw onboard UAV footage of Ali Abdullah in his pajamas being tossed into a French paddy wagon. We also collared a couple of other guys you might know, Ben Mallory and John Pitman?"

Pitman had tried to kill Charlie on at least three occasions in New York. Mallory, another Cavalry man, just twice. "Where are they now?"

"Put it this way: They'd better like vermin."

The U.S. Embassy in Barbados had flown in so many physicians and so much medical equipment for Drummond and Hadley that the consulate infirmary now looked like the ICU at Mass General. And everywhere there wasn't a medical professional, there was a marine guard. Charlie figured that he and Drummond were safer here than anywhere they'd been in months, or anywhere they might ever go.

Charlie entered Drummond's room — a curtained-off section of the infirmary, really. Drummond sat up in bed with obvious

416

pain. His generally wan appearance wasn't helped by the pale green light from the stack of machines or the intravenous tubes blooming from his arms.

"Good morning," he said.

It was a little past three A.M.

"How are you feeling, Dad?"

"Fine. Why does everyone keep asking me that?"

Charlie put him at a 4. He decided to try anyway. "Does anything seem strange to you about the Bream business?"

Drummond regarded one of the green curtains. "Pirate, right?"

"In a sense." Charlie hadn't expected much more.

"Plays first base, as I recall."

"That's Sid Bream." A Pittsburgh Pirate. Twenty years ago.

Weighted by frustration, Charlie took a seat at the edge of the bed, careful not to knock loose Drummond's IVs.

Drummond sat a bit straighter and smiled, restoring some color to his cheeks. "Right, Bream was the name of our pilot too," he said.

Charlie felt a trickle of optimism. "That's the one I meant."

Drummond paused to reflect. "Who was he, really?"

417

"That's probably the first question I should have asked." Charlie put it to Corbitt, chatting with a nurse outside the makeshift doorway.

Stepping into the room, the base chief shrugged. "Maybe you'll find out in the debrief."

"What debrief?"

"With Caldwell Eskridge, chief of the Europe division."

"When does he get here?"

Corbitt looked at Charlie as if he'd asked for the moon. "When do you fly to Langley, Virginia, you mean?" Corbitt said. "As soon as possible."

"Barring major medical advances in the next hour," said Charlie, "my father probably won't be able to get on a plane." Or out of bed.

"It's actually McLean, Virginia," Drummond said. "An interesting piece of information: Langley's not a city or town. It's just part of McLean, as Park Slope is part of Brooklyn. You need to go there, Charles."

"Do I?" Charlie wondered if his father's danger detector had been disabled. He turned to Corbitt. "Why can't Eskridge fly here?"

"The mountain doesn't come to Mohammed." Sensing Charlie's anxiety, the base chief added, "I'll be accompanying you."

Which did little to ease Charlie's anxiety. "Great," he said.

Drummond reached forward, clasped Charlie's arm, and drew him close. Although his father's skin was tepid, Charlie felt an infusion of warmth.

"Go to McLean, Charles." Drummond's focus appeared to sharpen. Or was it a trick of the fluorescents?

"But until about twenty minutes ago, the agency had us on their To-Kill list."

"You can handle it. I'm willing to bet on that."

■ ■ ■ ■

PART THREE:
LUCIDITY

■ ■ ■ ■

1

Eight days earlier, a man whose passport listed him as John Townsend Bream had flown from Puerto Rico to Paris to meet with an Algerian agitator he knew from his Air Force Intelligence days.

A three-hour drive from Charles de Gaulle and Bream was in Dijon, far enough off the security grid that countersurveillance didn't require too much effort. And because the city was the capital of the Burgundy wine region, the mustard center of Europe, and home to the most dazzling collection of medieval and Renaissance buildings in the world, there was always a large and diverse enough crowd that anyone could blend in.

Or so Bream thought until Cheb Qatada plopped down opposite him in an isolated booth in the back of an otherwise lively brasserie near the train station — a textbook clandestine meeting spot. The problem was, the bearlike Algerian had a tough time blending in anywhere. Although he shaved every morning while in Europe, he sported a five o'clock shadow by lunchtime, and it was now an hour past that — the best time for a meeting because the lunch crowd thins so that friend can more easily be distinguished from foe, or rather foe may be distinguished from genuine tourist. Qatada's choice to heavily pomade his thick black hair, giving prominence to a V-shaped hairline, made him stand out even more. Also his eyes were set close to an extraordinarily wide and flat nose. But his most remarkable feature was an almost constant toddler-like glee, odd given that the majority of his forty years had been spent on a serial rant — in the form of massacres of innocent civilians — directed at the French government.

"I'm looking to retire," Bream said.

"As opposed to living on a tropical island and flying once or twice a week?" Qatada spoke fluent British-accented English, at a higher pitch than the growl presaged by his appearance.

Bream gazed at the cricket game on the TV above the bar, without which the dark stone tavern wouldn't have appeared much different than it had a millennium ago. He used the mirror behind the bar to take an inventory of the crowd, inspecting for shifts in stance or positioning — that is, were they watching or listening to him? As new people came through the door, he assessed them: local businessmen, tourists, ladies lunching, etc. He would have preferred that one of his "associates" do the countersurveillance, but the mercenaries in his employ were all busy in Gstaad today, rehearsing a rendition for the new Counterterrorism Branch of the U.S. Diplomatic Security Service — as far as they knew.

"I was on the tropical island prospecting," Bream told Qatada. "Now I've got a prospect."

Qatada smiled, maybe at the cricket game, maybe at the play of light on his water glass — who knew? Bream had given him no reason to be happy.

He was about to, though.

"You know how for a party, you write a check and a party planner does everything?" Bream asked. "He gets you the band, the cake, the hall — all for the exact day you want?"

"What about it?"

"I'll run an op for you like that in two weeks, except instead of cake I'll serve up an ADM."

Qatada smiled again. "Sounds like quite a party."

"The venue I have in mind is the municipal marina three hundred and seventy-five meters north of the hotel hosting the G-20."

"The Grand Hotel near Mobile, Alabama?"

"Yeah, beautiful old resort."

"The French delegation is planning to stay there." Qatada spoke matter-of-factly. "I am guessing you knew that."

"Think of them as your guests of honor. All you'll be required to do is push a button, and you'll strike the biggest blow possible for an Islamic state." Qatada's al-Jama'ah al-Islamiyah al-Musallaha, known here in France as Groupe Islamique Armé, sought to oust the current Algerian government.

Qatada sat back, lips pursed with skepticism. "Does the Fountain of Youth come with this package too?"

Bream laughed politely. "You know Nick Fielding?"

"I hope for your sake that he is not your supplier."

"You mean 'cause he's dead? That's why I can get my hands on his ten-kiloton Russian ADM without any opposition from him." Bream paused while the waitress deposited their plates of steak fries, then waited until she was out of earshot. "You know you can practically throw a rock from my place on Martinique to Fielding's island, right?"

"No, I did not." Qatada was rapt.

"I watched his act for three years. Not only that, I watched No Such Agency watching him — I even got myself hired on as copilot for a couple of their charters. After giving an envelope full of money to one of Fielding's goons, I now know not only about Fielding's ADM, but that he took its hiding place to his grave. Since he died, legions of spooks have tried and failed to find it."

"But you can?"

"Yes. Then it's yours, plug and play. I just need five million down to cover my expenses and another seven hundred and forty-five mil on delivery."

The Groupe Islamique Armé's principal benefactor, Algerian oilman Djamel Hasni, could write a check for $750 million on any one of a dozen of his accounts around the world.

"If I told Djamel that you asked for a billion dollars, he'd think seven hundred fifty million was a steal," Qatada said. "His problem isn't going to be the sale price; it's going to be the salesman."

"He'll think I'm an American spook running a play for the United Satans of America?"

"Of course."

"That would mean that the Air Force faked my dishonorable discharge, that I flew clunkers for four years in exile, and that I damn near destroyed myself with the cheap local rum all to build up cover for an op whose objective is to bag a couple of members of an Algerian terrorist group that no one's heard of."

Qatada ceded the point with a nod, but remained circumspect. "How would you get the device into the States?"

"That's the easy part. I built myself an ironclad alias with access to a U.S.-flagged yacht that's a fixture at the Mobile Bay Marina. You ante up, I'll go get the yacht, cruise down to Martinique for a 'pleasure trip,' pick up a 'souvenir' along the way, then cruise on back to Bama."

Qatada winced. "Take it from an expert: Since 9/11, your Homeland Security can't install enough chem-bio-nuke detectors in your ports."

"You're part right. In Miami this scheme would never fly. Houston and New Orleans, ten miles before I even reached the coast, drones would shoot Hellfire missiles, turn my yacht into flotsam, and ask questions later."

"But not in Mobile?"

"Think of Mobile as the Groupe Islamique Armé of port cities: It's big, but no one knows much about it or really cares much about it. Cares enough, I ought to say."

Qatada shrugged. "Even in such places, the Americans can afford to give every other port employee a palm-sized gamma-ray spectrometer and litter the docks with sniffers and ICx rovers and probably many other new detection devices that we do not even know about."

"But there's almost nothing along the other hundred-something miles of coast."

"Except the Coast Guard and the Customs and Border Protection agency. You don't think al-Qaeda has spent thousands of hours trying to find holes there? Djamel has spent millions of dollars on computer simulations alone."

As a twelve-year-old, Bream had been undefeated in Tennessee Chess Association junior play, but he had dropped the sport in high school in deference to his image. Still he thought like a chess player. Now he saw checkmate in two moves. "The key is, I'll be cooperating with Coast Guard and CBP from start to finish," he said. "They'll have had me on transponder and satellite the whole time I'm in the Caribbean, plus five kinds of radar on top of that as soon as I get close to U.S. waters on the way home. A foreign national can expect a Custom and Border Protection 'welcome committee' on reaching Alabama waters. But most of the time, all a good ol' American boy's gotta do is check in with the CBP folks with a phone call, which I'll do during the night — they close at five every day. One in thirty times, they summon you across the bay to the commercial docks for an inspection the next morning, in which case I'll risk offloading the device before I go. One in ten times, they come to your marina for a look-see the next morning. But even if that happens, I'm still good because the ADM's concealed within a specially modified housing that does to spectrometers what fresh-grated bell pepper does to bloodhounds. And most of the time, all the CBP folks do is call you and say, 'Welcome home, sir.' "

And there it was, Qatada's smile, at full wattage. Although pleased, Bream looked down so that no one would remember his face, too.

2

The CIA's New Headquarters Building, a pair of six-story towers of sea-green glass, could have been mistaken for a modern museum. Hardly the dark fortress that Charlie, in the Hyundai's passenger seat, had been expecting. At the wheel of the rental Corbitt was whistling the tune of "We're Off to See the Wizard."

Although it was two in the afternoon, Charlie would have believed it was early evening, a consequence of the enervating trip from Martinique more than the overcast sky. A nagging sensation that he'd overlooked a clue to Bream's plans had kept him from sleeping.

As he extricated himself from the subcompact car, his eyes smarted from fatigue, and his reflection in the window shocked him: In the gray flannel business suit and dark overcoat the consulate had procured for him, he resembled his father in old photos.

He and Corbitt proceeded through a colossal arching entryway to the skylit lobby. Feelings of inadequacy buffeted Charlie, making the bitter wind an afterthought.

Leaving him with Eskridge and a young analyst at the door of a secure conference room, Corbitt said, not entirely in jest, "They only sent me along to make sure you didn't stop at a racetrack."

"But I have a hunch I'm missing something," Charlie said after detailing the events of the past few days. "What if India is a decoy? What if the real target is somewhere else, maybe even somewhere in the United States?"

Across the conference table, a giant surfboard rendered in aquamarine glass, Eskridge shared a look with the analyst, Harding Doxstader, a twentysomething version of his boss. Their look made Charlie think of parents who've just been informed by their child about the monsters in his closet.

"We've picked up a good deal of chatter that a Punjabi separatist group was in the market for an ADM," Eskridge assured Charlie. "If not for you, though, we wouldn't have any idea about Vasant Panchami, or even that the bomb was heading to India."

"What if Bream just wants you to think he tried to kill me and my father?" Charlie asked. "That way, our India revelation would carry more weight."

Eskridge shrugged. "If Bream had meant to use India as a decoy, eliminating you would have eliminated his means of decoying us."

Nodding, Doxstader scribbled a note on what appeared to be a sheet of white light hovering above the table.

"The thing is, he probably would have taken into account that my father could land a plane," Charlie said. "Also, if he really wanted to kill us, why not just shoot us beforehand on the beach?"

Doxstader said, "Sir, if I'm not mistaken, you said that, at that time, your father was suffering from extreme disorientation symptomatic of Alzheimer's disease." He checked his notes. " 'A four,' you said."

"Right, at the time, he couldn't have flown a kite. But Bream knew that my father had episodes of lucidity. And my father wasn't our only option. If Alice hadn't called, someone at one of the control towers in the area might have given us instructions over the radio."

Eskridge appeared to ponder this, pulling the knot of his tie to the point where it would take some effort to undo. "Mr. Clark, do you have any factual basis for your speculation that the target might be in the United States?"

"For one thing, I don't see Bream being on the level about his employers. The Injuns, he called them. Every bit of information he volunteered was tailored to a clever cover — it was only at the very end that I saw his redneck act for what it was."

"So he's more intelligent than he let on." Eskridge inspected his fingernails. "There's a fellow here at the agency. Summa cum laude from MIT, top of his class at the Farm, National Clandestine Service fast track. He had some home trouble. Now he works in Food Service."

Food Service gave Charlie a new line of thought. "You know, I asked Bream if he'd celebrate the sale of the ADM with a good bottle of wine — I was fishing for where he was taking the bomb. He pooh-poohed me. He'd be having Budweiser, he said, and a rack of ribs. Not exactly standard Mumbai fare."

"Probably just playing to his cover again," Eskridge said.

"What if it were one of the bits of truth mixed in to give foundation to the lies?"

"You'd be surprised what you can find in

Mumbai," said Doxstader. "There are now two hundred and forty-four McDonald's in India."

Eskridge remained intent on a thumbnail. "Alternately, if you've just sold a nuclear weapon to folks who have no compunction about using one, you don't want to stick around. You want to get bloody well back on your plane. Later, you celebrate, sure. At a good ribs joint, if that's your thing. Or a sushi bar. I don't see how it pertains."

With a sudden sense that he was closing in on the clue that had been eluding him, Charlie rushed his words. "Right after that, I asked him how the collateral would affect his appetite. I was hoping to bring his ego into play. He asked if my knowing he was kept up nights by thoughts of the victims made him less of a villain in my eyes. Then he said that he'd made the decision to go ahead anyway because it's the wake-up call *our country* needs."

Eskridge shook his head. "It's more likely that, as you said earlier, he wants the mansion. Ultimately, the bad guys all want the mansion. The good guys too."

Charlie pulled his seat closer to the table. "But if we walk back the cat —"

Eskridge turned to Doxstader to explain. "Old counterintelligence expression."

The junior man nodded, as if impressed. Charlie suspected they were mocking him, but he forged on. "He made so many disparaging remarks about the 'Culinary Institute of America' and other 'so-called' intelligence agencies. If the best and brightest were on this case, he said, he wouldn't have had such an easy time of it. Maybe he was one of you once. It sure seemed like he'd had the same training as my father. Maybe the intelligence community didn't accept him, or, in his mind, judged him unfairly. And now he wants to prove he was right."

Eskridge almost sneered. "The way horse-players do?"

"The thrill of being right drives a lot of people to do stupid things."

Doxstader looked up. "You know, the G-20 starts this weekend."

"The G-20?" Charlie said.

"The Group of Twenty. Argentina, Brazil, China —"

Eskridge cut in. "And seventeen other countries, including ours, who send deputies to chat about economic issues. The reason you don't know about it, Charlie, is the same reason terrorists wouldn't be interested: no sex appeal. I couldn't even tell you where they're holding the G-20."

"Mobile, Alabama." Doxstader set down

his stylus for the first time. "Gem of a city, precisely the sort of secondary target al-Qaeda's been focusing on."

He waited for a response from Eskridge, who focused on a cuff link.

Doxstader wasn't deterred. "Sir, a number of the top French officials are attending the G-20, including the president — something having to do with Mobile's French heritage. Also Mobile has close to a hundred miles of coast without anything near the level of security in a Miami or a Long Beach."

"And wouldn't the element of surprise be a selling point?" Charlie asked.

Doxstader nodded emphatically. Eskridge cleared his throat in an obvious effort to suppress his young colleague. "You probably don't need to know this, but we have another source corroborating the India story," Eskridge said. "A former intelligence operative, one of Alice Rutherford's captors, tried to sell information to our people in Geneva. He said that Ms. Rutherford was to be traded for an ADM by the United Liberation Front of the Punjab. A couple of weeks ago, the very same United Liberation Front of the Punjab had sent men to Martinique to try to buy the ADM."

"But suppose they didn't buy it," Charlie said.

"They didn't." Eskridge grumbled. "Not until yesterday."

The implicit blame stung Charlie. "Why would Bream be foolish enough to let some hired thug in on his plans? Even I would have known to make up a cover story for Alice's rendition."

"This thug was a professional spy, or at least he had been," Eskridge said. "He assumed he'd been false-flagged by Bream. Then he did some digging."

"And found the fool's gold Bream had left for him?" Charlie said. "Why would Bream have hired an untrustworthy ex-spy in the first place?"

Eskridge turned to Doxstader. "Share the company secret to catching bad guys."

Doxstader nodded. "They always make mistakes."

"The thing is, Bream knew enough to use the Indians as straw dogs," Charlie said. Eskridge's enthusiastic nod belied his growing impatience. "He could be trying to divert attention from Alabama, which, not incidentally, is to ribs what Switzerland is to cheese. Plus, I bet he really is a Southerner."

"You *bet?*" Eskridge turned to Doxstader. "What do we know?"

"Only that the actual John Townsend Bream has been institutionalized in Mississippi for nine years."

"That lends more credence to Southerner than if the institution were in New Hampshire," Charlie said, but to blank faces. "And he certainly had the dialect down, and the accent — a lot better than the cast of *Gone with the Wind,* anyway."

Eskridge rolled his eyes.

"You'd be amazed at the Russians' linguistic training," Doxstader said to Charlie.

Charlie wanted to hit something. "Why would Bream want us to think he's a Southerner?"

"It's an old spook trick." Eskridge pushed back from the table. "So you don't know who he really is."

3

Charlie planned to spend the next couple of days in Laurel, Maryland, enjoying some R & R at Pimlico Race Course. Or so he told Corbitt as they returned to the airport, alleviating the base chief's concern that Charlie would take his wild theory to the media.

In fact, Charlie drove a rented Ford Taurus 1,039 miles south. At Mobile's city limits the sporadic shacks and farmhouses alongside the country road mushroomed into a collection of genteel antebellum homes and buildings that met his conception of the old South. Until several taller buildings appeared, and from behind them, taller buildings still. The skyline rose, like flights of stairs, to futuristic skyscrapers. This was certainly not the quaint Southern city that his hasty Googling had led him to envision, a few square blocks of charismatic office buildings and a "downtown" swaying to the sultry saxophones from little jazz clubs, the air scented with smoke from ramshackle yet charming ribs joints.

The country road rose into an elevated modern highway, spiraling in apparent defiance of the laws of physics over what Charlie initially took to be the Gulf of Mexico. It was the sort of construction that caused people to stop and marvel. Charlie indeed marveled at it, and he marveled even more at the body of water, which extended to the horizon, like any ocean. Except *this,* unless the maps and signs were mistaken, was Mobile Bay.

He exited the highway at Water Street, a four-lane road paralleling the Alabama State Docks, check-in point for vessels from abroad. He drove alongside miles and miles of blackened iron piers, mammoth warehouses, and comparable container ships. Not only did the complex dwarf the city, an entire naval fleet could cruise into it without drawing notice from shore.

He had a feeling, like a cold coming on, that he'd greatly underestimated the amount of detective work that would be required to find Bream here.

He caught sight of a sign plastered onto the side of a warehouse — he'd seen one or two of them already, but only now did the significance register. It listed a Customs and

Border Protection phone number for arriving noncommercial vessels to schedule in-harbor inspections. If Bream were checking in with Uncle Sam, he could do so from any number of harbors on the ocean-sized bay.

Charlie sat outside Mobile's tourist information office with a map of Mobile Bay spread over his steering wheel. In the passenger seat was a pile of brochures that the zealous staffers had forced on him, including those of a charter fishing service, a children's museum, various historical sites, and local real estate agencies — in the event that he really, really liked the contents of the other brochures.

Gusts off the bay spat bits of garbage around the parking lot. Dark sheets of rain belted the rented Ford. The horseshoe-shaped bay itself was 413 square miles, or twenty times the size of Manhattan. Its shoreline was eighty-four miles, and there were another hundred miles of beaches on either side of its mouth. He had a better chance of finding a needle hidden in New York than he did of finding Bream in Mobile.

And here was one for the annals of idiocy: He had actually thought he could row a boat across Mobile Bay, if needed, to look for Bream.

Bream had taken possession of the washing machine on Monday, three days ago. A fast yacht would take seventy hours to get here. The G-20 kicked off tomorrow evening. Presumably sometime before then, when security would be tightest, Bream would arrive with the ADM. Unless he'd taken a plane.

Charlie wondered what his father would do now.

He had no idea. That was the problem.

He called Alice, needing comfort as much as counsel. Five rings and her voice mail kicked in. She was probably in a conference room that didn't permit incoming calls.

Just as well. He didn't relish explaining to her how he'd charged down to Alabama on little more than a hunch.

He glimpsed a small ad on the back of a local pennysaver, placed by a private detective named Dave LeCroy, who specialized in marital infidelity. LeCroy's black-and-white photo might have passed for one of a young, beardless Abraham Lincoln if not for the cell phone pressed to his ear. A comic strip balloon from his mouth declared, "I'll get your man!"

4

Shafts of sunlight appeared to part the clouds when Charlie parallel parked on a low-rent stretch of Dauphin Street, Mobile's answer to Bourbon Street according to the tourist information. The elaborate four-and five-story buildings indeed conjured those of New Orleans, but at eleven-thirty in the morning, Dauphin — pronounced *Doffin* by everyone here — was quiet, the bars still asleep.

Charlie entered a squat building whose ground floor tenants included a "gentlemen's club" and a tattoo parlor. A grubby flight of stairs brought him to a door stenciled with big gold letters: OFFICES OF DAVID P. LECROY, LICENSED PRIVATE INVESTIGATOR.

Charlie had barely knocked when the door was flung open by a voluptuous young woman.

"Hi," she said, adding, "I'm the receptionist." She wore a white blouse and a modest plaid skirt. Her lofty heels, the absence of hose, and the tattoo of dice on her ankle suggested that she worked at the club downstairs, and that she threw on the blouse and skirt when the detective had a prospective client. "Mr. LeCroy is expecting you."

As Charlie followed her through the tiny anteroom, he realized that she hadn't asked him his name. She gestured him ahead into a faux-teak paneled office, where the man from the ad shot up from his vinyl chair.

"Great to meet you," he said, pumping Charlie's hand.

"Same." Charlie heard the outer door shut and heels clicking down the stairs.

In real life, the latter-day young Lincoln was pushing fifty and stood no higher than Charlie's nose. He'd used a good retoucher for his ad — much of his face showed remnants of teenage acne. His hair was not his. And he'd put money into his mouth. Perhaps too much. Flashing a game-show host's smile, he said, "Take a load off." His eyes never once met Charlie's.

Sitting down, Charlie asked, "So how'd you get into detective work?"

"I like to help people." Leaning forward, LeCroy nested his chin on his hands, a

445

pointedly contemplative pose. Finally his eyes found Charlie's. "How can I help you?"

"I have a friend who arrived or will be arriving here from overseas this week in a private yacht, but I don't have a way of reaching him. He's not big on turning on his phone or checking e-mail on vacation. I was hoping that, as a licensed PI, you'd be able to access the port's entry database."

The screen saver on LeCroy's computer was a low-resolution photo of a naked blonde in the same chair Charlie occupied now. The detective clicked his mouse and she dissolved into a jumble of file icons. "Know the name of the boat?" he asked.

"No."

"What's your friend's name?"

All Charlie knew was that the name wouldn't be Bream. "Is there any way I could see a list of all the people who've arrived?"

LeCroy's eyes filled with understanding. "Let me guess: Your old lady took a cruise for two with a yacht owner you've never met and know nothing about, but would very much like to sock in the nose?"

"That sums it up well enough."

LeCroy smiled. "I have more cases like this than you'd believe."

"Then I have come to the right place."

Charlie decided that the private eye was probably better suited to this job than the CIA was.

"I can execute this search now." LeCroy tapped his keyboard. "It usually runs ninety-nine ninety-five. How does that suit you?"

"How does cash suit you?"

"Goes well with my leather billfold."

It took Charlie a moment to figure out in which of his new cargo pants pockets he'd placed his wallet. He dug it out and produced a hundred-dollar bill. Directed by a bob of LeCroy's head, he dropped it into the in-box.

"Okay then." The private investigator interlaced and stretched his fingers, the way pianists limber up. "So where'd the bastard take her?"

"Saint Lucia or the vicinity." Bream would have covered his tracks, Charlie thought, though it made sense to start there.

LeCroy clicked away at the keys. "Bingo!"

Charlie felt a shiver of excitement.

"Ronald Feldman and Annabelle Kammeyer, ages sixty-one and thirty-one, of Fort Walton Beach, Florida. Arrived here in Mobile from Saint Lucia on Tuesday the twelfth, two days ago."

Charlie's excitement dissipated. "Couldn't be my 'friend.' He was still in the Caribbean

447

Monday the eleventh. I don't think he could've gotten up here that fast."

LeCroy reapplied himself to the keyboard. "I'm gonna check a bunch of ports. It's possible the guy cleared customs in Florida or in Gulfport, Mississippi. Also a lot of folks get it out of the way in San Juan."

The Florida Panhandle and Mississippi were both thirty miles away. The residents of Mississippi would offer a strong argument that their barbecue beat Alabama's. Charlie could practically hear his prospects deflating.

The bulky dot-matrix printer behind LeCroy grunted out three sheets of paper. The detective snapped them up and perused. "Okeydoke, in the past forty-eight hours ending yesterday at four-fifty-eight P.M. — that's about as late as CBP stays open — we've got eighty-three private vessels that checked in one way or another and either passed inspection or were cleared without inspection."

"Can you tell me how many had a guy aboard between, say, thirty and forty?"

LeCroy ran his finger down the top page, counting to himself. "Thirteen so far. Plus a boat with a Jean aboard, age of thirty-one. Probably a broad, but could be a French guy, right?"

Charlie tried not to appear forlorn.

"Cheer up, kiddo. The game's just begun," LeCroy said. "Now's when I put the gum to the pavement."

"And do what?"

"Trade secret. Two twenty-five a day, plus expenses."

"How about two hundred, if you give me a for instance?"

"Fine. Between us: harbormasters. They make it their business to know which fish are in their harbors, let alone which boats."

"Aren't they supposed to be discreet?"

"Yeah, but they're also supposed to not accept donations for their kids' new video game console funds, if you get my drift."

"I think so," Charlie said. He liked the harbormaster strategy, but odds were LeCroy would offer bribes that Bream would smell a state away.

LeCroy flipped through his desk calendar. "I got spouse cases today and tomorrow, meaning I'm stuck in a car with a camera in a motel parking lot. After that, I'm yours. What do you say you call me then?"

"That fits my schedule perfectly," said Charlie, who intended to go visit the harbormasters now.

5

The posh Mobile Bay Marina sat a quarter of a mile up the beach from the Grand Hotel. The information Charlie needed was strictly proprietary. Finally, a task suited to a horseplayer.

At the track, a fortune could be made with the knowledge that a favorite was running just because "he needs a race," meaning he's not fit to win, so the jockey will "school" him — just let him experience competition. Much of Charlie's "job" had been wheedling such intel from grooms. The attendant in the Meadowlands owners and trainers parking lot often proved an oracle — just not often enough. At Aqueduct, the refreshment stand workers were Charlie's best sources. Amazing what an owner would let slip while waiting for his seventh Big-A Big-B — thirty-two-ounce beer — of the day.

In the waterside village catering to the

Mobile Bay Marina, the Grand Hotel, and a cluster of golf and beach developments, Charlie posed as a tourist. He was interested in chartering a yacht, he told the eager-to-serve proprietors in three of the quaint art galleries and boutiques crammed onto the short main street. He learned that the marina's veteran harbormaster, known to all as Captain Glenny, viewed her job as part sheriff and part priest. Refueling a cabin cruiser took in excess of an hour, during which time returning yachtsmen regaled her with their adventures. In twenty years on the job, she had become their friend and confidante.

Charlie sensed such a woman would look upon any bribe with indignation. Were Bream among her charges, she would alert him within moments.

Charlie took a page from the *Post* and *Daily News* beat reporters at the track. Their jobs, consisting of little more than reporting the order of finish and adding a dash of commentary, placed them at journalism's lowest rung. Nevertheless, their status as members of the media induced complete strangers to speak with the sort of candor psychiatrists rarely attain from their patients. The limelight acted as a powerful stimulant, even the few particles of limelight

451

emanating from a department whose existence newspapers didn't like to acknowledge.

Charlie's cover began with a stop at a nearby Sears. He bought a baggy pair of khakis, an oxford shirt, Hush Puppy knockoffs, and an extra-large synthetic wool parka. The idea was to look like a journalist as well as hide his identity from Bream.

In the same mall, Charlie hit Cheapo's, an office supply store. For $4.99 he printed himself business cards using the same name that appeared on his forged New York driver's license, John Parker, and billing him as Editor at Large for *South,* a new lifestyles magazine based in Tampa. He chose Tampa because it was far enough away from Mobile to preclude *Do you know?* questions. Also Tampa was the only place in the South where Charlie had actually spent time — albeit all of it at Tampa Bay Downs.

The Mobile Bay Marina stayed open twenty-four hours. It was probably never more inviting than when Charlie arrived, the bay a pastiche of blues and silver, the sun having brought the air to the precise temperature at which being outdoors felt most invigorating. Rustic docks and gleaming hulls and spars swayed with the mild current. From the parking lot, he saw no one about, though there might be yachtsmen below deck. He wasn't sure how to pass through the big entry gate without drawing their attention. Then he spotted the OPEN TO THE PUBLIC sign. It felt like a gift.

The instant he set foot on the pier, a middle-aged woman burst out of the harbormaster's office. She was stout and might have been pretty if she hadn't appeared poised to bark at him. Her spiky hair was cut short, exposing a sizable collection of gold earrings, worn only on her left ear.

"How can I help you?" she asked with a none-too-subtle undertone of "You are obviously not a wealthy yachtsman or someone a wealthy yachtsman would want to see, so what the heck are you doing here?"

"I'm a reporter," Charlie said.

She looked him over. "Doing something on the G-20?"

"Actually I write for *South Magazine.*"

"Uh-huh. Don't know it."

So much for the Limelight Effect.

"Lead times what they are, my story won't run until the spring issue. We're doing a piece on the prettiest harbors in the South, and so far this one gets my vote. Could you by any chance direct me to the harbormaster, Glenny Gorgas?"

"I'm Glenny." She took in Charlie's mock surprise. "Short for Glendolyn."

"Pretty name."

She warmed, but only by a degree. "So how can I help you?"

He needed to find out which yachts had arrived in the last day or two. This time of year, the number wouldn't be high.

"Do you, by any chance, have time to give me the dime tour?"

They walked the docks for twenty minutes, Glenny paying no attention to the sprawling golf course or the tennis courts, or the resort hotel itself, a town's worth of pert three-story brown clapboard buildings, many of which loomed over the marina. Her focus was on the two hundred or so yachts, which she referred to as if they were their owners. Passing a sleek and towering catamaran, she said, with pride, "*He* made a hole in one last weekend."

This was the opening Charlie had been waiting for. "Here in Mobile?"

"Mr. Chandler has a condo on the course at the Grand." She smiled. "Sailing for him is an excuse to play golf."

"Do a lot of the boat owners have homes here?"

454

"A few have condos here, but most live close enough, up in Montgomery or Birmingham. A handful in Tennessee."

"How many people do you see during the winter?"

She sighed. "Winter's a lonely time to be a harbormaster."

He stopped, pointedly looking around. There was no sign of anyone, just the groans of ropes holding yachts to docks. "Is *anyone* here now?"

The harbormaster brightened. "Actually, I had two parties in yesterday, and one the night before that. January and February I get the occasional excursion to the Caribbean or Mexico."

With manufactured fascination, Charlie scribbled each in his notebook. "It must be fun, when the people come back, to hear about their adventures?"

Glenny's step added a skip. "Best part of the job."

"Heard any good stories lately?"

"I'm expecting a really good one any time now, actually." She pointed to an empty slip at the end of the far dock. "Anthony and Vera Campodonico, retired couple, spent their whole careers at Auburn — he used to be a dean. Now they go down to the Caribbean and South America looking for lost civilizations and stuff like that. He actually writes books about it."

Probably not Bream, Charlie thought, given the Campodonicos' ages.

Glenny strode ahead. "And of course there's Mr. Clemmensen — Clem Clemmensen. Great guy. He just got in from Martinique." She smiled at a relatively plain cabin cruiser. "Even when he goes on fishing trips 'just to do some thinkin',' as he says, he comes back with yarns that involve either a girl or a barroom brawl, or a barroom brawl over a girl. Lately he's been cruising around trying to figure out what to do with the rest of his life. He made a bundle in flight simulator software and basically retired last year at forty. Not bad, huh?"

"Sounds like a good story," Charlie said, struggling to keep a lid on the high-voltage conviction surging through him that flight simulator software was a chapter in a cover story: Clemmensen was Bream.

Motion on the pier behind them seized their attention. Heading their way were two men in dark suits and sunglasses, one white and the other black, both athletic, clean-cut, and in their late twenties. Their stride was all business.

Once within hailing distance, the black

man asked, "Charles Clark?"

Charlie tried to appear relaxed.

The men shared a nod. He'd failed.

"We're Secret Service," the white man said. "We were hoping to talk to you privately, sir." For Glenny's benefit, he added, "We have to interview everyone in the vicinity with out-of-state tags. Standard operating procedure."

6

The Cavalry's not as dead as they're supposed to be, Charlie thought.

Because his hands were bound in front of him by plastic cuffs, each turn slammed him into the door or the window as the SUV sped away from the marina.

The black man drove. Washington, according to his ID. The Secret Service badge the white guy had flashed identified him as Madison. Either the names were flagrantly fake or a simple instance of truth being stranger than fiction.

As the sun fell into the woods lining the two-lane country road to the local police station, their purported destination, their SUV approached an identical black vehicle, which slowed as it drew near. Washington stopped so that he was even with the other driver. Both drivers' windows glided down. In the burgeoning darkness, Charlie could make out only a thickset man in the other car.

"How's it going, Wash?" the man asked.

"Can't complain — no one would listen. You?"

"Another day, another advance team packed off to Dauphin Street. You heavy?"

Washington glanced at Charlie in the rear-view. "A Class Three."

The thickset man yawned. "You boys hitting happy hour?"

Leaning across the seat, Madison said, "We sure hope so."

"I'll be waiting. Wash here's been ducking me at Miss Pac Man."

With a round of *Later*'s, they were off.

Charlie was almost convinced that Washington and Madison were indeed who they said they were. The laptop computer, bracketed to the console between the front seats, had a Secret Service gold star as its screen saver. The muted chatter from the police radio continued to include "Grand Hotel" and "protectees." And if these guys were Cavalry, he would either have been dead by now or on a waterboard.

But why would the Secret Service want him? Aside from the fact that he'd been exonerated — although it wouldn't be the first time in government annals that paperwork was slow to be processed — how did

459

they even know where to find him?

Bream might have told them. He could have seen Charlie through a porthole.

"So what are we supposed to talk about?" Charlie asked the agents.

Madison turned around in the passenger seat, no trace remaining of his happy-hour banter. "Mr. Clark, for a heads of state event prep, the Secret Service is required to conduct advance interviews of all Class Threes in a two-hundred-fifty-mile vicinity."

"I'm guessing Class Three doesn't mean VIP," said Charlie.

"It's an individual in our database who —"

Washington cut in. "Who, we hope, won't give cause for concern."

"How did you know I was here?"

"We received a tip from a civilian who has a working relationship with law enforcement."

"Not the private eye, LeCroy?"

Madison looked to Washington.

"We don't disclose the identities of paid informants," Washington told Charlie.

LeCroy must have snapped a photograph of Charlie with the Webcam he had used to produce his screen saver of the naked blonde, then sent the picture to his law enforcement "colleagues" in hope of collecting a reward for a tip leading to an arrest. Irksome, but better a betrayal by a two-bit PI than a setup by Bream.

"My record was cleared though," Charlie said. "It's supposed to be in the same classification now as driven snow."

Washington slowed the car, to better focus on Charlie in the rearview mirror. "Sir, then why your interest in private vessels arriving from overseas?"

"I'm glad you asked. I believe there's, like, a Class Ten at the Mobile Bay Marina, a guy bringing in high explosives."

The agents exchanged a glance.

"I get it, I sound like one of the people who tells you they've seen a flying saucer," Charlie added. "But just call Caldwell Eskridge, the director of the Europe division at the CIA. Or let me call him myself. I met with him at CIA headquarters yesterday about this matter. I'm almost certain the bad guy is passing himself off as a yachtsman named Clem Clemmensen."

The resort town's police station sat adjacent to a fire station and looked to be part of the same toy set. Sitting alone at the intake desk, Charlie waited for his claims to be verified and for the return of the personal

461

items he'd been forced to surrender upon arrival — "just a technicality," the duty officer had said. The policeman had also promised that, afterward, either Washington and Madison or one of the four cops on duty would take Charlie back to the marina.

An hour crept past.

Finally the duty officer reappeared. "Sir, I'm afraid we've got some not so good news."

Charlie braced for the latest.

"We need to charge you for possession of a forged United States government document — your New York driver's license. It's a Class Two misdemeanor."

This was good news by Charlie's standards. Teenagers were caught with fake licenses all the time. "So is there a fine?" he asked.

The duty officer, a gangly, twentysomething Southerner, had warm blue eyes and the gentle manner of a kindergarten teacher. "A conviction carries a fine of up to a thousand dollars or confinement for up to six months, or both," he said apologetically. "We'll need to hold you here. Bail will be set tomorrow morning."

Charlie's initial thought, practical joke, was too much to hope for. Best case scenario, this was indeed his sort of luck. Worst case, Bream had somehow managed to keep him on ice here. No, that wasn't the worst. The worst was that Bream or one of his confederates would be visiting.

Charlie decided to use his allotted phone call to solicit Eskridge's help. Although arrogant, the division chief wasn't stupid, and Charlie had a solid lead to give him.

After wending his way through the CIA's telephonic maze, Charlie reached an agent on duty in the Europe division who promised, "I'll get this to the chief right away."

Then, once again, Charlie was behind bars. In this case, wire mesh. The police station's "holding cells" weren't cells so much as a single small room divided in two by a wire mesh sliding gate, with windowless walls painted cherry red, so bright as to be depressing. A stainless steel panel would provide him a modicum of privacy should he need the toilet in the corner. He was the only detainee, however.

He sat on the concrete bench running the length of the back wall and stared at the lone door, a slab of metal with a glass stripe at eye level. The door would not open again until breakfast-tray time, he thought.

If he was lucky.

A few hours later the door to the next cell opened, with a hydraulic hiss.

The duty officer ushered in another detainee, a handsome man of about forty with a deep tan and the physique of a former athlete. The man's demeanor remained pleasant in spite of his circumstance.

Closing the door, the policeman said, "Don't worry none, we ought to get this settled right quick, Mr. Clemmensen."

7

The new inmate plopped onto the bench on the other side of the dividing wall. With a wave and conviviality better suited to a cocktail party than a holding cell, he said, "Hey there. Name's Clem Clemmensen."

Charlie wondered if he was in the midst of an illogical dream. "John Parker," he said, sticking with the name on the forged license in case Clemmensen was in league with Bream.

"They got me in for an expired fishing license, even though I wasn't fishing," Clemmensen said. His indignation quickly gave way to a smile.

You'd be hard-pressed to make this guy unhappy, Charlie thought.

"Were you even on a boat when they picked you up?" he asked Clemmensen.

"Yeah, I just came in from Martinique. French island, you know it?"

"I've heard of it." Charlie raced to connect Clemmensen to Bream. Could Bream have tricked the flight simulator software millionaire into transporting the washing machine to the United States? Or put a gun to Clemmensen's head and forced him to ferry the bomb here? "So what happened? One of your friends was fishing?"

"It was just me on the boat." Clemmensen sighed. "The young lady I was trying to lure aboard was spending way too much time with her scuba instructor."

Charlie grunted sympathetically. "So you just motored on home?"

"Not until she went to the disco with him." Clemmensen sat straight up, seemingly spurred by epiphany. "Know what I think's going on?"

"What?"

"The dang G-20. There's all kinds of screening being done by various local law enforcement agencies. Now me, I never done much worse in my life than drive over the speed limit. But on election days, I pull the Democratic lever, which sometimes doesn't go over well in these parts. It's just my luck that I get hauled in by the cops while the Campodonico bastard in the next slip rolls in tonight from a tropical rum binge and heads right out on a pub crawl. Rule is, you're supposed to stay on your boat until Customs green-lights you."

Charlie recalled the name Campodonico. Captain Glenny had been anticipating the Campodonicos' return from their latest adventure in the Caribbean or South America. But they were elderly. Or was that cover?

"Campodonico, the university dean?" Charlie asked.

"That's Anthony Campodonico," Clemmensen said. "I'm talking about Tom, the nephew — in this case, the acorn fell awful far from that family tree."

Charlie smelled blood. "I might know Tom, come to think of it. About thirty-nine or forty?"

Clemmensen chuckled. " 'South of forty' is all he ever admits to."

Charlie recalled Bream using similar phrasing. "North of thirty," he'd said when telling of his hoped for transition from Lockheed's Skunk Works to corporate jets.

What were the odds?

The door hissed open.

Clemmensen leaped to his feet at the sight of the duty officer.

"Sorry, sir, not just yet, Mr. Clemmensen," the kindly cop said. He turned to Charlie. "Your lawyer's here to see you."

8

"Actually, I do have a law degree," Eskridge said. "Yale, 1986."

Charlie sat facing him at one of the three schoolteacher-style desks in the tiny and otherwise unoccupied detectives' bureau. Doxstader stood outside the door, in the lobby, feigning interest in the M&M's machine, but obviously eavesdropping.

"If I were acting as your attorney, I'd have had you out of here before my helicopter left the pad at Langley," Eskridge continued. "But as someone whose concern is national security, I have a reservation that needs to be addressed first."

Charlie confessed, "I realize I haven't exactly taken a textbook approach to things, but there's a chance some good has come out of it."

Eskridge stiffened. "Do you have another tip for us?"

"No, not a tip —"

"Good. The Secret Service, not knowing better, believed you. They trumped up a charge to yank Mr. Clemmensen away from the marina. Then they inspected his yacht stem to stern. The closest they found to contraband was a bottle of Aqua Velva. Clemmensen himself is a speeding ticket shy of being Mother Teresa. And if he weren't such a good old good ol' boy, we'd have ourselves a flap now."

"I'm sorry about that."

"Good. Now —"

"There's one other yacht there that's just in from the Caribbean, registered to a family named Campodonico —"

Eskridge cut him short. "Listen, Charlie, you acted heroically in Fort-de-France. Everyone commends you; everyone is grateful. But if we were to go after anybody else without probable cause, we would be on a witch hunt, and we don't do witch hunts, despite what you may read on blogs. The people paid to do this sort of investigating are currently in India, based on good intelligence. To conduct an investigation based on anything less is begging for a flap." Eskridge paused to think. "Why is the name Campodonico so bloody familiar?"

From outside, Doxstader said, "The anthropologist."

"Ah, yes, right." Eskridge turned back to Charlie. "He writes coffee table books on indigenous tribal rock painting. My wife has given me several of them as Christmas gifts. So, yes, Campodonico is, in a way, a terrorist."

Charlie wanted to argue for an unofficial peek into the life of Tom Campodonico, but he recognized that he stood a better chance of convincing Eskridge to launch a new investigation into the Kennedy assassination. Tonight.

"So you have a choice to make, Charlie Clark. You can stay here — the company has no power to detain you. On the other hand, Mobile's finest may find — *or be supplied with* — ample excuse to prolong your stay in the drunk tank. Alternatively, you can leave the G-20 security provisions in the hands of the Secret Service agents and the more than nine hundred other specialists here from the Coast Guard, Navy, Air Force, Department of Energy, and Homeland Security. If you do, you'll be released at once and I'll see to it that your fake driver's license issue will cease to be an issue. All I need is your word that you'll leave town tonight."

"I promise," said Charlie.

Eskridge nibbled at his lower lip, seemingly unconvinced. "Where will you go?"

"A few hours drive from here, in Mississippi, there's a casino where I have a good relationship with a couple of slot machines."

"Congratulations, you're a free man."

"Thank you," Charlie said.

He had every intention of going to Mississippi tonight.

And returning to Alabama first thing in the morning.

9

Earlier that same night, Bream sat at the helm of the Campodonicos' sixty-foot cabin cruiser, entering Mobile Bay, the sky so dark and the water so gentle that if it weren't for the salty air, he might have believed he was chugging through outer space.

He dreamed of sitting at a bar, his fingers wrapped around a cold bottle of Bud.

The yacht had plenty of beer, and the plush cabin was much more comfortable than any of the seedy dockside dives that would still be open when he reached the marina. He'd been at sea for the better part of four days, though. He could have covered the distance from Saint Lucia in two days and change, but so as not to raise any eyebrows in the Coast Guard radar stations, he'd dropped anchor for one night at Saint Kitts and stayed a second night in Anguilla. Now he felt as if sea salt clogged his pores. Not much of a seaman, he longed for the "firma" sensation of terra firma.

And he was close. But he still had to pass Customs and Border Protection. Along the 95,000 miles of American coastline and in 3.4 million square miles of ocean territory, CBP had to contend with 15 million registered small vessels and another 10 million unregistered. And the agency's primary job was commercial traffic. Consequently, CBP agents boarded only about 45,000 small vessels per year, or 1 in 500. Under ordinary circumstances, Bream stood a better chance of being boarded by pirates.

Of course, illegally ferrying a nuclear weapon hardly rated as ordinary circumstances. An added worry was that the cutout from Lahore, Dr. Jinnah, might have figured out that he'd been an unwitting part of a false trail meant to lead the CIA to the United Liberation Front of the Punjab's door. An even greater risk was defrocked Air Force intel operative Corky Morrison, Bream's surfer boy "associate" — a little meth money and the mercenary would spill all he knew. Accordingly, when Bream had rendezvoused with the Zodiac near Saint Lucia, he had shot both men. His only choice. Live men tell tales.

The unbelievably resourceful Alice Rutherford had killed the remaining mercenaries

— Carlo Pagliarulo, Lothar von Gentz, and Klaus Wagner — saving Bream the trouble. And in helping Charlie land the plane, she had helped perpetuate the Punjab diversion. Otherwise Morrison, monitoring the flight, would have stepped in via radio.

And if Alice now reported what she'd learned about Bream, fine. He no longer existed, effectively.

Nosing the yacht into his slip at the sleeping Mobile Bay Marina, he telephoned the local CBP office. "Hey, y'all, Tom Efferman here, fresh back from the beautific island of Saint Lucia," he told the voice mail. As he'd anticipated, the office had long since closed for the day.

Tom Efferman was a damned fine alias. In 1976, in rural Blue Ridge, Georgia, a horse bucked, throwing five-year-old Thomas Efferman to the ground. The animal's front hooves slammed onto the boy's head, permanently damaging his brain. He subsequently left his mother's trailer only on Christmas, if he was able.

Four years ago, Bream — born in 1971 in Nashville and given the name Maddox Mercer — learned of the boy when hacking the database of an organization that delivered holiday meals to the homebound. Thomas Efferman's social security number was all

Bream needed for the state of Georgia to send a copy of the boy's birth certificate to an accommodation address he'd set up in Montgomery, Alabama. With the birth certificate in hand, obtaining an Alabama driver's license under the name Thomas Efferman was a relatively simple matter of passing the driver's test. The boating license was simpler still.

Prior to meeting with Qatada, Bream — as Efferman — had offered to rent the Campodonicos' yacht. The couple needed money, having underbudgeted their retirement and overestimated the sales of books about tribal rock paintings. In the Campodonicos' patrician yacht club social set, renting carried a stigma. Bream had figured that out in advance of contacting them. In person, he suggested, "How about we just tell folks I'm your nephew or cousin?"

Now he steered their yacht's starboard side even with the dock. Technically, he couldn't go get his Budweiser — or disembark at all — until he had either passed a CBP inspection or received the call from CBP releasing him. But the CBP folks were in bed, and the cops enforced the shipboard regulation with less frequency than they busted up penny-ante poker games.

As he bounded onto the quiet dock, two

Mobile policemen materialized out of the darkness.

Standing unnaturally straight, Bream said, with a slight stammer, "Evening, officers, how y'all doing?" As an innocent man would.

" 'Evening, sir," both cops said as they hurried past on the way to Clem Clemmensen's boat.

Bream guessed ol' Clem had backed the wrong sheriff.

10

As the radiant Mobile skyline shrank in his rearview mirror, Charlie thought of Arcangues, a French colt named after the village in Aquitaine. Arcangues had only raced on grass in Europe before being shipped to California in 1993 to compete in the Breeders' Cup on Santa Anita's dirt track. Sent off at odds of 133 to 1 and under a last-minute replacement jockey, Arcangues caught up to the powerful bay Bertrando in the homestretch, beat him to the wire, and became arguably the greatest in the history of long shots.

Charlie put the odds that he could securely communicate with Alice even higher. But even if he could tell her why he'd driven south and what he'd subsequently learned about Bream, neither she nor her NSA colleagues — who were busy grilling her in Geneva — could do anything about it.

When he called her on his cell as he drove

out of Mobile, he recognized that he would have to tell her a cover story.

"Eskridge must have given you an awful lot of confidence in the agency's efforts if you're on a casino crawl," she said. She spat out "casino" the way she might have said "brothel."

"He made a very strong case for my going to a casino."

"Wasn't it you who said the best chance you have at a casino is to stay outside?"

Although he'd braced for it, her implicit disappointment stung him. In Gstaad, she'd once called his life at the track "tragic."

"Haven't I ever told you about Joseph Jaggers?" he said.

"You said that you wanted to name a dog Jaggers, when you get a dog."

He'd meant when *they* got a dog.

"He was a nineteenth-century British engineer who thought that even slight imbalances in a roulette wheel might result in certain outcomes. At the casino in Monte Carlo he discovered that the ball wound up more often in nine of the compartments. When he started playing, he broke the bank."

"Ah. So you're headed to Mississippi to make a study of certain outcomes."

"I don't know. Maybe I just need some R & R."

He wished he'd simply said that he was going to hit some golf balls, or that he just wanted to lie around a pool and read sports magazines. Either would have sufficed to confuse his true target audience, the CIA personnel he believed were eavesdropping. It wasn't Eskridge's style to leave things to chance.

"How about, once I'm done here, we rendezvous at Le Diamant?" Alice asked. She maintained that the beach resort at the southern tip of Martinique received five stars only because there were no six-star ratings.

"Sounds great."

"Super," she said, but with so little of her usual enthusiasm as to cast doubt on the plan.

He hoped she would be proud of him when she knew the truth. At least the eavesdroppers now had corroboration for his three-hour drive to Choctaw, Mississippi. He wanted to give them all the help he could in tracking him to the Golden Sun Hotel and Casino.

He and Alice talked over next steps, dependent on the completion of her meetings in Geneva. He signed off with a cheerful, "Call me when you have the green light." He did not say that he intended to leave his cell phone at the Golden Sun when he fled.

11

Lake Geneva ranked as the largest body of freshwater in continental Europe. And arguably the most spectacular. On this sunny morning, the water outshone most sapphires. Alice liked Lake Geneva best for its public transit system: classic ferries that chugged between docks all around the lake.

Having sped through her morning debrief, she hopped a ferry at the Quai du Mont-Blanc in front of the Grand Hotel Kempinski. Boats made it easy to detect surveillance, forcing tails to stay close for fear of losing their rabbit. Alice was willing to believe that Geneva's transit system alone explained the city's status as the world's espionage capital. As a city, especially by European standards, it had all the excitement of a post office.

Covertly scanning the sixty-seat single-decker, she reminded herself that she ought to be reveling in her liberty after two weeks that had been the surveillance detection equivalent of scaling Everest.

Just take a bloody cab and be done with it.

Then again, after nine years of deceiving and killing players on other teams, it wasn't a terrible idea to keep an eye peeled.

She detected only one possible tail, middle-aged tourists with two toddlers. The purported family boarded the ferry at the last moment, right after she did.

Surveillants sometimes used children, and this mom and pop looked a bit too long in the tooth to be parents to such young kids. Then again, the couple could be young grandparents, or beneficiaries of the new wonders of reproductive endocrinology.

But what about the big pink teddy bear the girl dragged over the damp deck? Quite the cliché, a pink teddy bear. Regardless, if you love your teddy, you don't drag him around like a shot deer.

When Alice got off the ferry at the next pier, the family remained aboard, squabbling, suggesting they really were a family.

Leaving the pier, she took the train to Cointrin, Geneva's international airport, and bought a ticket for a direct flight to Atlanta.

The customs agent was a young American

with a belly indicating a fondness for the lo-cal *bräuhaus*. He studied her documents for an excessive amount of time, before finally asking, "So what's taking you to Atlanta?"

"A reunion."

"With bowls of potato salad and long-lost uncles, or the happily-ever-after kind?"

"No potato salad or uncles. Maybe the other one, though, if things work out all right."

The young man looked her over. "I'm pretty sure things'll work out." He waved her through.

12

Charlie drove northwest through Alabama's dense woodlands, the few gaps between trees filled by kudzu. The darkness was such that, if not for his headlights, he might as well have shut his eyes. He frequently changed lanes and took exits at the last possible second, but no one seemed to be following him.

Unless his minders were disguised as Mississippi teenagers either patronizing a McDonald's at State Line, Mississippi, or working behind the counter, he ate his Big Mac and fries unminded as well. The only person over the age of eighteen was the lanky man in a custodian's uniform, twenty-two perhaps, wiping down the men's room door.

Returning to the highway, Charlie considered that he was instead being minded via aerial surveillance or simply being tracked by the signal strength of his phone between cell towers. Neither posed a problem. As long as *someone* was tracking him. It was integral to his plan.

After another hour's solitary drive, a massive structure rose from behind a hill. It looked as if the moon had slipped out of its orbit, settling on the road ahead. Drawing closer, Charlie saw that it was a freakishly large golden sphere perched in front of a proportionate building boldly wrought in tempered steel and bronze-tinted glass. He had imagined the casino in the middle of nowhere in Mississippi as a neoned-up, big box store with a motel and a few golf holes, but this glamorous and luxurious complex was the Golden Sun Hotel and Casino. Any doubt was dispelled by the letters lining each side of the road — G-O-L-D-E-N on one side, S-U-N on the other — big as buildings themselves. Charlie chided himself for having underestimated the might of gambling.

From the parking garage he heard the distinctive rain of coins into slot machine payout trays. The dozens of other people leaving their cars — and, mostly, pickups — seemed to brighten at the sound. He wandered onto the gaming floor, a galaxy of slot machines — 5,465 of them according to a billboard with the digital numbers poised to change with each addition, a new take on the HAMBURGERS SOLD sign. Seemingly all of the ten million colors visible to the human eye were on display. The whirring reels, accompanied by bells and chimes, blended into one harmonious and mesmerizing chord. It wasn't just that the oxygen was purer in here, Charlie thought. It was like inhaling adrenaline.

In the chrome frame of a one-armed bandit, he caught the reflection of a curly-haired young man in a peacoat and fatigue pants. The thick-framed glasses would probably have thrown Charlie. But although the young man was playing a slot machine, he was looking at something other than the wheel, possibly a chrome band enabling him to view Charlie, and enabling Charlie to recognize him as the lanky custodian from the State Line, Mississippi, McDonald's.

Charlie felt as if he'd hit a jackpot.

Turning away, he searched for the VIP credit lounge. It would have been hard not to find. Its golden letters were almost as big as those outside.

But would they admit him? A VIP, in the gaming industry, was someone with assets. Does a person have a credit card, a debit card, even a library card that can advance cash now against overdue fees later? Then he's a VIP.

Charlie waltzed into the lounge, and with little effort obtained a $5,000 cash advance — it was nice to be able to draw on the family numbered account without fear that the transaction would incite an Interpol SWAT team. He also put $5,000 on the casino platinum card he'd been handed upon entry, bringing its balance to $5,020 — all new arrivals began with a balance of $20. A taste.

He needed appropriate clothes, which were readily available a few steps off the casino floor. Among other tuxes for sale at a store called Golden Man was the "High Roller" line; Charlie bought a size 42R along with a matching dress shirt, shoes, and a bow tie. He also tossed onto the counter a Golden Sun baseball cap and a windbreaker, as if on impulse. The total was $2,111. He paid in cash, hoping the lack of a paper trail in this instance would obfuscate his planned exit.

He checked into a hotel room, opting for a Chief's Suite at an extra fifteen dollars per night. The lofty space was furnished in an Ancient Rome theme, the walls and marble floor flecked with silver and gold. The bed was almost as big as a swimming pool. He wished Alice were here, if only to share his grin.

He called room service and ordered the "executive" surf and turf. While waiting, he changed into his tux, which was almost identical to those worn by the staff he'd seen carrying drink trays and pushing the linen-draped room service trolleys.

A few minutes later, at the sound of a gong, he answered his door and admitted a waiter who not only wore a tux like his, but was close to his height and weight. Their principal differences were twenty years in age, a slight hunch, and an overbite. Lucky, Charlie thought. He could mimic those.

He asked, "Sir, how would you like to make a thousand dollars?"

The man, who probably heard an equally unusual question at least once a week, didn't hesitate. "Depends what for."

"For reasons I'm sure I won't need to explain to you, I need to get out of this building without being seen by my wife, who unexpectedly just showed up."

Stooping so as to resemble the waiter and to keep his face from the view of security cameras, Charlie heaved the trolley down a service corridor, his planned change of clothes hidden in a food compartment.

He came to an exit leading onto a dark

dining patio, evidently used during warmer months. Abandoning the trolley, he crossed the patio, reaching an unlit spiral stairwell that took him down to a curb lined with six or seven buses rumbling at idle. Their exhaust created a fog laced with diesel fumes. His plan had been to make his way to the parking lot and find someone leaving the casino who would thank Jesus for the crazy Yankee who gave him three grand for a clunker pickup truck. But this was better.

Charlie fell into step with the grumbling and otherwise downtrodden crowd exiting the casino and boarding the buses. Throwing the windbreaker over his tuxedo coat and zipping it to the neck, he wove through shadows and climbed aboard the first bus in line, a sixty-foot-long Golden Sun coach destined for Hattiesburg, Mississippi's YMCA, according to the marquee.

He found a seat, the three dozen passengers scattered around the cabin paying him passing notice at most. The lone exception, a buzzard of around eighty lowering himself into the seat across the aisle. The old man locked eyes with Charlie and said, "Fun, but no money," then readied his blanket and tubular "snuggle pillow" for the trip home.

The bus driver, a fiftyish man with the

look of a commandant, took his place behind the wheel, snapped the door shut, and propelled the coach toward the highway — all without a glance at the passengers. The Golden Sun's management cared much more about gamblers on the way in than those who'd left.

13

The Brig reminded Bream of a utility shed. Decorated, barely, with a pair of model ships, a dartboard, and three beer company posters, it smelled of low tide even though the tide was now high — because the juke-box was out of order and the six solitary patrons weren't speaking to one another, Bream could hear the waves slapping the top of the pier.

Glad of the opportunity to be alone with his thoughts, he climbed onto a stool at the warped bar and ordered his Bud.

He found himself stealing glances at the young woman in a Princeton sweatshirt at the other end of the bar, as exquisite a specimen as he'd ever seen. Aphrodite with green eyes and a damned good attendance record at the gym.

What the hell, he wondered, was someone like her doing in a place like this?

Cliché be damned, he wandered over

and asked.

"Waiting for you to come to this side of the bar." She flashed two fingers to the bartender. "But just because you're the only man here who wouldn't be a shoo-in for the cast of a zombie movie, don't think I'm going to be easy."

"That makes two of us," Bream said. "I've already got an old lady."

"But you want a young one, don't you?"

Bream didn't say no. Maybe what he really needed was to take his mind off work. Settling on the stool next to hers, he asked, "So you got a story?"

At twenty-three, she said, she was over the hill as a fashion model. Tonight she was drinking herself into grudging acceptance that she would start law school in the fall. She had eschewed the Ivies for the University of Alabama so that she could help take care of her grandma, who lived nearby.

He was charmed. Three beers later and it was probably clear to everyone in the bar, even the guy facedown at the table beneath the dartboard, where this was heading.

Everyone except Bream. He was haunted by the thought that, as a consequence of the washing machine aboard his cabin cruiser, this latter-day Aphrodite would be transformed into red mist tomorrow.

He thought back to the conference in Miami in March 2005. He was a round peg then, trying to act square enough to work for Air Force Intelligence. And he was succeeding. He'd received a spate of plum assignments, the latest of which was an appointment to an interagency force to protect America from weapons of mass destruction smuggled aboard small oceangoing vessels.

The October 2000 al-Qaeda small vessel assault on the USS *Cole* had made it clear that waterborne attacks were high on bad guys' to-do lists. Such an operation in the United States wouldn't even have to be "successful" insofar as taking out a target. If it just shut down a single port, anxiety would spread through the global financial marketplace. For starters.

The director of the interagency force was a pompous Pentagon bureaucrat in desperate need, in Bream's opinion, of a punch in the face. And that was before the ignoramus hypothesized that modern surveillance technology rendered human intelligence obsolete. His measures mollified a naive public and Congress, but utterly failed to safeguard American ports and waterways. The rest of the committee proved a bunch of bobbleheads. Or, viewed another way, proficient bureaucrats: All reaped career laurels. All except Bream, who, after one long and excruciating day of meetings in Miami, finally punched the boss in the face.

The washing machine would deliver an invaluable lesson — a costly one, but Mobile was not Manhattan. More lives had been lost in single battles in Vietnam than would be tomorrow. It didn't hurt that Bream would nearly become a billionaire in the process. The money was of little consequence compared to the vindication, though. Imagining the expression on the Pentagon man's face when he had to answer for what had happened, Bream worked himself into fine spirits.

"Another round?" Aphrodite offered.

"I'd love to, sugar." He slid off his bar stool. "Thing is, I've got a big day tomorrow."

14

The sun sliced through the vinyl curtains of room 12 at the Country Inn, just down the main drag from the Hattiesburg Y. The light woke the man who'd registered late last night as Miller, paying in cash. The clock radio read 9:01. Charlie, who as a boy had admired scrappy Mets infielder Keith Miller, thought the five hours of uninterrupted sleep well worth the thirty-nine dollars. Unless the CIA had used the time to locate him.

He peeled back one of the curtains, half expecting to look into the barrel of a howitzer. The day was blindingly white. Three vehicles were parked in the thirty or so spaces, a pair of big rigs and a rusted Buick Skylark that looked as if it would have a hard time cranking up, let alone following the casino bus on the interstate. On the four-lane road fronting the parking lot, a handful of cars and pickup trucks waited at a red light.

Charlie found the Country Inn lobby empty. The middle-aged Pakistani man behind the reception desk, embroiled in a phone conversation that could only be spousal, didn't look up as Charlie exited.

The Dollar Store was a treasure trove. The shaggy blond wig Charlie selected, though probably intended for a woman, appeared fake only on close scrutiny — a man could wear it and pass for a biker. The horn-rimmed sunglasses, likely sitting on the spinning rack since the Dollar Store was the Quarter Store, might be taken as retro-chic and would certainly alter the contours of his face. He also picked out several sweat-shirts and a camouflage-print coat. If Esk-ridge's people were to ask young Mysti at the register what Charlie had purchased, they would net a dozen possible descriptions.

Getting into the spirit of obfuscation, Charlie bought three more wigs, a fisher-man's hat, and a purple poncho.

"School play," he said with affected sheep-ishness as he set everything onto the conveyor belt.

Behind the counter, Mysti smiled reflex-ively. Her gaze was fixed on the round security mirror overhead. Charlie saw the reflection of an elderly woman sliding a Christmas ornament — three for a dollar — into her blouse.

Leaving the store, Charlie started back across the street to the Avis two buildings down. He noticed security cameras on three of the car rental agency's walls. Even with the big blond wig and sunglasses, he would thwart decent facial recognition software for only a few seconds, if that.

Farther up the block, Hattiesburg Rent-A-Car, a spruced-up shed with a hand-painted sign and three dusty Chryslers in its unpaved front lot, looked more promising.

Closer inspection revealed that it too had a security camera in a plastic dome the size of a salad bowl suspended from the ceiling.

Charlie cursed car thieves if only as an outlet for his frustration.

Then he considered joining them. He had watched his father hot-wire cars often enough. Of course, he'd also watched Darryl Strawberry hit 450-foot home runs.

Necessity won. He returned to the motel parking lot, stopping to tie his shoe between one of the big rigs and the old Buick, a two-toner with beige side panels.

The easiest way to gain access to a vehicle,

his father had said, is by opening a door. People left them unlocked far too often. Charlie reached tentatively for the handle on the driver's door of the Buick, bracing for the car's owner to burst out of the motel.

The lobby door remained shut.

Odds were the Buick belonged to the man behind the reception desk. And odds also said a place like this didn't pay for security cameras in the parking lot.

Gingerly, Charlie pulled up the handle. The door opened, hinges croaking. The dome light flickered on.

Still no one seemed to notice.

He darted into the driver's footwell, pulling the door shut behind him. Careful to keep his head below the window line, he smashed his wounded shoulder into the radio. It stung, but he quickly stretched out across the floor, flipped onto his back, and studied the ignition barrel.

On its underside, he found a curved rectangular panel the size of a Pop-Tart and plucked it free. Now he needed to find the two reds from among the jungle of wires inside the ignition barrel. Nervous perspiration burned his eyes.

He spotted the reds. Without much hope that it would work, he touched their ends together.

The engine sputtered to life.

Charlie would marvel later. Now his eyes darted toward the lobby door.

The usual.

15

The scant sunlight had failed to burn the heavy fog off Mobile Bay by late morning. Although sixty degrees, the day remained too blustery and generally dismal for most pool or waterfront activities. A few joggers and bicyclists used the trails through the Grand Hotel's lush grounds. The G-20 security teams couldn't have been more conspicuous. Many of the agents wore shiny black coats emblazoned with SECRET SERVICE and HAZMAT and COUNTERSNIPERS. The conference wouldn't kick off until evening, but guard stations already formed a wall around the hotel's main lodge and surrounding buildings. Still more security types swarmed the grounds.

In hope of passing for one of the joggers, Charlie donned the running suit and Nikes he'd purchased at a strip mall on the way out of Hattiesburg. As he loped away from the hotel, he heard high-pitched squeals and giggles. A hedgerow parted, revealing children on a playground, well within the blast range of the plastic explosive in the ADM he suspected was at the Mobile Bay Marina.

He continued toward the marina. To someone on the lookout for him now, any of the wigs would be a giveaway. So he had also bought a battery-powered hair clipper and, standing at the mirror of the mall's deserted men's room, shaved back most of his hairline. The rest he trimmed into a buzz cut. Gel slathered over his newly bald areas made it appear that years had passed since he'd had any hair there. He added wrap-around sunglasses whose "fire-iridium" — the manufacturer's term for "red" — lenses would divert attention from his features.

Unfortunately, he wasn't much of a jogger. And propelling himself forward now proved an even greater struggle than usual due to the bullet wound in his shoulder as well as the two layers of long underwear he wore beneath his running suit, intended to make him look stocky.

A few yards shy of the marina's side entrance, he dropped his hands onto his knees as if catching his breath. No pretense necessary. A shiny white power boat that looked like a miniature cruise ship now occupied the Campodonico slip by the end of the dock. Reclining in a canvas chair on the stern deck was a man of between thirty and forty, face buried in a magazine. He wore dark glasses, a Grand Hotel golf windbreaker, and a pair of Bermuda shorts. He had dark brown hair and a goatee. The Bermuda shorts alone — really, the bronzed, muscular legs the shorts revealed — were enough for Charlie to recognize the glasses, brown wig, and glue-on goatee for what they were. Ever the peacock: Bream should have worn long pants.

Instead of feeling the thrill of being right, Charlie was stumped. He had no idea how to stop Bream. He could alert the Secret Service, but they'd probably just throw him back in the local drunk tank, and then, worse, alert Bream. The CIA might help, but not before cables for authorizations ate up the remainder of the day. Or Eskridge might have Charlie thrown back in the drunk tank.

Charlie weighed contending with Bream himself. The pilot had probably deemed it too great a risk to entrust his cargo to anyone but himself, meaning his plan was to charm Captain Glenny, then hang out on the yacht until he made the transaction. Or possibly he was waiting for all of the G-20 leaders to arrive, at which time he would switch to a car and drive beyond the blast radius. Thirty miles on the interstate ought to do it. There he would detonate the bomb by pressing a button on a remote control, or, if he had adapted the detonator, by dialing a cell phone.

Charlie wished he had a gun. He reeled from flashbacks of the pawn shops he'd blown past. With all of his damned preparation, how had he gotten to this point without even a penknife?

He considered luring Bream away from the yacht, then somehow getting aboard himself. Once he found the washer, he could permanently disable the detonator by dialing an incorrect code three times, activating its safeguard, a capacitor that would essentially fry the system. It would take him two minutes, tops.

But how could he get Bream out of the way, even for one minute?

Charlie looked around for a fire alarm to pull, then realized that Bream would just stay by his yacht. A boat surrounded by water wasn't a bad place to be during a fire. At best, the alarm would clear the marina, making Charlie's approach as conspicuous as if he'd set himself on fire.

What about a pizza delivery?

Less stupid, the more Charlie thought about it. As on several of the boats docked here, a few of the Campodonico yacht's windows were opened a crack to keep the cabin from getting stuffy. While Bream and the Domino's guy stood in the parking lot trying to get to the bottom of the delivery error, Charlie could squeeze through a window and into the cabin. Unless the Domino's guy brought the pie right to Bream's yacht. Either way, Bream might notice. As would Glenny — Charlie detected movement behind the frosted glass window of the harbormaster's office.

He was mulling a more discreet approach via the bay, capitalizing on the kayaks sitting on the beach at the hotel, when Bream stood up and locked the door to the cabin from outside.

Crouching behind a bush, Charlie watched the pilot straddle the starboard rail, thump onto the dock, and walk with purpose toward the parking lot. Possibly he was going to the little village to get lunch. Whatever he was doing, if it involved leaving the marina, he ought to be gone long enough for Charlie to gain access to the yacht. And it might be Charlie's only chance.

16

With a silent prayer to the nameless divine entities he called upon when one of his horses took the lead in a race, Charlie started jogging toward the marina. He tried to think of himself as a Grand Hotel guest, entitled to romp wherever he damned well pleased, and he hoped he projected this air. Particularly to Captain Glenny.

Bream had been gone for a couple of minutes when Charlie reached the pier. He exchanged a friendly smile with a man on a catamaran, then ran — although not too fast for a jogger — toward the Campodonicos' yacht.

There was no sign of anyone aboard. Charlie heard only the wind and the creaks of the yacht as it rose and fell in the water. Stepping onto the stern, he ought to have been nervous, but he felt something akin to exhilaration.

A few steps along the narrow side deck

and he reached one of the slightly opened cabin windows. The glass slid all the way open with a gentle pull. He fit through, barely, tumbling onto a cream-colored carpet and into a corridor lined with enough framed maritime maps for a museum.

He followed it to a spacious dining room with a table for eight. The adjacent kitchen had all of the necessary appliances found in a luxury home. Except a washing machine.

Holding his breath, he tiptoed down a spiral staircase, with solid mahogany steps, to the lower deck. A television glowed in one of the staterooms, giving him a start, but no one was there. The two other staterooms contained only tall beds and built-in cabinets.

Still no washing machine or sign of one.

At the end of the corridor was a closet. Without expecting much, Charlie pulled open its bifold door to find a surprisingly compact laundry alcove with plenty of shelves, a foldout ironing board, and, alongside a modern dryer, a cheap, boxy Perriman Pristina, still spotted with muck from the cavern.

Eureka, he thought.

He reached to pull open the top-loading lid when he heard a bolt snap above-deck.

Fear hit him like a bullwhip.

The cabin door creaked open. He heard at least two sets of footsteps.

"How 'bout a cold beer, Steve?" Bream asked. "I got you the nonalcoholic stuff."

"Very kind, thank you." A low, raspy voice with a strong Middle Eastern accent. "But let us get on please with the business?"

"That'd be just fine," said Bream, letting the door bang shut and tramping in the direction of the staircase. "All due respect."

Charlie considered the staterooms, distinctly lacking in places to hide. Ducking beneath the ironing board, he stuffed himself into the ten-inch gap between the rear of the washing machine and the wall. He would have tripped over the washing machine's tattered orange power cord, stretched into a wall socket, but there was no room to fall.

He sank to one knee. The space was dark and otherwise like the back of a clothes closet.

"While I'm thinking of it, you should have these, just in case you need to move the boat for whatever reason," Bream said, jangling something. His leather sandals came into view at the base of the stairs.

Charlie held still, hoping the jackhammer that used to be his heart wouldn't draw Bream's attention.

Stepping into the lower deck's corridor, Bream handed a set of keys back to Steve, a swarthy boar of a man, probably twenty-five, with close-set, black eyes. His crisp Levi's and shiny new Florida Marlins jersey and Converse All Star high-tops ironically accentuated his foreignness.

"Thank you kindly," Steve said, pocketing the keys. He looked around until his eyes settled on the washing machine. He stared.

Charlie's heart nearly leaped out of his mouth as Steve advanced for a closer look. Charlie used muscles he hadn't realized he had in order to hold still.

Steve pointed to the washer's control panel. "So is this button actually the trigger?"

Bream stepped up, so close Charlie could have reached out through the gap between the washer and dryer and touched his knee.

"You mean the start button?" Bream leaned forward and clicked it.

The blood drained from Steve's face.

The machine belched and the length of hose running past Charlie swelled, filling with water from the copper piping on the wall. Water splattered into the washer.

Taking in Steve's disquiet, Bream chuckled. "The water trickles in for about five minutes, then drains out and the machine turns back off. It's a little special effect in case a customs inspector happens to turn the thing on, which they do sometimes."

Steve heaved a breath of relief. "I was not ready yet."

Steve is about to martyr himself, Charlie thought, and Bream is fucking with his head. Whatta guy.

"Check this out." Bream flipped open the lid.

Steve looked in, surprised. "No water."

"The water goes into a special compartment in the back of the machine."

"Ah."

"Of course, if the inspector opened the lid, it's game over. There's no way of disguising the bomb." Bream pointed into the washer. "See the three dials there?"

"Yes. The progressive action links. I received thorough training with them from Doctor Zakir."

"Good. You'll be glad to know that to save you the trouble, he dialed in the code to arm the device. Then he paused it, two seconds into a ten-minute countdown. Here . . ." Bream handed Steve a device that looked like a TV remote control. "The good doctor rigged this, too. At game time tonight, you simply click the big red button and the countdown resumes at nine minutes and fifty-eight seconds. If you need to pause for whatever reason, click the button again. It's basically a play and a pause button in one. The batteries are fresh, and you've got more up on the kitchen counter. If for whatever reason the remote malfunctions and you need to use the PALs, the code's here." Bream pointed to the area of the control panel where, Charlie recalled, the serial number had been engraved onto a strip of metal.

Steve nodded.

"So you ought to be all set." Lowering the lid, Bream turned to go. "The fridge is stocked with all your favorite stuff — don't worry, all halal."

"And you will be where?" Steve asked.

Bream turned toward the staircase. "Outside the blast radius."

"What if there's a malfunction?"

"If anything goes wrong, Cheb Qatada knows how to reach Zakir or me — I know you've got the boss on speed dial." Bream inched toward the stairs.

Charlie was eager for him to leave. It would mean contending with only Steve.

"Well, good, then, Mr. Bream," Steve said. "Thank you most kindly."

"The kind thanks are for you, Steve."

Bream bounded toward the stairs.

He stopped just shy of the first step and spun back around, eyes on the laundry door. "That folding door was open when we came down here, wasn't it?"

Steve nodded.

Charlie's blood froze. He needed an exit strategy. It was right up there with a weapon on the list of omissions in his planning.

Bream knelt, studying the floor.

Could he detect Charlie's footprints on the linoleum?

He sprang into the master bedroom, refreshing Charlie's hope. Because the laundry alcove looked prohibitively small, Bream and Steve might not think to look behind the appliances.

A moment later Bream returned from the bedroom with a Glock capped by a silencer. He faced the washing machine. He couldn't possibly see Charlie, but the barrel of his gun was on a direct line with Charlie's face.

"Please come out now and save me from putting a bullet hole in my nice dryer," he said.

17

Charlie rose, his legs burning with pins and needles. And fear. "I owe you a big thank you, J. T.," he said.

"This is who?" Steve demanded of Bream.

"Nobody." Bream was extraordinarily unflappable.

"Nobody in the grand scheme of things," Charlie said. "But for our purposes today, a CIA asset."

Steve muttered something in Arabic.

"He's lying," Bream said. "He's just a gambler." He beckoned Charlie with a wave of the gun.

Charlie held his ground. "A gambler who attended a debrief at Langley the other day, and recalled your saying that you were going to celebrate the consummation of your arms deal with a rack of ribs. It took an analyst about a second to figure out that you were targeting the G-20."

"Don't worry, he's not CIA," Bream said

to Steve. "Even the lousiest gamblers get lucky now and then. This is just some sort of cash grab."

Steve's eyes widened with panic. "What if he is not alone?"

"He's alone."

"How do you know this?"

"He plays the horses for a living; CIA wouldn't let him near an op. And if he did have someone with him, they would've tipped him off that we were on our way here, or at least tried to waylay us, to give him time to get out."

Steve paused for a moment. "Mr. Bream, the plan is to detonate ahead of schedule should anything go wrong. This was part of the deal, yes? Already very many people of consequence have arrived at the Grand Hotel, including almost all of the members of the French delegation —"

Bream extended his palms. "Whoa, we're getting way ahead of ourselves. Trust me, Chuckles here is a lone mutt."

"With all respect due, sir, it is not an issue of trust."

"Good point. Let me prove it to you."

"How?"

"If he had any backup, they would be here by now." Bream leveled his gun at Charlie and pulled the trigger.

Charlie dropped behind the washing machine. The bullet tore the air above his hair, clanking into the dryer. An odd hiss came from within the dark maze of ducts and hoses. Suddenly his shirtfront felt wet. Blood? A chill encased him. He noticed a spray of cold water from a rupture in the length of hose running into the washing machine.

He slid behind the washer, hoping Bream would be reluctant to shoot through the bomb.

Steve waved in horror at the water pooling in the alcove and slicking the corridor. "What about all this?"

"Water won't hurt anything." Bream advanced to the gap between the washer and dryer, sidestepping the pool of water forming on the floor. "This device is designed so it could sink to the bottom of Mobile Bay and still detonate."

His gun was close enough that Charlie smelled the spent cordite.

Times like this, his father usually came to the rescue. Or Alice.

But neither even knew he was here. No one did.

"I am still not confident," Steve said. "If I am with your CIA, I would let him die, so that we believe they do not know about us."

Bream sighed. "They don't know, okay. Sure, it makes strategic sense to sacrifice a man. They'd never do it, though, for fear of the Senate investigation alone."

"Maybe so." Steve aimed the remote at the washer. "But why take the chance?"

Bream bristled. "You really need to hold up there."

Steve held the remote at the washing machine like a fixed bayonet.

"Listen, there's a girl I want to get out of the red zone, not to mention myself," Bream went on. "Half an hour of lead time was part of the deal."

Steve slid a thumb onto the big red button. "Clearly and irrevocably, the will of Allah has changed." He clicked the remote. The conic bulb on the gadget's head glowed red.

The bomb mechanism whirred to life, the washing machine housing vibrating against Charlie's rib cage.

Bream fired the silenced Glock.

An image came to Charlie. A memory of the living room in the chalet. He and Alice on the comfortable sofa and Drummond in the armchair. The three were engrossed in one of their games of Scrabble. An interesting piece of information: Even Alzheimer's couldn't prevent Drummond from laying

515

out seven-letter word after seven-letter word.

Now, feeling nothing save the spray of cold water, Charlie peeked around the washing machine.

Steve's forehead had a red hole at its center. He collapsed, revealing a splash of gore at head level on the wall behind him.

"He was planning to die here anyway," Bream said, as if seeking absolution.

"Let me convince you not to use the bomb," Charlie said.

"Among other reasons that you won't be able to convince me is I don't get a red cent if there's no explosion here."

"Suppose I told you that you won't get the explosion you have in mind. The penthrite and trinitrotoluene in the bomb are the genuine article, but the U-235 is fake." Charlie decided not to mention that the device, designed to trick customers into initially believing they had achieved a nuclear detonation, would still yield an explosion sufficient to kill the children in the playground, all of the security agents, and a high percentage of the hotel guests and staff.

"Not true. Just this morning, Vivek Zakir, a Nobel-caliber nuclear physicist, confirmed the enriched uranium was grade-A."

"This device was designed to fool even Nobel Prize–winning nuclear physicists. This is what my old man did for the CIA. His team replicated the old Russian ADMs because the uranium pits are fixed so deep, you can't adequately test —"

"Good story." Bream advanced to the appliance alcove. "Even if it were true, a hundred pounds of plastic explosive still yields a big enough bang to suit my purposes."

"Fine. Sell me the bomb instead. I can pay you more than you'll ever need."

"Sounds like I'm about to hear another whopper."

"You know about the treasure of San Isidro?"

"Yeah."

"My father found it. It was on one of those little islets off Martinique."

Bream lowered his gun. "You've seen it?"

"Yeah. An entire roof made of gold, taken in panels off a Venezuelan church."

"If that were true, why the hell would you come here?"

Charlie tapped the washing machine.

"Then you're a fool. And even if you found El Dorado, I'd be a fool to trust you." Splashing into the alcove, Bream aimed his gun at Charlie. "In fact, I'm a fool to be talking to you at all."

"Thank you." Charlie plunged the washing machine's tattered power cord into the water.

With a bestial wail, Bream flew up in the air. As Charlie had hoped, Bream's sandals had made him vulnerable to the current; Charlie was protected by his rubber-soled running shoes.

Bream landed in a heap over the washer and lost his hold on the gun. Charlie caught the weapon, spun, and pointed it at him.

The pilot's muscles quivered. His breathing, however, appeared to have ceased, and the color drained from his skin.

Charlie turned sideways, slipping through the gap between the appliances. He knelt by Steve's body and pried the remote control from the terrorist's hand. He aimed the device at the washing machine and clicked. The conic bulb illuminated.

But the detonation mechanism within the washing machine continued to whir.

Gun still trained on Bream, Charlie stepped closer to the washer and tried again.

No change. Maybe the water had shorted the remote control? In any case, he could enter the code by hand. If enough time remained.

07:55, according to the LED adhered to

the inside of the washing machine's lid.

Plenty of time.

Charlie looked at the serial number atop the control panel. The metal band he'd used in the Caribbean had been removed, replaced by a strip of tape with different numbers. He realized why with harrowing clarity: There was nothing wrong with the remote control. The Nobel-caliber scientist, Dr. Vivek Zakir, had been clever enough to build a remote control to be used to initiate detonation only. He had removed the real serial number for the same reason, as a failsafe in case the martyr developed cold feet in the 9:58 between pressing the button and the hereafter.

Unable to recall the actual code, Charlie knew of no way to stop the detonation.

18

07:34.

Charlie could call 911, explain that he was aboard a yacht with two dead bodies and a nuclear bomb, although it wasn't really nuclear — part of a secret CIA program — yet it still packed enough high-grade plastic explosive to take out a good percentage of the people in the vicinity, and it had been triggered, so you really ought to hurry.

If he succeeded, the bomb squad would then have 00:04 to arrive and do its job.

Discarding that idea, he dug the boat keys from Steve's pocket and raced up the stairs. He intended to untie the yacht and drive it as far from shore as he could. A mile or two out, the device might detonate causing relatively little harm — the fog and general gloom had kept most boaters home.

Needing first to untie the heavy ropes tethering the yacht to the dock, he charged through the cabin door and onto the deck at the stern, where he found himself staring into the barrel of a shotgun.

Time seemed to slow, adrenaline again shifting his senses and thinking into higher gears. He had anticipated myriad obstacles and plotted countermaneuvers. Still the sight of Glenny made him jump.

"Stop right there, Mr. Pulitzer. Hands up where I can see them."

He raised both arms above his head. "Just listen for a second."

"No, sir." Squinting through the sights, she tightened her finger around the trigger.

"Just one second, please."

"One second." She eyed the pale sky. "Time's up."

"The man you know as Tom the Campodonicos' nephew is actually a very bad bad guy." Glenny's finger didn't move. "This boat currently has a bomb with a hundred pounds of plastic explosive, enough to take out the marina and everything within a quarter mile. It's going to detonate in seven minutes. I have no way to turn it off, so I need to get it out of harm's way."

Glenny paused to reflect. "Bullshit. You're a yacht thief."

Glancing at the parking lot, Charlie sighed in relief. "Here's the Secret Service. They'll straighten this out."

She turned to look and saw only a deserted marina. When she looked back, readying a curse, she found Bream's Glock leveled at her by Charlie. She blanched.

"If I were the bad guy, you'd be in some trouble now," he said.

She acknowledged this with a grunt. And fired the shotgun.

Having anticipated that she would, he dropped to the deck. Through a scupper, he saw the thick bowline split in two, freeing the yacht's bow from the cleat on the dock.

Swinging the barrel toward the stern, Glenny said, "I saw Tom this morning passing my office two different times with Arab guys who kinda kept looking over their shoulders." She blasted the stern line free, destroying the bulky metal cleat in the process. "You'd best shove off, shipmate."

"Thanks," Charlie said, barging into the wheelhouse.

He glanced at the LED he'd ripped from the washer. 04:58.

He inserted Steve's key into the ignition, weighing the odds that this key, like the remote, was a dud. The engines roared, churning the surrounding water.

On the dock, Glenny shouted into her cell phone and waved Charlie on.

The yacht's controls were similar to the

Riva Aquarama's, a good thing as Charlie would have thrust the throttle in the direction common sense dictated was reverse and accidentally sent the yacht into the parking lot. He managed to back away from the dock, clocking the wheel. Shifting into forward, he launched the yacht toward what he thought was the middle of the bay. The fog, essentially low-lying cloud banks, made it impossible to tell that he wasn't simply hugging the coast. Or about to crash into it.

The twin-tiered, state-of-the-art navigational equipment was of no more use to him than it would be to a caveman, with the exception of the hot-pink ball compass, a novelty item held by a rubber suction cup to the windshield. If the compass was working, the boat was headed due west. Toward the center of the bay.

He stood at the wheel, using all of his weight to absorb blows from oncoming waves.

When the clock flashed 3:00, he had put more than a mile between him and the marina. Or far enough.

Now to get overboard with the life raft.

Lest the yacht continue smack into a commercial freighter, he cut the engines, plummeting the dusky vicinity into graveyard silence broken only by the slapping of the water and his own heavy breathing as he ran out onto the bow.

He slid to a stop and tore away the Velcro straps binding the bright red Zodiac raft to the inside of the railing. About ten feet long, it had a stern-mounted outboard motor that looked like it had plenty of zip.

The raft wouldn't budge. A padlock at the end of a thick stern line fastened it to the yacht's uppermost rail. Charlie looked on the back of the lock. No miniature keyhole. He might be able to cut the line with a knife or saw, however. And a couple of minutes.

He had 1:43.

He considered diving overboard and swimming away. Hypothermia beat disintegration.

Instead he held the barrel of the Glock two feet from the padlock. He shielded his face, and pulled the trigger. Either the sound or the shrapnel stabbed his eardrums; he couldn't be sure which. Regardless, there was no longer any trace of the lock.

He heaved the Zodiac into the water. Trying not to think about the fifteen-foot drop, he straddled the rail. He glimpsed the LED blink from 1:00 to :59 as he leaped.

His weight and momentum torpedoed him into water that felt so cold it should have been ice.

He resurfaced to find the Zodiac drifting away, faster than he could swim. Ordinarily. Lungs shrieking for air, he reached the raft, perhaps seventy-five feet from the yacht, or a good thousand feet closer than he needed to be.

As he climbed aboard, he jerked the cord, starting the little outboard motor on the stern. Grabbing the tiller, he set a straight course. The raft shot ahead like a dragster just as a blinding flash cleaved the fog, followed by a boom so intense that his hearing quit, replaced by sticky blood and maddening pain.

A tower of water of biblical proportions rose from the disintegrating yacht. The force of the explosion swatted a helicopter out of the sky and tipped over sailboats as far away as the eastern shore.

The Zodiac shot into the air like a kite, Charlie clinging to it until he was no longer able to stay conscious.

19

He awoke at the center of a flock of tiny, sylphlike particles of light. He was seeing stars. Spectacular, but probably the result of a concussion, judging by the pain.

Shaking his vision clear, he found himself on the Zodiac, the motor still bubbling away, though icy water streamed through the holes in the hull, swamping most of the bow.

Chunks of the yacht had hacked into his running suit. The two layers of long underwear notwithstanding, blood coated him. Each wave that sprayed his wounds felt like a hundred fresh cuts. Still he was alive, and the knowledge that he'd succeeded in getting the bomb far enough away from shore relegated the pain to mere discomfort. He felt himself smiling, ear to bleeding ear.

A police boat sprinted from the eastern shore toward the shaft of smoke that had been the yacht, a quarter of a mile away.

Through the scattered fog, he could see two more police boats charging from the opposite side of the bay.

As his hearing began to return, he discerned from the tumult of waves the whine of a motor, spotted the motorboat, and made out a figure at its helm. A woman. Hand held as a visor against the vapor, she was scanning the area where the yacht had been.

Alice!

Even in hazy silhouette, she was beautiful.

"Where are you?" she called out.

"Here," he croaked through a throat caked with salt and blood.

She didn't look his way.

He swallowed, then tried again. "Alice." It came out as a wheeze. Something was seriously wrong with one of his lungs.

She steered away from the Zodiac.

Fog was resettling over the bay, shrouding the police boats in the vicinity of the yacht's wreckage. Charlie doubted he would be able to get to them, meaning his survival would come down to a race between Alice and hypothermia.

He thought of firing the Glock to draw her attention. Before he could reach for it, the Zodiac's bow rose sharply. He turned and looked over his shoulder.

Bream clung to the stern.

Charlie considered that he was hallucinating.

"She's looking for me," Bream said weakly, but all too real. Somehow he'd made it off the yacht and then clung to the Zodiac's stern line.

"A lot of people are going to be looking for you." Charlie reached for the Glock.

It was gone.

"You don't get it, Charlie Brown. She's *with me.*" Bream still hung on the stern to the right of the motor. Evidently he lacked the strength to climb aboard. "I knew you and Daddy were in Switzerland because *she told me.*"

Charlie recalled Drummond wondering if Alice orchestrated the rendition herself.

"That would mean she had herself kidnapped and shot at," Charlie said.

"Exactly." Bream seemed to exult in the revelation. "The whole point of the rendition was to give her an alibi. For her 'captors' we handpicked mercenaries who had a track record of running to intelligence agencies to get cash for tips, so the CIA would establish that she'd been the victim of a rendition. That way, who the hell would ever think she was helping me?"

Charlie regarded Alice through the thickening fog. She was leaning over her motor-boat's prow, still searching the waves and calling out. He made out a gun in her right hand.

"And she just happened to phone right when the plane was going down?" Charlie asked.

"We wanted you to give the spiel about Punjabi separatists," said Bream.

"Otherwise she would have let the plane crash?"

"Otherwise we wouldn't have set you up in a plummeting plane in the first place."

"So it was nothing personal? Just another day at the office in Spook City?"

Biting back a grin, Bream nodded slowly.

"You're just telling me this to distract me, aren't you?" Charlie said. And hoped.

"You're learning." Bream raised the Glock. "Just too late."

He had difficulty steadying the barrel, what with his lower half still submerged and lashed by waves and the rest of him swaying and lurching along with the Zodiac, but at a firing distance of six feet, even with gale force winds added to the mix, he would have excellent odds of hitting Charlie.

"You need me alive," Charlie said.

"Really? Why's that?"

"Cheb Qatada isn't going to pay a dime

for your services. You'll want to know where the treasure of San Isidro is hidden."

"Why would you tell me?"

"To distract you." Charlie kicked the tiller as hard as he could. It swung the outboard motor toward Bream. The whirring propeller blades sawed into his pelvis. Hot blood pelted Charlie's face and stippled much of the raft.

Bream tried to scream but got a mouthful from a wave. Still he fired.

The bullet severed the handle from the rest of the tiller. Charlie rolled toward the stern, snatched the handle, and swung it, batting the Glock away from Bream. The gun took an odd bounce off the stern and splashed into the bay.

Propelling himself away from the raft despite obvious pain, Bream plunged into a dark wave and, somehow, fished out the weapon.

Charlie dove for the far end of the raft.

Bream wrestled the tide to put Charlie in his gunsights.

The tinny sputter of a motorboat grew louder, capturing their attention.

The bow sliced apart the fog, showing Charlie a washed-out image of Alice at the helm. She was squinting down the barrel of her pistol, pointed at him. The sight was more painful than the bullet would be. All he could do was brace himself as she refined her aim and fired.

The air shook with the report. The bullet drilled through the haze, missing him by a wide margin.

Bream gasped. A wave swept aside a large lock of his hair, revealing a purple cavity in the side of his head. Another wave clubbed him, driving him to the bottom of the bay.

Charlie wondered if, in reality, Alice had shot him — or if Bream had shot him — and he was now spending his last throes in reverie.

A moment later, the motorboat was close enough that he could clearly see Alice's face. She was smiling.

"Need a lift?" she asked.

He glanced at his raft, all but underwater. "Where are you going?"

Setting down her gun, she gathered up her bowline and tossed him the end. He caught the rope with both hands, then held on tight while she pulled the remains of the Zodiac toward her. When he stepped off, grabbing the motorboat's bow, the raft disappeared altogether beneath the waves.

"There's something I need to tell you," he said as she helped him aboard.

"What's that?"

"I love you."

"Same." She stood on her toes and kissed him.

20

Charlie liked to say that the best thing in life was to win money at the track. And the second best thing was to lose money at the track. In the three months after Mobile, he lost hundreds of thousands of dollars, not counting his bourbon tab, which wasn't far behind.

At least the losses came at Keeneland, the historic Kentucky race-course famous for the Blue Grass Stakes as well as for its tonic effect on horseplayers. Sitting in the august grandstand, breathing in the horses and hay and fresh-mown bluegrass, Charlie often felt as if he were drifting back in time. He sometimes turned toward the thunder of hooves half expecting to find Seabiscuit in the lead.

During the final week of Spring Race Meet, Charlie was joined in the grandstand by his father. Drummond's heart had healed entirely in Martinique and, after nine weeks in Geneva, his mental condition had begun to show improvement. In Kentucky, he was happy just to be in his son's company.

On their third day together, a few minutes before the final race, Charlie said, "I'm going to make a run downstairs. Need another cup of burgoo?" The robust meat stew was a Keeneland specialty, and a favorite of Drummond's.

Drummond smiled. "That would be nice, thank you."

Charlie headed to the aisle, then turned back to Drummond. "This is your sixth cup of burgoo, and you've yet to impart an interesting piece of information about it."

Drummond lifted his shoulders. "I don't have one."

"With a name like burgoo, we ought to be able to find one."

Leaving him to soak in the sunshine, Charlie went to watch the post parade, in particular Queen of the Sands, a stocky dark brown mare with a white star between intelligent eyes. Her illustrious ancestry included two Derby winners. Her owner, Prince Mohammed bin Zayed, seemed to have a golden touch of late, although rumors swirled that his gold was in fact a new detection-defying anti-inflammatory drug that could mask pain, allowing horses to run faster.

Charlie was known to bin Zayed less as a horseplayer than as the son of Drummond Clark, the retired spy who had recently purchased a château in Switzerland with the proceeds from the illegal sale of a Russian atomic demolition munition. Rumor was, Drummond had another ADM.

Bin Zayed, the chief benefactor of an international terrorist network, suspected that Charlie had learned the location of the second bomb from his father and might be persuaded to give it up to pay off his gambling debts.

The CIA had fed this information to bin Zayed through cutouts in Saudi Arabia.

In truth, Charlie's betting and bourbon were just cover. Alice, waiting in Paris, understood. His real reason for being in Kentucky was to sell a washing machine.

ACKNOWLEDGMENTS

Thank you to Phyllis Grann. Detailing her excellence as an editor would make this book too heavy to lift.

Richard Abate is the Albert Pujols of literary agents.

Novelist Chuck Hogan has been the Kevin Youkilis of writing advisers. Incidentally, Kevin Youkilis is the Chuck Hogan of hitters.

In the same league, on national security matters, are Elizabeth Bancroft, Fred Burton, and Fred Rustmann. I'm indebted to them as well as too many members of the Association of Former Intelligence Officers to mention (just as well as most would probably prefer going unmentioned).

Thank you to Roy Sekoff and the *Huffington Post* for allowing me to report on the intelligence community and learn, among other things, that the men and women of the clandestine services are our most underrated heroes.

I'm also grateful to the members of Doubleday's incomparable marketing, publicity, and sales teams — notably, Rachel Lapal, Adrienne Sparks, and John Pitts — and to Doubleday's Edward Kastenmeier, Sonny Mehta, Jackie Montalvo, Nora Reichard, Bill Thomas, Zack Wagman, and Michael Windsor.

Thank you also to friend and Internet guru John Felleman, who gives Web sites an added dimension.

Additional thanks to Rachel Adams, James Bamford, T. J. Beitelman, Tim Borella, Patrick Bownes, Glenny Brock, Cindy Calvert, Rachel Clevenger, Columbia Pictures, Jennifer Donegan, Peter Earnest, Linda Fairstein, David Flumenbaum, James Gregorio, Amy Hertz, Melissa Kahn, Joan Kretschmer, Olaf Kutsch, Robert Lazar, Kate Lee, Donna Levine, Ray Paulick, Michael Perrizo, Christopher Reich, Jake Reiss, Hilary Reyl, Raya Rzeszut, Keck Shepard, Malcolm Thomson, Barbara Traweek, John Waddy, and Lawrence Wharton.

There would be no acknowledgments section, nor pages preceding it for that matter, if not for my wife, Karen Shepard, a swell wife with a sixth sense for story structure.

Finally, thanks to anyone else who has

read this book to this point.

Please send any questions or comments to kqthomson@gmail.com.

ABOUT THE AUTHOR

Keith Thomson is a former semipro baseball player in France, an editorial cartoonist for *Newsday,* a filmmaker with a short film shown at Sundance, and a screenwriter who currently lives in Alabama. He writes on intelligence and other matters for the *Huffington Post.*

LARGE TYPE
Thomson, Keith, 1965-
Twice a spy